Goin' Up To Cripple Creek

by
Raymond Walter Seibert

Published by Advanced Concept Design Books
Lago Vista, Texas

This Book is dedicated to my best companion, my wife Anna Jean, whose faith in me has never wavered, whose love has sustained, and money has supported.

Acknowledgments

The first time that I ever viewed Cripple Creek, my wife and I came in from Divide from the North, and got as far as the Mollie Kathleen. I must admit that I am an inveterate rock hound, and my wife will swear that I lost all my marbles a long time ago. I insisted that we come to the area to 'check it out.' I had read some intriguing stories about a cave of gold, and I wanted to photograph the buildings and machines. My wife also does not understand me shooting photographs of machines. I don't get why she doesn't get it. They are just too cool.

After one glance at the old historic town in the distance, I lit out across the back side to Victor, and was amazed at the active gold mining machinery in the area. We studied some road signs at the visitor center we found along the way, not open, but the sign in front had this interesting logging road that was not long, and I thought we would explore South, and then come back. Everything went along fine for several miles on Phantom Gulch Road, and I must admit that there were modest disclaimers, but the sign said 'maintained', and like I am saying, it looked good, for a while. It looked good up until we came to a bridge that said, "No Vehicle Over 26 feet in Length Allowed Along This Road. Extremely Dangerous Road Ahead."

But the bridge was in brand new shape, so, in spite of the screaming, and promising that I was 'only looking for a place to turn around,' we came around a curve to another bridge, one lane, with boards old and weathered, and no boards, where there should have been some, nothing straight down for 150 feet. This was a bridge that I had seen many times before, in my nightmares. No place to turn around, I proceeded for the next 18 miles trying to turn around. At one spot between two rocks, with a 3000 foot drop off where there should have been a road shoulder, I met a man coming the other way. He had such a disgusted look on his face, when I refused to go to the outside, and backed into his lane, until my mirror was touching the rock wall, and obstinately shook my head, and made him go around me on the wrong side, on the cliff side. You who have made this run, from either end, will know the exact spot that I am talking about. Fun, huh, like partners in crime, we did a dangerous thing and lived to tell the tale.

Needless to say, my wife did not come back to Cripple Creek that day, nor would she have ever, as far as she was concerned. But, I began to develop an interest in the story, as there was no placer gold, it really should not have been of exceeding fascination, but I kept coming back to the story, and the more I read on the Internet, the more fascinated I became. The story of such phenomenal growth and the money and energy that had been poured into the area, was almost unfathomable.

..................And then, there was that cave of gold.

But, what brought me back to Cripple Creek, was Jack Dempsey. As I learned of a few of the people involved in the early history of Cripple Creek, I heard of Dempsey, and it was a name that I recognized from the fighting lessons that Uncles and friends, and my father gave. These men never failed to mention Jack Dempsey, and I could tell that they idolized the man. So, when I ran across a book called, "Kid Blackie" on the Internet, and on Ebay for $120 dollars, I noticed it, but it was too rich for my blood. Still, it was an interesting place to start, and by this time I was seriously searching for a good and not overly told story. One that had no politics in it, I said to myself. Just a pure adventure story, one that would be easy to write, and stay away from the big questions, like religion, and politics, and keep it simple. Well, you will see just how that worked out for me.

Still intrigued by the story, I had found that the Cripple Creek Library held a copy of "Kid Blackie" in the reserved section, and that it could be used in the library, but could not be checked out, and was not available on line. In the late summer of 2006, I had been a very good boy, and as a reward, my wife agreed that I could go to Cripple Creek for a couple of days to research the early Jack Dempsey biography, and photograph the Aspen in the area, that is, if she could get on over to Salida in time for the Philip John Brooks concert at Bongo Billy's.

I later sweetened the deal with a Mt. Antero aquamarine jewelry. But, that is another story.

When we arrived in Cripple Creek, we located the library and Nancy Fromm was very kind to show me to the book that I was searching for, and using one of the library tables, and surrounded by yelling children in shifts, which was one of the nicest parts of the day, I proceeded to make copious notes on Dempsey's early life from this book. My wife, Jeanne, got us a wonderful old hotel room at the Independence Hotel, and it has the quaintest flush mechanism that you lean back against, oh, there I have told you too much information. Oh well, she would not let me take a picture of it, and so it will not appear on the blog, so you will just have to take my word for it or go there and see it for yourself.

I was considering the trip a total success, as I found the information that I was after, and a plan was trying to take shape in my head. I visited the Mt. Pisgah cemetery the morning that we left the area, and while there, looking randomly for Susan Anderson's grave, a friendly voice hailed me, and asked, "you want to see a really interesting grave," he called.

"Sure," I yelled back and joined him uphill, not quite all the way to the back. "Who you got there," I ventured when I came in speaking distance, "one of the lady's of the evening," I guessed.

"Pearl DeVere," he pointed. We stood without speaking for some time.

I introduced myself and he introduced himself as Christopher Hanson, and said that everyone called him Pete, and that he was on the committee to restore and care for the Mt. Pisgah cemetery. We visited a bit, and I was once again impressed by the openness and hospitality of the people that were the natives and lived in the area year round. It was refreshing and very pleasant to bask in the warm glow of the people here in the District. I found this as a pervading attitude in researching the characters, who open-handedly gave friends, and new comers alike, a chance to share in the bounty that the land gave in fun, and in resources. After Pete had shown me both the Susan Anderson grave sites, my wife and I toured the Cripple Creek Museum, and met the marvelous ladies there, who are full of stories, and knowledge (They have all been helpful. Thank you, Betty Tritz, Jan MacKell Collins, Jean Schaal, Marlane Smutka, and Nancy McDonald.). Then wandering down to the Museum Gift Shop, it was my very good fortune to meet Johnna Luck. As I was perusing the book shelves, Jeanne decided to try the manager, and ask if they would like to sample our Pinon Pine Incense, that I make, and acquire the sap from Ben and Debbie Sandoval, who are the owners of Tiwa Kitchens, just outside of the Taos Pueblo, on the Pueblo side of town. Johnna was very receptive to carrying the incense in the store and took five packages right away, and in talking to her, admitted that I was considering writing about the area. She was very encouraging, and this is a real positive, as she offered to plug me into several great sources of information. Now, with the idea new in my mind, I had three people in as many hours, be positive and helpful to me on this project. You must write, in order to know how very unusual this is, and how much this stuck.

It was just a week or so later, that resting from the long trip, and still mindful of the notes that I had jotted down, I had a dream. I was standing in the Mt. Pisgah cemetery, and everyone was standing at the head of their graves, and yelling things at me. It was very real, and made a great impression on me when I awoke, as they were arguing over whose story was the most important, and trying to tell me things that had happened to them. I was not surprised, as there didn't seem to be any hook to hang the story on, and I could not get a handle on it, and although, I thought that I had a natural ending to the story, I could not find the beginning and had spun my wheels on the beginning in frustration. So, dreaming about it, seemed just a normal, if somewhat bazaar, and vivid experience.

It was a couple of months later, that one morning, I was sitting at the kitchen table at my office and had drifted back to around 1889, trying to visualize what it would have been like for an old cowboy to be poking around looking for gold, and I may have been typing out a few lines, but was deep into the fantasy, walking along with Bob Womack, just a little below the present position of the old assay office, in the year of whenever that was, when the phone rang. Now the office phone is very rarely

anything of much importance, and it is usually someone selling something that I don't even have time to talk about, so, if they are rude enough to call me about it, I am rude enough to just hang up. So in this frame of

Table of Contents

Preface The Vug Wave

The wave moved inexorably upward, forced by its own momentum and the unspeakable pressure which gained a megapascal with each one hundred and fifty feet that it ascended. The penny sized slug of molten gas moved along the line of least shear, mathematically predetermined to be a forty-five-degree angle, but varied by material inclusions, and grain distribution. As it gained pressure, the vug wave moved faster. Once opened, vast amounts of superheated plastic material cracked the rock all around it and the sudden release of pressure on the side of the fissure vaporized the material shooting the hot vapors into every crack and fissure that was formed. As it moved faster, it gained momentum, and as it moved forward and up, the hot plastic magma burst through the mantle of the planet moving ever faster upward through the tough schist, and granite that stood in its' way to release the pent up pressure which was reaching fifty thousand megapascals every ten miles of ascent, until many thousands of times over atmospheric pressure, it sought release at the surface of the earth, but long before it reached the surface, pressures had reached levels high enough and the superheated metal vapors, were so hot, that the rocks bulged like a clown had blown into a balloon, slowly at first, and then with a thrust of movement until the chamber had formed. The pressures equalized for a moment, and then began to build again as more super pressurized, vaporized gold, shot upward from miles beneath the surface to the earth, and began to deposit in gold crystals on the edges of the crevice, as the vaporized gold hit the cooler edges of the bubble of the cave that had been made of raw heat and pressure.

The pressure and the wave renewed itself and carved deeper into the rock over it, ever pressing upward in an attempt to escape the earthly confines. The rocks split in three directions, and headed up three sides of the collapsed caldera, that was the old magma route that the vug pressure wave had followed. Climbing high up the sides of the caldera, the waves in sequence smashed the hydrothermal quartz veins in all directions, infusing them with the vapors, depositing metals of all kinds, and cracking and popping the surface rocks, which burst into the air releasing the pressure below them, and then settling back onto the surface helter skelter, in what would be seen many years later as a confusing and undecipherable pile of strata. One solid gold rock weighing over seventy pounds, was blown out a vent and traveled sixty miles to a sight where it was over looked for a hundred years until a bulldozer operator building a road in nintee-eighty=seven noticed it, and got down to take a look.

Safely hidden from view, at the twelve-hundred foot level, the chamber cooled, and a natural wonder of the world as had never been created, filled with layered gold crystal, waited for the startled eyes of man to thus behold.

Chapter 1. Pioneers, Homesteaders, and Prospectors

Levi Welty worked the wagon and team around a boulder and pulled the team over to rest for a moment, as they were rising three feet in height to everyone hundred feet they went forward, and it was the most that the team could do to make headway up Ute Pass. "Them boys sure did leave a bunch of boulders in the road," he observed to George. George grunted his agreement and got down off the wagon to roll a smaller stone out of the path. Maybe they would get to the top without breaking a wagon wheel.

While he was heaving the stone to one side, his brother Alonzo appeared at the crest of the next rise, several hundred yards above and up the pass and waved his hat at the men below. Levi yelled at him, "Alonzo," with an edge in his voice, and Alonzo immediately disappeared back over the crest. George climbed back into the wagon, and they started up the steep and rocky pass again. Alonzo caught up with his brother Frank, who was resting his horse under a Pinon pine at the top of Ute Pass.

From there, the view was magnificent, with Pike's Peak rising, massive to the south, and the west Pike's Peakarea, that had come to be called South Park, stretching out to the Western horizon some sixty miles of alpine flat land. The flat land stretched out brown and yellow in the early afternoon sunlight.

"Pa's throwin' a fit," Alonzo informed Frank, who let a smile flicker across his face, "we should'a took some ofthem stones out of the ruts. He's gonna give us what ferwhen he gets up here."

"Ah, let him stew," Frank shot back, and plucked a stalk of feather blue stem in his mouth, and tying his reigns, let his horse browse the sparse green grass that had found some purchases in the edge of the shade. He propped himself up against the pine and determined not to worry about until Levi caught up. Alonzo looked nervously back along the trail checking for dust, with a frown on his face. "He was the one wanted to bring the wagon and chuck. I wanted to ride in and look around and high tail it back to the Springs." With that he lay back and rested in the insect hum of the afternoon. Alonzo gazed out to the West and after a few minutes got a spy glass from his saddle bag and studied the land directly to the West for several minutes. Before long, he could hear the creak of the wagon timbers, and the snorting of the horses, as they pulled the last grade to the crest of Ute Pass.

Since they wanted to stay close to water for the stock, they had to make an early camp. It was the next afternoon when Alonzo and Frank rode into Judge Castello's Ute trading post.

"Welcome to Florissant, men," the Judge boomed out as he strode out to meet the men. He rubbed his hands together in anticipation of the food he could sell the men, as they had obviously worked up an appetite along the way. "Alonzo and Frank Welty, howdy boys," he recognized them.

4

"Howdy Judge," Frank hallowed him, Pa and George are comin' along in a wagon directly. He handed the reigns of his horse to an Indian boy that came out at the direction of Judge Castello, running up from an encampment of some number of ponies and people a short distance across a little gully cut by the trickle of a stream. Alonzo followed the boy back to the stable.

Levi thought the Castello Ute trading post a primitive but neat establishment, with the old log part that had served as the original store, now added onto with rough cut sawed planks nailed vertically on the outside, with a lapping board over the top to cover the seam where the rough cut planks met on the wall. That meant that the Judge had a sawmill up and running and Levi could smell a business opportunity right off. Frank had stabling and lodging arranged by the time Levi and George pulled in, and as soon as the men had stored their gear and unhitched the team of two mules and turned them over to the stable hand, they sat down to a dinner that the Judge had started to prepare when the wagon hove in sight. He fried up thick slices of smoked ham, scrambled eggs and onions, with white and sweet potato slices fried in the ham fat. When the men had their fill, the Judge joined them at the table to get acquainted.

"Judge," Levi Welty took his hand and thanked him kindly for the grub and lodging. "Me and my boys are honest, peaceable, and hard working men," he began, and we just need to get a little ahead of the crowd, if you know what I mean," Levi opened his palms toward the Judge, who nodded and lit his pipe and said that he understood fully the pressure of too many people. "We're running some good stock, and we have a good thing going North of the springs there at Colorado City, but you might have heard, people are pushin' in and the grasshoppers was pretty bad too. That Seldomridge is a big operator, and he has been pushin' a lot of sheep up to the Eastern Slope just *mind, and mostly somewhere in the last century, I answered the phone.*

"This is Johnna Luck, in Cripple Creek, and I sure would like to get some more of that incense," a voice said. Now, at the moment, I was standing just a few feet away, but a little more than 100 years earlier. It was one very strange experience, and I had to pull the phone away and stare at it, and then look around the office kitchen to get myself together before I could answer. Realizing who I was talking to, I quickly asked if she still had "Kid Blackie" on the self for the right price, and we did a trade, in which she sent me many more books, that have been of the utmost help. This was the beginning. Special thanks Johnna.

Renee Caldwell and Rosa Uhl, at the Florissant Museum, have open handedly helped me with whatever information was known to them, and pointed me at several good pieces of reference literature of the area.

The Heritage Center has lately opened and is a great source of Cripple Creek history, and Tom Cooper was most helpful there, as well as many other workers, and Congressman Doug Lamborn's Deputy District Director, Joe Rall. All of these sources are available to everyone, for free.

A very special thank you goes to my hosts at the "Last Dollar Bed and Breakfast", Chip and Kathy Gregg, who have made me welcome over and over, with a place to stay, information, food, and a wonderful place to write over ten percent of this first work in the Gold Trail Series.

Lastly, and with utmost appreciation, my editor, my cousin Norma Melrose, who has painstakingly reviewed the manuscript many, many times, removing awkward structures and correcting my atrocious spelling.

north of that newly plotted town of that railroader, Palmer, Colorado Springs." He spit out the name hard. "Anyway, here is the thing, Judge, we need to get in and squat on a good piece, that has got some water, on something that is just about to be surveyed and opened for homesteading, like this county here and the Platte River area. Now, I was wondering and hoping you might oblige us a lot of lookin' if you had an idea where a man might get set up to ranch some of this high country."

The Judge set back and puffed his pipe and hurumped, a bit and gave it some thought, then just gave a wink. "Levi, if I was you, and wanted to run some cattle up here, I know of a fine little alpine valley South and East of here that no one has cut a road to yet, and few people have ever seen, but it's a good one, no doubt about it."

Levi and the boys drew in close and stopped eating to hear what Judge Castello was saying. Seeing he had their full attention the Judge continued. "This here creek out there is Twin creek we call it, so, go on and follow the Forty-Niner's trail another couple miles West, and come to what we call Four Mile Creek. There's a road of sorts turns down the canyon and goes along the rim of Four Mile Canyon and down to Four Mile. There's a couple homesteads goin'a be down that way with a few families squatin' down there and a teacher runnin' a school, but beyond that, you will have to cut your own trail for the wagon. You need to go on down Four Mile Creek to the junction of what we're callin' Spring Creek right now, for lack of a better name, although we got two other Spring Creeks in the county." The Judge made an irritated noise and then continued. "Now go on past a couple of small gullies, but after the junction of Four Mile and Spring Creek, follow on down to the next little tricklin' steam you come to and turn up that gully, and climb to it's source about two thousand feet higher, it'll be a feat cuttin' a wagon road in there, but it can be done, and there you have the prettiest little alpine valley, all nestled in just Southwest of the Peak."

"No one has got those water rights," asked Levi?

"It's a small stream, but I've seen the stream in mid- summer, and it runs good and clear and strong. I think a case of dynamite would open it up some."

"That or close it off, I've seen that happen too."

The Judge shrugged and puffed his pipe. The men talked among themselves and soon they wanted to go over the directions again, so Judge Castello got out a map he had drawn of the area, far from complete, of the places that he had been, mostly the South Park area, but at it's edge, including the alpine pasture noted Southeast of the store.

Levi thanked him, and paid him, and got ready for an early start the next day. "Judge," Levi added, being the good business man, "me and the boys are going to be back and forth a lot from Colorado City, and we already do a little freighting around, you know, just to pay for the grease and wagon wheels," Levi laughed, "so feel free to use us, if'n you're needin' anything trucked up from Colorado City."

"No doubt Mr. Welty, that that will be," the Judge agreed, although he himself had wagons on the move, he always saw a man as a partner, instead of competition, and as a result, made money, coming and going. "No doubt, Mr. Welty," he warmly shook his hand good night, as Levi assured him, they would be up and gone before daylight. Levi had what he wanted and having put in eggs and ham in the wagon, would get on down the trail before breaking for breakfast. He liked the hospitality of the trading post but had not liked parting with hard earned gold in order to camp. But it had been a necessary expenditure of hard won capital.

"One more question Judge," Levi lowered his voice a notch. "What about them Ute's camped out there.

"They won't give anyone any trouble at all," Judge

Castello assured him.

"They never go up to the top of the pass anymore," George, standing close to his father asked?

"They say that there is no need for them to guard the pass anymore. That the white man guards the pass, and no Comanche will ever again come up the pass. They figure that we done them a big favor, and their hunting is mostly all North and West of here, and it is vast, and uninhabited by any people of any type, lousy with game. Vast elk herd, deer. We don't never have no trouble with the Ute's."

Levi nodded his approval of everything that he was hearing and bid the Judge good night.

They made an early start, with everyone rested and well fed the night before, Levi pushed on. They followed the road down along the flat terrain and past the Thompson cabin. Little Anne Thompson came hobbling out on her crutch and watched as the men past by. They wound their way passed the Florissant Fossil beds and through the grove of giant stumps of fossilized prehistoric Sequoia and Red Wood that had been covered over by ancient ash and mud and then uncovered in recent geological history. Many of the stumps were over twenty feet in circumference, and the stump reaching up to as high as forty feet, stood as silent sentinels as the men passed by them. The road through the fossil beds led a bit east but it was already cut and used. Beyond this homestead the going got more difficult and the road less traveled. Just short of Four Mile and Spring Creek, by just before noon that day, Levi pulled them up and fed them, as he intended to make a long day of it. In fact, they made six long days, finding the route to the creek and cutting a wagon road in. Late on the eighth afternoon, Alonzo rode back in to tell them that he had seen the source of the spring and that the valley was everything that the Judge had said and more. That the steep sides of the valley offered protection, as well as it would naturally hold the cattle, and that there was water and grass aplenty. He was obviously pleased and Levi pushed on with all his might, chopping, and rolling stones, and making way pushing up the gullies toward the glen that was now so close.

When he finally came out into the high alpine valley at the top, he was astonished and pleased with what he saw. Stretched out in front of him lay a beautiful and peaceful alpine valley several miles in circumference, nested into a bowl of a rolling depression, surrounded by aspen groves on all sides. The cone of Mt. Pisgah rose on his right, to the west and to the northeast rose the massive bulk of Pike's Peak. Never had he seen a more peaceful and serene site. Alonzo 'halloed' him from the source of the spring, and from where he was standing. Levi had already picked out the perfect spot for his house in the head of the valley, near both timber and water, and with a commanding view.

After they had looked over the spring, he set them to staking a cabin site. "Alonzo," he gathered the boys around and fed them with hard tack jerky from an elk he had killed and smoked the previous March. They ate their fill between some hard biscuits, that they had cooked earlier, and were left over and saved. Levi was frugal and made the boys that way or at least tried. "Both you and Frank go back down and cut out as many head of cattle as you can manage, ones that will follow the bell cow and bring some feed to keep'um moving and see how many head you boys can move on up here. Me and George will get busy chopping logs and dragin'um in with the mules. We can get it laid out by the time you two get back, and then when it comes to heavy liftin', we'll all be able to pitch in and make short work of it. We got to move fast, cause winter comes quick and hard up this high. We got to get places ready for the stock and try to get a spring house built to keep the animals out and keep it free of ice, as

9

much as possible. This valley is gonna' get mighty cold in the dead of winter." Levi shook his head, and the men took this as a sign that they had their instructions. They went about the task of making bedding for themselves and tending to their individual stock, as light was failing and night was coming fast.

It was almost three weeks later in mid-August when Alonzo and Frank managed to get eleven head of mother stock with a big almost yearling heifer or steer, still following a mother just beginning to be heavy with another late summer calf. Somewhat out of the preferred rhythm, but very suited to this venture. The big calves, who were still trying to nurse would follow along bawling at their mothers, while the mothers would not stray far from the bell cow, being as they were heavy with calves and needed the sweet feed to start to bag. With this plan, in a couple of months this bunch would amount to over thirty head and was easy to move. Frank rode ahead and yelled out to George and Levi that they were returned with a small herd. In a few minutes, Levi could hear the tinkle of the bell around the bell cow's neck, that soon turned into a loud clanking as the cow made her way across the rough ground, and the clapper clanged against the crude brass bell. Soon the bawling of the doggies following their mothers could be made out, as they bawled and tried to get the mothers to stop and let them catch up and suck. They would occasionally be able to catch up and get ahead of the mothers and stop their path and get a pull on one tit, before the mother pulled away from the teeth of the big babies. Levi saddled up and met them on the slopes of Mt. Pisgah coming toward the spring from the West around the base of the mountain, and George went to pull the railings on a makeshift pen that he and Levi had constructed with branches that they had trimmed from the logs that they had drug up for the construction of the new cabin.

When they had the cattle penned and had given

them some sweet feed to settle them in, the men stood together, with arms resting on the railings and surveyed the little herd together.

"We'll keep'um penned here for a few days and gather hay for'um and get'um used to the sweet feed at the same time every day," Levi told the boys. "That way, they won't stray far from the spring." He scratched the nose of 'Princess' the year-old calf of the bell cow, who was the family pet, and followed Levi around like a dog on some days. They all petted her, as they were all fond of the little heifer, as she was in training to be the new bell cow when her mother became too old to trail anymore.

"The calves have got to be branded, before we can turn them loose," Frank observed to his father.

"Did you boys think to put in an iron," Levi questioned? Frank looked flummoxed and hung his head. Alonzo gave a little laugh but shut it up when Levi snorted at him. "Boys, I ain't always gonna be around to do your thinkin' for you." He shook his head at them and started up the hill toward the tent that they had pitched next to the cabin lay out.

George and Levi had amassed a dozen logs next to the cabin site and two tiers of logs set in a rectangle on a flat spot of ground. Alonzo and Frank were impressed that the other two men had been obviously very hard at work. They had also hand scythed some tall summer grass and rolled it into bundles and brought it in for the mules, and in preparation for the stock that had come in. The next morning broke clear and bright, with just a nip of cold in the morning, warning that winter was coming at this high altitude, which Levi judged was above nine thousand feet, and maybe close to a thousand feet higher in some parts of the grassy bowl that surrounded them. The trees on the edge in the morning light flashed a shimmering glimmer. At higher altitudes, the aspen leaves were beginning to quake in the breeze, and some were starting to turn, as the higher altitudes near the timber line, had already begun to experience frosty weather. It was this high altitude that gave Levi his only doubts, as the valley seemed a perfect place for ranching, except for this one fact. Levi had already noticed that there was very good land and water available in the Four Mile area, when they had come through.

The beginning of the construction of the cabin went without a hitch. When they had the house roughed in Levi started on a spring house over the spring to keep it from being fouled, and to assert total ownership of the water, as this was the concern that had driven him from the lower valley above Colorado City, as more and more of the water sources had been fenced with this new thing called 'barbed wire'. Levi had hated that cursed wire, and was going to enclose the spring with logs, and then he would not string any wire in the valley, nor need to in order to show that he was in control of the spring, even if they were only squatters at the present time. All through the remainder of the shorter and shorter days, with Mt. Pisgah making each day that much shorter by blocking the evening sun from the valley, he pushed them as hard as they could all four work.

The first days of September were coming fast and cold weather would not be far behind. Construction went well on the spring house for several days, but as the construction got higher, the going got slower and tougher. It was going very well, all considered and the weather was holding for them in a perfect Indian summer, and the men had reached a level just above shoulder height, where the hands, during lifting, had to change positions. First a boost of the log was underhanded, and then at shoulder level the hand position had to be changed to lift the log higher and put it in place in the notches. Levi had cautioned the boys that if a log was too heavy to call for help, they were young and strong, and impatient to get the job done.

Levi was on the west side, chinking mud into the cracks of the logs, and Frank and George were setting a log on the uneven and sloping south side, which sloped toward the creek from the west and east and sloped downhill on the south side. The logs were not nearly as long as the ones used to build the non-windowed sides of the cabin, which had been heavy and everything that the four men could do together. They had been stacking and notching at an easy pace all morning and Levi had sent Alonzo up to the cabin to start the noon meal. George was on the east end and Frank on the west, and as they started up with the next course where they would have to change hand positions, George had questioned Frank if he could lift his end.

"Frank," George asked, "can you manage your end all right?" Frank who was a little smaller than George, and a little touchy on the subject, as George always beat him at Indian wrestling shot back, "you just get your end up little brother and I'll be there with mine."

Both men grabbed their ends of the log and lifted; George got his hand position changed first and not noticing that Frank was having a little trouble with his end, changed his hand position and started on up to set his end in the notch. Frank had barely got his fingers turned back toward him and was feeling for a good grip, when George started on up with his end. The higher that George got his end, the more he raised was putting the whole load on Frank, and as Frank desperately went for the notch on the top on the log, a knot, that had been only partially trimmed, caught right before the log went into place, and George thought that it was alright, set his in the saddle. Frank lost control of his end, and instinctively dropped it and stepped back, yelling at George, "Look out George." George had no time to move, and just gave a grunt of, "Huh," before the log rotated, rolled out of the notch, and came slamming to the ground. The log caught George just below the knee on the

13

right calf and swept him off his feet. George screamed in pain, as he fell. Levi, hearing the clamor not knowing what was happening, thinking of a snake, or some other kind of trouble, grabbed at his shotgun, that was always near at hand.

In his haste, he failed to notice that as he pulled it up from where he had it leaning on a bush, one of the triggers caught on the bush, and as he pulled the gun toward him one of the hammers partially pulled back, but not enough to set. Being caught on the bush, Levi's hand slid along the barrel top, and fortunately, his hand caught a little on the beads on top of the barrel, but the flap of skin between his thumb and forefinger on his right hand lapped over the bore, just as the bush pulled off the hammer and let in come forward with enough force to set of the percussion cap on the bottom of the shell. The discharge blew away the flap of skin, and the powder and shot burned his face as it went by but did not hit him.

Alonzo, hearing the shot, came running down the hill, and as he approached the spring house from the cabin, saw Princess the pet calf, bellowing in pain, with a broken leg, laying down and stuck in a boggy spot in the middle of the creek. As he came around the corner of the construction, on the south side he saw Frank bandaging Levi's hand and trying to staunch the blood that was flowing from the wound. George was on the ground, laying across the log, that had done the damage. George was groaning and going into shock from the blow.

"What the Hell happened," he asked?

Levi looked up at him and then at the carnage that was all around, and figuring that it all explained itself, quipped, "Boys, this sure is one cripple creek we got here."

They made a litter and rolled George onto it and took him back up the hill to the tent that they had set as temporary quarters while they finished the cabin. Levi

14

tended to wash his wound, and George's, and sent Frank and Alonzo out to put the pet calf out of its' misery, and dress it out for what meat could be salvaged from it. It was still bawling pitifully from the bog. Levi, counting himself lucky, after examining himself in a hand mirror, and seeing the burn up his face realized that he had dodged a bullet. He heard the report of Alonzo's rifle, and the pitiful bawling of the pet stopped, and he thought to himself that at least Alonzo was a good shot and had made short work of the task with a well-placed round, to end the suffering of the little heifer.

Turning his attention to George, he tried to clean him up some, but with one hand and the trembling that had come on him, the most he could do was use some cold spring water to wash his own wound and pour some whiskey that they had bought from Judge Castello. He had managed to get George's pants leg cut up to the wound and was trying to wash the blood away but could not get his boot off from the dried blood. He did not like what he saw of the wound.

It took the other two boys a little over an hour to field dress the calf, and get it hanging in a tree, to keep it clean. They came into the tent looking very chastised.

"Pa," Frank pleaded, "it wern't my fault, "he started in plaintively. "George lifted too fast and didn't wait for me to get a grip."

Levi held up his left hand to stop the protest. "No sense in that Frank, just help me cut his boot off and get him cleaned up."

Both boys pitched in with great care for their brother, as the emergency caused them to come together in one spirit. As they heated water and washed the wound, George became a little more coherent and told them that the leg was numb, which pretty much confirmed that it was broken. It was not a compound fracture, and that was good as there was no bone sticking out of the skin, and it had gotten a solid whack, but appeared to be a green break, with the bone not displaced. The worrisome thing was that the wound had a gash where a little stub of a chopped limb had dug into the skin. They cleaned it as best they could, but Levi had suspicion that there was still wood under the skin that he could not get out, and he knew that this would fester. He watched the wound off and on all that night and sent the other two to bed. By morning there was a redness that Levi was very unhappy about and George was starting to run a fever, which might have been a normal thing, but was one more thing that Levi was worried about.

Alonzo and Frank had moved their bedrolls into the partially finished cabin and about daylight, Alonzo heard Levi come in and felt his father give him a little shake.

"Alonzo," he said quietly, "you get yourself some breakfast, and make me a little too. We'll let Frank sleep, as he is going to have to handle all the chores. As soon as you can get everything washed and put away, go as fast as you can to Judge Castello's and see if there is anyone around that can do any doctoring, cause if we have to take him all the way back to Colorado City, it's gonna be really rough on him, as we don't have time to take the wagon, and a traverse is gonna be a bad trip down the gullies and down the canyon. We may have to take him down anyway, but if'n we can get him some attention, we might stave off the gangrene."

At the mention of this feared word, Alonzo said he would get food at the Ute trading post when he got there and lit out as hard as his horse would go, and kept up a canter, or on flat ground a dead run, just short of running the horse to death, and made the store well before noon.

Judge Castello came out on hearing him ride up, and knew from the lather on the horse that something was terribly wrong.

"Judge," Alonzo called out to him,"George got a leg broke, and it's got a bad cut, Pa sent me to ask if'n

16

there was a doctor closer than Colorado City?"

"Get down and come on in the store, and I'll send someone after the Doc we got around here." Alonzo dismounted and handed his reins to the same Indian boy who had tended stable the weeks before. "Piala, saddle a fresh mount with this saddle," he slapped Alonzo's saddle, "and saddle a horse for you, and go to 'Dirty Woman's' house at Four Mile, tell her to be ready to help with a broken leg, with a cut," Judge Castello made a knife like movement along his leg, and Piala nodded that he understood. He and Alonzo entered the log part of the structure that served as the dining and kitchen area, and as the Judge got some food together for Alonzo, he heard a blow-by-blow description of the accident. In a few minutes, they heard the sound of Piala's horse riding out at a gallop.

"This Doc," Judge Castello began, "is a midwife, mostly, to folks around here, but she's good with wounds, though, folks think she is a bit odd," the Judge squinted his eyes a bit, and Alonzo wondered, between big bites of ham, what that might mean.

"Oh, how's that," he inquired?

"Well now," the Judge lit his pipe and held his hands palms up," now you can trust that she's a good Doc, but she's a bit gruff, sort of talks like a man, cussin' and all. She just talks odd for a woman. And then, she's," the Judge paused and scratched his beard, "well, she's a might dirty," he confessed. "We all call her 'Dirty Woman'.

"Well, that's a good one," Alonzo blustered, "I'm sure gonna get a lickin' from Pa, bringin' some foul mouthed dirty old midwife up to doctor George."

Judge Castello held out his hands in a helpless shrug, as he often did, "I'm'a tellin' you she's good with cuts," he stabbed the air with his pipe stem, and then pulled a draw on the end and added with another shrug, "she's the best we got around here, and with a bad cut, by the time you can get a cripple back to a doctor, down in civilization, well," the Judge just shrugged his helpless shrug again.

"Dirty Woman, huh," Alonzo asked again.

"Just call her Doc," the Judge warned, "cause we don't call her 'Dirty Woman,' to her face," he cautioned. Alonzo acknowledged he understood.

"You go back down to Four Mile and find the last cabin on the right hand fork up in there. Piala will be watchin' for you and maybe find her there and helped her get ready, so you take a little time to grab some grub and then take that fresh mount that has your saddle on it. You can trade me back my mount when this gets sorted out."

Shortly, Alonzo took the fresh horse, and made good time, came to the four-mile junction, and group of squatters, waiting to file their homesteads. He made his way between the cabins, up a trail to the West, and soon found Piala, and the cabin. Even with the Judge's description, Alonzo was not ready for Dirty Woman. Piala was in front of the cabin half dug out, with his horse's reins and the reins of a large donkey that was packed with gear on one side, and an old side saddle for a lady on the other. Taking in the animal first and working his horse up the hill and around the front side, he was suddenly eye to eye with a filthy, and ragged, mud soaked, old crone. She was smoking a corn cob pipe and staring at him right in the eye. He tried not to react, but he was startled and reined his horse around in a circle.

"You come up here, cause you got somebody hurt," she boomed out in a strong voice, more of a statement then a question.

"Yes'um, that's true," Alonzo gulped, and confirmed her statement. He gawked at her for a full ten seconds, and she gathered a bag at her feet, and stubbing out the pipe with a finger that she used to cut off the air and save the tobacco for later. She made way to the donkey and situated herself into the side saddle, where she waited for Alonzo to move out. When at last he did, he had just turned to go, when she yelled at him.

"Hey, you dumb cowboy, come lead this donkey. I don't know where we are agoin' but don't you lead me over any rough ground, now you go around it, and don't pull me straight up no steep spots neither, if you know what's good fer ya."

Alonzo came back and sheepishly took the reins of the donkey from Piala, and he could see from the Ute boy's eyes that he was relieved to be free from his part of the job. There was something that made him very uneasy about this filthy woman, but he felt he had no choice, as Judge Castello had assured him that there was no other that had any skills in healing. Alonzo was very careful to choose the path that would keep the donkey coming along as well as possible, as the path up the draw to the new Welty cabin was steep and strewn with rock and sudden changes in elevation. But whenever he looked back at the Doc, she was rocking along in apparent contentment, occasionally she would yell at him to stop for her to light her pipe and take a puff, and in this way, they made it back up to the Welty construction site by late in the afternoon.

Levi was anxiously waiting and watching the western rise around the edge of Mt Pisgah and saw them coming as soon as they came over the ridge on the extreme northwestern edge of the cone.

"Pa, this is the Doc the Judge sent for, and there ain't no one else," Alonzo said in defense and introduction all at the same time. Levi had a chance to study them as they made their way toward him, and he was perturbed by what he saw.

The Doc didn't wait for a helping hand but got down spryly off her side saddle and began to unhitch her bag. "Boy, come take my donkey with you and care for him," she ordered. Levi approached with some doubt in his eyes, and Alonzo just stepped around him with a shrug, saying the Judge said she was good, and led the animals down toward the spring house, to water them after the trip up.

"Levi Welty," Levi introduced himself and stuck out his hand.

"Richards," she ignored his hand and hoisted her gear. "Well," she said, "show me the sick one, cause time is a wastin'," she rejoined. Levi, with his mouth agape, led her to the tent, next to the cabin under construction, that had been the quarters for all three, but now had become the sick room in which only George was laid on a cot. Levi and Frank had taken turns watching and bringing him water, and helping him to limp to use the toilet, so that he did not have to use a bed pan.

"This is my son, George," Levi introduced George on the cot, and Frank as he left the tent. "I guess that Alonzo introduced himself."

"I never asked," said Dirty Woman, "and he didn't say. I don't expect no manners from the young," she observed to Levi, as she knelt and pulled back the blanket to look George's leg over. "Bring me hot water and whiskey and keep a fire going to heat some implements like needle's and knives, and such." She looked up at Levi, "and make sure it's a hardwood coal, nice and hot and clean that you heat things on, and then when I call for them, you bring'um to me straight away, as fast as you can, in this cloth." She held out a cloth from her tote bag that was filthy with matted dirt. Levi took it, reluctantly, and did as he was told, preparing water and whiskey and fire.

They looked in on her from time to time, but unless she had asked for an implement to be heated, she shooed them away in firm terms, as soon as they put their heads in the tent. After a while they fixed a supper and talked among themselves, with her still cleaning and probing and stitching the wound, until it was late and the boys slept, and finally Levi dropped off to sleep, propped against the wall next to the fireplace that was under construction and being used all at the same time.

Levi awoke with a start, as the face of the Dirty Woman was right in his, and he could see in the morning light, the glistening of the grime that was on her face and matted in her hair.

"You got a bad burn on your face," she explained. "It's got a need for some salve," she offered.

"Oh, it's not too bad, just a powder burn. Could a been a lot worst, as the gun accidentally went off on me and just missed blowin' my fool head off."

"Too bad," she said solemnly. "It might have improved your looks some," she quipped without a smile. Levi flinched and looked at her. "Hold still." She took a tentacle of a dessert plant leaf that she carried in her medicine bag, and splitting the leaf, applied the sap to his skin. She got herself some coffee from the pot on the ashes of the fire that they had kept going all night. She drank the black coffee at the cut, at the edge of the construction, where the door would be. Levi stirred the fire higher, adding wood a little at a time.

"How is George," he ventured after a while.

"He's going to be fine, it never was very bad, as breaks go, it was just a green break and the bone didn't separate, just cracked into, but not much out of place. The cut had some splinters in it, but they're out now, and there never was any proud flesh much, but that's taken care of now. He's got a splint on for a few weeks, and a bandage that has to be changed. I'll be back, she left for the tent, then went off down the stream into the woods and was gone a few minutes and returned.

"He's hungry," she reported to Levi, "and that is a good sign," she loaded her corn cob pipe and lit a twig at the fire and took a puff on her pipe. "He's going to

21

recover just fine, and my job is done here, if you'd oblige that boy that brung me up here to take me back, I got things to do, so I'll be on my way."

Levi roused Alonzo and got him ready to lead the Doc back down to Four Mile. Before she left, she instructed Levi in the use of the dessert plant Aloe, for the promotion of healing, and in three days, the stitches had to be cut and pulled out, which she cautioned should be done with whiskey to stop any blood, and to bring him to her if any pus developed that didn't crust quickly. With that, she relieved Levi of a twenty-dollar gold Eagle, which he grumbled about, but paid, as he had to agree the boy's leg and life was worth it.

Finally, arriving back at her cabin, Alonzo bid her farewell and started home. At last, she was able to heat a tub of water, but first, she lifted the contents of her bag out of the medicine kit, and carefully unwrapped the wiggly, white, maggots, and placed them back in their box of putrid flesh, where they could at last feed. There had not been much to feed on, on George's leg, and they were hungry after the long trip. She folded her outer garment and placed it in the slime of the box with the maggots. Then, at last she could get into the heated water, and wash the maggot slime out of her hair, and off of her skin, where she had placed it, when Piala had rushed up and told her that someone had a broken leg, and a cut, and a man would be coming soon to get her. She had not wanted to infect his wound.

It was not too long after dark that Alonzo returned to the camp, but the moon was up, and he could see his way along the now-familiar path. He found his father sleeping and George was awake and wanted some water, and help limping to take a leak. So, they settled in for a recovery, and a first winter, and soon, building the new corral was the interest.

It was very early the next spring when Levi stepped out on the cabin porch, and gazed to the east along the ridge line, high up on the timber line. A shot rang out, and Levi could make out an elk running along the edge of the timber and coming behind him, someone was riding, with the reigns in his teeth, and taking shots at the big elk as he ran.

Frank joined Levi and sipping coffee, watched the chase all the way across the top of the valley, until it disappeared across the rise in the valley to the north.

"I think that was Bob Womack on Whistler," he observed to Levi.

"Looked like him, alright," Levi agreed. "He told me about being up this way hunting and lookin' for gold." Levi threw the rest of his coffee on the ground. "He was talkin' about gold this, and gold there, like all the other tom fool, tender feet cowboys, gold crazy, and lazy. Wouldn't hardly keep the fire hot for the brandin' irons, you'd look around and he'd be talkin' a blue streak with some other cowboy, keepin' him from doin' his job, too, and talkin' about gold." Levi spit where he had thrown the coffee, in farther show of his disgust for all such activity, so much the more, since he had been a crazy, tenderfoot, prospector, when he had come to Colorado, and had taken up ranching as a reasonable way to make a living on the open range. Here he was still surrounded by open range, whereas, in the East Slope pastures, barbed wire was fast freezing out the small operations, and as fast as homesteads could be consolidated, large operations, by syndicate of owners, were bringing railroads, and even cities, like the new city of Colorado Springs that the railroad man, General Palmer had brought into the Eastern Slope range.

Levi finished his breakfast chores, and continued to expand the corral and barn area, which had been the focus of his attention. They had heard several more reports from the rifle from time to time, heading north and west into the wilderness of canyons at the foot of the western side of

Pike's Peak. It was near noon when Levi noticed that the cattle had all stopped grazing, and were looking to the north. Soon, he could hear the whistling of someone, and the snorting of a laboring horse, and a scraping sound, of poles being dragged on the ground. Within a few more moments, he could make out the long nosed, long face of Bob Womack, and the face lit up, when he saw Levi, and stood his six-foot bean pole frame up in the stirrups and waved his hat. His frame almost dwarfed the little horse he was riding, which was straining already with the load of elk that it pulled on the traverse, that was made of two slim poles. Even though the little horse was all heart, coming along with this whole load made him grunt and give a snort of protest, every few steps. Bob got off and led the pony the rest of the way down to the spring. Levi walked down from the other side and met him there.

"Howdy," Bob Womack called out cheerily, then pulled out a red bandanna handkerchief and blew his big, long nose, and wiped it twice and stuck the bandanna back in his back pants pocket. Frank walked up, and began to admire the elk, the dogs had come down and Frank kicked them away from the carcass, which had been field dressed, and when the dogs realized that the offal was back up the trail, understanding what was going on, the smart ones headed back up the trail looking for the reward they would find and the other dogs tagged along. Levi shook Bob's hand and moved to examine the elk.

"Saw Alonzo, and George working cattle," Bob observed, "and George looked fully recovered, and hardly limps at all." He got Whistler loose from the traverse and let him get at the water. "They told me about ya'll moving' everything up this way, we're having' the same trouble as you with the Sun View operation, the big operators are coming' to control all of the water, and all of the grain'." Bob shook his head.

"Well, there is plenty of open range up here," Levi

confessed, "and it gets a mite lonesome for company here abouts. I reckon that I would welcome a few more squatter's that were ranchin' and didn't want to put the range under barbwire."

"Well, you know the Womack's would never cotton to anything but open range, why it and mining, are the only hope for the small man and without him this country would belong to the Ute's or the bears and lions."

They were in agreement, and their interests ran side by side. Bob brought news from the Eastern Slope, and the Welty's were hungry to hear what he had to say, and one thing Bob Womack liked to do better than prospect, or ride Whistler through the mountains hunting, was talk and drink. However, when Bob pulled out a pint of whiskey, and passed it around, Levi declined and looked disapprovingly of Frank taking a second pull on the bottle.

Fortunately, Bob put the whiskey away, seeing Levi's disapproval, and they had a good visit all around in the newly finished cabin. Levi was proud to show off his hard work, and Bob was interested in everything that Levi and the boys were doing.

When he bid them farewell the next morning, they had quartered and boned the elk, and put strips out to dry as jerky, to be smoked. Bob carried a hind quarter of elk, wrapped in burlap and salted to hold it on the way down to Sunview Ranch headquarters, where his sister reigned as regent for his father, who was ailing. Bob was often away hunting and prospecting the mountains of the Western Slope around the Peak and even farther afield.

The visits to the cabin in the lovely valley became more and more frequent, and many times Bob brought a field dressed elk or mule deer into the Welty cabin. He usually left almost all of the meat there for the Weltys, and they were glad to see tall, talkative, Bob Womack ride up.

Chapter 2. A Hardscrabble

"Sarah Elizabeth Yates, stop pickin' them flowers and come on right now," Peter Yates yelled at his daughter. The force of his voice set the baby in his arms crying, and he jiggled the infant to try and quiet it, but once aroused, it cried out in hunger.

"Oh, Papa, just a few more," the eight-year-old called out to him from among the field of wild columbine, but she began to make her way back toward the wagon, poised at the edge of the Somerset Cemetery. She stopped to place a few more flowers on the grave. "Mama loved them so much," she said as persuasion, as she placed them among the others on the new wooden marker that showed the traces of new dirt around its base. Peter Yates turned his head away, and his eyes brimmed with tears. What was he to do now?

Sarah bent to trace her finger along the neatly chiseled letters, spelling out the name. Mary Elizabeth Yates, on the next line, Dearly Beloved, and carved below, May 4, 1852-March 31, 1884. The young girl lingered her finger on the last mark and began to absently retrace her path backwards.

"Come now child," her father's voice softened and almost broke. "We have to get this baby back to Mrs. Olmstead, and we've a way to go."

"I'm coming, Papa," Sarah turned, and dragging her toes, started toward the big freight wagon, where her father stood, waiting for her to hold the baby, so he could climb into the driver's seat above the right wheel. Sarah turned for one last look, but a squall from the hungry infant brought her on the run.

"I don't know how I would make it without you,"

26

Peter Yates told his daughter, as he handed the child for her to hold, while he climbed into his seat. "I'm going to carve a marble marker for your mother, out of the purest, white marble that I can find at the quarry," he tried to soothe the hurt away from them both. The heat was already leaving the day, and at this altitude the thin dry air would cool fast. Feeling the wagon move, one of the big dray horses stomped his foreleg impatient to be on the move and the wagon moved slightly, as Sarah handed the infant up to her father so that she could climb aboard. The wheels moved a few radians and then rocked back near Sarah's foot. "Ho, Clipper," Peter commanded the big gray dray horse. Clipper held still but snorted his eagerness to move and tried to turn his head to look past his blinders that were built into the harness of the head gear. "Whoap," Peter cautioned again, and the big horse's ear flinched where he was expecting a disciplinary crack of the rawhide whip. Both horses stood stock still as Sarah climbed into the bed and gently took the squalling child and cradled him as she sat down with her back to the crossbar of the seat. The baby cried a lot. She pulled a rag from her pocket and positioned the hard rock candy in the center, and twisting it a turn, gave it to the baby to suck on through the rag. The infant quieted immediately.

The wind began to change, and gusts came in a swirl around the mountain plateau that had become the graveyard for the budding little community called Hotchkiss, after the family who had first settled there the year before. They had come in soon after the Ute's had been forced out, as a result of the Meeker Massacre two and a half years earlier, in September of 1879. Enos Hotchkiss had struck it rich with his Golden Fleece Mine in Lake City, and had scouted the area before the Ute's had been forced onto the small Northern Utah reservation. He had known that the relocation was inevitable and had brought a number of pioneers into the North Gunnison area the next year. Peter Yates had freighted ore for Hotchkiss at the Golden Fleece mine and had decided to join the influx of settlers into the area, unaware that his wife, Mary, was pregnant with their second child. The winter had been hard, and the soddy that they used cramped, and wet.

They had just begun to settle in when Krakatoa had exploded half a world away, and soot had spread worldwide. A black frost had killed the corn on the Fourth of July in 1883, and the winter was cold with meager food supplies, and what there was to be bought, expensive. Mary had never had much fat on her bones, but was never fragile before that winter, but the cold winter and the pregnancy had gone hard with her, and without proper vitamins, the baby's head had gotten large, and she had gotten frail. The labor had been hard, and there was no doctor. A midwife and neighbor, Mrs. Olmstead, of limited experience had tried valiantly, but mistakenly to ease her pain with opium, that had only increased the labor to over eighteen hours, even though it was Mary's second child.

She had become listless from the loss of blood, and after a couple of days of not being able to eat or drink, had weakened, nodded into a coma, and died. The boy baby was blue and would not breathe. Mrs. Olmstead lay the dead baby to one side, and in her frantic attention to staunch the bleeding of the mother, lay the body next to a hot anvil of iron that had been heated in the fire, and was being used to keep water hot. It had burned the child severely on the back, and he always carried the scar, but it brought life to the body, in a gasp of pain, and then a wail of life. Harry had cried out just as his mother faded from this life. Mrs. Olmstead saw a flicker of recognition cross Mary's face, and she handed the baby into trembling weak hands, as she slipped away, Harry got the nourishment of a dying mother.

They searched high and low for a wet nurse, and finally a Ute woman was found that would bring her infant and come act as wet nurse to the struggling baby. Harry was an unhappy infant and cried a great deal. His brain had been deprived of oxygen for too long. The restlessness, and crying were the first signs.

Elizabeth was mother to Harry, there was simply no other way for the family to exist. Her memories really began with Harry's birth, and the responsibility that she was under from her mother's death. She loved her father, and the two made a workable unit, and Harry grew, but he was always a handful and given to tantrums.

That night, the Olmsteads brought a light and sat the sad little family down to a stew and corn bread. "I'll need to leave Sarah and Harry with you for a few days while I deliver a load of coal over to the Yule Marble Mine. Tatum's steam marble saw uses up coal at a fierce rate. He's payin' in money and stock in the mine, so I'm in the mining business now, I reckon," Peter bragged.

"Peter," Mrs. Olmstead assured him, "you know that the kids has a place with us when you're in need. Heaven knows, with my seven, another two won't be noticed, and Sarah does so well to watch out for Harry, why they're nary any trouble at all."

The next morning Peter hitched the team to his freight wagon and headed out at first light. He would return in a few days. This would become the routine of Sarah and Harry's lives until that fateful day when Peter Yates didn't return, and their lives changed forever. When word came that her father had been killed in an accident at the marble mine, Sarah was devastated. It was only the beginning of things that would be numbly endured in the chain of events that led to her becoming an orphan, along with brother Harry.

Arturo Marquez walked on Ferdinand Vandeveer Hayden's left side, and Bob Womack walked on his right, as they looked toward the rim of Mt. Pisgah and Bob told them of the little Alpine Valley spread out east of that formation. They had been doing a survey of the South Park in the Platte River country to the west. Upon the completion of that part of the survey, which was to be opened for settlement, Van Hayden's orders put him looking at the territory to the south and west of the Peak. In stopping to replenish supplies at the store of Uncle Ben Requa, and remaining for several days, enjoying the good cooking and comforts, word got out. Bob Womack was on an errand for his sister Lida who had sent him for thread at Uncle Ben Requa's store, and while there met with his relation, Theo Lowe, who recommended him to Van Hayden as a guide for the area, and Van Hayden benefited from much good advice from the affable Bob.

Van Hayden, who enjoyed Uncle Ben's ham and other good food, decided to stay at the store and let his second in command lead the party east toward the Pikes Peak.

Now, Bob guided the elected party of surveyors to the homesteader's house of the Welty's. The hound dogs announced the approach of the party of thirty, or more men, some part of the party, and some just hanging around the edges for the gambling and crumbs of subsistence, and food that followed the party of men from place to place. Some out of no more than curiosity, and a chance to go camping in the mountains.

Arturo was there on an exchange program from the

University of Seville and had come with the terms of the grant that had funded Van Hayden's commission from the Department of Interior. He was young and knowledgeable, and from a wealthy Spanish family. His dark eyes were alive as he surveyed the valley in front of him.

He saw a line of purple rocks on the mountain side in the distance that looked very familiar to him. He pointed it out to James Woods, the second in command under Van Hayden, "Possible sylvanite ore vein exposed in that ridge in the distance, sir. Do you see the purple outcropping running north to south along that ridge," he pointed the interesting geography out to Woods.

"Yes, indeed," Woods agreed immediately, as he undid his field glasses which he wore, and surveyed the other side of the valley. "We have a very interesting caldera, here," he observed. He paused for several minutes before giving the order to move on to the Welty cabin.

"Think it is worth a look tomorrow?" Arturo ventured to ask.

"Definitely," Woods clipped. "We'll start there tomorrow and take some samples. "Rough territory," he observed, as he rose a little in his saddle and rubbed a sore ass, that did not like to move so many miles in a day. He was glad to get down and shake hands with Levi Welty, who immediately set about meeting the needs of the party, by selling them three good beeves, and set his sons to show them where to corral the horses, and butcher the beef. The men began to settle in for the night.

After supper in the Welty cabin, Woods sat with Levi, and Bob Womack, as Arturo Marquez looked on over Bob's shoulder, as they spread out maps that were had of the area, and added benchmarks, and herms of any earlier survey, as well as landmarks that could be found and would further clarify the area. He was marking several papers that joined at the edges and had latitude and longitude lines imprinted in a grid on them.

The next few days they gathered samples and survey readings of the entire area. The party rejoined Van Hayden at Uncle Ben Requa's store and the party moved on.

As the years went by, one gray and silvery sample of ore sat on the table as a paperweight, and Stefano Marquez played with it from his earliest memory. He puzzled over the rock, and as he grew, before his father was killed in the cave in, he heard fantastic stories of the country from which the sample had come. The stories were filled with adventure, with Indians, and bison, and elk, and beaver. His father's eyes would be alight, and he wished he could see these things of wonder. He looked at the rock and he wondered.

Later, when he went off to the School of Mines in Sophia, he carried the rock as a paperweight. It had acquired an even more special meaning after his father's death in the cave in of the mine where he worked. It was a keepsake from his childhood that put him in touch with the memory of his mother, taken by a pneumonia, and his father, taken by an accident. Stefano Marquez's felt his fate intertwined with this memento of his.

For several months he had been telling them about a survey that had been made and directed by an agent of the government, from Ben Requa's Store, and that Bob had provided them with information about the creeks, and the lay of the land. He had been introduced to the survey team by his relation Theo Lowe, and now one of the survey party had sought Bob out at the County Clerk's office. Bob had found him there one day, and this man Woods had told him that some of the survey team were very excited about the formation around the alpine valley where the Welty's were. Woods informed them that it was a volcanic formation and could contain gold. Levi had laughed in Bob's face at that one, and told him in no uncertain terms, that he had seen plenty of prospecting himself at Leadville, and that if there had been a single speck of gold in the area, he would have seen it.

Now, failing to get anyone interested down in Colorado City and the Springs, the County Clerk, Howbert, had teamed with Ben Requa, and they had over one hundred men headed up to the area above the Welty cabin to blow a prospect hole. Bob Womack was among the leaders, and Levi had told him that although he would welcome a few more ranchers in the area, he had seen Leadville, and people diggin' holes all over the place and explosions going off at all hours. This had not been his vision of alpine paradise. However, he was confident that without a doubt, they would find nothing, and soon leave, because had there been a spec of gold, he would have found it.

Bob had come in early this morning and told him the men were on their way from Florissant and would be at the Welty cabin by dark. Levi had welcomed them all, as it was unstoppable anyway, and was glad to meet the men in charge and see that some order was going to be maintained, and that beef that might be needed was bought from Levi and not stolen.

Bob had brought the main organizers up to meet Levi and have a talk at the cabin.

"Levi," he began, "you know Irving Howbert, the El Paso County Clerk," with that Howbert took over and Bob fell silent to one side.

"Mr. Welty," Howbert began, "we're much obliged that you would let us camp out around your good water here, and we were hoping that you might sell us a beef or two, since we have some hungry men to feed, and we have some provisions but not near what we will need in the long run."

"That can be done easily, Mr. Howbert," Levi was quick to see a business opportunity, and this was going to be a good one.

"You might remember Henry Wood here," Howbert introduced the party leader, "and you know Uncle Ben Requa." Ben nodded as he and Levi had been acquainted for many years, as Ben Requa's store was in Fountain, on the other side of Sunview, the Womack place on the south of Pike's Peak.

"You might remember, Mr. Welty," Wood spoke up, "I was in the Hayden survey party, when we came by here last year. Some of the team was very excited about formations that were evident about a mile south and west of here, in a site that we marked as 'Eclipse Gulch', there were volcanic formations that samples proved later to have gold content."

"Is that a fact," said Levi, he was beginning to see a bonanza here. "That sure is a surprise to me."

"Mr. Welty," Howbert continued to introduce the responsible men to him, "this here is Clay Croft, this is Brown, Jones, and you know Rowdy Magee." Howbert let the men shake hands all around and then continued.

"These men are paying the bills, and staking the claim, so they will be responsible for their people. Course, we got some, just followin' along, and we will try to do the best we can to keep them in line."

"That's fair enough," Levi agreed. Frank and Alonzo drew in close. "You boys go on down and cut out three steers that will weigh close to four hundred pounds each, and get'um up to camp for these men," he sent the boys on to do the wrangler work. "Now," he turned back to Howbert, Woods, and Uncle Ben Requa and the rest, which including the men gathered around was more than one hundred men with donkey's, tools, wagon's, and several women of unknown intent, following in the background, "just don't foul the spring, and don't rustle my stock, and we are good, gentlemen."

"We intend just that Mr. Welty," Howbert assured him. With that, the men began to break up to make camp, with some of the leaders going off with Alonzo and Frank to tend to the beeves and the general layout of the camp. Some went on toward the Gulch that was their destination, some two miles across what was known as Lone Tree Hill by some. Bob Womack stayed behind and talked with Levi Welty.

"I told them they didn't need no guide, when we first met back at Uncle Ben's Store, but they said that they wanted me to lead them in, but with the wagon's and the explosives that they are cartin' I judged it best to come around by Florissant and up your wagon road."

"Bob, that was just fine, like I told you when you rode in and said this little party was a comin'," Levi scratched his head. "But, there ain't no gold up here Bob, 'cause I would have found it long ago." Levi shook his head in wonder. "But I can get a good price for some beef and who knows, maybe someone will stake in by the time that they give up. I could use a few neighbors. They say that the Ute are no threat, but I been looking at a piece

35

down at Four Mile, where there are a few more people. The winters are mighty hard up here."

"Really," Bob's interest perked up right away, he also smiled because he had heard some talk about Levi visiting 'Dirty Woman', down at Four Mile, "you'd consider selling out the squatter's rights on the spring?"

"If'n we all file on land down at Four Mile, then we'd have to abandon this piece here, suppose the Womack's might want it?" Levi put the question to him.

"I'll advise for it myself and take it up with Sam and Miss Lida this very evening."

"No hurry," Levi advised. The four-mile land won't be open for a few more months, and it will take some time to move."

Bob left early in the afternoon, and heading back over the mountains to the Sunview in the South of the Peak, he was feeling very excited about the possibility that Levi would sell the Womacks the rights to the spring, on what they both now called Cripple Creek.

When he rode into the yard at the ranch house, he could hear his sister's strident voice, and the plaintive, complaining, of his new sister in law, Ida, his brother William's new wife, recently come from the East, as a bride. Bob slipped in the back of the house and avoided the cacophony of noise, as the two females went at each other in an endless squabble over territory. Sam had fled into the back room and was sitting in a corner when Bob crept in the back, a look of complete consternation on his face. They sat together in the gathering gloom as the confrontation rumbled to a close, with William's new bride going completely hysterical, and fleeing to her blanketed area, in the main room, which was all the privacy there was.

"Levi Welty offered to sell us his squatter's rights up in the Cripple Creek pasture, spring and all," Bob conveyed with some stifled excitement. He had come at an excellent moment.

"Praise the Lord," Sam exclaimed, "it's a godsend. For sure it is, I can't take it much longer. These women are gonna' be my death with all this argue, and fuss, argue, and fuss, then cry, cry, cry." Sam's voice reached a high and cracked over. His practical side came out. "Did Levi say what he wanted for the place? You've seen it. Could William and Ida live there?" Bob hid his disappointment that his father would not think of him as the owner of the property but would put William and Ida in there.

"It's a right nice work, but it needs a floor, and a cleaning, you know with four men livin' up there in the one place. I'm sure they would be reasonable, cause otherwise, they would just abandon it"

Sam got a picture of that and scratched the scraggle of beard on his chin. "I'll have to ride up that way and take a look," he mused.

"Irving Howbert has seen the property several times, and he will vouch for it as a good piece of ground," Bob told him, knowing that if it came to convincing Miss Lida, she respected Howbert's opinion.

"It's always been good advice to the Womack's," Sam affirmed a fact. Howbert had advised them very well from the start of their time in the area, when the mining played out around Idaho Springs, and Sam moved the family into ranching, as he had made a small fortune of over ten thousand dollars in various endeavors in the mining camps around Idaho Springs. He had once hit and sold a very nice silver lead, that became an important money maker in the area, after a great deal of money had been put into it, which was always the trouble with hard rock mining. A great many factors affected the net production of a hard rock mine, and Sam had sold out and brought his family and his boys to the plains at the eastern edge of the Rockies, where Irving Howbert had told him about Sunview, and that the grass was strong in nourishment if seemingly somewhat scarce at times of low moisture.

"See if you can get him to set a price, Bob, and if he says to tell him how much you would give, tell him that you don't like to set a price on another man's goods. Then just be still and wait him out."

"Pa," Bob protested, "you act like I ain't got no sense at all."

"And don't go up there drinkin' with them and talkin' about it neither."

They both glared at each other, and let it lay there. Bob stalked off to the barn where he had a little hideout office of sorts, with rock samples and bits of treasure that he had picked up in the Colorado wilderness. He sat on a bale of hay and twirled an old Spanish Roule that was on a part of a Spanish spur that he had found. He would never get his father's respect, but he would do what was best for his brother and sister and the family as a whole, in deference to his own best interest. The Womacks moved as a unit, and Bob worked within that framework.

It was close to a month before he could get back to Eclipse Gulch, and the Woods-Requa party. When he did he found a much depleted and discouraged crew. Uncle Ben Requa had gone back to store keeping in a few days and was complaining about hiring men to do his part of the mining work. The few remaining were grumbling, and the work was proving to be slow and hard, with the dynamiting going slow and the timbering necessary because of the crumbly rock that was likely to slab off and fall on the tunnelers.

Levi would not talk about a price until he had filed on land at Four Mile, and so, Bob, discouraged, had nothing to report to Sam. Sam shrugged and held out all through that winter.

By the next spring the Four Mile area was up for pre-homestead settling and the Welty's were ready to make a move. Sam waited until the last, then Bob, William, and Sam rode up to the Welty cabin.

"Levi," Sam shook his hand. They gathered around and Alonzo, Frank and George were all there. "Our family is a needin' a little more room, Levi, and I heard that you was filin' on a homestead over in Four Mile."

"You heard right Mr. Sam," Levi respected the older man, although he was very little older. "We're movin' already and need to sell out these improvements here and the claim to the spring."

"You know what kind of price you might ask for the claim," Sam inquired.

"Yes sir, it's worth two thousand dollars for sure, but I need to get five hundred, for all the work and the claim on the water."

"That sounds like a very fair price," Sam stuck out his hand.

"And two pigs," Levi added as he grabbed Sam's hand. They shook and laughed, "cause were gonna' be hard pressed to keep up with meat and all in the move." After all, Sam had accepted really fast. Levi didn't know about the two fussing women, or he would have raised the price.

"And two shoats," Levi confirmed adding the approximate size to the deal. It was a good deal for both men, and that is always a good deal.

Within a few days William and Ida had moved in, and Bob had a small room of his own. He had to keep his whiskey hid down at the spring house, but it was a workable solution, compared to the cramped situation back in Sunview, and if things got too dicey at Cripple Creek, which everyone was happy to call the place now, as the Womack's came from a Cripple Creek back east, Bob would high tail it back to do Miss Lida's bidding, and when that got tiresome, he could come back and do chores for Ida. This worked fine, until Ida got with child.

Chapter 5. Jake Gets His Cow

Jake Hoopoleith was saddle sore and mad, as he had been looking for that missing cow and calf for half a day, and was convinced that the maverick bovine had doubled back on him in an effort to hide the calf, that everyone knew she had. They had Pied up at the dugout, and she was peaceful, but crazy old Pied had done took off. He patted his horse, Jack, on the neck, "Dang it, Jack, if'n we don't find her sorry hide soon you goin'a have a kack biscuit on yar back, and I'ma goina have one on my butt." He eased himself up on his feet, and standing in the stirrups, gave his rear end a rest for a minute and let some air dry the sweat that was forming between him and the saddle. He had been this way a few moments, when from his higher vantage point, he saw some movement of brown in the brush. He kicked Jack in the sides hard with his gut hooks, and the big gelding was moving at top speed in a spurt of motion, so that Jake had to reach up and grab his hat and fix it down hard on his brow. He reached down and loosened the thong that fit over a brad that fixed his throwing rope to the latigo holding the saddle. He could feel the strain on the old latigo, and he hoped like hell it would hold. It was Pied, alright, and she took off. "Ye Hah," he yelled, "Jack, I been airin' my lungs, and that old Pied was hid out here all along," he whipped his reins to urge the big blazed faced horse to even greater effort and plunged into the brush after his cow. He fixed the dally to his saddle horn, "Gonna have to rope her and stake her out to find that calf," he consulted with his horse, as there was no one else around. He 'aired his lungs' some more at the crazy old Pied, admonishing her in superb cowboy epitaphs for having hidden the calf, because now he had to catch her sorry hide and tie her up until she started bawling

41

for the calf when her bag strutted. That could take until evening, and he might not even get the calf to answer right away, and he might have to move her around some, although, he thought that he knew where she had it hid out, as he caught her up that way when she was coming due, and she had probably gone back to her birthing spot or near it.

He had ducked several limbs and pushed the big horse right through the brambles and brush on the forest floor, and jumping some fallen logs from a past flood, broke her out into the open along the creek bank. The creek was only about six feet wide at this point, and a few yards farther down, the creek broke out into a deceptive clearing, that was a treacherous marsh. "Uh Oh," Jake eased up on urging the horse perilously forward. Some of this ground was firm and old Pied seemed to be making' it on a fast trot, and Jack had the reigns slack, and feeling the excitement of the chase, made for the trotting old Pied, whose bag had enough milk in it to slow her down. Jack was gaining ground fast, and Jake, catching some bones gleaming white in the sun, like a warning sign, ignored the danger of riding breakneck through the marsh, swung his rope.

He loosened his rope through the Hoolahan a couple of coils, and expertly snapped a loop about six feet around, and let the wind from the speed of the ride open it up behind him and on his right side, as he was right handed. Jake seeing old Pied veer off to the right, side stepped quickly to even more right, and when Pied swung her head to look, the horse was coming up fast on her right side, and Jack turned her back to the left and dashed any hopes of a run across the creek and into the tree line on the other side. Man and rider worked as a team, and now they closed on the target in a spurt of speed from her left side, as she took a look down her right flank as she ran, and failed to see the man with the rope swing a loop around the wrist, for the

42

heft of it, and then one for distance feel, and then a throw. The loop dropped clear of Pied's horns, and settling down along her neck, fell in perfect position, except for the marsh. Pied shied left and tried to run, but went down headfirst, and front feet first into a deep marshy hole. She bawled, and then screamed as her front, left leg sprained, and she went down headfirst into the creek bank, twisting her neck under her body until she was practically folded in half. Jake's momentum swung him out and around the edge of the marsh, man and horse tryin' to stay away from what was an obvious edge. They were partially successful, in that they stayed away from the marsh, but the force on the latigo, holding the saddle onto the horse, was more than the old leather, which was rotten from being wet, and unsoaped for some time, gave way. Old Pied went one way, and horse and rider went another. Jake was launched a good twenty feet, in a high arching fall, in which he knew he was going to eat gravel. He was turning side flips in a clockwise spiral, and put out a right hand to break his fall, knowing from experience, this was not good, as he would have liked to take a rolling tumble shoulder and back, if he could, but he just couldn't get around before the ground came up and hit him, and he heard the sickening snap of his right arm breaking.

Jack took a rolling tumble up the slight rise on the left toward the tree line, and came to rest, legs straight up, tangled in the rope with the saddle swaying in the tension between the horse and old Pied, whose neck was pulled even farther around by the rope and saddle and tangle of the horse's legs, so that her head looked detached from her body. She struggled to move, along with the horse, to the effect that the saddle swung in an arch straight at Jake's head such that he had to throw his good arm up to protect his head from being hit by the flying saddle swaying back and forth. He took the blow on his left hand, and rolled clear, about the same time Jack got untangled and kicked

43

free of the rope with the saddle falling square on top of the spot that Jake had just vacated.

Jack, finding that he was free from the rope and saddle, had all he wanted of this nonsense, and lit out up the hill, after shaking himself all over and turning with a snort, as if to say, "Next, time gut hook yourself." The last Jake saw of the big blaze, he was disappearing into the tree line headed uphill. He could hear him breaking sticks as he ran free through the brush, while his own breathing came under control, and now the pain was beginning in his right arm.

Pied had managed to untwist her head and was standing with her front left leg held off the ground. She was shocked still, and the rope hung around her neck and connected by the dally that still held tight to the horn of the kack, just sitin' on the ground, with the busted latigo trailing out behind.

Jake came to himself and lunged for the saddle, just as Pied found out that she could move the kack about with some ease, although, she was hoppin' about in the creek on three legs, but there was plenty of fight left in her. Jake hadn't come this far to let no maverick crazy old cow get the best of him, and he reached the kack, and rolled up in the rope where that dang old Pied wasn't goin' nowheres, he thought. About that time, Pied bowed up, and took off down the creek, hoppin' along, dragin' Jake and the saddle.

Jake was wizzin' along down the creek riding the saddle and tangled like hell in the rope. Fortunately, old Pied went round a curve in the creek and Jake stood and cut across, so that the rope went slack. Then, he had what he needed. He got the rope around a snag on the creek bank, just as Pied hit the end of it and did a flip in the middle of the creek, with a terrific splash, from which she came up bawling, and holding her hurt front, left foot up, and tried to set the leg down, and picked it right back up again. Jake pulled Pied in with his unbroken left hand and snubbed her up to the snag. Then he tied her off, at which time he gave to and aired out his lungs at her with every curse word that he could bring to mind, in a long string of epithets. He pulled the broken latigo out of the saddle and using it like a razor strap, beat the poor old cow in the face and neck until he hadn't strength to hit her or curse her anymore. Pied hung her head and made not a sound and blinked her eyes fast, in case any more blows were coming, whenever Jake looked up at her.

Finally, after a long time, Jake got up and gathered some stout branches with no bark and well-seasoned. He bound them to Pied's front left leg as tightly as he could with the leather thong, and then wrapped the rope tightly on the outside, and unbraiding the end of the rope, split it and tied it off on the opposite side, making it fast and permanent. "I ought to shoot you," he observed to Pied, as he turned her loose from the snub, and he led her out of the creek, and off the marsh, and down the creek trail to the house in Arequa.

Pied limped along as well as she could, not wanting anymore of the leather strap, and somehow knowing that this had to be. Jake put his arm in a sling made of the latigo and the leather thong that he had recovered as soon as he had begun to wrap the rope around the splints of dry sticks. He kept a couple of wraps of rope around his left hand just in case Pied had any more, but he figured she would come along now, and he figured right. She followed him right on to the porch at the half dugout, and he got her some straw to hold her. It was just getting absolute dark when he finally, awkwardly opened the door to the soddy house and entered. "Betsey," he yelled for his sister, his mother turned from the wood stove where she was stirring a pot, and replacing the heavy lid on top of the vittles, she crossed the tiny room and taking Jake's left arm, guided him to a seat at the table that formed the center piece of the front room. "Jake, my good gracious, son, what has happened to you, let me pour you some coffee," she turned in one motion to the big coffee tankard of blue enamelware. It was her pride that she always had this precious brew available, if somewhat rerun, as never a drop was to be wasted.

Pouring Jake a big steaming mug, and adding some heavy cream that was saved back, she soon heard the whole tangled story unwind, and about that time Betsey came in, and Jake told it over again, leaving out some of the tangles, and emphasizing his brilliance in the capture, except that he felt pretty sure that he had broken his right arm. Mama Posey, upon examination, pronounced it, 'broke bad, across the big bone." She pulled it straight, and about the time Betsey was tying it off with some splints and strips of old cloth torn for the purpose, Sam roused up from the back room, and moaning at the rumatiz that wracked his body, and painful pleurisy that was the result of horses kicking him in the ribs at various points in his long life, came through the door of the back of the house, that would have been a sod construction on the plains, but was backed to an ancient adit, or drift worked into the side of the mountain, up away from the creek. No one knew who had dug this cave into the mountain side, or why, but it made a good back room for the house. "Ma," Sam said in a shakey voice? "Go on back to bed Sam, It's jus more trable." She shook her weary head, filled with gray hair at fourty two years of age. Sam limped back across the threshold and back into the cave. He could learn what happened in the morning, sometimes he felt better in the morning.

Jake started in on Betsey, "That calf has got to be found." Betsey tried to soothe him and assured him that he could go out lookin' for the calf early the next morning, after he had some rest and food. "Naw, Betsey," Jake bellowed at her, "ya can't leave him out there for tha

46

wolves, Bet, he's just a baby, remember how he sucked yar thumb and fanger, now Bet we got to have him, he's the start of our herd." And he haranged at her and badgered her until she agreed to go out the next morning. Then when the moon rose, he came at her again, with the same tug on her emotions, that he knew would overcome her fear of cougars, and the dark.

"Sis," he pleaded with her, "you can use my Winchester, if your afeared." So, in the end, as a full spring moon rose over the pass to the northeast, Betsey put on a poncho, and big floppy hat, and tucking the Winchester under the poncho, stepped out into what was fast becoming a cold night for spring. Betsey Hoopoleith was no more than a waif. The family chopped some juniper cedar, and sold it around to ranchers, and farmers who needed a corral, and didn't want to take the time to chop their own. She stood then about four feet, and nine inches, but the wide brim hat crowned a good three inches above that, making her close to five feet in her boots. Her hair was the color of an Indiana corn field at harvest, just like back in Posey County Indiana, which was where they had come from, and where Mama Posey came by her name. She strode out with purpose, and Jake yelled after her, "She's up that second draw north and back up in the meadow beyond the snag at the bend. She was up thar, hangin' about, when she was due, and I know she birthed that calf right thar, somewhar's."

"I'll find'er, if'n she's up thar," Betsey sat out determinedly enough, but the night was cold, and the rocks slippery with condensation from the evaporation of the heat of the spring day. She had to work her way carefully along the not so well-defined creek trail. There was enough moonlight to see, but not to tell exactly where a rock was, or a shadow. She faltered many times but kept the Winchester firmly in her grip. She found a walking staff to help pick her way, and being right-handed, shifted

the gun, to her left, as she hadn't seen or heard anything
threatening since leaving the house. She had navigated the
trail all the way back up and past the snag, where Jake had
finally been able to stop Pied, and would have made it into
the meadow, except for one slick rock, and a little marshy
spot right at the meadow's mouth. The stream diverged in
rivlets and then remerged. Her foot hit a rock in the
shadow, and down she went kerplop, on her backside. She
jumped up instantly out of the water, as the shock of the
cold hit her like a knife. She shivered, and moaned with
the chill, and tried to beat some water out of her clothing,
and the poncho, but she had managed to keep the
Winchester high and dry, out of the water. She knew that
she had to go back to the house immediately, but the
meadow was just ahead of her. She made little sucking
sounds, and quiet moos, like the calf's mother might. But
the calf never made a sound, and she would have missed it
for sure, if she hadn't stepped right over it in the
moonlight. She dropped straight down beside the calf and
grabbed it tight in case it tried to struggle. Even though it
was almost newborn, it still weighed half her weight.
"Gotcha," she said in triumph, and then began to
immediately to soothe the cold and frightened animal and
rub it to warm and reassure it. Soon it stirred and began to
respond, with little whimpers, at first, and then a good
bawl, then it tried to stand up, but its' legs were asleep
from so long in one spot, and it had to try several times
before it made a solid footing.

Betsey was totally chilled, and her teeth were chattering
loudly, as she put her thumb into a little comb of honey,
she was carrying wrapped in a waxed paper. She brushed
the thumb against the calf's lips, and the calf went for the
thumb, like it was a tit. She gave him several tastes, and
moved him around a bit, and about dawn, she and the calf
moved off down the canyon, with her moving him along as
fast as she could. He would sometimes balk on her and

she would have to let him try to nurse, but he wasn't getting exactly what he wanted, although it was good enough to keep him moving all the way back to the house. A little after sunup, Betsey and the calf made it down the canyon, by the creek trail, back to the little house in Arequa.

Mama Posey was waiting on the porch, watching out for her youngest, and smoking her corncob pipe. This was something that she saved for big stress or a big hoedown. She sat it on the porch rail and helped Betsey to get the calf back with its' limping mother. With the corral gate open, and Jack not coming home, Dan, the only other horse of the Hoopoleiths, decided to make a dash for freedom, and high tailed it thru the gate. Mama Posey tried to head him off, but Dan smelled a runabout, and some fun, and would have run right over her, if she hadn't given way, and let him go. "If that don't beat all," she shook her head as the big black lifted his tail and ran off down the valley.

About the time they got the calf squared away, and got back to the fire at the house, Posey discovered Betsey was wet. She stripped her out of the wet clothes and built up the fire and wrapped her in a blanket. It was too late, however, and Betsey took to the sniffles and then a fever set in, as she had pushed her body way past its' limit. Within twenty-four hours, she had a raging fever, and Mama was applying poultice cures and herbal teas to her around the clock. So, there they all sat, a sorry lot of humans, the next evening when a wagon came rattling up the road from the South.

Sam had come out on the porch at the sound of the approaching wagon, and inspite of the rumatiz, which was still getting him down, squinted against the failing light, and could just make out the form of their distant neighbor, Arkansas Toothpick, driving the wagon which was approaching.

"Glory be, Posey, the Toothpicks isa' comin'," and hobbled off the porch toward the approaching wagon. Posey put more coffee in the big blue enamel pot, and threw some more wood on the cook fire in the little stove. Jake woke up and came out of the back room pulling on his suspenders. Betsey came drooping out from the loft, and pulling a blanket around her shoulders, sat on the front of the porch and leaned her head on the rail, as if she hadn't strength to sit up. Soon the pot was boiling, and Mama had everyone with a steaming mug, out in the yard and around the little table. They had been down south a piece to trade at a fair, as Arkansas was a part time blacksmith, who would shoe a horse for a neighbor, but his passion in iron was the making of knives, which is partly where he had got his name. Sam and him fell into talk about a deal for some red cedar post of good size and length, that Toothpick wanted for a new corral. Sam wanted the knife as a present for Jake, who had a birthday coming in a month. They couldn't quite agree on a fair trade and argued back and forth as to the value of each commodity and labor in producing. This was just the opening tussle in a negotiation that might go on for some time, as Toothpick was very proud of his forge hardened, and oil dip quenched blades. He worked the red-hot blades in coal, pounding and folding the grain of the metal, knowing just how to make it hard steel, without being brittle, an art won thru many hours of pounding over a hot forge. He had lost his real name, somewhere along the way, and rumor was that he could do more with a knife than just forge them, and that was what got him in the trouble that made him leave his name behind.

He soon realized that Sam was not buying today, and tossing the last of his coffee down and thanking Posey for the third time, and flattering the good quality and strength of her coffee, which was a show of wealth of the little family, he wanted to do something kind for them seeing

50

them all stove up, and in the shape they were in, and asked them to a hoedown that was happening, for which he was playing the fiddle. He regretted saying anything as soon as he spoke, realizing that the Hoopolieth's were in poor shape. They made a laughable rag tag bunch, hunched on the porch eagerly hanging on each word of their personable neighbor. Posey spoke up for them right away with regret in her voice.

"We kain't go; all broke up; Sam's down with th' rumatiz; Betsy's got th' fever; Jake's got 'is arm broke; old Pied broke 'er laig, and the hosses is run off. So, ye see, we kain't go. But if you all 'ill come over to Cripple Creek," she gazed along the porch, trying to improve the family's morale with a little joke, "we'll he'p ye out th' best we can fur yer hoedown."

"Well," said Arkansas, "when I get finished on Saturday over yonder, we might jus' come on back and do a little fun here for you folks." And with that, Arkansas rolled his wagon toward home, as the Hoopolieths waved and hollered bye and urged him to keep his promise, Posey promising a fine peach cobbler, if he did, until he was out of sight up the road.

Jake cared for the calf and saw that Pied was fed and turned out for exercise. The calf tried to get the runs, and Jake had to milk Pied out with his one good arm, and she had to be hobbled for that. He had some trouble with the tits with his awkward left hand, but he got better at it fast. Dan came edging around the perimeter of the pasture, having failed to find Jack, and got lonely. Betsey coaxed him up with a bit of sweet feed made of whole corn kernels, and grains of oats, rolled in sorghum syrup. She was almost free of fever and felt well enough to move about the yard. Sam's rumatiz eased a bit with increasing warm weather, and Mama rocked and smoked her corncob on the little porch. And that is the way that they were a few afternoons later, when a whole troop of Toothpick's,

51

nephews, and cousins, come whoopin' up the road to Arequa, driving a short horn heifer, with Arkansas riding on Jack, and making sure the heifer didn't turn aside, and get away from the group coming along behind.

Arkansas dismounted in front of the cabin, and removing a venison quarter from the saddle horn, let Jake take the reins of the big brown. "He ran all the way to Sidley," he laughingly observed to Jake. And then giving the venison haunch to Posey, he told her, "Posey, I sure hope you make that peach cobbler." Posey lit out to carve the meat and prepare it and soon had a cobbler to go with it.

"Sam," Arkansas said, "I'm gonna need those ten post, and ten more like'um. I brung ya tha knife that we talked about, and this here heifer for the other ten."

"That's shore a good deal to me," Sam mused "but I can't tak'er. With Jake laid up, I couldn't get them post to ya anytime soon."

"We can argue about that later," Arkansas had his fiddle brought up by one of the boys, that was waiting for the order, from his tribal chief. Arkansas had Scot blood in him. Another lad brought up the bag pipes. Arkansas chose the bag pipes and the whole clan marched to and fro in the afternoon light, until all that wanted to try and play, were out of breath. It was getting dark when they had built a fire outside and ate venison and peach cobbler. Then Arkansas, finally, picked up the fiddle and began. Arkansas Toothpick played a song called Devel's Dream that the fiddlers in the Appalacian Mountains had played in the Georgia and Carolina gold fields.

He played and Mama rocked, and old Pied patted her bad leg on the ground. Old Sam worked his rumatiz out of his hips, and Jake was jumpin' and flapin' like a chicken with his broken arm. Betsey had so many cousins and nephews that they all just joined hands at last and danced in a circle. Their faces glowed in the firelight. The fiddler called tune after tune.

Arkansas Toothpick was sawin' out another Irish jig on his fiddle. Something about the way Jake was flappin' his arms to the music and hoppin' on one leg, and the way Pied kept puttin' her lame leg on the ground and lifting it in time to the music, made Arkansas, suddenly put an extra note in the jig, and singing out loud and clear, sang, "Goin' up to Cripple Creek, goin' on a run. Goin' up to Cripple Creek, to have a little fun." Arkansas bowed out that extra note, and right there, an American classic fiddle piece was born. Jake got to hoppin' so fast he lost his balance and fell back in the camp fire. All the sweat, and oil of days of exertion, caught on fire, as Jake beat at his rear end and ran for the stream, Arkansas hit the last note, just as the hiss of steam came up from where Jake plopped himself into the creek. "Ahhh," Jake gave a satisfied sigh just managing to keep his butt from getting badly burned. A snicker from Betsey, soon spread to a roar of laughter, as they all had tears running down their cheeks, from the absurdity of the whole situation.

Bob Womack was looking for a cow he lost from his little herd. Bob kept a sharp eye on the ground, and one out for the cow, because he had the gold fever, and he always watched the ground he was covering. Besides, it paid to watch your step. This morning in the sunlight, something caught his eye. He stepped closer and reached down and brushed away some dirt at the base of a rock just behind the boulder, and at the outside of a bend in the creek. It was an odd rock, of a purplish color, hard like granite, but very unusual. Bob turned it over and over in his hand looking at it in the sunlight. He was cautious, as he had looked at many ore samples over the years. But, he thought that he was not fooled this time. Gold has a certain heaviness to the ore that distinguishes it from other ore and rock. Bob got that tingle, he knew that this time he was not fooled. He began to search around for more. He squinted into the morning sun and checked the hillsides, marked his position with a small cairn of rocks stacked one on top of the other, and then began to slowly move up the stream, searching as he went. He didn't see another one like it. but he knew it was there. He had always known. The people around had scoffed, but he had told them all, that there was gold in the Cripple Creek Area around Poverty Gulch, and gold that had been washed into the stream. He caught a red color of a cambric cotton shirt, and figured it to be Jake Hoopoleith out on his ranch rounding up what cattle he could find. He waited for Jake to approach and haled him down.

"Whoa, there Mr. Hoopoleith," Bob hollered at him. Jake reigned in and brought the big Brown around to a stand.

"Well, Mr. Womack, I reckon we both got some brands out here in this alpine land." Jake eased his hat back on his head, and took a big red bandana from around his neck and wiped the sweat band where the hot sunlight had moistened his scalp.

Bob looked off in the distance and let the big horse of Jake's nuzzle the ground at his boot looking for a mouthful of grass to chew around the bit. Jake let him go slack, and that was a good sign that he wanted to take time to talk. Bob let the horse graze a minute. "I hear that your folks are moving South, are you a'goin that way too?"

"Mama is already gone on to Raton, and Pa and my sister been over there for three weeks, so I just have to round up the strays, and get the last of the kit and kettle." Jake stepped down out of the saddle and stretched his legs a little.

"Let me round up for you and sell your brand, and I'll send you the money, if you like."

"That would be mighty nice of you Bob."

"What are you and your folks gonna do with your land and house?"

"Probably let the claim go back and abandon the land and house, no one would give nothing for it."

"Now I wouldn't be to sure of that," Bob said, with a twinkle in his eye. "I might need a line cabin up this way and title might be nice, if the price was right."

"Well, now there is a thought, I'm sure Pa would be good with it. He paid a ten cent per acre abstract fee, each of the four of us filed on a forty acre section, so we got one hundred sixty acres all in all, two filed in Ma and Pa's name, two filed in mine and sis's name over in the court house at Colorado City."

"That's sixty-four dollars, and say another thirty six for the house?" Bob questioned hopefully.

Jake didn't hesitate a minute, but stuck out his hand, "Mr. Womack, you done bought yourself a one quarter of a square mile, right smack in the middle of Poverty Gulch, bless your soul."

"Well, Jake, it'll suit my wants, fer what line work I want to do, and keep me from comin' all the way up from my sister's place in the Springs."

They both shook on a good deal, and Bob Womack was camping' in style at his cabin, finally out of William and Ida's hair. He was on his new ranch, by sunset two days later. He and Jake went over to Colorado City and recorded the deed transfer, and Bob packed some things from his sister's house and lit out back to his new porch. He pulled out his whiskey flask and had a big party in the afternoon sun that next sunset, at which he mused on the fact that fortune was many times a matter of timing. Having mined this nugget of enlightenment, he then built the stove up and snored through the cold night and the next day.

He was close to the bonanza now; he felt it. He was out scouring the creek beds in the area, every minute that he could break away from his chores on the ranch. He was finding little bits of color every now and then, but it didn't seem to make any sense. No float trail uphill could be found, at least not at first. Sometime in May of the following year was an interim election year, and a durn good reason for going into Colorado City. He went to see what the boys was talking about, and what might be happening in the East. Drinking a few beers, Bob pulled out a gnarled looking stone from his overalls and set it on the bar. "Boys," he addressed the bar room, "Ya'll been having a great big laugh out of me for years, but this time I got the proof."

A general chuckle ran up from the room, and Major Demary, who was at the far end of the bar, mimicking Bob's distinctive high-pitched drawl, called out, "Gold, it's gold." Someone in the back mockingly yelled out, "It's Gold, it glitters in the sunlight." Another voice hooted.

"OK boys, that's good enough from you all, this sample is gonna shut your mouths for good. You been hurrahin' me for years, and I keep on telling' you young know-it-alls that ther' is a mountain of gold up ther' on the Western side of The Peak, and this here ugly ole rock," he kissed it a slurpin' kiss, and took another pull on his beer, is gonna settle your hash.

Theodore Lowe stood back from the end of the bar, next to Major Demary, and came around to where Bob was drinking.

"Would you mind, Mr Womack, if I had a look at that rock. I'd be real curious to see some gold."

"Indeed, you would," said Bob, in a slightly drunken swoop, plopped the rock into Lowe's hand. "Take a good look at it Theo my lad, cause it's the rock that is gonna to change things around here. Yes sir, you boys are a'gona laugh out the other side of your faces."

Lowe inspected the sample for a long time, and took it close up under one of the lamps for inspection, and was joined by several other men including Henry Cocking, who came in for a closer look than the rest, and then gave Lowe a knowing look, and then put on his best poker face. "What you gonna do with this here volcanic float," Lowe gave the sample back to Bob.

"Well, I guess I'll have it assayed up in Denver," Bob allowed with a pleased smile on his face.

"Have you got the minimum assay weight of this same sample," Theo asked him matter of fact. He made it seem that he had some knowledge of the process, when in fact, he didn't know if there was a minimum or not, but it buffaloed Bob for the moment, and brought a further chuckle from the men standing closest. Bob had to set his beer down and scratch his head on that one. "I got a friend in Denver," Lowe continued, "and he works for an assayer in his office, and I reason he owes me a favor or two as we been in a tight place once or twice durin' the war." Theo

57

paused to let the import of this camaraderie sink in on Bob, who was throwing' down another brew. "I expect I can get him to do what they call a short assay," he was gettin' pretty creative on the new ale himself. "I'll be up in Denver next week, and I can carry it up there and get you an assay, for sure."

The alcohol had hit Bob's blood, but good, and he reared back and hollered a big yahoo. The bartender got a worried look and watched his gun hand, knowing that at this point his patrons sometimes put a few bullet holes in his ceiling, and other spots. But Bob was just feeling flushed and after thanking Theo for his kindness and handing him the rock that was going to change everything in his life, he ordered drinks all around, and noticing the bartenders now otherwise worried look, soothed his fear, "I just sold three head of cattle to the army supply, so I got good army dollars to spend, and they're a burnin' a hole." With that he pulled a wad of notes from his pocket and slapped them on the bar and Burt started pouring everyone the shot or beer of their choice.

It was high summer and past by the time Theo came back from Denver with a report, but it was exciting enough to get Henry Cocking out on the rough road up Phantom Gulch to the bottom of the feeder stream that the Womacks had named Cripple Creek, partly from incidence and partly from nostalgia, as they had come from an area named the same in Virginia. The two passed a bottle back and forth at regular intervals, and this was impeding their progress over the rough rock that rose around them like a jumble of ice sheets in a glacier, only this tumble and folding was of granite, with millions of years of carving by the water and wind to further sharpen and weather the surfaces. They picked a path worn by mules and men, up the winding canyon and crisscrossing the tumbling stream over and over, keeping their feet wet. Henry let out a good string of epitaphs each time the way was blocked and they had to cross.

"Don't break that other bottle," Lowe warned Henry. "Were gonna need it to loosen the old man up. Try to get him to show us exactly where he picked up the rock."

"I know somethin' about these formations," Henry claimed. "I was up a Leadville for over a year, and I guess I learned a thing or two."

They had come around a small grove of trees in a bend of the stream, when the house, rough logs with unchinked holes that a man could stick his fist through, came in view, with an inviting little curl of smoke rising up from the chimney. Theo "Halloed" the house real loud and friendly with a little lilt in his voice.

"He ain't never shot at nobody up here, has he," asked Henry a little nervously?

"Naw, old Womack'd give ya the shirt right off his back. You never met a better old cowboy. But now it don't never pay to startle a man, and walk up on him, with no warning."

Womack came out on the porch pulling up a suspender on his long johns, as he was dressed against a nip that had come in the air at this altitude, even though the summer was still in bloom at lower elevations. He halloed back for them to come on up to the house and motioned them inside to the fire. He scooped up a load of wood and stepped back in the cabin to build up the fire. Theo waved the bottle that he had Henry carry up the canyons with jubilee at Bob and the old cowboy got a twinkle in his eye right away.

Henry and Theo found a little path that led up to the cabin and made their way up and around to the entrance. The cabin was tiny and the three men filled it up. They shook hands all around, with Bob saying, "Boy's glad you could get up this way, as I don't see many out this far."

"We brought you some good whiskey," Henry offered.

"Much obliged," Bob took the bottle and took a hearty

pull.

They sat by the fire and both Henry and Theo stretched out their feet and rested their legs. It was a walk of over ten miles, and they had been at it since before daylight, as not knowing whether they would find Bob Womack's place, had to be prepared to return to the City or find themselves sleeping in the open on the trail.

"I got good news on that sample that I took to Denver," Theo ventured with a serious import to his voice. Bob sat up in his chair and leaned closer.

"Weren't pyrite, was it?"

"It assayed two hundred dollars to the ton," Theo handed Bob a slip of paper.

"That's pretty near ten ounces to the ton," Henry chimed in with excitement in his voice. Theo pulled out the bottle that he had carried along the road up Phantom Gulch Canyon and waved it in front of Bob's face. "That calls for a drink, I say." He broke the tax seal and handed Bob the bottle.

"I'll vote fer that one," Bob took a good pull on the bottle, and then grimaced, as the alcohol burned his throat, down to his stomach. "Ahh," he chortled, and the two men looked knowingly at one another. "Glad you boys come up, gets mighty lonesome up here, of course, I got my brother, and his wife and child up at the cabin on the other side of the creek, but they don't want me hangin' around all the time, and we ain't partnerin' on any cattle or nuthin'." He lowered his voice at this, "And they think I'm plumb touched in the head about gold being around here," he winked, and touched the side of his head with his index finger.

"Well, we know you ain't crazy any, Bob," Henry offered encouragement. "Say, where'd you find that rock we had assayed, anyway?" Lowe gave his companion a stern look, as they had agreed that they would let the old cowboy drink for a while, and then Theo would be the one

60

to broach the subject of the exact location of where the sample had been found, that he had transported to Denver, and had assayed.

"I'll show you boy's exactly where it come from, and it ain't far from here, neither." Bob had a shine of contentment in his eye from good whiskey, a warm house, and friends by the stove that he was gonna make rich. He told them, as they plied him with drink. He told them about the dreams of a mountain of gold, with a solid gold heart, that beat in his dreams like a live thing. The two men eyed each other, and shrugged and shook their heads, and tried to convince him to come away and show them immediately; they could not wait. But Bob had things just the way he wanted and was in no hurry to play his hole card. He scoffed at their attempts to rush him, and broke out his best fat back, and put a big batch of black beans on to cook and soon had it bubbling away by bringing the little stove to heat with glowing coals. He placated them with a promise to show them everything the next morning, "And, boys, he confided to them, there is some more interesting finds, and I got a cairn built on every site. Yesiree, I'm gonna track that gold right to its source." And, with these assurances, and the camaraderie that was established by the confidences and the fire and food, Theo, and Henry let their feet rest from the long walk up from Colorado City, and eagerly embraced Bob's suggestion of a friendly card game. They were careful not to cheat the generous, drunken cowboy out of very little more than the cost of the whiskey.

The next morning, Bob was up early, in spite of the bender he had pulled. Cocking and Lowe were still asleep, and Bob made the coffee and put on the sourdough from where he let it work, in an old can of Red Man Chewing Tobacco. He built up the stove and had some scrambled eggs going when the other two men began to awaken to the good smells and the heat.

"Bob," Cocking asked, "when are you going to show us where that volcanic tuft came from?"

"It's a short walk from here up the gulch to the north, and we can go there as soon as you boys get this grub put away. When the men were finished, Bob took up the pans, and taking them a way outside, put some sandy dirt in the pans and dusted them out down to the old layers and then placed them aside to soak up and dry. Bob led the way out of the gully to the north, and as they walked along, Bob pointed out some of the interesting things about the formations that the gully had cut through. He was mostly gassing, as he knew very little about the things that he was pointing to, but it served to draw the men's attention to the rocks in some detail. Cocking and Lowe kept picking up shiny rocks infused with mica and examining the stones with care.

"That's just mica, mica everywhere," Bob told them when they were particularly intrigued with a stone. "There ain't no gold in that formation at all. You can pick them little flakes out and mash them with your fingernail and see how soft the specks are, too soft for gold." The men continued up the gully to the north, until they came to a stack of rock that Bob pointed out to them. "That stack tells me where to turn up hill and we go that a way." Bob pointed up the hill and led the men in that direction.

When they had proceeded about two thousand yards toward the crest, they came to another stack of rock that would have escaped the notice of Henry and Theo, if Bob had not pointed it out to them.

"That piece of volcanic float was laying on top of the ground, right there," Bob pointed at a spot on the ground. The other two men began to search the area, turning over rocks that took both to lift. After a couple hours of scouring the area, the two men grew tired of looking and began to complain.

"There ain't another damn rock here that looks

anything like that rock we had assayed," complained Theo.

"I know that is true," agreed Womack, "as I have searched every rock on the side on this hill in all directions, and have not come up with a single other rock like it."

"Some Indian might have carried this in here from anywhere," observed Henry.

"Or," chimed in Theo, "the way these things go, it could have blown out of an ancient volcano all the way from Creede. That purple rock looks a lot like the formation that is around the Bachelor Mine that is there." Both the men stretched and worked the kinks out of their backs and gave each other a look that said that there was nothing more to be gained here today.

Cocking dropped a rock he had been holding. "Guess we better head for the Springs, Theo," Henry observed that if they did not leave soon, they would be stuck for the night, if they did not want to travel in the dark part of the way. A cloud crossed Bob's face, as he liked the company, and spent far too much time in isolation from other humans. He was loath to spend much time at his brother's cabin, as was under considerable criticism from both the other adults, who were aghast at the amount of drunkenness that Womack practiced.

"You boys are sure welcome to stay the night and look around some more tomorrow. I got some good grub that I can fix up and all the whiskey ain't gone yet," Bob looked hopefully at the other two, who both shook their heads.

"Of all the ground we covered, and nothing showing, Bob, I just don't figure there is any use," Henry replied.

Bob snorted his disapproval, "I been searching these hill sides for thirteen years," Bob rejoined to them, "and I know that there is gold here." They made their way back to the cabin and gathered their gear, leaving Bob the rest of the whiskey, as they could get more in town and had brought it for him, so that it seemed totally ungracious to take it away. Bob turned to start back toward the cabin, and they drifted off down the hill.

"It is sure nice to have company," Bob called after them. After a brief farewell wave, Bob watched the men make their way back down the gully toward Phantom Gulch Road and resisted the lonesome impulse to tag along to the Springs. Besides, Bob had seen something that he wanted to investigate that the other two men had not seen, as he had noticed a line of fault that he had not seen before, bearing a little of the purple color of the telluride that he had found earlier, that had been blown from deep below and lain and tumbled down the hillside, all those eons ago.

Chapter 7. (April Eighteen-Eighty-Four) Ol' Mose

A hint of springtime began to penetrate into the winter den and tickle his nose. He rolled and changed positions and grunted a couple of times and let out a deep sneezing cough. Another smell penetrated his olfactory glands, and a message of danger was carried to his huge emiglia in the back of the mammalian brain. He shook his giant head and came awake with the adrenalin shot that came with the realization that two scents were present. He smelled man, and he smelled cordite. A man, no, two men were near, and they carried the guns that had stung him so many times. He growled and bit at his back where a bullet was lodged next to his backbone, and it caused him constant irritation.

"He's in there alright," Bob Womack told the other men as he crawled back from the entrance to the den. "I heard him growl. That Ol' Mose has already caught our scent."

Bob Witherspoon straightened and stepped back from the mouth and rubbed his two day stubble. Reckon he's got another entrance to the den?"

"Mose has always got a second entrance and maybe more in every den that has been found. So, I reckon that he has one here."

Whistler, Bob's horse, staked out some yards away with Witherspoon's mount, made a nervous whinny. Both men looked toward the horses. Both horses were milling nervously, and both horses' eyes were wide with fright.

"I'll be darned," Bob exclaimed. "He's done broke out of the other entrance. "That's one cagey bear."

Both men headed for the horses, and as they moved away from the mouth of the den, they could hear brush being broken with tortured snapping and cracking.

"He always cleans his main entrance, but he leaves

himself a dense second exit," Bob threw over his shoulder, as he swung onto Whistler's saddle, and reined him down slope parallel with the crashing sounds. "Won't be no use trying to follow that trail. It'll be a tangled mess."
Whistler responded to Bob's reining him down slope and took off so fast that Witherspoon's less responsive mount, was soon left behind. Bob turned his rifle and settled it into the holster mounted just in front of the saddle horn. He would need both hands free for the pell mell plunge downhill. Whistler was plenty familiar with the chase. Bob and he had chased many elk, deer, and bear, along the Four Mile creek, and they soon hit the junction, near the bottom of the draw, and turned up the north bank of West Four Mile, watching for the broken trail of brush, and the prints that would appear in the soft ground on the bank of the stream. Ol' Mose was estimated to weigh about a thousand pounds when he emerged each spring from hibernation, and half that much again, in the fall when he settled in for the long Colorado winter. That kind of weight would leave plenty of evidence were he to cross the stream. Bob cut the trail, and followed along the streams North bank, where it tumbled along from the West. He moved uneasily in the saddle and pulled up to wait for Witherspoon's horse to catch up.

"Whistler's getting tired," he observed. "Ol' Mose is into some rough country down in Eleven Mile Canyon that he knows good. I'm going to head down to Currant Creek and get on the stage road and drop by Frank Welty's house and tell him that we flushed Ol' Mose from his winter quarters. He's got a buffalo calf for sale, and I think it might make just the pet for my little niece," Bob observed, as he reined a tired horse away from the twisted, and dense trail that the bear always choose, and down along a more forgiving growth, and slope. Eventually, miles of rough brush country later, they broke out on a road of sorts, that ran back toward the south and Cannon City. They took this south for several miles, before they would reach the turn off that led back toward Frank Welty's homestead.

All along the way, they were meeting an increasing number of men headed in the other direction. It didn't take long for Bob Womack to get curious, and he stopped one floppy hatted traveler on a mule.

"Howdy, stranger," he questioned the man. "Where are all you feller's makin' for on this here road?"

"I'm agoin' up to the Mt. Pisgah gold strike. I just come in on the train to Cannon City, and am followin' the trail to the Mt. Pisgah gold strike."

Bob explained to the man, that Mt. Pisgah was a days ride east, but the fellow just mumbled that he was following the other fellows along the trail, and left Bob pulling his hat off and scratching his head. "Now what in tarnation do you suppose that's all about," he said to himself, more than his saddle buddy.

"Suppose somebody struck gold up on Mt. McIntyre," Bob Witherspoon asked?

"Not a chance," Bob scratched his chin. "I've been all over that country up there hunting elk and lookin' around. It's just the wrong kind of ground for placer prospecting. Somethin' ain't right." Bob said this to himself many times under his breath, as they made their way along the road, passing man after man and sometimes buggies, and even a stage came by headed the other way. Eventually, they reached the turnoff to Frank Welty's and Bob Witherspoon, having had enough of the ride, and wanting to be home, gave his reasons and split off toward his home. Bob continued on along the road at a leisurely pace, stopping at a crossing of West Four Mile Creek, and letting Whistler drink, graze, and rest for close to an hour, before arriving at Frank Welty's in the early afternoon.

Frank was out tending the mules that he used in his freighting business. The buffalo calf was following like a pet, right behind him.

"Hallo," Bob doffed his hat and called out loud, and put Whistler in a run, sliding to a stop, outside the corral. Bob always liked to arrive with a bit of drama.

"Howdy, Bob," Frank Welty grinned up at him. "What brings you down to this neck of the woods?"

"That's a fine little buffalo calf you got following you," Bob dismounted and dropped Whistler's reigns over a railing. Whistler immediately began to look wide eyed at the bucket of molasses coated oats that Frank was using to lure the mules to him, and the buffalo calf stopped and tried to gage the horse's intentions.

"He thinks he's a dog the way he follows me around when I'm doin' my chores," Frank observed. He scratched the calf's ear, and then bent it, and shoved away, so that the gate would open and give Bob room to come into the corral.

"Stay, Whistler," Bob told the horse, who had made a move to follow him inside, to try and get his muzzle into the coated grain. The smell was just too irresistible after the long hours of exertion, and the horse tried again to follow. Bob swatted at him with his hat, for failing to obey, but Frank grabbed another bucket nearby, and poured a small amount of grain into it, and set it through the railing for the horse to try and chew around the bit in his mouth. He came up out of the bucket mostly slobbers, but he was getting a taste and that was settling him down. The buffalo calf stuck his head up to the railing, and his nostrils flared as he tried to catch a whiff of the grain in the bucket.

"Sure is a tame little thing," Bob reached and rubbed the calf behind the ears.

"Just a big pet," Frank affirmed. The mules stomped impatiently, and he moved to a trough and poured some of the grain. The mules bit at each other, establishing a pecking order, and Frank moved to a second trough and poured a little more for the animals that had been excluded from the first batch. Bob continued to scratch and pet the buffalo calf. The calf looked longingly at the trough that the mules were feeding from but knew better than to try to approach them.

"Frank," Bob began, "this is sure one friendly little critter. Ima's daughter is goin' on five years now, and she makes a pet out of everything, but she gets lonely not having any children around her age, and I was just a'thinkin' that this here buffalo calf would make a perfect pet for her. You suppose that you might sell 'em to me?"

"Well, I might consider that, he's weaned off the bottle, and more nuisance than pet to me. What do ya think he might be worth?"

Bob studied on that a moment, and pulled at his hat, scratched behind his right ear. "Well, I sure do hate to put a price on another man's stock. What do you reckon he might be worth?"

That put Frank to scratching his head, and he figured, and studied on the question a minute, and set the oat bucket down where the calf could get the last few grains left in the bottom.

"You sure would be makin' a little girl happy," Bob put in as a bit of a wedge. Just then, the men's attention was drawn toward the road, as a rider was coming fast toward them.

"Looks like Captain Grose," Frank observed, shading his eyes. "He's likely come to tell you about the gold strike over at his place," Frank said with a skeptical grunt.

"Is that what all those men are doin' on the Currant Creek Road?"

"It's just plumb crazy," Frank shook his head. "Best I can tell, Chicken Bill paid a couple of old bums, one named Bradley, and a surveyor, whose name I can't recall, to come up here and stake a claim that they call the Teller Placer. They staked it on the slopes of Mt. McIntyre, over

69

on some government land that borders Grose's property, land that he has free range rights on, and has been running cattle on during the summers."

"Chicken Bill Lovell," Bob questioned? "That Leadville shaft salter that got caught in the snowstorm, and got found buried in feathers of chickens that he e't up?"

"That's the one," Frank confirmed, "and they're saying that the merchants in Canōn City is in on it, too." Both men turned to face the rider, and Bob placed an arm on the corral railing and fingered Whistler's reigns to keep the horse from being startled by the rider coming on fast.

"Howdy, Bob, Frank," Grose said, trotting up, and reining to a halt, with great purpose, and importance.

"Captain," both men acknowledged the man's standing from war time.

"Bob," Grose began, "have you heard about the gold strike over at the base of Mt. McIntyre?"

"Ain't heard a word about it," Bob quirked an eyebrow in mock surprise.

"Well, this here's your lucky day," Grose began his pitch. Two prospectors, one named Bradley and a surveyor named Miller, done struck a rich placer load just north of Kittridge's ranch. It done assayed at over a hundred ounces to the ton!"

"A hundred ounces to the ton," Bob repeated! "Why that's amazin'," Bob shook his head in disbelief.

"Maybe more," Grose continued. There callin' it the Teller Shaft, and there are fifty are more placer claims staked out all around. "Tim Hussey, and the Houghtons, and Pat Walsh are already up there with good claims staked out, so you better high tail it up there and stake yours, if you don't want to miss out altogether." Grose clasped his hands together. "Why there's a town sprung up overnight." Grose was obviously pleased.

"Guess I'll have to get up that way and see what's going on," Bob agreed.

"Well, boys," Grose wheeled his horse, "I got to spread the word," and he spurred his horse into a full gallop, like a posse was on his trail.

"Well, what do you make of that," Bob mused?

"Money changing hands," Frank shook his head. It could be hauling tender feet in by the wagon load, but it just seems like plain stealing and worse. Them boys is mostly destitute miners come down from Fairplay, and Leadville, cause the opportunities is played out up there, and they're milking the last dollar out of 'em with this hoax."

Ol' Mose crossed the Arkansas River at his crossing at Spike Buck on Tallahassee Mountain, playing in the water at the crossing. He splashed sprays of water into the air with his great paws and puzzled over the change in light that appeared in the air.

Once, so rudely awakened, he wandered far into the north of his range. In the springtime, he followed the berries up the streams and gullies always bearing northward. Crossing into the Gunnison River valley, he ranged into the high country far up the Gunnison to the ranch house that he had come to know through the years.

He had watched for years as the operation had built up. He had taken many a yearling steer, and many a suckling calf, when the elk had moved into the mountains where they were harder to catch. The slow-moving cattle were no match for Ol' Mose, who was known to have taken over five hundred cattle from ranchers by 1889. He had watched the ranching operation go from a small outfit to a considerable spread with many men and horses.

From that spring when Bob Womack had run him from the den in Eleven Mile Canyon, he had made five round trips to this most northern part of his range. This day, in 1889, a noise of angry voices drew him near.

The man that built the ranch was furious mad. That

71

was obvious to a bear in the woods. Ol' Mose watched as the man slapped and yelled at a young girl with him in the yard. It seemed right for bears but somehow didn't look right for people.

Peter Yates had been hauling coal to Nat Tatum for the steam saw that he used to cut the marble at the new Yule Marble Mine. He had been receiving stock in the Mining Company that Tatum had formed. So, when Peter was pinned and killed under a falling slab of stone that sloughed off unexpectedly, Tatum found himself as executor of his partners estate, as Peter had died without a will, and the money owed the partnership had to be accounted for.

Rafflen Janeck had come to the upper Gunnison area as soon as the Ute's were forced out. He had actually staked a homestead claim before the treaty date.

Ranching had made him successful, but as coal was discovered and then later the outcropping of marble, pure white marble, some thirty miles southeast of his ranching interest, where he now ran hundreds of head of cattle on the open range of the high country, other men with money began to arrive. He had come even before the Treaty of 1878 had opened up the area. He had picked up quite a few extra dollars during those years killing buffalo for tongue and hide. Then he had bought the bones, from the bone pickers, and ground them into bone meal for cattle feed. The high protein bone meal stimulated the appetite of the cattle in the feed lots, making them put on extra pounds and therefore, more money when they reached Chicago.

Money and land, Raff Janeck had. Now, as he looked around, he saw men with wealth from natural resources coming into the area, like Hotchkiss and the men that followed him from the lake area.

Another thing that these men had, was a wife. He

had always had to go to the seamy side of Denver. Janeck had grown tired of the lonely life he led at his wilderness ranch.

And so, it is no small wonder that while talking with Nat Tatum, the owner of the land where the newly discovered marble was located, upon the learning of Peter Yates death while moving a large block of marble at the quarry, a light, or rather a dim lantern of an idea began to glow in Raff's lizard brain.

"Who's going to be executor of his will, and whose going to look after those orphans," Raff asked, with fained concern?

"I guess that as Yates' partner, I would be, as his wife is dead, and his boy is not of age yet," Tatum pulled at his long white beard. Elizabeth, being a girl, and women having no legal standing, was not considered. "The Olmstead's are taking care of the young'ens. Mrs. Olmstead midwifed the boy's birth, and not only did the mother die, but the boy was damaged; blue baby. You know, he's a little shy of a few cards. Olmstead wants me to apprentice the boy here at the quarry, so I'll probably have Olmstead sign apprentice papers on him, as he's a guardian to the boy."

"That girl's about marrin' age, ain't she," Raff blurted out?

"Jes' about," Nat looked appraisingly at the other man.

"She's takin' a shine to me," Janeck blustered. "I seen it several times. Her daddy and me done talked," he asserted. What he didn't say was Peter Yates had turned the idea down cold, as Elizabeth was too young to consider even thinking about courting.

"I see," Nat, who owed Peter Yates money for coal to keep his quarry saws running, and had been trading Peter shares of the Yule Marble Mine, as it was known, from the previous owner, suddenly understood a way to absolve himself of a problem, and perhaps profit from the whole business. "Raff, why don't you come by this evening for some supper, and I'll invite the Yates children, as well?"

"Well, Nat, I'd be much obliged for an invitation like that," he put out his hand, and the two men shook on the deal.

The first time that Nat Tatum brought Raff Janeck to the Olmstead's place, they said that they were there about some legal problem with the Olmstead's Homestead filing. Elizabeth didn't understand much of what she heard, but she noticed Raff Janeck kept looking at her. It wasn't the first time that she had seen him leering at her from some spot in town that she was bound to pass, when she came to the store, the one dry goods store in what was becoming known as Hotchkiss.

It was a very few weeks after that, when Mr. Olmstead told Elizabeth that she was a very lucky girl to be getting married to Raff Jeneck, that he was very wealthy, and a person in the country to be noticed. Elizabeth's mouth just flapped, and no words of protest would come. The shock of her father's death was still vivid. Now this just couldn't be, but it was. She stood before the altar in a white dress on that day, and did as she was told. She mouthed the words she was told to say in a voice that even she could not hear. And then, that night had been unspeakable. The liquor, his disgust at her ineptness. He made no show of love and never wasted a chance to denigrate her. Early on, he had locked her up in a room, but when her spirit was broken, he let her out, except when he beat her. Then he would lock her up again, until the bruising healed some.

It was when she heard that Harry had been apprenticed off to someone, knowing that he would not do well among people that did not love him, and be patient with him, that she was shocked into pondering her situation, and determining that her father would not want her to let these things happen to Harry and to her. She began to watch and began to form a plan. To these ends, she complied with Janeck, as she knew that she must. He was pleased, and began to dress her up, and show her around to the ranch hands and even trips to town.

Elizabeth watched for her chance and tried to learn where her brother had been sent. She heard that he was apprenticed to Nat Tatum by Olmstead, in the beginning to become a stone worker. The contract was seven years, but they didn't get along, so Tatum had 'sent' the boy with Arkansas Toothpick who had picked up the indenture contract for some steel, and tools, and had sold the boy as a stable hand in Creed. That was as much as she had been able to learn.

The day that she had left him, she had satisfied him and bore his drunken breath for the last time. After he was asleep, she went to the hiding place, where he kept the money from her father's estate. There were several gold and many silver coins. She picked them up one at a time and placed them silently into a sack, being careful not to let one coin clink against another. There were fancy papers saying *Stock Certificate of Yule Marble Co.* She had no idea what they were, but she took them also.

Slipping quietly out of the ranch house, she went to the barn and hitched the mare to the small surrey. Then slipping away, she headed for Mrs. Olmstead, hoping to get her brother, and some advice.

She had only gone a few thousand feet, when she caught a glimpse of the huge brown form. A mile further, she saw him again. It had to be Ol' Mose from the size, and he was trailing the mare, maybe stalking. The surrey had to make its way downhill in a zig zag pattern of switchbacks down the mountain side, while the bear came straight down the hill to a point that she must pass. Four times she was sure that she saw his great face staring at her

76

from the roadside bushes when the horse had passed. He made no threatening moves but simply watched her pass.

She thought she saw the bear in a hundred shadows along the road. What the animal had been doing, she could not understand. The bear had watched her slapped around on that day of her wedding, and now he was here to watch her flight.

Mrs. Olmstead did what she could and spared what she could. She was sorry that Harry had been indentured to Tatum at the quarry, she had spoken against it. Men will do, she sagely advised. She had no news of Harry except the news that she had already given, that Arkansas Toothpick had taken the boy from Tatum, and that he had apprenticed him to a livery in Creede. Elizabeth thanked her and assuring her that she would be all right to be on the road, headed out. It had been a good choice, because Raff was on her trail by daylight.

Mrs. Olmstead took a big chance denying that she had seen her, as Raff could see the surrey tracks in the sand in the road ruts. Still without her help he could not determine which way she had gone. He was aware that she had a brother, but knew nothing of his fate, nor cared. That had given Elizabeth some time, as he went to Montrose, and then on to Uray, and over Red Mountain to Silverton, before he cut the high trail across to Creede.

Creede Colorado was about as lawless a town as ever was, and Elizabeth drove her surrey right into the middle of it. From questions that she asked at the livery stable, she was able to find out that her brother was not good around horses, and the man had sold his contract to the manager of the Orleans Club on Creede Avenue, and as far as he knew, the boy was busing tables, and washing dishes, at the place just up the street. Elizabeth paid him to feed, water, and curry her horse and stable her for the night. The man looked closely at the money in her purse, that she was careless enough in her haste over her brother, to let him see. She didn't realize that she had already run across the tentacles of the Shell and Pea Gang.

Soapy Smith dealt faro in the Orleans Club. He said that he owned it, but in fact he was always in debt to partners. He had fleeced many men at Leadville, and when the ore began to run out he moved to Creede during the lawless years, at the height of the silver rush there. He was good-looking and a slick talker, with a knack for relating to people and dazzling them with his wit and charm; a pure snake underneath. Within minutes after Elizabeth had stabled her horse, the spy at the stable, where they picked up newcomers to steal from, had carried the tale of a woman in town, young and pretty, and alone. The spy had also seen her pay with good silver coming from a heavy purse.

"She was lookin' for someone, a brother," Sanders told the boss. Soapy looked over at the retarded boy he had bought from the livery owner, Bates, when the boy proved bad with horses. Soapy had the boy washing dishes, cleaning spittoons, bathrooms, and sweeping floor.

"Boy," he yelled. "Harry, come'er," he commanded. Harry looked up from his sweeping, and like an obedient dog, sidled over in his clumsy sideways gate.

"Boy," he questioned? "You got a sister?"

"Sister, Sarah," he intoned in his sing, song. He stood with a goofy and expectant smile on his face.

Soapy waved him away. "Go on, go on back to sweeping," then thought better. "Go back in the kitchen and clean up."

Elizabeth poked her head into the saloon just a moment too late to see Harry disappear into the kitchen area. She pulled her shawl in a determined manner and pushed through the swinging doors. She locked eyes with Soapy Smith, and then turned away toward the barkeeper, who talked with her a moment, and them pointed at Soapy Smith's table. Elizabeth came determinedly on toward the knot of men at the faro table.

"Are you the proprietor," she asked Smith?

"You're here to play faro?" He countered with a sly smile.

"I'm here looking for my brother," Elizabeth explained in a no-nonsense way. "We were orphaned when father was killed, and the Olmstead's had his care. He was apprenticed to Mr. Tatum at the rock quarry, who sold his papers to Mr. Toothpick, who sold them to Mr. Bales at the livery, who tells me he sold them to a Mr. Smith, the owner of this saloon."

"That's a mouthful, little lady," Smith chuckled and pushed back his bowler hat with the deck of cards in his left hand. That brought men slowly to either side of the door. Elizabeth saw it.

"Are you Smith," she asked again?

"I'm Soapy Smith," he affirmed, "but this here is Mr. Smith, and there is another Mr. Smith." The two men pointed at shook their heads in the affirmative. "In fact, Soapy asserted in innocence, "they're all Mr. Smiths." All the men shook their heads 'yes' with the joke.

"I'm willing to pay for my brother," she attempted to cut through the hurrah that she was getting. "I have money," she told him.

Smith fingered the faro chip in his right hand. "Well, I'm never adverse to a good deal," he said. "But he's become a very valued employee," he continued. The men with him laughed a sinister and leering laugh that made Elizabeth's skin crawl.

"He's slow, and can be stubborn," she countered, trying to bargain with limited resources. "What do you want for him," she asked point blank?

"He cost considerable," Soapy began, "and, he eats a lot." The men laughed. "And he's clumsy, like you say. He's broken a lot of glass, so he owes for that. Room and board for three months. He took a guess at the most she might have in that purse and then doubled it to make sure she couldn't meet the price. "Over eight hundred dollars, all told," he asserted. "More than you can pay."

"You can have it now," she said. Bring me Harry."

"Well now, not so fast, missy," Soapy reappraised her through narrowed eyes. "He's not here," he lied. "I got him doing work at a farm. And besides, I have to consider what I have invested in him total. It's sure more than eight hundred dollars," he was back peddling, trying to understand how much she would pay. "You come back this evening about dark, and I'll send someone out to bring him in," Soapy told her smoothly in his most beguiling voice.

When she had left, he told the men, "Sanders, take that boy and take him to the bath house and clean him up."

"We gonna sell him to her," he asked incredulously?

"Hell no," Soapy spit at the spittoon, "but a shiny penny is better crow bate. When she comes back, just show her back to my office. I'm going to lighten the little orphan's purse, and then when I finish with her, you boys can have her in one of the cribs 'til we get tired of her skinny little ass."

They all laughed and got ready for the excitement. It wouldn't be the first time that they had shanghaied a woman alone, stolen her money, and then trapped her into the life of a crib prostitute. The Gang pimped or 'protected' half the whores in town. These were the ones on the lower end that no one else was interested in protecting. Creede was a lawless and wide-open western town.

Elizabeth thought about getting a room for the night, but upon survey of the town, she changed her mind. This was no place for her or Harry, not even for one night. She ate an expensive meal of poor quality, from a tent eatery on the western edge of town. The crib houses were on the eastern edge and she saw and turned away quickly during her exploring. Late in the afternoon, she went back to the livery stable and began to prepare the surrey.

"Yes, miss," Bales said coming out of the tack room that served as office, and had a stove needed even on summer evenings in the high country.

"I need to harness my horse and surrey," she told him.

"Taking to the road at night," he questioned?

"Yes. I have a need to," she explained. She looked nervously around. One of the men at the faro table had followed her about town, but she had gone in a shop and out the back to give him the slip earlier.

"That can be dangerous on a dark night."

"My mare has a sure foot," she reassured the livery man that she knew what she was doing.

"Hmmm," he put a pipe back in his mouth, and started for her horse in the second stall. "Guess you found your brother then," he questioned her as he moved toward the stall, gathering up a hackamore from a bale of hay to lead the mare into position for harness.

"Mr. Smith says that he will have him brought in when he finishes his farm work at dark."

"Brought in," Bales questioned? "He never sent that boy out of town before. Won't let him out of the saloon for fear he'll get lost."

"That makes no sense," Elizabeth wondered at what was happening.

"You better watch that Soapy Smith," the livery owner warned her. "He's bad through and through. If'n I'd known then," he shook his head. "Well, I would have never sold him your brother's papers."

"Might I ask," Elizabeth inquired, "how much did you pay Arkansas Toothpick for his indenture?"

"Arkansas wanted seventy dollars, but we made a deal at sixty. But, the boy was no good with stock. They

81

could be a danger to each other, so I made up a hand bill and posted it. Soapy Smith inquired, said he needed a dishwasher and busboy to sweep up. I had to make a deal for forty dollars to get him off my hands. He could throw some real corker of a fit for no reason I could tell."

"So, Soapy Smith paid forty dollars for his indenture papers."

"Well, I don't know's Arkansas ever signed over any papers. I saw some as applied to Stone Mason and such craft. Didn't apply to me," he shrugged.

So her brother had been sold into slavery, without so much as indenture papers to give the terms. She was angered but sobered by realizing that it could have been worse for a feeble-minded person in that environ. The livery man tried to help her with the harness and surrey, but she moved much faster than he, and soon he stepped backward, and smoked his pipe and watched her expert work. She had studied to do this job well and fast.

She tied the horse on the street west of the Orleans Club. She was suspicious and cautious now, and she crept around the windows just at dark and saw Harry in a pantry area, stocking, and out on a porch area, where a stove boiled water and Harry reached in a cage and took out a chicken, wrung its neck and lay it in a box until it stopped flopping, then submerged it in the boiling water. She worried, knowing he was clumsy for this type of work. He almost knocked the pot off several times in his movements to get it all done. At least she knew where he was.

She made her way to the entrance, slipping two buildings down before emerging on Creede Avenue. There were several faro tables in play. As the bartender came around and started to escort her to Soapy Smith's office in the back, a man with a smirk tried to lure her into a shell and pea game at a table.

"Take a chance, and watch the pea," he chanted. "Never can tell which shell it'll be." He shuffled the shells and palmed the pea. "There's money on it, if you can tell me which shell covers the pea?"

She didn't answer. She had no idea what this strange game was about, nor had she ever heard of The Shell and Pea Gang, or she would not have been walking into this trap.

Soapy Smith welcomed her into his office with elan. He offered her a cognac, which she accepted, but did not drink it, other than to touch it to her lips.

"I have brought your eight hundred dollars for the indenture."

"Well," Soapy paused solemnly, "there are considerably more expenses, when it is all tallied up." He pulled open a desk drawer in front of him and removed some papers and placed them on his desk, importantly. He fingered the leather case that was in the drawer beneath the papers and opened it to reveal a syringe with ten cubic centimeters of seven per cent morphine solution. He removed the syringe from its holder with one hand and moved it a small amount to where it was easily reached as it sat slant wise on the case, fully readied.

"How much, exactly, do you have against my brother," she asked?

He paused and pretended to look the papers over, pretended to figure. "Three thousand will about square it up," he grinned at her.

"That's unreasonable," she burst out. "I haven't that much money. He couldn't possibly run up that kind of debt."

"It's true," Soapy sympathized. "Perhaps you and I could work out some sort of trade," he made a lurid face, licking his lips. His inference was clear.

"The Marshall at Pueblo will be sure to hear about the way a mentally retarded white boy was enslaved in Creede. She got up and turned to go.

"You leave this room, and you'll never see your

brother again," Soapy said smoothly, just as she reached the knob. She found it locked, and was about to turn back toward him, when he was on her, pulling a handkerchief from an inside coat pocket. He whipped a scarf from the pocket wrapped in wax paper. When the scarf came free of the paper, he held it over her mouth and nose and a cold pungent smell invaded her senses when she gasped for air.

"You're not going anywhere, bitch," he whispered in her ear. She tried to scream but breath wouldn't come as her diaphragm was frozen with drugs and fear. "After I deliver you to the arms of Morphious, for just a kiss, I'll use you for my pleasure, and then my men will have you in the crib, and your brother will clean your chamber pot."

Elizabeth passed out. She awakened lying on the office couch. She had not gotten as strong a dose of chloroform as Soapy had intended, and when she awakened, she groggily saw him fingering the syringe with morphine with his back to her. It shocked her system with adrenaline and fear, but she had to remain still and clear headed, as she had many times with Raff Janeck to keep from getting beaten, if she showed any revulsion. She could feel him standing over her.

He removed his belt, a preliminary to his future plans, and tied off her arm using the belt as a tourniquet just above the elbow of her left arm. He was searching for a vein when she snatched the syringe from him, twisting in the tussle for the needle. He was off balance and fell across her, as she came up with the syringe.

She slapped it into the back of his neck and slammed the plunger home with the flat of her palm. Soapy grunted at the sting of the serum solution.

He staggered up off of her and grabbed the back of his neck and pulled out the needle point and held the syringe in front of his face. His eyes began to cross and as he began to slump down, his pants began to slowly drop down to his knees with a final plunge. Elizabeth had to be quick to move to keep him from falling on her a second time.

She wasted no time in gathering her things, the papers on the desk, and the gun she found in the top drawer next to the case where the morphine had been stored. She slipped out of a back entrance that led to a porch off to the west side. She crossed to the back where Harry was plucking feathers and burning pin feathers with stove kindling lit from the stove fire.

"Harry," she called him quietly. He looked up with no recognition at first. "Harry, it's me."

"Sarah," he asked unsure?

"Brother," she went to him and hugged him. He shivered in a deluge of conflicting information coming at him.

"I've got to get back to work," he stammered, keeping to his immediate task.

"No, Harry," she coaxed, "you can come with me."

"No, no, sister," he was getting excited and confused. "I got to get back to work," he insisted. "They got my contract," he mimicked what he had heard, though it meant nothing more to him than only who told him what to do.

"I bought your contract," she had a bright idea. "You're mine, now, little brother." It was a tone of voice and a sentence that she had said hundreds of times as she tickled him when he was just a baby, and he responded to it with a regressed memory and a childish laugh.

"You did," he questioned?

"You do what I say now," she instructed him. "So just drop that chicken back in the feathering pot and follow me."

She turned and took a step, then looked back. Sure enough, he dropped what he was doing and shuffled after her. "Where we goin', sis," he persisted with endless questions. He always needed to know his destination, only

85

she didn't know.

"We're going to the big city," she told him. "We're going all the way to Colorado City," she said as she led him to the next street over, and they reached her surrey. She was relieved that it was just as she had left it, with her mare a bit impatient with the waiting. The horse stomped on the back leg to signal its irritation. She hurried Harry to get in, then looking nervously around, untied the reins and the hobble she had on the mare, and with a sound slap of the leather, set the mare going at a good clip out the south road toward Wagon Wheel Gap, and on down to Alamosa, where she figured to sell the horse and surrey and take a train to Pueblo and on to Colorado City.

They arrived in Colorado Springs in the afternoon three days later, and touring the town in a horse drawn hack, she and brother made their way west toward Colorado City and eventually Manitou Springs. Harry was enthralled with everything he saw and shrieked with delight at the new wonders of man and nature. They wound through the Garden of the Gods, as it was starting to be known.

At a side street in Colorado City, she had noticed a sign in a window advertising for a seamstress. She could sew. This was a possibility, if she could talk her way into the job.

She chose a boarding house where she could purchase a room for the night and then walk to the place where the advertisement for a seamstress was in the front of the house. She would be able to leave Harry for a short while and apply for the job.

The next morning, she gave Harry careful instructions not to leave the apartment, and she went out to see about the sign for the seamstress job. She walked the short way to the house, and the sign saying 'seamstress wanted' appeared on the side of the well-presented small gingerbread house. She went inside.

"Hello," a tall, middle-aged woman with the mannerisms of a dowager greeted her. "I'm Innes Burns, how can I help you?"

"I've come about the sign," Elizabeth pointed toward the sign on the other side of the door.

"Yes, do come in and sit and have tea," the lady invited. It was the best thing to happen to Elizabeth in years.

It was a few days after Elizabeth's good luck in Colorado Springs at the seamstress' house, that Raff Janek arrived in Creede. It was not many hours before he had met Soapy Smith, and they had discovered a mutual interest.

A curious rock sat in the Seldomridge feed store
window. It had been there for some time. It seemed
almost a year, when this afternoon, Ed De LaVergne,
walking a route he took almost every day, noticed it and
came over to the hardware store window to take a look.
Maybe the afternoon light caught a glitter, or maybe it was
the upcoming blowpipe course that he signed up to take
with that professor. Ed casually observed the stone, and
then looking a bit closer with keener curiosity, he entered
the store to question the clerk about the unusual window
display. Harry Seldomridge was studying over some
paperwork, when he looked up to see Ed De LaVergne
walking purposely toward him.

"Hello, Harry," Ed greeted him, and then without
waiting for the young man to answer him, added, "Where
did you get that gold ore that you have in the show
window up front?"

Harry broke out in a smile from ear to ear. Finally,
he would have an inquiry about the sample that had set
there for literally months, with not one curious inquiry.
He would be able to tell that cowboy Womack, and that
dentist Grannis, one of which came by every day to pester
him about anyone that might ask. "That there sample
come from Bob Womack's El Passo Load, that he has
discovered up at Cripple Creek. He and that dentist John
Grannis, are looking for partners to help develop the
claim."

"Bob Womack," Ed questioned? "Is that the drunk
cowboy that Major Demary is always making fun of."

"That's him. He's got an old shack up on the
Western face of The Peak, in a place he calls Poverty

Gulch. He's been up there for years, scratching around and insisting that there is a mountain of gold there for the finding."

"A Mountain of Gold," Ed repeated. "I just finished an assayer's course, from Professor Henry Lamb, and he told a few of us at the end that we should check out the Cripple Creek area."

Harry was excited to hear this news, and Ed was considered a knowledgeable mining man, as he was known to have managed mines in New Mexico and Colorado. The two men walked together to the front of the store and picked some of the samples up off the windowsill and began to examine them.

"It don't look like any gold ore that I have ever seen," Harry confided.

"Hmmm," Ed De LaVergne just mused. He had seen this ore before. It was rare, but he had seen samples of a gold-silver bearing tellurides from the Red Cloud Mine, North of Denver. It was called sylvanite, and the geological report of the original survey of the area that had been done by Ferdinand V. Hayden had made mention of the ore, in that old government report. Hayden's party had also marked out the boundaries of the ancient caldera of the extinct volcano of the Cripple Creek area. De LaVergne kept that information to himself. "Harry," he slapped the young man on the back affectionately, Do you think that you could arrange for me to meet with Bob Womack."

"I'm sure that he would be eager to meet with you Mr. De LaVergne, as everybody here abouts knows that you are about the most knowledgeable mining man in Colorado Springs."

"Good, good," Ed could be extremely affable when he took a notion. "Let's give it a couple of days to percolate, and say we set it up for Saturday evening."

"Sure thing, Mr. De LaVergne," Harry agreed to

set up the meeting. Ed went back to examining the ore. Harry was beaming when Ed left. He liked Bob Womack and owed him several favors, so he was very pleased to be of help, and in such an exciting prospect.

But on Saturday evening, with several people gathered to hear what was said, Bob Womack failed to make an appearance. Ed paced impatiently, taking out his pocket watch to check the time.

"Bob's a good intentioned feller," Harry defended him more than once. "It's just he's unreliable sometimes, like when he gets to drinking."

"Which, I hear," Ed added, "is most all the time." He disgustedly twisted the watch fob, spinning the watch back and forth. "Well, this is a waste of time," he shoved the watch back into the watch pocket of his pants. "If he comes in later, send for me at my brother George's house. If he doesn't show, we'll have to try to put it together again, in a few days."

"Sorry, Mr. De LaVergne," Harry apologized.

"Thanks, Harry." Ed stalked out with Fred Frisbee in tow, his brother's clerk from the De LaVergne furniture store across the street. The twilight had faded into a dark and moonless night.

At that moment, a few miles away, Bob Womack was having a raucous drunk. He had been drinking since coming into town in the early afternoon, and he had a first-class bender going on. The bars lined the city limits, where Colorado City and Colorado Springs met. Years of ridicule had been working on Bob, and it all just burst out. He had mounted Whistler and ridden down Tejon Street at breakneck speed.

"Eureka," he yelled in a bleary intoxicated whoop. He started trying to shoot out the new electric arc street lights that had been newly placed. He might have even hit one, had the Bobbies on patrol not come running. He still had sense enough to holster his gun when they came around the corner and confronted him.

"Bob Womack," the first one to him yelled, "get off that horse." He grabbed Whistler's reins and Bob attempted to turn the horse and make a break for it. The first one got hold of him and held on as Whistler tried to turn on his back heels. Another Bobbie grabbed him from the other side, and the two men skinned him off the back of the horse. He hit the ground hard, and that sobered him a little more.

"Ah, what'ch want to go and do that for," he blathered. "You boys is spoilin' the fun, and you're out of your jurisdiction" he complained again. "I'm not even in your city." Two more Bobbies had arrived, and when they tried to take his gun, he put his hand on the butt, and pushed down. "Nosiree," he howled, and tried to pull away.

They all knew who he was, and they didn't want to hurt him, but they couldn't let him loose either. One of the new arrivals had a night stick out and wrapped him soundly on the head. They got the gun away from him.

"Ouch," he yelled. "Police brutality," he yelled at the top of his voice. A few heads poked out of the buildings around, having heard the shooting and scuffle and tentative, at first, then seeing that the shooting was over, a few came out to watch the fun. The four men picked Bob up by the arms and legs, and carried him back to the Springs' City Hall, where the jail was located in the basement, beneath Fire Station Unit 1. Bob yelled 'police brutality' halfway there. He was pretty much passed out by the time they got there and tossed him on the old cot that was set up in one of the cages. He merely muttered to himself that they shouldn't treat a rich man that way.

Bright and early the next morning, Jimmie Burns, the Fire chief, and several others were sitting around the fire house drinking coffee and talking politics. Jimmie Doyle came through the front into the kitchen area of the

91

fire station. He nodded to the men, poured himself a cup of stiff firehouse coffee, and proceeded to seat himself next to his best friend and mentor, Jimmie Burns.

"Morning Jimmie," Burns quipped.

"Morning Jimmie," Doyle returned. It was a routine that they did often. "I thought that you might have a plumbing job going on somewhere. I been over to your sisters' house this morning, running errands for their sewing. Have you seen that new seamstress that they have hired?" Doyle had come to the Springs with the three sisters when he was a teenager. They had taken the orphan under their protection, and their brother had joined them from New Orleans, to make sure that the sisters stayed safe in moving West.

"No," Burns confessed he had not. "Work is slowing down, and it's startin' to worry me some. What's the name of the new woman?"

"Elizabeth somethin' or other. Don't remember what her last name is, but she's a looker," and then added the Portland Maine, "Eeyoughah," expletive, to reinforce his claim.

"Is that a fact?" Burns sat up to ask more, when a pounding on the boards beneath them, that shook the floor, grabbed their attention.

"Who do we have as guest this morning," Doyle asked?

"That damned cowboy, Bob Womack, started shooting at the lights on Tejon Street late last night. He was whahooin' real good." The pounding on the floor started again with renewed intensity.

"I guess he's discovered where he's at," Doyle got up and moved to the wooden peg on the wall which held the jail keys, and lifting them down, proceeded down the inner stairs to the cells in the basement. Burns ran a hand through his dazzling white hair, and watched as Doyle disappeared, and in a few moments the voice of Bob

Womack could be heard, whining and complaining, coming back upstairs.

"Them boys roughed me up bad last night," he started in a petulant way. "They didn't have to be so damned mean about it, and I was on the Colorado City side of Tejon anyway, they was out of their jurisdiction." His hair was standing straight up in the back of his head, stiff with muck from the street. He rubbed his nose on his shirt sleeve back and forth, and took a look around the room, seeing if he had any friends in the crowd that might see his case in a sympathetic way. "You boys are gonna be sorry that you treated me this way. I'm going to be a rich man, and then you men are gonna be sorry, yes siree. Ya'll been horrahin' me for years, while I tried to tell you that there is a mountain of gold over on the west side of the Peak, at Cripple Creek, and you had your fun. Well, I done struck it. I got the El Paso Load staked, and the assay done come in at two hundred fifty dollars to the ton. Even Ed De LaVergne is a lookin' to jaw with me. I done had bankers, and businessmen all over this city want to stop me, and find out about my gold mine." He was surprised to see that the room had stopped still to listen to him. "I was just lettin' off a little steam and tryin' to wake this town up to the fact that Bob Womack has been tryin' to tell you for years. Cripple Creek is full of gold."

"Here's your gun, Bob," Jimmie Burns got it off the wooden hook on the wall next to where the keys were kept and handed the gun and belt to Bob. "You're probably going to have to go to court over this one, Bob. You may have some damages to pay, and there may be a 'disturbing the peace' charge."

"Oh, I don't see that I did that much harm," Bob patted his hair down, and took the belt from Jimmie and held it by his side. He wiped his nose on his sleeve again, and tried to beguile his listeners with as innocent a look as he could muster. "But I'm agonna have plenty of money, so fine me all you want."

"The gun's unloaded, and we're keeping the bullets as evidence in the case. That's what Marshall Dana ordered last night. "What's this about a gold mine?"

Bob was really surprised to see the men watching him eagerly, hanging on his words, and really listening to him. "You men need to take a look at this," Bob fumbled in his britches pocket, and digging down deep, came up with a little piece of gray rock. "This here is high grade ore from my gold mine, The El Paso Load." He handed it to Jimmie Burns, who took a close look at it, walking to the East window, where the strong sunlight was streaming in.

All the other men in the room began to gather around and crowd together for a better look. Bob never got interest like this before, and it made him smile and spry right up.

"Don't look like gold to me," said Jimmie Doyle, who had been first in line to see the sample after Jimmie Burns was willing to relinquish it.

"That's cause you don't know what you're lookin' at," Bob retorted. "That's Sylvanite, and it's a mineral loaded with gold," Bob gestured toward the sample, and dug around in his pocket, failed to find what he was looking for, and dug deep into his other front pants pocket, came up with another sample, and passed it to the now packed group of men, all straining for a better look.

Bob got himself cleaned up a bit and headed to the hardware store to pick up supplies. After he had gotten what he needed he walked about and talked to almost everyone that passed by, as Bob knew many people. He also became aware that people were starting to take interest in him, and he was asked about the El Paso, or his gold mine, or questioned about Cripple Creek every way he turned, and this was very pleasing to him, after years of trying to convince people in the Springs that there was gold on the western side of the Peak.

When Jimmy Burns arrived at his sister's seamstress shop, later that day, he had a fantastic story of gold in the mountains and was at a fever pitch to quit his job as a fireman, stop contracting plumbing, and head for the west side of the peak to find his fortune. His sisters managed to reason him into a more practical frame of mind, but they were excited too. Elizabeth was there to hear all this, and she was quick to see the potential. The real money in any mining camp that she had ever heard of was made selling food to hungry miners.

Bob always made a visit to the El Paso County Court House, where all the courthouse cronies gathered. It was always the best place to find the best tidbits of information in the community, even before things might hit the papers.

"What's this I hear about you staking a mine in Cripple Creek," Frank Howbert, Irving Howbert brother asked him? That drew the interest of many of the men standing around. He got questioned by the County Treasurer, McCreery, by Commissioner Plumb, Judge Kinsley, and the real estate developer Charlie Tutt.

"Bob," Judge Colburn suggested, "I think it would be a good idea if you would go talk to that carpenter, Stratton, as he's been all over these mountains, and probably has more prospecting experience than anyone around."

After the talk at the courthouse wound down, Bob did go hunting for Stratton on a job site that he was running and working on. He found him doing some gingerbread decorations on a fine house.

"Howdy Bob," Stratton greeted him, as he walked up, but kept on working.

"Will," Bob started hesitantly, "Judge Colburn said I ought to come by and talk with you," he said by way of introduction.

"That right," Stratton kept working a curl with a small coping saw.

"I got a mine staked out up at Cripple Creek, and the assay come in at two-hundred-fifty dollars per ton."

"That's a good assay, eleven ounces per ton," Stratton kept his head down, and kept sawing. He was not pleased to have this reprobate cowboy slowing his work and taking his concentration off the complicated scroll work.

"I got a piece of the ore right here," Bob fished a sample out of his pocket and held it out to the disgruntled carpenter, who finished the scroll, and leisurely put his saw aside and accepted the ore.

He glanced at it only a few moments and then handed it back to Bob.

"You ought to come up to Cripple Creek and look around. There's more veins up there still to be found, that's a good possibility."

"I've been in the area," Stratton replied and went back to his saw. "Don't look promising to me."

"Well, Judge Colburn asked me to come by and ask you to come to Pisgah Park and look around a bit, as he thinks you're the most experienced prospector in the area. If you'll come up and look around a little you can bunk in at my place there in Poverty Gulch," Bob made what he considered a hospitable offer.

Stratton physically started at this suggestion. He shrugged it off, and kept working. "It's not likely that I can get off my work here and break away anytime soon."

Stratton said no more, and Bob hung around awkwardly watching him work a few minutes more, and then dejectedly turned and went back to his horse and mounted and rode away without another word. When he got back to the main part of town, the paper was out. The headline caught his eye and he bought a copy.

The Reported Gold!

The story told of a gold strike in Florissant some eighteen miles northwest of Cripple, and the upshot of the story was that the strike had proven to be very small amounts of copper. There was also a short paragraph reporting a young ranch man's report of a rich vein found in the vicinity of Mt. Pisgah, and the paper was waiting for more development before the Gazette would report more facts, in consideration of the possibility of printing misleading information. They did credit Dr. J. P. Grannis as heading the company that had been formed to establish the claim. The story both pleased and disturbed Bob, as he smiled at being called a young ranch man, at forty-seven. Bob enjoyed being called young, and being mentioned in the paper at all, was a first for him, at least in any positive sense. Still, Bob realized that the coupling of the story with the Florissant false strike and also joined with the Mt. Pisgah directions would only dampen interest here at the Springs. Feeling dejected, he made his way to his partner's dentist's office to give him a report of the interest that was stirring.

"John," Bob told him when he the dentist was finished with his patient, "we're going to have to develop the El Paso a little more, and I'm going to need more money for dynamiting, and a windless and rope. That means a small headframe, so I need lumber, nails, and such."

"Bob," Grannis told him, "I'm out of money myself," he was beginning to wish that he had never grubstaked the crazy cowpuncher.

"Ain't you got credit at the bank," Bob asked him.

"They're going to want collateral, Bob, and I don't own nothing," and then gestured toward his dental equipment, "except my equipment, and damn it all Bob, I can't risk that."

"Goldarn, John, we're sitting on a gold mine with a

good assay. Surely, they will take that claim as collateral."

"I doubt that." Grannis rubbed his chin. "I hate to fold up the cards now," he agreed. "I'll go talk to them, but I'm getting in over my head here, and I just don't see how I can risk my equipment by putting it up to guarantee the loan."

"John," Bob pleaded, "we got to have some money to develop that claim a little further, or else it's just gonna sit, and nothing is gonna come of it. I can see that for sure."

Bob made his way back to Cripple Creek by way of Florissant, chagrined, and disheartened. It seemed like things were never going to break right for him. Just when it seemed he had it in his hands, it slipped through his fingers, like sand.

He hung out at Judge Castello's store in Florissant. He gave up on convincing anyone in Colorado Springs, and talked it up to the Judge, and several people that came by the store, and a small smattering of people that lived in the Florissant area. He stayed there for three days, sleeping in the feed shed. He talked the strike to anyone who would listen. At least he wasn't being horrahed like at the Springs. Several men took an interest. Several had already been to Cripple, and with George Carr's directions, had staked off claims near Bob's El Paso Claim, and by the time that he returned to Poverty Gulch, it had been determined that a miners meeting would take place on the fifth of April at George Carr's house at The Broken Box Ranch.

Emma Carr spent the first few days in April baking and cleaning, getting ready for the big meeting. She fussed over every detail. She was an energetic woman of good graces, with a good heart, pert face, and an innocent sex appeal, that made all the men around her pretty much putty in her hands. So, it was a right thing that she would run this show.

Frank Castello was the first to arrive on the morning of the 5th of April, and he brought mule loads of whiskey and beer. Bob joined him soon after his arrival, walking up from his shack at the head of Poverty Gulch. He started sipping Frank's liquor, just to make sure that the day got off to a good start, and they were all in good humor that this momentous day had arrived. This organization had been a fantasy of Bob's for years, and he was soon in rollicking good spirits.

Soon others started coming into the valley and made their way toward the ranch house, that was the original cabin that the Welty's had built, but now with a second floor added to one end of the structure. Ed De LaVergne arrived with Fred Frisbee and his wife Claire. The Piggs arrived from their property at West Four Mile, and the Welty's came from Four Mile. About another fifteen people drifted in over the next hours from Florissant. Emma Carr made them all feel welcome with copious amounts of food, pie, and coffee, and her husband George traded stories with the men and cheered things with generous sips of the Judge's whiskey until the little place was buzzing with people and good feelings.

When Emma had finished feeding everyone until their bellies were full and they were sated, they began to gather everyone into the kitchen area of the little house.

Bob Womack, who had been sipping the bourbon all day, was given a chair in one corner of the kitchen, and Ed De LaVergne, Fred and Claire took an opposite corner.

"Folks," George Carr's big voice boomed out, "Let's get this meeting underway. Ya'll gather round in here in the kitchen and doorway where we can all hear each other," he called over the crowd noise. His voice rang out above the hubbub, as he was used to calling the local square dances. People began to move toward the kitchen and take places, and as soon as everyone had quieted down a bit, Ed spoke up from his corner.

"Now I was just wondering," he began, "since Bob staked the El Paso Load, several of us have found superior leads and staked them. Now in the interest of generating the most interest in the new district that we are going to determine here today, it seemed in all of our best interest to name the Discovery Load as the claim with the best assay. That," he explained "will get the most newspaper coverage and bring the best investors and will be a benefit to everyone involved." He let this soak in for a few moments, and there was no immediate reaction from the group one way or the other.

Emma Carr, however, saw right through him. She realized in a moment that he was putting in a bid to defraud Bob Womack of his rightful place as the discoverer of the Cripple Creek district. She was quite fond of Bob, had spent many good evenings listening to his stories, and knew him to have a generous spirit and a good heart. She had also seen him be the butt of jokes by almost everyone, and she even enjoyed a good natured laugh at him from time to time, as he was a truly funny person, in attitude, appearance, and manner, but she was having none of this, and saw it as an outrage taking place in her kitchen.

She grabbed a chair from the table in the center of the room and set it down with a resounding clap, climbed up and stood on the chair seat, with her jaw clinching, grabbing a rolling pin from where it hung behind the stove. "Everyone," she boomed, "raise your glasses to Bob Womack, The Discoverer of Cripple Creek!" She waved the rolling pin over her head menacingly as part caudle and part Queen's Mace. Every glass went up, and a 'here, here' sounded out from the little group, so that even Ed De LaVergne had to raise his with the rest.

Now, with that point settled, the group got down to

the business of forming the Mining District. Several preliminary points had to be voted on and set in the record first. Frank Castello spoke up to begin, as they were all drinking his whiskey and beer. "We're going to need a moderator that's in charge of the meeting, and since we are enjoying the hospitality of the Carr's, I nominate George Carr as President of the Meeting." "I'll second that," Ed De LaVergne spoke up, remembering the fine treatment that the Carr's had given to him and Fred Frisbee on an exploratory trip a month earlier, when George and Emma had furnished them a place to stay while they combed the surrounding area for several days. The others immediately gave voice assent, and George took over the order of the meeting.

"The first thing we need to do is name the new district," he informed them.

"I vote for 'Womack' as the name of the district," Emma Carr put forward.

"I think we should keep a well-known mountain, to guide people to the site," Warton Pigg proposed, "so let's name it Mt. Pisgah." This brought up memories of the old hoax, and several people saw Bob Womack shake his head 'no' before he took another pull-on Frank's whiskey.

"It should have the name 'gold' in it," said Claire Frisbee, who had recently become an expert on the subject, "so I propose 'Gold Heaven' as a good name." That seemed to fall flat on the ears of the mostly male grouping.

None of these seemed to catch, although 'Womack' had the most favor. Ed De LaVergne stepped forward and George gave him the floor.

"We need a simple name that everyone associates with the region," he explained "and this area is fairly well known to everyone around as 'Cripple Creek', so that being the simplest, is probably going to be the best overall."

This argument seemed to carry the day, and George put 'Womack' to a vote, against 'Cripple Creek'. By a show of hands, 'Cripple Creek Mining District' carried by a few votes.

"Next task, as I understand the way this should go, is we need to define the limits of the mining district by nearby geology. Ed," he summoned, "would you bring that Van Hayden survey map in and unroll it here on the kitchen table and let's all take a look at it."

Ed got out the map and spread it on the table and then pointed out the limits of the old volcano as they appeared in yellow on the survey. He explained the geological limits of the old volcano and then suggested that the district be bounded by mountain peaks that defined the outer limits, and slightly beyond the survey of the old volcano. That would mean Mt. Pisgah on the West, Rhyolite Mountain on the North, Big Bull Hill at the base of Pikes Peak on the East, and Straub Mountain on the South. This met with everyone's approval, and George moved them on to adopt the rules to govern the new district.

They adopted the Mining Law of 1872 as the rules that would govern the claims, the same laws and customs that had governed the strike in California in 1849, that had been formalized by Congress some eighteen years earlier. This was quickly affirmed by a voice agreement, and they got down to the local customs within the law, which were basically, how much land was in a load, or placer claim, and how many men could go together in each case.

"Ed," George Carr called on De LaVergne again, "you know more about the details than anyone else here, so would you explain the details of a claim?"

"Basically," Ed spoke up again, "there are two types of claims, and only a couple of things to decide about each. There are Load Claims, which are hard rock claims, and Placer Claims, which are sedimentary. The Load Claims are governed by law as being the ground inside of a rectangle being three hundred feet wide by fifteen hundred feet long," he explained. "The claim must be recorded with the County Clerk's office and can be made in the name of one man or many, with no limit. Each man or group of men can make as many load claims as they want, as long as each is properly staked with six stakes and posted with the names of the claim and the names of the claim owners. These have to be on open range and proven each year with one hundred dollars' worth of development to the claim each year. Also, a load claim can be patented by a survey, and an initial investment of five hundred dollars' worth of labor at the site," he paused to look around and see if he was being understood. Claire Frisbee had a puzzled look on her face and she spoke up.

"Why would anyone spend five hundred dollars of labor and probably twice that much for a survey, when they can hold the same thing for a hundred dollars a year?"

"In other districts," Ed explained to her, "claims have been jumped by people moving the stakes and signs, and fighting has occurred over these types of claims. A patented claim is much harder to contest, and much easier to defend, when there has been a survey and substantial work done on the claim. Also, we will all probably make some marginal claims, that we will mean to prove, but will abandon. Assessment work becomes a problem on that type of ground, and yet, you never know where the outcroppings are, that are beneath the surface. Surveyed and patented claims can simply sit until if and when they become valuable. Plus, a surveyed claim will sell for a higher price." He let the implications of the two paths sink in for a moment and then continued.

"Placer claims are a bit different," he began again. "They are limited to twenty acres per man, and include the dirt down to bedrock, so only the loose sedimentary fill. But here we have a choice. We decide how many men can go together to form a placer claim, and each member draws twenty acres, with the entire claim being the size of the number of men involved times the twenty-acre limit."

Nobody thought that there would be much placer gold at Cripple Creek, and looking at the size of the overall district, and by common agreement, the group decided to limit placer claims to eight men, and one hundred and sixty acres. Ed did not explain to this tenderfoot crowd that placer claims had been known to become platted town sites.

"That takes care of the business of this meeting," George told them, "And I want to thank Bob Womack for his perseverance and generous spirit for making this all possible for us."

At this point Clair Frisbee patted Bob on the back, and with a groan, Bob fell out of his chair and passed out onto the floor.

After putting aside things on the kitchen table, some of the men placed Bob on the table to sleep it off.

Outside, some of the men who figured to work for the men who had money to stake claims and work them, had piled logs up in a great bonfire. The music started, and they danced and laughed like wild Indians, or wilder Irishmen.

Elizabeth Yates set up a table and gave out slices of pie and introduced herself to everyone that would come by the table. She had heard that the Broken Box Ranch was going to become a town site, and she intended to have a restaurant on the main street. She had her inheritance money, and now would be the time to invest it, she was certain.

Chapter 10. The Letter

Stefano Marquez looked down on the mining operation that he was working on. It was his first job out of the School of Mines in Sophia, in Spain. This gold mine was all he knew for the last four years, and he was sick of it. He dreamed of active prospecting in the United States. He had grown up on legends of the fabled Golden City of Cibola. The wealth that the Spanish empire had acquired during the Sixteenth Century was the myth and lore that every Spanish youth learned, and playing at Conquistador was the game that they played in the streets of the city, and at the Hacienda. His father had worked for the mining interest in his hometown. Stefano had worked all his life, as his father had let him help with the office cleaning when he had completed the days' schooling and was through with his studies. That would sometimes go far into the night, and Stefano was not afraid of hard work or long hours. Under this direction he had grown strong and lean, light and of Castilians heritage by his mother, he had the unusual blond hair and blue eyes of the minority of the Spanish population.

He noticed that the post for the day had come from Barcelona, and his professional journal was in the stack. Picking it up and sitting down facing the door and looking down from the office, where he could see who was approaching, he allowed himself a quick peek at the periodical.

His eye caught a report from Colorado from a new mining strike from a town whose name was translated in the Spanish for this distribution, and had been translated as Lame Stream, Colorado. As Marquez read further, he was intrigued by the description of the gold telluride that was the ore of the new find. It was a purple color with dark spots of small size in the matrix. Stefano gazed at the paperweight from the Van Hayden survey, and then across the mine pit, at the purple rock at the entrance of the adit that ran into the hill directly across from where he was sitting. He knew that this unusual ore was sylvanite, and perhaps calaverite, named after the Calvarias County, where it had originally been discovered, lately made famous by the world famous Mark Twain. Stefano knew of these things through the trade journals that he subscribed to, ever since the college training had opened that door.

He was aware of it in another way also. His father had done an internship with the Hayden Expedition. Arturo was from a wealthy family, and he could afford the travel to the United States of America and applied and was accepted into a geological survey group that was sent out by the American government to map the potential wealth of the West. Ferdinand Vandeveer Hayden was paid to survey the Western Pikes Peak area and open it for settlement, since the Indians had ceded the territory in the treaty of the previous year. Arturo had brought back such stories of the Colorado area. He had brought back many, many rock samples of the area around the Western Pikes Peak side, and South. There had been a great deal of excitement among the members of the Hayden Party, and they were sure that precious metals were present in the area. Arturo had brought back more than interesting rocks, he had brought wonderful stories, about buffalo, and Indians, and a land, strange, beautiful, and far away.

Stefano made up his mind. He would give notice and prepare for the trip. He would book a ticket to New York from the Spanish Coastal Port. He would go to Colorado.

He looked at the article again and found the name of the discoverer of the El Paso Load. He pulled out pin and paper and wrote a letter to Bob Womack, Lame Stream Colorado.

Horace Bennett was having his breakfast at his favorite eatery near his real estate office in Denver, when his partner, Julius Myers came excitedly into the restaurant.

"I've got good news this morning," he practically beamed with the news.

"What have you got this morning Julius," Bennett looked up from the morning paper in his hand.

"There has been gold discovered on the Broken Box Ranch, and a miners meeting was held, and a mining district has been formed."

"You don't say," Bennett was doubtful. "Another Mt. Pisgah," his eyebrows raised at his partner.

"Ed De La Vergne is in on it, staking a mine that he calls The Raven. Ten or more claims have been filed so far."

"So that place is going to be more than a personal fishing stream for your trout fishing," Horace loved to needle his partner about the dud of a real estate buy they had gotten for a bargain from that eastern dude Ellesworth, who had paid seventy-five thousand for the land, and sold it to Bennett and Myers for five thousand down, and twenty thousand that he would carry. Myers loved the fishing and was hell bent to have the property. It was leased to Carr as the Broken Box Ranch.

"That's not the only claim that De La Vergne has staked. He's joined with several other men in staking a placer claim, just north and east of the edges of The Broken Box. They call it The Hayden Placer. I'm sure I don't need to tell you what that means."

"Hummp," Bennett saw immediately. "They mean to platte a township."

"You know it."

"Well, I doubt that there is ever going to be a need for a town out there. But we might be able to platte and sell a few of those worthless acres."

And so, the first day that Bennett and Myers put up lots for sale Elizabeth Yates was one of the first in line to pay her nine hundred dollars cash for a lot on the new street called Bennett Ave. She had a tent up by the end of the day, and two days later her stove arrived from the Springs, and she was selling pies.

Tents sprang up everywhere. The Whoever Shall Come revival tent set up just up the street from what came to be known as Elizabeth's Place. It was a wild time for the young community with two competing cities, and eventually when consolidation became necessary and desirable, an election for a common Mayor was held. George Carr was in the lead, until he and Bob Womack got drunk and decided to rope the competition and drag them down the street. Folks didn't take to it well, and George lost the election.

With an elected town council and mayor, the city moved forward as a modern city right from its beginning, with water, sewer, and electricity, and with a few telephones.

When the post office moved from Hayden's Placer to Cripple Creek, no office existed for several days, and when the postmaster from Hayden's Placer brought down the last mail, including the dead letters, Stefano Marquez's letter to Mr. Womack, Lame Stream, Colorado was in the dead letter file. The flowery handwriting with all the flourishing, was intriguing to Elizabeth, when the letter ended up at her restaurant in her care.

The Florissant stage depot had naturally formed around the train depot, which had formed around the original house built by Judge Castello. His son, Frank, took over in 1884, and, with the gold strike going on at Cripple Creek, the depot grew into a bustling operation. Horses stomped and snorted impatiently, waiting to go the last leg of the journey. They knew that sweet feed and water would be waiting after the trip. This team had brought the stage from Cripple Creek to the train depot, and they would be changed at Four Mile with another. A new team would be put in place for the pull from Four Mile uphill to Cripple Creek.

Stefano Marquez found a shady spot and turned a log on end. He perched himself at the southwest corner of the platform and caught what little breeze was stirring in the Spring morning sunshine. The morning had been cold at this elevation, but now, the morning sunlight had penetrated the mountains, and the dry air had heated rapidly as soon as the sun had risen above Pikes Peak in the distance to the east. A train whistle blew. The Colorado Midland Railway train had brought Stefano up Ute Pass just as the sun was turning the eastern horizon pink. He had been stunned at the change in scenery. After the previous day of traveling across the flat land prairie of Kansas, the mundane topography had abruptly given way to the foothills of the Rockies. The bare ground of Pike's Peak and the majesty of that great uplift had been hidden from him by the darkness the night before, and the Colorado Midland Railway train had pulled out toward the west before daylight. The walls and red rock formations of Ute Pass had hidden the Peak from him, but now, in the morning sunlight he was able to study its massive structure rising high into sky, with its summit intermittently visible through the mist and the morning clouds that wisped around its crown. Closer, he watched a large hawk hover on the wind before it suddenly folded its wings and dove on some unsuspecting prey.

He shed his coat, and as the dry air warmed rapidly in the morning sunlight, he rolled the sleeves of the calico shirt he had purchased during a train stop in St. Louis some days before. He had been cautioned at Ellis Island that there might be some prejudice against Spaniards, and although his skin was light colored, and he had learned English from a native of London during his college years, so that his voice betrayed none of his true heritage, his clothes still spoke his origin very clearly, and he had looked at the clothing around him, and then copied the styles by purchasing new clothes along the way from New York. His lace and ruffle Spanish style shirt had been the last to go, as he was very fond of its European styling. He had reluctantly discarded it in St. Louis and donned a more Western style. He absently rubbed the material on the rolled-up sleeve, thinking and remembering the long train trip, and the many transfers, after the long boat trip from LA Harve France, where he had embarked on his journey.

His attention refocused in the now as the Midland Terminal Station Master pulled the baggage handlers back and gave the flagman a wave to signal that the train was ready to leave. The flagman signaled to the engineer that all was in readiness, and with two longs and a short from the whistle, repeated twice more the Colorado Midland train began to chug slowly away from the terminal, headed out to the west across Wilkerson Pass, across South Park, and north to Leadville. Stefano pulled a gold pocket watch from the watch pocket of his corduroy western suit and checked the time. He looked fondly at the antique gold watch, the only thing he had from his father. It was an excellent time piece, made in Germany, and belonging to his grandfather. It was his only remaining family tie. He noticed a pointy headed man, about his same age watching him closely. The man had a pronounced limp, and his attention made Stefano uneasy in a way that he could not fathom. Another man approached him with a limp, and he heard him say 'Otto' as he passed the other crippled man, who turned his attention from Marquez, and swung swiftly to face the other, revealing a wooden leg. He did not return the salutation. The man came to a stop in front of Stefano and addressed him in a Colorado, western drawl.

"Frank Castello tells me you're a lookin' for the least expensive way to get to Crik, young feller," the broad-shouldered man addressed him. He stood on one leg and relaxed his game leg in a hip shod way.

Marquez squinted against the bright, clear, morning light, and stood up to face the man. "Steven Marks," he shot out his hand in the way that he had watched the western men do. He had shortened and americanized his name on advice at the Ellis Island disembarkation point. The name had been the suggestion of the immigration officer who had interviewed him and registered him as a new applicant for citizenship, and this was the first time that he had occasion to use it. "I would be pleased for passage to Lame Stream," he said slowly, to get the pronunciation just right.

The man got a puzzled look on his face, and then introduced himself, "George Welty," the man gripped Stefano's hand firmly, and pumped it enthusiastically. "This stage goes to Cripple Creek. We're nothin' fancy," he explained. "No springs, but we got leather slings on the coach, which is better than the old hard mounts," he held his hands out palms up, with a shrug. It was not as much of an apology as it was an explanation of just the way things are.

"Yes, Cripple Creek," Stefano corrected himself. "What is your fee, one way, from here," he asked?

"It's a long uphill walk to save a dollar and a half," Welty pitched. "I'd let you have the shotgun seat on the outside for a dollar, that's the best deal I can make you."

"Outside will be fine," Steven agreed. They shook on the deal, and Welty asked him to sign the passenger manifest, and then waited for the payment. Marks fished his money from his wallet. George took a curious look at the type and make as it was longer and thin compared to the western wallets he was used to seeing. It was curious, but he said nothing about it.

Welty turned away to tend the stage and started for the corral then turned back. "You handy with a rifle, young feller," he asked?

"I know nothing about firearms," Marks returned without apology.

"Well," George scratched under the back of his hat. That was a third puzzlement. "No matter. We never have any trouble, anyway." He turned toward the stable. "Piala," he yelled at a young Ute Indian dressed in western corduroy, and a home spun shirt. His hair was long, shoulder length, but the face showed keen intelligence, and he rose quickly from the fence rail he was sitting on, at George Welty's call. "Bring that fresh team up here and let's get'um hitched. Piala tore out at a run for the horse stables, and soon returned leading six horses by halter ropes, with three reins in each hand. Piala left three reins looped over the right back wheel of the coach and led the other three into place along the tongue. The horses seemed to know where to stop, but the second in line bit the rump of the lead horse and got kicked at by the leader. Piala scolded the two unruly horses and when the leader bowed at him, he grabbed the horse's left ear and bit it harder and harder, little by little until the animal got the message, and stood stock still. The two settled into position and gave no more trouble. George, who had been loading the luggage on top of the stage, and in the back boot, took charge of the other three. Soon, they had the reigns run through the eyelets that guided them along the backs of the animals, and George climbed into the driver's seat, checked the reins, checked the brake for proper throw and tightness.

"Aboard Cripple Creek stage," he yelled. This call echoed two other larger coaches of an Overland Concord Stage style that had pulled out minutes before. The bigger coaches had been pulled by a team of six up with matching blacks on the first one. These coaches had springs and fancy gold leaf lettering on the sides and trimmed in gold leaf designs along the edges. Whips cracked and they moved out the South Road toward Four Mile, and each stage was crammed high with luggage and people inside and on the top. The horses hitched to these two big coaches were almost twice the size of the ones hitched to Welty's coach.

People began to vie for seats on the little Welty stage. Two women were left standing as the men rushed for the inside seats. Two big men in lace up boots and cheap corduroy, and four more men in impressive western suits, complete with cravat and stick pin, also climbed inside. Steven stood close to the front, and George motioned him into the seat beside himself. Four other men piled on the top and situated themselves as best they could among the baggage that filled every inch of the top of the coach. George noticed the women being rudely left aside, and he climbed down from his coach. He opened the coach door and looked over the men inside. "Mr. Burnside," he nodded to one man. "We need room for these two women," he stated flatly. No one inside the coach moved. George's eyes narrowed and got hard. "The District needs good women a lot more than slickers, and prospectors," he barked at them. "It's just goin' to haf to be shanks mare for some of you guys," and when no one moved again, he grabbed the boots of the two roughest

113

looking and pulled them out the door. "I hate to get rough," he said, "but it's the law. Fourteen is all I can take, and no strap hangin'. You two boys is just goin' to have to get out. Get a move on now, I ain't got all day for gabbin'. You'll haf to catch the next stage in a few hours," he informed them. Piala was holding the reins of the two lead horses until everyone was positioned and then stepped to one side.

Steven was leaning over the left side of the coach trying to peer in, and he heard two of the men introduce themselves. The wooden legged man introduced himself as Otto Floto, and the other introduced himself as Oscar Burnsides. The woman gave her name as Kitty Barbee, and her daughter Mabs, and then asked the man across from her if he knew her husband Jonce Barbee. He laughed and said that everyone knew Jonce Barbee, and that Jonce was a fine man and his best customer.

"Hi'up," George slapped the reins and yelled, "Gee, gee, Dan," as he brought the coach around in a tight half circle to the left, then, "haw," as he straightened them onto the road to Four Mile Station. The lead horses ears lay back with the strain of pulling and perked upright whenever Welty yelled a command. Welty pulled a bull whip from the area below his feet and let it uncurl to the side of the coach, spun it high over his head in a circle, and expertly cracked it over the head of the leaders, who then began to strain forward. He swung the whip in a figure eight over the heads of the men on the top and bringing his wrist down, cracked it loudly again right above the heads of the lead team. Soon, the horses had picked up the pace into a loping gallop, and the wheels began to sing against the ruts of the road.

They began to pass dozens of men walking with implements of all kinds tied to packs and carried in their arms. Some had pots and pans, and almost all carried a shovel. These were rag tag, and scruffy, bearded men with

114

sad and determined faces, and as they passed Steven could see anger and envy in their eyes. But they were not all sad men, and one played a fiddle as he drove along in a handmade horse cart, with his dog beside him.

"Jesse," Welty hollered and waved. "Jesse Cook," George explained. "He'll be playing at the Social Club up at the Crik on Sunday night."

Cook rode along in a slow plod, playing a lively western tune. "Goin' up to Cripple Creek, goin' on a run," he sang. "Goin' up to Cripple Creek, to have a little fun," Steven heard him sing out, as the stage barreled past.

They rode along in silence for several miles with Welty talking to the horses once in a while, when one would take a wrong notion. The men on top hunkered down against the wind coming at them from the speed that the coach was making. Occasionally, Welty would crack the whip over the horses to make them keep the pace up.

"We're a comin' to the petrified forest," Welty broke the silence about thirty minutes into the trip. They were passing a very neat log house on the right and a sign advertised 'eggs and butter'. A stout woman waved to the coach from some distance away. "Howdy Mrs. Hornebeck," George halloed her and then cracked the whip again for good show. In a few minutes they came to the largest stump that Steven had ever seen. It was over twelve feet in diameter and stuck up some three feet above the surface. The coach passed within three feet of its edge. It glistened from the silicification that had replaced the original wood. About a mile or two farther on they emerged into a low spot in the terrain and passed through many petrified stumps. Most were at least six feet across and some twice that. Steven's mouth fell open in amazement. Some of the stumps rose as columns to a height of twenty or more feet.

"What type of trees were these," he yelled against the wind and wheel noise?

"Don't rightly know," Welty shook his head. "They say there's some bigger in the Redwoods out in Cal-i-forn-i-a," George made five syllables out of the name.

Steven could tell from the depression that the trees had been silted over by an ancient lake eons earlier, and then the lake had eroded in more recent times to reveal the remnants of the forest of huge and ancient trees. Europe had nothing like this, and he marveled at the natural wonder.

They soon left the petrified forest behind, and as they traveled down stream along side West Four Mile Creek, they began to pass huge rock formations of metamorphic sandstone and great boulder of granite or schist, which was the earth's mantle, and rarely made an appearance at the earth's surface. The silicification of the forest had obviously come from the minerals that were in the sand, which had weathered from the ancient upthrust crust. Obviously, to him, huge geologic forces, and volcanic activity in ancient times had been at work here long ago.

The path was generally downhill, but they occasionally crossed a mounded hillock, only to come back to the stream and run alongside or cross back and forth at fords, as the stream meandered slowly down the valley. George let the horses walk on the short uphill jaunts but cracked his whip at them and made up time on the downhill runs. They were spent and lathered with a thick white sweat along their withers and flanks by the time the white church and the buildings of the little town of Four Mile came into view. There was nothing small about the corral at Four Mile, as dozens of horses grazed along the roadside. Ten to twelve barns of various sizes completed the corral structure, and one big Concord stage was pulling out as they were pulling in.

The horses snorted and shook themselves when the stage had pulled to a stop, and they looked about impatiently for the men that would relieve them of the harness and give them feed and water and curry the sweat from their coats. The passengers unwound and began to climb down off the top and emerged from the inside of the coach. George laid the reigns loose across the top of the driver's seat, and climbed down, immediately examining the braking system. "Harry," he yelled, and a blacksmith working at a forge in a near building looked up from the hot coals that he was holding a piece of steel into that he had been working to flatten. Harry waved that he had heard, and then turned his attention to the steel that he was working on, watching it closely, and just as it lost its red glow, he quenched it in oil, passing the steel from its Austenitic phase, and stuffing the surface with carbon atoms, making a hard but somewhat brittle Martensitic surface, yet to be tempered through repeated heating and pounding, until the steel had come to a hard yet pliable consistency. A true art, that took years of experience to understand. Laying the quenched piece aside he wiped his hand on the leather apron that he wore and ambled toward the coach.

"Harry," George pointed under the coach, "I'm getting a problem with this brake rod tensioner." Both men squatted to look under the coach.

Marks climbed down from the seat and began to stretch and look about the yard. Bustling activity was all around him as stable boys unhitched the horses, who blew, and stomped in impatience to get loose from the coach. He walked to the porch of the main building and the smell of potatoes, greens, and frying sow belly wafted toward him from the separate kitchen area that was visible through the back of the building. He noticed a line of people developing to the rear of the kitchen. He knew that was the outhouse, and he would have to join that line soon.

Five men grunted and pushed on the stage, and he went back to help. George Welty was pushing on the top of the left rear wheel, and Steven fell in beside him at the back. "We're going to be delayed here a'while," George explained. "Blacksmith has got to do a little repair on the brakes, fore we can go up to Crik." They pushed the stage over to the front of the blacksmith shop, and then Welty dusted himself off with his hat. "I'm goin' after some grub," he turned and walked off to the main building where several women were laying out a meal for travelers that were hungry.

Steven sat with the others and ate the potatoes and collard greens that were brought out, and tried the gravy, which was half grease from the lard that was used to cook. He left the sow belly alone, as the smell was unfamiliar, and seemed not to be fresh, with a crusting of salt. There was little to do all afternoon, and he sometimes wandered over the yard, and sometimes scratched the ears of a friendly horse or donkey that moseyed up to look for hay or comfort. He noticed Otto Floto had walked out away from the yard and was curious when he saw him talking to two riders that approached him from the road. The three stood in close conversation for a short while, and then with a furtive look around, the three split up, and Floto ambled back toward the stables, and stretched out on a raised walk in the shade of one of the outbuilding and leaned his back against the wall, pulling his hat down and folding his hands across his chest. The wooden leg showed plainly where his cuff was pulled up. Steven watched the blacksmith work, and a woodworker worked on the braking system. They replaced the working parts of most of the brake system and some metal parts had to be heated and shaped and tempered, and this took considerable time.

It was very late in the afternoon, and the sun was sinking quickly behind the hills and road that led toward Guffey, when Welty finally had the coach hitched, and was satisfied with the work that was done. The evening air was cooling, and the sun was just edging below the far mountain range to the West, when the 'All aboard for Crik' was sounded, and they began to load, and got underway. It was soon dark, and the stage rolled on in what seemed total blackness to Steven, but the horses seemed to know their way. They kept a slower pace, and the swinging, and sway, and the iron wheels crunching in the gravel made for a hypnotic feeling, and Marks had trouble keeping his eyes open. They had just pulled a long grade, and come around a gradual turn, entering a thick stand of Aspen trees. There was a quarter moon up now giving a hint of light, when suddenly the horses shied, and abruptly stopped. A dark shadow was across the road, and Welty gave a curse, and got down. He walked forward, and then called, "We got a tree down in the road," he barked, "some of you men get out here and give me a hand." Several men got down off the top, and Marks went forward with them to help with moving the log out of the way.

All six of the men from the top of the stage, along with Steven, and George, were fully engaged in moving the tree. They had swung it a little, oouching it a few inches at a time. "Funny," George said with a suspicious tone in his voice. He left his position near the top of the tree and walked around to the butt. "Why," he exclaimed, "this is a healthy tree, and it's been axed."

At that moment a dull light shown from behind a tree to their right, about waist high off the ground, and a voice boomed out at them. "Stand easy boys," the voice called through the dark. "We've got you covered, and we don't want to haf to shoot." A leather flap was dropped that had covered the light, and a revolver showed plainly in a handheld down low, waist high. A masked face was barely visible in the dim glow.

Moments later another voice called to the inside of the stage. "You gents in there wake up and step out here, and don't try nothin' stupid, and nobody gets hurt." Now, another leather cover came off, and a dull glow showed near the coach. The bandit rapped his gun barrel on the coach's door window on the left side, opposite from the side the first bandit had appeared from. A hand opened the coach door, and the gruff voice spoke again. "Get out, and don't be slow, if'n you value your life."

Otto Floto was the first to emerge from inside the coach. "You," the gunman pushed Floto with his free hand, while keeping the inside of the coach covered, "hold them horses. We don't want nobody hurt cause the horses got skiddish." Floto did as he was told. Oscar Burnsides emerged next, followed by the other two men inside. "Keep your hands up, and no funny business," the voice commanded. The two women were slow to come out, and the gunmen seemed little concerned about this.

One of the gunmen covered the people from behind, and one from the front. The first bandit kept them covered from the back and the one that had emptied the coach pulled a tightly woven burlap ore sack from a coat pocket and popped it open. He relieved Floto of his wallet and rings first and then went down the line. They came to Steven next to last and cautioned him to keep his hands up. The robber went straight to his inside pocket on his heart side, opening his coat with the gun barrel, transferring the long European wallet to the sack, and then reached for Steven's antique gold watch. When Steven reached to stop him by grabbing the chain, the thief cocked his pistol and put it right in Steven's face.

"I'll blow your fool head off," he threatened him. Steven let the watch go, and the man tore it loose from the fob that fastened it to a belt loop.

The woman and her daughter were emerging from the coach. The little girl was still half asleep, and they brought them over to the line of men and looked them over. One continued to cover them while the other brought the lantern close.

"I'll be damned," he said, "Lou, look how this pug-nosed kid is tryin' to hold out on us, and cheat us."

"Shut your yap," the other warned him.

"You leave her alone," the mother wailed in an excited voice.

"Keep still," the one in the back warned," or I might just take them garnet earrings that you're a wearin', and see what you got in that fat purse of yours."

There was something lurid in the remark, and the other bandit barked a wild, and distinctive hyena sounding laugh.

The front bandit came closer to the little girl, and a silver dollar showed where her mouth was not large enough to contain it. Drool dripped at the corner, and the mouth gapped from the effort. The bandit reached in his sack and pulled an identical coin, and placed it into the girls open mouth, on top of the other coin. Then, without another word, the two backed off into the Aspen grove, and in a moment, had put out the lanterns that had been strung on their cartridge belts, and disappeared.

"First time I ever seen a prospector double his stake before even getting to the district," one of the men laughed at the child. They placed the women and her daughter back inside the coach and finished removing the tree out of the road. Soon, they were underway, and Welty picked up the pace, as fast as the dark would allow. Steven was devastated. He was now flat broke, knowing no one, in a foreign land. He wondered what he would do. The prospect seemed poor indeed.

Welty moved the horses along, cracking his whip, and yelling at the leaders. He was sullen and angry, and concentrated on moving the stage, which leaned as he took the curves at the top safe speed. He slid open the little front window under the driver's seat, and Steven could hear Oscar Burnsides' voice booming out from inside with indignity.

"Soon as we hit town," Oscar swore, "I'm asking

Win Bonyton to form a posse and see if they can pick up the trail. Win is the best man for the job. This hijacking has got to stop. Someone is going to be killed. We must pursue these bandits, or they are only going to become more brazen."

Up top, the men behind Steven laughed and talked about how smartly they had avoided being robbed of most of their goods. Knowing that it was a possibility, they had prepared with gold coins to throw down, while hiding most of their money in among the luggage on top. There had not been enough time or light for the bandits to do a very complete search of the coach and luggage. That had left most of the men with most of their possessions. Steven had not been that savvy.

Soon, the horses pulled the last grade around Mt. Pisgah and came to the top of the rise overlooking the town to the east. The whole bowl of the ancient caldera spread out in front of Steven, and he immediately recognized it as an ancient collapsed volcano. Even in the pale moonlight the high ridges surrounding the town were obvious. Lights twinkled from the campfires of tents surrounding the main part of the budding town, and a few lights shone from buildings that had sprung up along Bennet Avenue.

Welty shook his whip loose and started to crack it one after another until the animals were in a full run down the hill, and he kept it up all the way into the center of town, until reaching the beginnings of the rise on the other side of the bowl, he stomped on the brake, and pulled the reigns back hard, until the six animals, foaming, and snorting, with sweat slinging off them, practically sat down on their haunches, and with the wheels locked, and sliding, came to a perfect skidding stop directly in front of the Palace Hotel. He did this performance every time that he roared into town, but he put on an extra show of speed because of the robbery. There was always a large crowd to welcome the stage, no matter the time of day, and tonight, the crowd was even larger, as Welty had yelled the news of the robbery to the few homesteads along the way, and someone had ridden at breakneck speed, in the dark, over to Limekiln, where a phone existed, and news had spread by the new-fangled device to Cripple Creek before the stage rolled to a stop. A cacophony of yelling and hubbub broke out at the station, which set donkeys to braying and dogs to barking, so that lights began to come on all over the town and people began to emerge from doorways, and stood in night shirts, leaning from windows, and yelling to find out what was going on.

One man always met the stage, no matter the weather or the time of day. He just loved to see Welty roar to a sliding stop, and to see what new passengers had come to what he considered his city. Bob Womack made his way to the front and took the mail sack from George Welty as he passed it down and swung down from the stage driver's seat.

"Who was it, George," Womack asked in his high-pitched voice? "Any idea?"

Winfield Scott Boynton pressed to the front in time to hear Bob's question to Welty, and George began to recount the experience.

"No one that I recognized," he shook his head. "One of 'em did make a mistake," he recounted, "and called the other Lou. That made the other bandit real mad. He got kind'a off kelter, when he saw that little girl holding a silver dollar in her mouth," George indicated Mabs, and her mother to Boynton. "They cut a tree down, a big one, and that stopped us. It was pretty dark, and they had their faces covered with handkerchiefs. They had lanterns tied to their belts. There seemed to be only two, but there might have been more that we didn't know about."

"This is all similar to a couple of other robberies

that have happened on the Shelf Road, but now they seemed to have moved over to the Florissant Road."

Oscar Burnsides joined the other three men, and listened to George's description. "Win," Oscar put in, "I sure would like for you to organize a posse and see what you can find. Maybe, if you can find out where they had their horses staked, you could pick up the trail."

"I'd be glad to do that," Boynton replied. "George, I'll need you to show me the exact spot where you were waylayed."

"Won't be hard," George shook his head, "there's a big tree down to mark the scene."

"I'll get some men who can ride, and shoot, and tell them to join you at daylight," Bob Womack volunteered. "I'd go myself, but the rumitise, has got me stove up, with the change in weather."

"Jonce," the men heard the woman from the coach exclaim, as she and the little girl rushed to a man approaching.

"Must be Jonce Barbee's wife and little girl," Boynton observed. "I better talk to them and see if'n they saw anything that would help." He pulled away from the other three, after confirming that he would be ready at first light the next morning for a hard ride, and a search, giving Bob instructions to have the men ready for several days on the trail, and warning him not to choose any drunkards, or slackers. He made this point because he knew that Womack had been drinking that night and had a habit of it. Womack got a bit of a frown at the lack of confidence that Win had shown, but assured him that there would be no drinking, and that all the men would be serious, not out for a party.

Steven had sat for a few minutes taking in the whole scene, and as Boynton pulled away to talk to the Barbees, he slowly, and dejectedly climbed down. Womack immediately noticed the young man, and greeted him. "Bob Womack," he stuck out a hand in a friendly greeting.

"Steven Marks," he shook hands, he was dazed, and sleepy. The gun in his face had given him an adrenalin rush, which had worn off long ago, leaving him exceedingly tired, and he looked around him, a bit in a fog.

"Did they get much from you," Bob questioned him?

"Everything," Steven choked it out.

"Don't worry, son," Bob counseled him, and then turning to Oscar Burnsides, "Oscar, this man is going to need a cot for the night. Just put it on my bill."

Steven was stunned and speechless, but through his fogged brain, he finally made the connection. "You're Robert Womack, the discoverer of the El Paso load," he recognized in amazement.

"I guess that's my pain," Bob agreed, and then, as Bob always enjoyed being a celebrity. "How did you know about that?"

"It was news in the Geological Review, which I received as a member of the Society."

"Never hear'd of it. Where in tarnation did you get that?" Bob was puzzled.

"It's a review of all mining claims that are filed worldwide," Steven informed him. "I saw the notice in Europe, and that is what brought me here. My father was in with a group that was on the Van Hayden survey."

"Well, I'll be durned, you are talking way back. I guided Van Hayden's party to this valley," Bob shook his head in disbelief. Then a puzzlement crossed his face. "I don't remember any Englishman in that party," he looked questioningly at Steven. Steven made no reply. He was satisfied that the English accent that he had picked up from his proctor at the University of Sophia, in Spain, had given him a London pronunciation to his speech. The Spanish were definitely unpopular at this time in the United States, and he was not eager to have his heritage known. He had picked up too many negative conversations, and the general opinion was that there was a war coming between the two countries.

"So, you're an educated man," Bob ran a sleeve across his nose, as he was self-conscious in the presence of men of education, and always aware that his big long nose had a habit of dripping.

"I have a degree in Geology," Steven informed him, and a master's degree in mining engineering."

"Gol' durn," Bob was really pleased.

Oscar Burnside, who had gone up the street to his saloon to see how things were going, came back at that moment. "Young man," he informed Steven, "if you're wanting to sleep on a cot with some cover, and not on the floor uncovered, you had better come along right away. There's not enough room for a sardine up at my place, but I am trying to save you a cot. You had better claim it right away, or you'll have a fight for it."

Steven turned to follow Burnsides, then turned back. "Mr. Womack, I don't know how I will ever repay you for your kindness tonight."

"Don't worry about it son," Bob shrugged. "You just do the right thing, and it will all work out. You run along and I'll check on you in the morning. I got's to see if'n I can round up some men to try and pick up a cold trail." Bob turned away, looking over the remaining crowd to see who he might draft. Steven followed Burnsides uphill to the West along Bennett to his saloon.

Burnsides took him to a back storage room, where three men already lay asleep on cots crammed so close together that there was barely room to walk between. The whole barroom had been crammed full, and men slept on the stairs leading to the second floor. He saw the woman and the daughter from the coach follow a man up the stairs. He accepted a tattered wool blanket from

126

Burnsides, that he had pulled from a shelf in the storage room, and lay down on the cot without pillow. His head hit the wooden bar across the end of the cot, and his feet stuck out of the blanket and off the other end, but it made no difference, as he was exhausted, and sound asleep within a few moments, in spite of the cacophony of sounds coming from the adjoining room.

Chapter 12. Cupid

The next morning, Win Boynton and eight other men, including George Welty and Alonzo Welty, left Cripple to investigate the robbery site. A rain shower had passed through, and the men were doubtful that any trail would survive the downpour. Bob Womack had tried to recruit several men and met unenthusiastic support. It was a Sunday morning, and the men of the camp regularly used the day to rest. Womack didn't press the issue, as there was a special event that had been in the planning for some time.

Womack returned around midnight to his cabin in Poverty Gulch. He stepped carefully around at least a dozen tenderfoot camps. No one objected to men camping out in Poverty Gulch, as it was not part of the plotted township, and Bob made everyone welcome. There was more than two hundred greenhorns from the Springs and elsewhere that had clustered in camp sites around the bottom of Myers Ave., between Bob's cabin and the start of buildings and lots at the edge of the old Broken Box Ranch.

He rose early, just before first light, as was his habit, when he hadn't been drinking, which wasn't usual for a Saturday night, but this Saturday night was different. He put on his best duds and walked the two hundred yards down the north bank of the eastern branch of Cripple Creek, which ran down the center of Poverty Gulch. As he walked along in the early morning light, he encouraged anyone awake. "We're havin' a Sunday School and Church service at the Buckhorn, this morning," he told them. "Y'all come." He got little to no response from the sleepy and stiffened men. The rain had soaked the camp.

A fog had settled over the valley pouring in from the south and west over Mt. Pisgah. The men were cramped and cold, as a May chill had descended.

He walked on, and as he got to the edge of Myers Ave., walked west for several blocks, then turned north for one block, where Burnsides bar was located in the bottom of the new structure that was the Palace Hotel. He arrived in time to see Win Boynton, Alonzo, and George Welty, and Jonce Barbee, whom the Welty's had loaned a horse to from their stable, and four other men that Bob did not recognize, who had joined them, ride off toward the Florissant Road. Otto Floto stood watching from the open door and Bob touched his hat to him. Floto made no response.

Bob poured himself a cup of coffee scalding hot, then poured it into a saucer and blew on it to cool it some, and drank the steaming coffee from the saucer, as usual.

Oscar Burnsides finished wiping down some tables and glasses and came over to talk with Womack. "Mornin' Bob, did Win get off," he asked?

"They just rode out," Bob nodded toward the front door.

"Not much chance of pickin' up the trail, if the rain was as heavy down toward Four Mile. Pretty rocky ground in spots and they won't have much trouble coverin' their trail anyway." Burnsides ran a hand through his hair and then took a close look at Bob. "What're you so duded up for Bob," he quizzed?

"Headed to the Sunday School meeting at the Buckhorn this mornin'," Bob said proudly. "Father Volpe is going to lead it. We've got the makin's of a real town. Last count we had over two thousand souls around."

"And maybe three hundred a month comin' in from all over the place," Oscar beamed.

Joe Wolf, the manager of the Place Hotel, came down the stairs from his office on the second floor, dressed to the nines with cravat and stick pin, black coat, high topped boots, with a spit shine. He nodded to Burnsides, ignored Bob, and walked over to the front door, where he stood in quiet conversation with Otto Floto.

"Some good, and some bad," Bob's eyes narrowed, as he watched Wolf and Floto in conversation.

They split apart, and Floto went off south, and then west along Myer's, and Wolf stepped outside signaling to Amos, the boot black to put a fresh shine on his boots, which were already glassy. Wolf never payed the old black man, and got a free shine every morning for letting him set his shoe shine stand up by the front of the Palace's entrance.

Burnsides watched Bob with curiosity, wondering that Bob would be involved in organizing a Sunday School. The old cowboy never ceased to amaze him. The man seemed like a contradiction. "Where's this here Sunday School goin' to take place," Burnsides curiosity got the best of him?

"Over in the back of the Buckhorn."

Oscar went from curious to amused. "The Buckhorn," he exclaimed! "Whose gonna' conduct a service over there?"

"Father Volpe is'a comin' in from Victor. Bishop Matze is'a sendin' him after Portales requested it."

"Why that's a bar, and a rough one too," Oscar laughed.

"We got that all covered up," Bob retorted. Count Portales hired Walter Paris to paint a bunch of canvases to lay over the roulette wheels and faro tables. We been workin' on this since June," Bob defended. Oscar just got more tickled.

"Who's a'gonna come to such a fracas," Burnsides hooted?

"Wal," Bob scratched his head, "Mother Duffy's gonna have her girls attend, "Bob offered.

"Bob," Burnsides chided, "them's sportin' women!" He reared back in his chair and guffawed.

Bob was turning a slow red. No one defamed women in front of Bob. They were all sacred, no matter the persuasion. "And, so who needs religion more," he shot back? "Them girls can change."

Burnsides knew Bob pretty well and saw him getting his dandr' up. "OK, Bob, he softened. "Sounds like you've got it hitched. I got to get back to work," he excused himself.

"Say, Oscar," Bob questioned him, "Where'd you put that Marks boy, that came in on the stage last night?"

"He's back in the pantry, back in the back, behind the kitchen, on a cot with three others," Oscar inclined his head toward the back of the hotel. "I don't know where we're gonna put any more people. Just can't stack'em any tighter."

"What'd I owe you for his lodgin'," Bob offered?

"Uh," Oscar stopped and looked at Bob, "I guess two bits'l do it."

Bob followed Burnsides to the counter and poured himself a little more coffee, reached in a pocket, and lay a five-dollar gold piece on the bar top. Oscar looked at it, then picked it up. "I reckon that'll cover a cot, bath, and breakfast for about five days for the lad," he bargained.

"That'll about do it, I suppose," Burnsides turned toward the register, and rang it open, bit the coin, and flexed it to make sure it wasn't leaded, then dropped it in the till.

Bob drank the rest of his coffee, then made his way back through the kitchen, and found the pantry. Stefano Marquez was having a fitful dream. He kicked and moaned in his sleep. The snake eyes of a man with a thin mustache bore into him. The man in the adjacent cot had already gotten up and left, but a burly young kid was just picking his head up when Bob stepped to the door.

Stefano moaned, "Que como va," in his sleep and kicked his legs fitfully.

"Damn Mescan," the kid retorted, and kicked the adjoining cot really hard.

In his dream Stefano heard a loud gun shot, and started awake. It was the two cots braces coming together with enough force to crack loudly.

Bob came around the door in time to see part of what had happened. "What's goin' on here," he barked.

"Got a damn Mescan here," the burly boy spit.

"Burnsides don't allow no spittin' in his pantry," Bob told him.

"Who are you?" The bully boy squared, and his eyes started scratching toward a rifle that he had propped behind his head in the corner.

Bob saw his eyes go searching. "Jus' leave that iron alone," he placed the palm of his hand against his gun butt and pushed it away from his body. "Ain't never shot a man, but I've killed many a skunk. You need a cup of coffee," Bob informed him, "and you need it right now. Leave that rifle right where it is, and you can pick it up later in the day from Burnsides."

"I ain't leavin' my gun," the boy blubbered.

"If 'n I pull this gun," Bob warned him, "I'm agonna lay your scalp wide open with the barrel. Your choice."

Steven had come awake and sat up on the cot, but stayed stark still, trying to understand what was happening. Nothing moved for several seconds, and then the burly kid stood up and eased around the cots in the narrow pantry. Bob moved aside, staying out of reach, and let the boy pass.

"You ain't gonna forget Frank Hayden," the boy got the last word, and his freckled face, and shock of red hair disappeared through the kitchen and into the bar below the hotel.

"Not likely to forget such bad manners," Bob agreed with his assessment, more to himself, than to Steven.

"What happened," Steven asked?

"I'm not rightly sure," Bob said in his high nasal twang. He turned sideways and duck walked to the pantry rear and retrieved the rifle. He checked the chamber and was not surprised to find a live shell loaded. He ejected the shell onto the cot and pushed the spring down to keep a fresh shell from entering the firing chamber, replaced the shell in the magazine. "You better stick with me awhile Mr. Marks," Bob said. "Outhouse is out back," Bob pointed with the rifle. "Join me in the bar. I'll order us some grub."

Marks did and found some water in a tub outside. Several other men were getting washed up. There was a light frost on the metal rim above the water line, and the ice-cold water shocked him fully awake. Crossing through the kitchen the good smells of bread and meat cooking, made his stomach rumble, and when he entered the bar, Bob was sipping coffee from a saucer, and the rifle was still on the bar. Burnsides wiped his hands and sat the gun in a corner. He looked curiously at the stranger that had come in on the stage with him.

Steven took a chair beside Bob, running his still wet hands through his disheveled hair to try and smooth it. He had no idea what to do next. The shock of the robbery, and the consequences that would follow, with him being without money, was beginning to set into sharp focus in the early morning light. He closed his eyes, and lowered his head a bit, and just patted the stray hair down with his hands still wet from the icy bucket of water out behind the kitchen. When he looked up, he saw that one of the girls from the kitchen had set a plate of eggs, and bacon with fried potato, sliced, and covered with green chili. He tested the mix slowly and then gave himself over to the ravenous hunger, that followed the excitement of the previous night.

Bob drank his hot coffee and watched the young man in silence, letting him eat. After a few minutes, when Steven slowed in his wolfing the food, and looked up sheepishly, Bob put his saucer down.

"You best hang out with me," Bob slid back from the table a few inches.

"Mr. Womack, I can't ever repay your kindness," Steven began.

"Lad," Bob held up his hand, "that's an insult to a cowboy, in this here land, we all help each other, and no 'thanks' is necessary." Then more seriously, Bob asked, "any idea what had that fella riled up?"

"I was awakened with him kicking at me," Steven was puzzled.

"Hmmm," Bob mused? Just the same, you'd better stick with me today."

"I've not any money," Steven confessed honestly, more to himself than to Bob.

"We'll take care of that later in the day, when the assay office opens. I been thinking that's the best place, to put your talents to work, quick like."

"Is there one needing help?"

"They're always needing help, so much fire assay gets done that the men who do it don't last long. Most shops keep a sign out."

"But, will they be open on Sunday?"

"This is the World's Greatest Gold Camp," Bob informed him, "but first, we're agonna' take care of your spiritual life," Bob fixed him with a grin, as he knew he had a volunteer that couldn't refuse, "by takin' you to Sunday School." Steven looked amazed at the old cowboy, who was so full of surprises, and let himself be swept along by his good fortune.

"After that, we'll see about a job, and then, this

134

evening at the Squaw Gulch Amusement Club, we'll see about getting you introduced around, "Bob had a twinkle in his eye, as he rose, and lay coins to cover the meals on the bar. It was a signal to go, and Steven followed him, out the front door and on to Bennett Ave.

From the Palace, Bob headed east along Bennett, past Johnny Nolan's Saloon, to the Buckhorn, Nolan's main competition, a few doors away. As they came through the swinging doors on the front, a big boned woman with piles of hair, and red, rouge cheeks, broke away from the circle of people she was with, and hailed Bob.

"You scrawny, mule hided cowboy, I'll be damned if you didn't show up on time," the big woman threw a bear hug around Bob. "You look good, honey, clean up real nice."

"I told you I'd be here with bells on," Bob returned the jest. "You got everything decked out real good."

The woman turned and faced Steven. "And, who you got here," she asked?

"Mother Duffy," Bob gestured, "this here is Steven Marks. Come in on the stage last night; got robbed."

"Well, damn those thieves. I hope they catch'em, and hang'em," she swore. "Well, well, well," she clucked as she gripped Steven's shoulders in her vise-like grip. "My girls are gonna' love you," she tossed out and then whooped with laughter. "Should I introduce him now," she winked at Bob?

"Naw," Bob pulled Steven away from her. "I got some people I want him to meet first, "and then remembering his cowboy etiquette, "if'n that's what he wants."

"I'm sure that it would be exciting, Mother Duffy, but I'd best go along with Mr. Womack," he sensed the pressure, and hoped he didn't offend.

"Suit yourself," Mother Duffy shrugged, and

turned back to talk to a man in priest clothes who had tapped her shoulder.

They made their way through the crowd. There was a bar all along the right-hand side of the room, and six to eight girls in gaudy, but nice clothes sat swinging their legs and chattering among themselves. Tables were arranged along the left side of the room, and inter spaced between were gaming tables for faro and roulette. They were covered with painted canvases, and three men were examining the paintings closely, along with several other people, who were looking closely at the paintings.

"That there tall fellow with pipe and beard, is a European Count," Bob pointed him out to Steven, "Count Pourtales, and he had them pictures painted by Walter Paris, that other feller there with him. The third man is George Carr, and with him is his wife, Emma, the sweetest woman in the camp," Bob beamed. "Come on, I'll introduce you." He led Steven over to the group. The high crown of the roulette wheel could be inferred, and cupids chased cavorting cherubs around the canvas. Steven immediately noticed a striking similarity between the faces on each, and the face of the woman Bob was taking him to meet.

It was at that moment that he really looked at the woman who was next to Emma Carr. She was examining the canvas cupids with a knowing smile. She was of a slight build, but there was something sturdy and yet graceful in the way she touched the canvas and smiled.

She felt the pressure of Steven's gaze, and their eyes locked. Steven realized that he had been staring and quickly looked away, beyond her to the bar, and unfortunately to the gaze of one of the bar girls, who winked at him. Steven saw the girl turn and see the bar girl's wink, and he reddened. When he looked back, she would no longer look his way, and although he tried to catch her eye the rest of the service, she totally avoided his attention. Steven, however, could not get over the feeling that one of the Cupid's arrows had found its mark.

Bob brought him over to George and Emma Carr and introduced him. The Count and artist Paris were too much in serious conversation over the art work to be interrupted, and Steven kept hoping that Emma Carr would introduce him to the woman next to her. Just at that moment, Mother Duffy called the meeting to order, and shouted 'Quiet' until the room settled. The bar girls got very stiff postures and sat still on top of the bar. The crowd drifted for seats.

"I'm turnin' this here first Cripple Creek Sunday School over to Father Volpe," she shoved the good Padre forward. Bob and Steven ended up near the front door and behind the Carr's and their friends, as the seats faced the back of the barroom.

Father Volpe began with a Latin blessing that fell mostly flat in the almost totally Protestant gathering. Mostly, he had memorized church catechisms, but that was obviously not going to work here. Like most priests, his extemporaneous oratory was somewhat lacking, but he gave it a valiant try.

He knew the ten commandments in English pretty well, so he cobbled a sermon about gold, the lure of gold, the golden calf, and the ten commandments. It would have been long, rambling, and disconnected, and mostly falling on deaf ears, except for a miner that barged through the front door wanting breakfast.

"I need some grub," he demanded in a loud voice.

"Sir," Mother Duffy addressed him in her most diplomatic tone, "if you will just wait until our Sunday School is over, we'll be glad to fix you up."

"Ahh, the Hell," the prospector shot back at her. "What do I care for all this Sunday School business? I want some grub, and I want it now," he bellowed!

Mother Duffy began to turn a purple, red around

137

the roots of her hair, which quickly spread along her cheeks, and down her arms, until a frightening transformation had occurred.

Mother Duffy took two steps forward and turned a little sideways to give the astonished offender a good look. She raised one arm, pulled her frilly sleeve up, and flexed her huge bicep. "I'll teach you, you good for nothin' son-of-a-bitch, to come in here, and bother the first Sunday School we ever had in this town!"

The prospector turned and ran for his life, but Mother Duffy was on him quick as a cat, and grabbing his shirt collar, and pants' seat, increased his momentum, hurling him through the swinging doors, and halfway across Bennett Ave.

The good Father said a closing prayer, in a rather hurried fashion. The meeting broke up in groups. Some went to talking among themselves, and others gathered around a piano at the back, and kept it going with some songs. Emma Carr was coaxed into doing a lovely rendition of 'Amazing Grace', and when Steven looked for the woman again, she had disappeared.

"Howdy, cowboy," a feminine voice said.

He turned toward the voice and saw the girl that had winked at him when he had nervously looked away, standing with her hands on her hips.

"You're new around these parts," she twisted flirtatiously.

"Yes," he answered matter of fact. He was still looking around for the woman who had been with Emma Carr. She followed his gaze.

"What'ch lookin' for," she questioned?

"It is all new to me," Steven told her. She was a pretty girl, with dark brown almond eyes, a red satin dress, slightly dark skin, telling of a heritage from native, or Mexican parent, somewhere in the past. High cheek bones were accented with a hint of rouge.

"Where'd you hale from," she continued.

Some of the western vernacular was strange to his ear, but he guessed at her meaning. "I've come from New York," he told a partial truth. This had become his standard answer whenever he had been asked this question.

"You're a long way from home," she mused. "How long you been in town?"

"I came on the stage last night."

"The one that was robbed," she asked?

"Yes," he said flatly.

Bob had finished telling Emma and George Carr how much he enjoyed the efforts. Bob always effused good feelings, as he told Mother Duffy what a success it had been, and admired how she had kept order. He had worked his way around the remaining crowd, and came back around to Steven, at that moment.

"Birdie," he addressed the girl. "You can chase him around at the shindig tonight down at the Squaw Gulch Amusement Club," he told her. "Right now, I've got something more important for him than flirtin' with you."

Birdie's expression had already changed to disappointment, figuring that if he had been robbed, she might be wasting her time. Now Bob was adding insult to injury. "And what is so gol'dang important, Bob Womack," she turned to Bob, and put her balled up fists on either hip?

"Guyot is probably up at his assay office by now, and I'm a'gonna try and get him a job," Bob told her.

"In that case, I'll see you later at the stomp," she winked at Steven for a third time, figuring maybe he was a potential future customer, and then turned and walked away toward the group of girls, some who were still sitting on the bar swinging their legs.

Chapter 13. The Assay Office

"Come on," Bob told Steven. "We got a ways to walk up to Squaw Gulch," Bob led off through the swinging doors. Steven followed him out of the Buckhorn, and downhill toward Meyer's Ave from the buildings along Bennett.

Their progress was slow, as Bob stopped to jaw with half the people that they passed. They walked south on Third Street to the bottom of the hill, passing by Myers and the cribs and dance halls, and saloons that proliferated along that part of the town.

Being Sunday morning, there was only scant activity among the scatter of foundations and partly finished structures. They crossed Cripple Creek at the bottom on flat stones placed in the creek bed for that purpose and continued along the southwestern bank, past Poverty Gulch. Gold Hill rose above them North of the gulch, and the saddle that joined the next ridge. Bob Kept up a stream of conversation, pointing out landmarks, 'hallowing' people that they passed.

"This here is the limit of the township," he pointed out to Steven. "See how this tent city has sprung up," Bob spread a hand toward the south. There was a hodge podge of tents and shacks closely packed together, some wood, some sod, with rusting tin roofs, or roofs of boards and tar paper. People moved about, and small curls of smoke rose from cooking fires. Women could be seen tending the fires. Men stretched and pulled their suspenders over their shoulders as they emerged from out houses. Most of the dwellings were concentrated along the stream, which was dry, except for holes of water Steven thought the arrangement chaotic, and the whole area seemed squalid

141

and unwholesome. He noticed the proximity of the outhouses to the stream, and the thought of typhoid, and dysentery crossed his mind.

"My cabin is up that away," Bob gestured toward the top of the Gulch, "just over that rise." Steven could see many tents, and open camps, with hundreds of men moving around open fires. Many of the men in that direction seemed to simply have a bedroll rolled out on the open ground. "My family used to own where the town is, but we sold it several years back to some black boot ranchers, Bennett, and Meyers, who laid out the town after the District was formed," he said, without a trace of regret. "My cabin's on government land. That's why all them Greenhorns is up there campin' out, cause nobody cares. Most will give up in a few days. They'll be replaced by new ones with the fever. More and more is comin' every day. We got close to three thousand souls scattered out across," he said, with a hint of pride in his voice. "I spent many a month up here in years past without seeing another living soul, and I can tell you, it gets a might lonely with nothin' but the wind for company."

"Is there any ground unclaimed," Steven asked?

"Most anything with any promise is staked, clean across the top and down the sides. It's been six to eight months since a new area was opened. There are abandoned claims around, but it takes money to buy in, and money to develop. Then the ore has got to pay freight over to the smelter at Pueblo. At that, the assay don't always rightly tell what's gonna be recovered in the end. It's a matter of luck and determination. There are many prospect holes where one man gave up, and the next dug a few more inches, and hit it big," Bob gave him an appraising look.

Steven thought of the more than seven hundred dollars that he had carried the night before, and the anguish of his situation washed over him again.

"We can take a short cut over that ridge," Bob pointed uphill, and they started off again at a brisk pace. Steven had trouble keeping up with the older man, and his heart was soon pounding, and he was sucking air like a bellows. Bob noticed and slowed to look around from time to time. "You'll soon get used to the altitude," he led on. "Air's a little thin, up this high."

They reached the top of a ledge that led around a ridge where a trail was worn around the circumference of a low rising hill. There was a hole dug just off the trail, and Bob stopped to peer in. A man was swinging a pick vigorously at the bottom, which he had dug down some eight to ten feet.

"Well Lafe," Bob called. "I thought you had a vein over by the Ajax."

The man stopped in mid-swing and grinned up at them.

"Lost it in a poker game Friday night,"

"You got to stop losing them good claims, Lafe," Bob chided him.

"Ah, Bob," the man shot back, "I ain't got no use for money," he complained. "I jus' get drunk, and spend it all on whores," he laughed.

He was a grizzled old prospector, Steven observed, as he climbed out of the prospect hole, probably much younger than he looked.

"Ain't got nothin' left but my pick and shovel," he complained. "Don't even have a chaw of tobacco."

"Well, I can fix that," Bob dug in his pocket, and pulled a plug tobacco and a knife and cut the man two plugs. "There's one for now and one for later."

Lafe stuck one in his mouth and one in his pocket. "Much obliged, Bob," he grinned, showing a mouth full of bad teeth. He had all he needed for a good day.

"Watch that game at the Clarendon," Bob warned him. You know Joe Wolf runs a crooked wheel."

"Bob," Lafe squinted against the bright morning sun, which had just risen high enough to pierce the Aspen and pine, "you know that the fun of it is the finding. The money's just gonna fall through the holes in my pockets," Lafe grinned a big, tobacco-stained grin, and spit a stream of juice against a neighboring rock ledge, as if for added emphasis. Then without any more talking, went back to picking away at the bottom of the hole.

"Lafe was one of the first experienced prospectors to listen and come up to Cripple," Bob told, as they walked along. "The whores weren't far behind," he smiled to himself. "The first one set up a tent just below my cabin, and Lafe was her best customer, and he took it out in trade, givin' her an eighth interest on paper each time. After a couple months, one day she come by my cabin and asked me to help her understand what he had written, and what was goin' on," Bob laughed his high-pitched giggle. "She had notes for twenty-eight-one-eighth interest."

Steven had to laugh at this thought several times as they walked on around the base of the hill, curving southwest.

"Owned that mine three and a half times," Bob grinned back at him. "She's now a rich madam with a store on Bennett, and six girls workin' upstairs for her. She sold that mine for real good money," he laughed again.

As they rounded a curve in the trail, the forest opened up and below them, an alpine valley came into view with several buildings visible. "That there is the town of Anaconda," Bob pointed to the valley below. Everywhere men moved like ants crawling all over an ant hill. The trapezoidal shape of head frames dotted the landscape around the valley with the X shape of the cross supports the prominent feature inside the frames. Some were large, and some smaller. Mules struggled to pull wagons or slid on their hindquarters as they angled down the steep slopes with wagons with side boards piled high with ore. Men stood on the brake levers and the screech of metal rivet on steel rims echoed through the valley in an eerie sound, as men cursed, and cajoled the teams. Crys of "Whoa", and "Hi yup" mingled with the cracking of whip, and the shouting of men, the braying of donkeys in a cacophony of sound, punctuated by muffled underground explosions, or the blast of surface charges. Wagons reached the main road, and turned south, slowly moving in an almost continuous line, with empty wagons coming the other way, or stopped to let the loaded wagons take the inside to pass, away from the crumbly outside edge and drop off to the valley floor.

"This here is Squaw Gulch," Bob pointed uphill along a natural bowl that faded back into the mountains above them. "When digging first started, we found an old skeleton of an Indian woman up toward the top, and that's where it got its name." They stood for several minutes watching the spectacle around, below, and above them. Finally, Bob pointed toward a cluster of buildings a little higher, and up the center of the sloping bowl, "that's Barry, named after my friend Horace Barry, who founded it. He's mayor, and that big building near the center is the Squaw Creek Amusement Club, and town hall. That's where the fandango is tonight," he said with obvious pride. "I'm the only member not in residence," he bragged. Then pointing across Squaw Gulch, and part way up the side of the low hill bordering the gully, he pointed out a small log building. "That there is Guyot's assay office, where we's headed." Heat poured from a steel pipe coming through the roof at the back, betraying the presence of an extremely hot fire, probably coal or coked coal with very little smoke, showing a very well bellowed fire at a very high temperature. Bob led off in the general direction of the assay office, picking his way with obvious knowledge of the myriads of trails that intersected all along the way.

The roads were busy, and sometimes they had to wait for a wagon to pass where their path crossed a road. Within a few minutes they had made their way to the assay office, where a neatly lettered sign above the door informed, "Guyot Assay Office". The door was open and heat poured from inside, accompanied by the roar of a bellows fed flame, as they stepped inside.

The inside of the office glowed red from the red-hot glow coming from the edges of the furnace doors. In a few moments, Steven's eyes adjusted to the light inside, and he could see familiar machinery against the side walls. Most were small ore milling machines for grinding the ores of various sizes. There was an L shaped counter giving working space on the right side, and across the middle directly in front of the doorway. Several men stood with sacks stacked at their feet, and on the counter waiting to be attended. Two men in heavy leather aprons and asbestos gloves were tending the furnaces. Three young boys continuously pumped bellows that fed air into the superheated coal. Each time the bellows were pumped the furnace let out a roar.

A short, stocky man nodded to Bob as they entered. He looked over his wire rimmed glasses at them. His countenance was weathered as leather, and a classic Gallic nose was the prominent feature on his face. A worn and worried looking man stood in front talking to the man behind the counter. He was thin with a floppy hat. He turned to look at who had come into the room. His eyes had dark circles around them. His face was thin, but tanned. His body stiffened when he saw Bob, and so did Bob.

"Womack," he nodded, as he spoke the one word.

"Stratton," Bob returned the one-word salutation.

Stratton turned his attention back to the man behind the counter. "What about the sample from The Independence," he asked?

146

"A little better," the man behind the counter said. "But the telluride is unoxidized, and it's going to be hard to recover. The last sample would just about pay shipping," he shrugged. The old man looked crestfallen, and his posture slumped even more.

"Damn it, Guyot," Stratton growled. "I'm worn-out carrying samples over here. Pueblo just can't recover enough to make The Washington or The Independence pay, and I'm just about tapped out, and worn out."

"Well," Guyot pulled his glasses off and lay them on the counter, you might try the Frenchman in Anaconda. They have been getting some good results, and it would give you a comparison, just to be sure." He paused and let Stratton soak it in for a moment. "Of course, when you're ready to sell, I can give you a seller's assay," he lowered his voice.

Stratton looked beaten. "Fix me up a seller's assay on The Washington," he shook his head back and forth in chagrin. "I'm finished with Cripple," he announced loudly. "I'm going back to The Springs and back to carpentry."

"I'll fix that up for you Win," Guyot told him.

Winfield Scott Stratton turned abruptly, and Bob moved aside to let him pass. He walked determinedly out the door of the assay office, turned uphill around the side of the building. Steven watched him trudge over the rise to the north.

Guyot wrote notes and attached them to the bags of samples that Stratton had left on the counter. He picked up his glasses, and adjusted them on his face, glanced along the counter, and being satisfied that his help was taking care of the customers on that end, turned his attention to Bob and Steven.

"What can I do for you this morning, Mr. Womack," he asked?

Steven stepped back inside and approached the

147

counter and stood beside Bob. "N. B. Guyot," Bob motioned toward him, "I'd like for you to make the acquaintance of Mr. Steven Marks." The two men shook hands. "He's a mining engineer, come in on the stage last night."

"Is that a fact," Guyot's interest increased, as well as the firmness of his handshake. He took his spectacles off for a better look, and appraised Steven up and down.

"Stage was robbed last night," Bob quipped.

"I hadn't heard," Guyot returned

"Young feller had his money stole'," Bob told him matter of fact. "He could use a job right away."

"Well," Guyot's interest was pricked, "know anything about assay work?"

"Yes sir," Steven answered him in the affirmative.

"Where was that learned?"

"In mining school, in Europe," Steven hedged the question.

"Humm," Guyot thought a moment. "You know about acids?"

"Yes sir."

"How do you make Aqua Regia?"

"It is a fifty percent mixture of hydrochloric acid titrated slowly into nitric acid."

"What is its use?"

"It will dissolve gold and platinum, and no other acid will do that. That is why it is termed the 'king of waters'," Steven translated from the Latin.

"How would you assay for precious metal in ore?"

"Gold ores are usually analyzed by fire assay. The first step in the assay is the separation of the gangue, and the concentration of gold and silver in a lead button. This is usually done in a shallow clay dish sometimes called a crucible."

"We call it the "scorifier" in these parts," Guyot put in.

"Scorifier," Steven repeated the word. "In the scorifier, the gangue of ground ore is heated with an excess of lead and borax for flux. Much of the lead is oxidized and forms an easily fusible mixture with the silicates and borates. The rest of the lead collects the gold into solution, along with the silver, also. When cooled, the lump of metal lead, gold and silver is found among the forms and separated. The next step is the separation of the gold and silver from the lead. The button is heated in a small cup of bone ash called," Steven struggled for the word, and used the French, "petite cupola..."..

"Small cupel," Guyot followed the thought with encouragement.

"Yes," Steven continued, "the small cupel is made of bone ash, and when the lead is heated, it is oxidized with the ash, leaving behind a small globule of gold and silver."

Guyot nodded for him to go on.

"The third step is the separation of the silver from the gold, and this is done by flattening the glob with a hammer and then treating the flattened metal with nitric acid to remove the silver. However, care must be taken to make sure that there is an excess of silver so that the reaction can proceed, and sometimes silver must be added. With the crystals of silver completely dissolved the finely divided gold remaining may be fused and weighed. If any of the platinum group metals are present, they may be separated by precipitation with hydroquinone in a 1.2 Normal solution of hydrochloric acid." He paused for a moment to try and think of anything that he had left out. "A precipitate of silver nitrate is formed from a solution of dissolved silver in nitric acid, by one of several reagents, depending on the type of ore and the expected associates in the ore body." He paused a second and then continued to elaborate. "Also, all metal hydrides, and metal chlorides are soluble in pine resin, which can enhance the

149

precipitate, with platinum group metals, with rhodium being precipitated first at room temperature, and then palladium, at a slightly elevated temperature, and lastly the platinum at temperatures of seventy degrees centigrade."

"Is that a fact?" Guyot was more than impressed. He was shocked at having such a talent in front of him. "What do you know about gold tellurides?"

"Oxidized gold tellurides will in some ores give up gold in fine beads when simply heated to a temperature around twelve hundred degrees centigrade."

"Young man," Guyot stuck his hand out, "you got a job, pays three seventy-five an hour. When can you start?"

"N. B.," Bob broke in with a grin, "let him dance tonight, and start in the mornin'. Give me a chance to get him introduced around a bit. He's gonna need a place to stay. You got any room for him?"

"All I can offer is to spread some burlap sacks in back in one of those ore sheds," Guyot jerked a thumb toward the back of the assay office, "that's about the best I can do. It's a roof, and some walls to keep out the wind."

Bob looked at Steven and shrugged.

"It has to do, and it is close to my work." Steven accepted and counted himself lucky. "Are you sure that I will not be in the way," he asked?

"If you are, we'll just roll you over," Guyot laughed. "There's not much heat out there, but nights won't be much below freezing often this time of year."

"Thank you, Mr. Guyot," Steven shook hands one more time, and he and Bob made room for business that was lining up to get ore assayed

.

Chapter 14. Fandango

Bob led him back to the building where the dance was taking place that night. People were already setting tables and preparing the stage for the musicians. Bob immediately found a dozen people to jaw with, and after Steven had wandered around the building several times, Bob was still talking. Finally, he noticed Steven and joined him.

"You better walk on back to Alonzo's and get your gear and get cleaned up for the fandango." He pressed a five-dollar gold piece into Steven's hand. "That'll cover your storage, and get you a bath at the Clarendon, but just pull the duds you need and clean up, then go get the rest of your things. Don't trust nothin' at the Clarendon, but you don't haf to worry at Guyot's cause he keeps an armed guard on that ore shed twenty-four hours a day. Get Guyot to show you around, so the guards won't shoot you," Bob chuckled. "We have a little thieving going on with 'high grade'," he cautioned.

"I couldn't take money from you again, Mr. Womack," Steven protested, and tried to give Bob his coin back.

"Nonsense, you got a job now, you'll pay it back, or pass it on. Don't matter son, and call me Bob, Mr. Womack is my father, if'n you meet him sometimes."

Steven was moved by this old cowboy's generosity. He had been very lucky to have found a guardian angel. He shook his hand warmly, and as he turned, Bob patted him on the back in assurance that everything would work out. Steven was sure that he had never met a finer man.

He made his way back across the hogback ridge

line, the way they had come. A breeze had sprung up from the north, and he passed several groups that carried baskets, and seemed to be in a festive mood. Soon, he broke out of the pines and aspens, and rounding a curve in the trail, saw the bustling town of Cripple Creek spread out below and could clearly see the outline of the old collapsed caldera, like a bowl before him.

Making his way to the Welty's livery stable, he stayed to a higher trail that joined the township at the eastern edge, where Bennett Avenue dead ended into a road leading north. A sign in disrepair with peeling paint pointed north along the road, and said, "Hayden Placer." Walking directly west, he passed several saloons, and more than one of the working girls gave him an appraising look. He continued on the north side, as the sun felt good, and walked past the Buckhorn, and then passed Johnnie Nolan's at the corner of Bennett and Third Street, completing the circle that he and Womack had begun a few hours earlier.

Glancing over to the south and west down Bennett Avenue, he noticed a small eatery squeezed between two taller building, with a sign above the door. It was tiny and almost a shack up against the buildings on either side, which rose to dwarf it. A sign above the door said, "Elizabeth's Place." As he came directly across from the small store, wonderful smells emanated across Bennett and wafted to his nose. His mouth began to water, but the thought of spending his money before he had reclaimed his gear, and cleaned up, was out of the question. Suddenly, his heart skipped a beat when the face of a dark-haired woman appeared in the doorway. She smiled at him. She was the woman that he had seen in the Sunday School with Emma Carr that morning. The one that he had looked for and had disappeared while Emma had sung. He felt himself blushing from a sudden change in blood pressure, and again averted his eyes, and walked quickly on. He silently cursed himself and wondered at his reaction. Women did not normally make him nervous, and he was rarely shy. It was as if he fled from her gaze, when he really wanted to go to her. He felt that it must be his present circumstances that made him feel this way.

He hurried on toward the bottom of Bennett St. where Alanzo Welty's livery stable was located on the corner. In the front yard of the livery were hitching rails at the back of a turnaround area, layered over with wood chips and saw dust. A small cluster of buildings with low roofs served as an office and loading area, for passengers and cart rentals of various sorts. At the moment, a fine surrey with red painted spokes and wheels was pulled to the front. A spirited black horse pulling the surrey stood hitched to a rail, stamping a hoof, impatient to go.

Alonzo was helping an elegant lady in a flaming red satin dress into the surrey. "You're sure that you can handle this stud horse Miz De Vere," Steven heard Alonzo ask?

"I can manage quite well, Alonzo," she touched his sleeve reassuringly, "please don't worry," her voice dripped with southern charm.

Steven saw George in the back and made his way around the surrey and toward the door. As he did, he made eye contact with the woman. She was an exceptional beauty. Making his way to George, he moved around harness, and gear stacked all around.

"Mr. Marks," George acknowledged, as he approached. "I am sorry for the loss to you last night," he went on. "We rode out early, and found where they hid their horses, but we lost their trail on rocky ground north of the holdup site."

"They had a plan," Steven shrugged. He glanced around the stable among the assorted paraphernalia. George followed his gaze.

"I've got your gear, and suitcase, more like a

153

trunk," he chuckled.

"I might have to leave some of it here a couple more days," Steven bargained. "I've a job at the assay office over in Squaw Gulch, but I haven't been paid yet, as I haven't worked yet."

"You lost a bundle, I heared," George quired?

"All my money," Steven said. "And an heirloom gold watch of great sentimental value."

"Sorry about the watch," George sympathized. "That sentimental value almost got you killed," he remembered the night before. "Anyway, when you get ready for your trunk over at Squaw Gulch, or wherever, let me know, and I'll get it delivered. Until then, it's safe and sound right here in the storage.

"I'll just need to get a few things in one of the small bags," he followed George toward a locked section, and waited while he worked the lock and hasp.

"Is that surrey a rental," Steven asked?

"The one with the red wheels," George replied over his shoulder. "She's a looker, and she's for rent."

"Are we still talking about the surrey?"

"Pearl De Vere is a looker, too," George smiled. "Her and that surrey make quite a sight."

"Who is she," Steven asked?

"She's a madam, runs a place down on Myer's Ave. She come in from Creede, where she had a place there. Now, she's got the Homestead House on Myer's. Fancy place, fancy women. Too fancy for me," George shrugged, and slapped a hand down on a nearby burlap bag. "Here's your git. Let me know when you're finished, and I'll lock up."

Steven carefully thought through the next few days, and what he might need. He had never considered beginning without money, and things that he wished to purchase would just have to wait. He would have a little money in a few days, and he could get by until then.

He said his thanks to George on the way out and crossed Bennett St. headed uphill and east. As he passed 'Elizabeth's Place', he peered in a window and saw her waiting on a customer at a table inside. She looked up and saw him and smiled. Flustered at being caught looking through the window, he walked on quickly and took a right turn at the next corner. He walked over a block to Meyer's Ave. and made his way to the Continental Hotel, and purchased a bath, haircut, and shave. An hour later, for the five-dollar gold piece that Womack had given him, he felt like a new man.

It was getting late in the afternoon, by the time that he started back to Squaw Gulch. There were now a number of people on the trail going in the same direction. He had company along the way, and people talked about the weather, and who was going to try and come to the hoe down. He left the stream of people at the fork in the trails that led toward the Squaw Gulch Amusement Clubhouse, and Guyot's assay. Continuing up the trail to Guyot's Assay, he waited until Guyot noticed him. Guyot motioned for him to follow. He took him to a guard shed behind the assay office in a cluster of small buildings spread in roughly a semi-circle.

They entered the shed. "Who's on the seven to four tonight," Guyot asked a man inside?

"Pearce," the man answered.

"Hummp," Guyot grunted. "This here is Steven Marks. Gonna be working with me up front. Find him a place to camp in one of the storage sheds," he instructed. "Be sure to tell Pearce about him." Then he introduced Steven to the man. His name was Mat Perkins, and Mat showed him a shed nearby.

"There's a stove in this one," he pointed over the sacks. A twisting path led among the bags toward the back of the shack. A lantern hung from a roof member. Three cots were set up at the back. Matt turned to go to the warmth of the guard shed as a chill had set in with the evening. "Be sure to lock up," he said. "The keys stay in the guard shack. Pearce will be here at seven, so check in," he cautioned.

"I'll have to, in order to unlock," Steven stated the obvious.

"Just make sure you don't startle no one," the man warned. It had ominous overtones. Perkins went out and left him to organize.

He made room for his goods and used a small bag with clothes in it for his pillow. He found a cover in a coarsely woven woolen blanket in a box at the foot of the back cot. He could make out fine for a few days. He had seen the outhouse, and he could clean up at the hotel every few days. He would stay passably clean. It would have to do until he could do better.

After he settled in, he walked about, studying the assay office and grounds from all angles. It might be dark, with no moon, when he made his way back tonight.

The sun was disappearing fast behind the Sangra De Christo mountain range in the west. He followed their curve to the south. It was a majestic view, and he allowed himself a few moments to gaze at the horizon. Grand vistas spread before him in all directions. He could not help but feel hope returning to his spirit, which had been crushed a few hours before. And in a positive frame of mind, he set out for the dance, across Squaw Creek gully, to the Squaw Creek Amusement Club. Strains of music had come intermittently from the building a little up the gulch and across the tumbling slope of the valley, formed by the wet weather creek.

As he drew near, he could see women moving with baskets, and men moving with bottles in their hands. The music became livelier and more organized, and a caller began to chant the words to a popular square dance. Good smells and warmth exuded from the open doors, as he

156

approached. Bob Womack, and another man stood at the door, giving scrutiny to everyone that entered. A big smile broke out on his face when he saw Steven.

"See ya made it back," he called, slapping the back of the person he had been talking to, as they entered. "Welcome to the Squaw Gulch Amusement Club," Bob called, just as the music broke into a full round of 'Chicken in the Bread Pan, Kickin' Out Dough'.

Through the door Steven could see part of the dance floor, and beyond, the raised platform that the musicians played from. He could see two of the fiddle players, and recognized one as Jesse Cook, the man along the road outside Florissant, that had been playing as he rode along with his dog the day before, which seemed like a week ago. Bob motioned him inside and pointed toward a table piled with food. "Get some grub, before it's all et up," he warned. The stomping of the dancers and the sounds of the music made it difficult to hear. He nodded that he understood and moved on into the building.

Near the entry, and to the immediate right, tables ran along the side, with women behind them, dishing up portions of the food to hungry dancers. The platform for the musicians was at the far end, and between the two spread a sea of eager dancers. The whole floor was in a swirl of motion. Steven could see Emma Carr dishing up food at the tables, and recognized her husband, George, as he called the moves from the platform. The musicians behind him cranked out a steady fountain of sound. George called from the platform, a popular call, "Chase That Rabbit":

"Ladies to the center, how you do?
Right hand cross, an' how are you?

Swing six when you all get fixed.
Dance, ladies, like pickin' up sticks."

157

The crowd moved to George's commands, and the pounding fiddle jig. The crowd pulsated with movement and laughter, all moving together.

"Chicken in the bread tray kickin' up dough,
'Granny, will yo' dog bite?' No, by Jo."

Swing corners all.
Now yo' partners, promenade the hall."

The entire crowd on the dance floor swung from the four corners, to the edges of the inside perimeter of the building, so that the entire crowd was lined around the edge, and then began a merry and proud march all the way around the hall, with George Carr stepping off the platform and leading the promenade.

An elegantly dressed lady with dark hair was bent over at the end of one of the tables near the middle, setting a saucer with a generous slice of cake on the floor in front of a dog of obvious mixed breed. The animal was well trained enough to wait until told it could have the treat, before gobbling it with vigor.

When Elizabeth stood and straightened her skirt and petticoats, she noticed Steven watching her. The parade of dancers was approaching around the perimeter, And had rounded the far corner.

"Parade you ladies 'round the floor," George bellowed.

"It's still way early, so pass that door."

Steven moved closer to the tables to let the parade pass him by to the outside. When he moved within hearing she said, "It's the fiddler's dog," she shrugged with a smile. "The dog gets cake, or Jesse Cook, the fiddler, won't play," she explained. Steven had thought to answer her, when the parade of people, skipping, strutting, majestically strolling in elegant finery, to chicken- walking in comic overalls, came alongside, and George reached out and hooked Elizabeth's arm and she was pulled into the stream of the promenade. She managed an over the shoulder glance back, as George called out from his place in the parade;

"Promenade your ladies all the way home.
Chase that rabbit all night long.
All men outside, ladies bow in,
Rabbit's got t'get home, before tha full moon,
Promenade!"

Steven's last look disappeared as she bowed under George Carr's arm and continued on the inside away from the wall. He was about to turn back toward the table and the dog eating cake beneath it, when a hand near the end of the line caught him in a vise like grip and pulled him into the line with the dancers. When he could see who was pulling him along, he saw the tobacco-stained whiskers of the old prospector, Lafe, that they had talked with at his prospect hole earlier in the day. The wizened old face, now with signs of inebriation added to the juice stains, broke out in a broad smile from ear to ear, and chuckled, pointing to the bandanna tied to his right forearm. Steven joined the parade in a two-step shuffle, understanding that the handkerchief stood for type of sex, and since the feisty old man kept to the inside, he was marching with the women.

The overall form of the dance was not unlike certain European dances of the time, only a bit faster, and there was a free form style, where each dancer might be proud or humorous, or almost any style short of lewd. Any follies type ankle showing or Spanish fanning of the skirts was totally absent. The ladies presented themselves with almost Victorian decorum. George ended the parade when he reached the musician's platform.

"Chase that rabbit to th' ground."

The dancing stopped, and the two fiddlers

immediately turned their attention to a brown, short necked jug parked behind the chairs and instrument cases.

George Carr gave Elizabeth a final whirl, and they laughingly talked for a few moments. Steven had ended in the pronominal near the opposite corner. "Thanks for the stroll, pardner," grizzled, old Lafe beamed out at him through stained whiskers. "You cut a fine rug, young feller," Lafe laughed. "You can pard with me any ol' time, yes sirhee." At that moment, one of Lafe's old-time friends caught up with him. "Whalen, what'ch got there?"

"Ute's choice, from down in the Springs."

"Naw, Joe, do tell, you throwed a good loop," Lafe turned his attention from Steven to the other man.

"Come on outside, and we'll give 'er a pull," Joe Whalen invited him.

"Don't mind if I do," Lafe clasp him around the shoulder, and the two men started jauntily toward the door.

When Steven looked back at the bandstand, Elizabeth was standing still, searching the floor. She looked his way, and they made eye contact. Steven had an awkward moment as he wanted to walk to her, but could not, without some pretext. She smiled and started walking in his direction. He took a few steps toward her. He could feel himself flush, and he noticed an increased heart rate.

"Can I offer you some cake, cowboy," she made an assumption from the boots he was wearing, and also the clothing generally fit the type.

"Thank you very much, madam," Steven bowed slightly.

"Hmmm," Elizabeth mused at his choice of words. "I may be a Miz, but no madam, thank you much," she quipped. The word he learned had a different connotation in proximity to the brothels along Bennett and developing all along Myers Ave. It took him but a few moments to discern the difference in meaning and understand the irony in her reply. He had enough presence of mind to not try and correct the mistake, just not make it again. They walked on a few paces in silence. "So, what's your handle, where you from, how long ya been in the District," she was experienced with making small talk at "Elizabeth's Place".

Steven wanted to say Stefano Marquez. He stopped the impulse, and heard himself say, "Steven Marks."

"When did you arrive," she asked?

"Friday night," he told her.

"Were you on the stage that got held up," she asked, looking at him closely.

"Yes, unfortunately, my fate."

"Tough luck," she mused, "it's happening more often."

"Now it is your turn," he bantered back, wanting to change the subject. He did not want her to know that he had humiliatingly stood and let himself be robbed. "What is your name," he redirected.

"Elizabeth," she told him.

"And, do you have a last name, Elizabeth," he probed.

"Sarah Elizabeth Yates is my full given name," she didn't lie. She just didn't tell him the whole truth. This had never made her uneasy before, but this time it did.

"And, have you been in the District long," he inquired?

"I've known George and Emma Carr from when Bennett and Myers Real Estate leased then the Broken Box Ranch, before there was a District, and this whole area was scrub brush and alpine pasture." They had arrived back at the cake table. "You must be hungry, Mr. Marks, please take a seat at one of the tables, and I'll fix you a plate. Do you like fried chicken?"

"I'd be much obliged," he imitated a colloquial term of gratitude, "fried chicken would be good." She

161

turned toward the buffet line in front of the tables. He found a seat vacant, and in a few moments when two seats came available, he moved and claimed them both. He brushed a few crumbs away with the back of his hand.

In a few minutes, she came toward him with a heaping plate of fried chicken, mashed potatoes, dripping in churned real butter, and corn on the cob, which was tiny and just budding this time of the year, in mid spring, and ate cob and kernels, boiled and soaked in butter. Also, she had placed a few pickles of the same type of budding corn. He dug in with gusto. She left, and was soon back with a glass of lemonade, which she sat in front of him.

A seat had cleared across the table, and he had saved one next to himself. She looked back toward her task at the cake table, and as there was no activity for the moment, took a seat opposite him at the table. He was shy to eat with her looking on, but his hunger overcame his shyness.

She, on the other hand, was not shy about watching people eat. She watched people eat all day, every day in her restaurant. She thought that there was a great deal to learn about a man by just watching him eat. This one was enjoying himself, and in no hurry. She also liked him asking her questions about the town. People in Cripple Creek were open and sharing with newcomers.

"I assume that the restaurant that I saw you in the other day is yours, since it carries your name on the sign," Steven questioned?

"Yes," she told him. "I came in and bought a lot the first day that Bennett put them up for sale. That is, thanks to Emma.

Steven wondered where she had gotten the money. "So, you are the owner of the property, and the business," he asked?

"Free and clear, and in my own name," she answered, catching the drift of his question.

"And, can a woman hold title," he doubted her with honest curiousness? "I thought that women did not have a legal identity in the United States."

"That depends from state to state, now, and Colorado is just a little more sane," she stated strongly, "a little ahead in its time," she gave him a sideways glance to fathom his reaction to this. "Women have property rights, and" she added proudly, "we're going to get the vote in the next election!"

"Is that so," he teased her assuredness.

"That is so, Mr. Marks, you may bank on it," and then seeing the twinkle in his eye, added, "You may call me Miz Elizabeth."

He laughed at her manner. He understood the suffragette movement was worldwide. It was evident in every place that he had traveled. He fiddled with the pickled corn with his fork. "What is this," he finally asked?

"Little tiny, pickled corn," she made like eating corn on the cob. Then self-consciously thought it was a little too cute. She wondered to herself, why was she flirting with this man. She didn't have time or room for anything else in her life. And then, there were all those very bad memories, in the way, yet to deal with in some way, someday. She shook her head unconsciously back and forth; No. Steven saw it and wondered what was going on in her mind.

"Where did you come from to Cripple Creek," he asked to try and hold her at the table. He knew that she would go back to the cake table at any moment.

"Well," she took a long stretch at the table, and straightened her full skirts. "From the Springs," she began. " I worked there as a seamstress for the three Burns sisters, there. One day, their brother Jimmy came into the shop talking about this crazy old cowboy, who they had arrested for being drunk and disorderly, who

163

claimed to have found gold in the mountains just west of the Springs. That was that lovable old ruffian over there at the door," she pointed at Bob Womack. "It turned out to be true, a mining meeting was called, a District was formed, a town was plated, lots were put up for sale, and I had some money from sewing," she paused here to catch a breath, "so, I bought one, and here I am."

"Very industrious, very commendable," he nodded and complimented her. She looked to see if he was mocking her, and then seeing he was serious, the slightest flicker of a smile crossed her lips.

"The restaurant has been good to me," she told him. "Better than sewing, at least for the time, as there is more need of grub for the men, than finery for ladies, that mostly don't want to live permanent in a gold camp. But, give it time, and it'll make a city," she nodded positively. "For now, it makes me a living, with a lot of hard work."

"Did you make any of what I am eating," he asked?

"Do you like it?"

"Now, that's a trick question," he smiled.

"Yes, I made it all," she said.

"In that case," he paused for effect, and acted like a gourmet, or judge at a wine show, "I think that I will be often coming to your restaurant." He smiled, and she watched him dig into the grub.

Some couple came to the cake table and the fiddlers began to pick at their strings. She got up and went back to her duties at the table. It left Steven feeling cut off, abruptly, and he tried to stop watching her. Later, when he looked back, she was gone. He spotted her among the stomping, swirling dancers, as George Carr's voice could be heard calling overall.

Steven finished his dinner and enjoyed the lemonade. He began to be sleepy in spite of the rancorous noise of the crowd and the instruments. The adrenalin from the robbery was finally leaving his system. He was

164

almost shaky, tired, and was staring into space, when a voice calling his name brought him out of it.

"Steven, would you like to dance," he heard. He looked up to see Elizabeth holding out a hand to him.

"I don't really know the steps," he said, but he reached for her hand.

"You'll learn," she said. "We won't stomp on you much." She tugged on his hand and led him to the dance floor, just as the thumping of strings stopped and the fiddles broke into a jig of sorts.

"Chose yo' partner, form a ring," George Carr boomed. The crowd split into several circles of eight dancers in each, with Elizabeth and he paired in one, with three other couples.

"Figure eight, and double L swing," he called. Two of the men stepped forward, and forming a figure eight instead of a ring, the others moved in concentric circles, swinging around the center of the figure eight. When Steven didn't know where to go, someone gently pushed him in the right direction. Elizabeth laughed at him trying to keep up. People gestured with their faces and eyes, at their feet, to try and show him the steps. Slowly he learned. He got a second, and in this case a third, or fourth wind of strength. He felt like he could dance all night.

"Ducks in the river, goin' to the ford,
  Coffee in the little rag, sugar in a gourd."

Once he got the overall dance pattern, he could see that it repeated no matter what the words, unless from time to time the whole form changed, and a new somewhat similar pattern was formed, to be repeated. He knew many of the basic forms, but they had grown in expression on the western plains and mountains.

"Swing 'em once an' let 'em go,
  All hands left an' do-ce-do."

He still stumbled, and Elizabeth laughed, but he

was learning faster now.

"You swing me an' I'll swing you,
   An' we'll all go to heaven, in the same ol' shoe."

Steven suddenly, moving in unison, had such a feeling of community with these people, like never before in his life. Not at least since childhood, since way before the death of his parents. He felt as if he belonged, and when he passed Elizabeth in the dance, her touch was an electric tingle. When they joined as partners to promenade, he felt warm all over. She squeezed his hand from time to time, and it would send a jolt through him, like a shot.

"Chase that possum, chase that coon,
   Chase that pretty girl 'round the room.

Her smiling face would flash by him. Other faces flashed round and round.

"How'll you swap, an' how'll you trade,
   This pretty girl for that ol' maid."

Once lit up, the fiddlers played and played. They competed with each other to see which could go through the notes the faster. They played up and down the scale in crazy free form ways, and played circles around the guitar player, who played a series background cords, to back up the melody carried by the fiddlers. On and on, they went, with the crowd getting wilder. Sometimes at about midnight, Steven was exhausted.

"No thank you," she was saying. Steven looked through exhausted eyes. The red hair man from the cot at the hotel pantry was trying to cut in. Elizabeth was protesting. It was a blur to Steven. He reached to remove the man's grip on Elizabeth's arm. The next thing he knew, he was flat on the floor, and his face was numb. Someone rolled him over on his back.

"Steven," someone called. It seemed to be Bob Womack. He wanted him to get to his feet. Bob supported him as he helped him walk off the dance floor to a little alcove near the front door. "No problem, folks," he heard said. "Fiddler, strike up a tune." The music started again, uncertain at first, and then picked up as if nothing had happened.

He sat in a chair, and someone cleaned and bandaged his face. After a while, Bob Womack came in. "Steven, that feller says you started it."

Steven couldn't think of what to say.

"He certainly did not," Elizabeth spoke up from where she was cleaning the blood off Steven's face.

"Well, your say is good enough for me, Miss Elizabeth," Bob stated flatly and left the room. In a few moments, they could hear him shouting in the next room. A voice shouted back.

"Old man, you got nothin' you can hold me on," the voice of Hayden yelled. "Give me my gun, and I'll quit this flea trap. Too many Mexicans for my Texas taste."

"You cur, you defame Texas, and any self-respectin' Texan. Now, I'm Sergeant at Arms for this hoedown, and I'll say what's what. You committed an assault and battery."

"He laid hands on me first," Hayden defied him.

"I'm goin' by what the lady says," Bob told him.

"What's goin' on in here, Bob," a third voice broke in.

"That's the sheriff from down in the Springs," Elizabeth told Steven quietly.

"Hayden, you're mine," the voice said. "Bob, he's already wanted for a brutal assault on an old woman down in the Springs that was befriending him with some handy work, and a place to stay. He beat her and robbed her."

There was the sound of a scuffle, and someone yelled, "Stop him". There was the sound of a bone being cracked by metal.

"Damned if I ain't been headed to do that since early this morning," they heard Bob say.

"How's that," the sheriff questioned as he rolled Hayden over and cuffed him.

"Well, I caught him kicking this same feller at the hotel this morning."

"So, he has a quarrel with this man? Maybe I should talk to him also and see what the story is?"

"Naw, I know for a fact, they got nothing to do with each other except maybe someone snored too loud. They was on adjoining cots last night, at the hotel. The other feller is a fine young man, got robbed on that Welty stage Friday night.

"All right, if you vouch for him. Let's get this yahoo in a wagon, and I'll send deputy Peter Eales with him down to the jail house in the Springs."

Bob went to call some men. The sheriff stepped into the room with Elizabeth and Steven and stood, but didn't say anything. Just looked around. Bob came back with two other men, and the four of them grabbed Hayden like a sack and hauled him out the door to the wagon.

Bob came back in after a short time, and waited until Elizabeth had finished bandaging his nose with tape on either side of his face.

"That's real nice, Elizabeth," Bob told her. "I know where he is staying, and I'll take him on over there," he told her.

She was slow to move, making tiny adjustments to the bandages until Steven winched. "Oh, all right, Bob," she finally stood and moved to the door. She stopped and turned back. "Steven, I'm so sorry," she said, and then disappeared around the door.

"Can you walk," Bob asked?

"I think I can," Steven croaked in a low voice, and then added, "I may need some help." He got shakily to his feet. They made their way slowly.

"Should I get a buggy off someone, or can you walk on over to Guyot's."

"It's just a short way," Steven assured him. "I can walk it."

"All right, hos," Womack supported him along the way, as they cut straight for the assay office, picking their way slowly over the dry bed of Squaw Creek. Eventually, they arrived at the office, and made their way to the guard's shack, as Steven had been instructed to check in. Pearce was nowhere to be found.

Checking outside, Steven pointed out the shack he was camping inside. The lock was off and the hasp open, with the door ajar a crack. A dim light shone and shadows moved in the flicker of the slit of light.

"I'm staying in that one," Steven indicated.

They stepped to the door, and Bob opened it then stepped back. He had seen two men inside bent over a sack near the middle of the heap of sacks. "Pearce," Bob called loud before he opened the door again. "It's Bob Womack," he called through the crack. "I got Steven Marks here, beat up bad." He opened the door, slowly. The men retied the sack top and started toward the front to the door.

"Yeah, Mr. Womack," Pearce came forward.

"You boys look like two house dogs caught in the chicken coop," Bob narrowed his eyes at them.

"What's that supposed to mean," the other man with Pearce growled.

"I know you, Crumley. You tended bar over at the Concord. I seen you talkin' with your boss, Joe Wolf. Highgradin'," he stated.

"We's just spreadin' some rat poison," Pearce held his hands out, palms up in innocent protest.

"Yeah, there's rats in here, all right," Bob agreed with him. "Help me get Marks on his cot." Steven was collapsing again.

Each of the other men grabbed a leg and Womack held Steven under his arms, and they carried him through and across the jumble of sack, and deposited him, with some twisting onto his cot. He was more or less unconscious in moments. He vaguely remembered Bob starting a fire in the stove, staying for some time, and eventually he was alone in the dark. The warmth of the fire felt good. It had been some incredible day. He slumbered on past dawn.

Winfield Scott Stratton came through the door of Guyot's Assay Office with a smile on his face. He lay a bag of ore on the counter, and since Guyot was busy with some paper work, Steven stepped up from the furnace he was tending, and taking off the heavy gloves, and laying them on the counter, shook Stratton's hand. The old man had a happy look on his face for once, and Steven had always liked him.

"What can I do for you this morning Mr. Stratton," he asked?

"Got several bags of samples I need an assay on," he said, as he shook Steven's hand. His hand was calloused from rock work.

"This looks like pretty good ore, Mr. Stratton," Steven investigated the contents of the ore sack.

"I'd like to know the results as soon as possible," Stratton looked stern and worried. "I'm Winfield Scott Stratton, young man, and your name is?"

"Steven Marks, sir."

"Steven, I'd appreciate you keeping this assay private. This is important like."

"Don't worry, Mr. Stratton," Steven assured him. "It would be unethical and against the honor of my college of mining engineering to ever let any customer know of any customer's business. Mr. Guyot has a very strict policy about loose talk."

"Did you say something about college," Win asked him.

Steven took the sacks back to the course milling machine to start crushing the ore. "Yes, I have a degree in mining engineering."

"That so? I'm a carpenter by trade, myself," Stratton told him. "I done thrown away everything I've earned tryin' to find a gold mine," the dark eyed, silver haired, whisp of a man seemed to shrink even further under his old felt prospector's hat, stained with years of use.

"Well, I hear you've got the Washington under option, so I guess this is from The Independence," Steven chatted idly, not seeing the chilling effect that his speculations were having on Win Stratton. "This is really high grade ore Mr. Stratton. The assay is going to be real good." Steven crushed the first rock. "Give me a couple of hours, and I'll have a fire assay done. We'll know more then."

"You might know," Stratton began, hesitatingly, "I've got The Independence optioned."

"No, I didn't know that," Steven looked back, and then came back toward the counter. He realized that Stratton may have found something after he sold the option to purchase the mine to someone.

"Yeah, a San Francisco syndicate. A pompass fat cat speculator representing them named Pearlman. He wanted the Washington, but I got sick of him and wouldn't sell, then offered him The Independence instead, for a ridiculous sum, and I'll be darned if he didn't snap it up. There's a story," Stratton shook his head in chagrin.

"Maybe not so ridiculous," Steven looked back toward the ore.

"I'd appreciate your discretion," Win said.

"You have it completely," Steven reassured him.

Stratton was back for the assay in a few hours. Steven showed him the charting. The samples had assayed consistently with each sample bag, once tallied, telling a wildly rich story of twenty ounces per ton, which with the government controlled price of gold set at twenty dollars to the ounce, amounted to three hundred dollars' worth of gold for each ton of material mined and milled, after milling and shipping expenses, and labor costs were paid. Steven gave him the good news, but Stratton only seemed more darkened, more shriveled. He took the report, and folded the paper, let out a deep sigh, and left without saying a word.

Steven didn't see Win Stratton again for more than six weeks. He looked for a house to rent in Anaconda or Barry but found nothing. He wanted to stay close to the assay office. Summer would be over soon, and he would need better quarters then. He had managed to save some money. He had walked over to Cripple and eaten at "Elizabeth's Place" several times. The food was very good, but she seemed always busy. Then he heard someone moving around in the back, above the kitchen area. He discerned that it was a man, and decided that there were unknowns about Elizabeth, and that he should go slow. An infatuation was tempting, and delightful. He was lonely, but caution was called for. Still, he thought of her often. He had plenty to keep him busy and Cripple was a long walk, when he didn't know exactly why he was taking that walk. Early on, he had been embarrassed by the purple bruising of his face, and that had slowly faded. Still, he needed to save money, and the temptations of Myer's avenue, or even a good meal at a restaurant would tax his earnings, and these things kept him in the near area of the assay office.

It was near the first of August that Steven saw Stratton at the assay office again. Guyot was in Pueblo, and Steven had the office alone at the time. Stratton was a completely changed man. Dark circles still clouded his expression, but now a positive euphoria glowed from underneath.

"Ore from The Independence," he proudly announced. "Pearlman gave up the option, a day early," he laughed. Steven had never seen or heard of Winfield

Scott Stratton laughing. He was considered the most serious man in the district. Steven came forward and opened the first ore sack.

"Looks good, Mr. Stratton, as good as your last sample maybe."

"Better," Stratton hooted. "I own these rocks."

Steven began to tag the sacks and fill out the form that went with each sack. "That's real good news," Steven congratulated him.

"Did you tell me that you're an educated man in mining," Stratton asked him? "I seem to remember making note of that."

"I studied and worked in Europe," Steven told him.

"Where?"

Steven hesitated. There it was again, the problem. "I'm an American," he said first. "I've applied for naturalization."

"Yeah, that's fine, half of us are first generation immigrants. You say you worked in mining? Where at?"

"Spain," there it was.

"Spain," Stratton said, puzzled. "You sound British. You look British."

"My language instructor in college was English," he explained.

"You're sayin' you're Spanish," Stratton questioned?

"I've been told that that fact may not be accepted by all."

"No doubt," Stratton shook his head. "Hard feelings about Mexico by Texans. Still what Maximilian did and who he was, being a European, just don't set right with Americans. Still   Cleveland's got quite an appetite for new territory. See's a world empire, him and Teddy Roosevelt. Spain is in their way. They been whipping up feelings for some time. You're right to keep it under your hat, young fella," Stratton advised the same as many others.

"It seems prudent," Steven shrugged. He found the charade awkward sometimes, like when trying to explain who he was to Elizabeth. It made him uneasy to lie about himself.

"So, ever seen ore like these tellurides," Stratton went back to his inquiry.

"That is what brought me here to begin with," Steven told him. "The mines I worked in for five years, right after I finished my college work, was a brachia tube formation, like this one. That is what caught my eye when the El Paso Load discovery was announced in the "International Geophysical Review". It was a sylvanite deposit much like where I was working, and this as you may know, is a rare type of formation."

"What did you do there," Stratton was curious?

"Everything from mapping to inspection, calculation of loadings and bracing, design of headframes and pulley systems, to the analysis of ore."

"Mapping," Stratton mused.

"Drifts, strike and dip, keeping track of levels, powder rooms, air holes and volumes of air, enough to keep men alive."

"I'm a carpenter, and a good one," Stratton bragged. "I've got a working knowledge of trigonometry, enough to do roof trusses. But" he paused and thought how to say, "I don't know beans about spherical geometry," he held out his hands palms up and shrugged.

"Spherical geometry is one of my specialties," Steven told him. "I had a full year of instruction and then used it almost every day at the mine."

"Then you can figure strike, and dip, and apex?"

"I can survey any area you want, in three dimensions. I've done it for years."

"After you get this assay done, and get your work done for the day, I'd like for you to come visit me up the hill at The Independence. I've got some formations that I want to show you. And I mean to pay you for advice. I won't have you walk up there without it."

"I'd be glad to come up and look around this evening," Steven agreed. "Will you be back in for these results?"

"I know about what amount they are going to assay, so I'm in no hurry. Just bring the reports with you this evening, and weigh me in, and stack a spot with this ore," he indicated the sacks. "I'll be adding more to it and tell Guyot that I need him to tag and ship each day. The Independence is going to start shipping to the smelter in Pueblo, sometime in the next few days." There was something relaxed, almost calm about this fidgety, nervous, old prospector. Stratton seemed a different man as he turned and told Steven that he would see him later and that he would have supper waiting, so come on when he closed.

It was a high mountain sunset that early August night in 1893, when Steven climbed toward The Independence Mine, and what was to be an extremely fortuitous meeting for both men.

Stratton saw him approaching the cabin and left off talking to a man working at the headframe. They walked halfway to meet each other. They stood and looked south, from the slope high up Battle Mountain. A beautiful sunset graced the sky purple and neon orange to the south and west. The sun was setting behind the Sangre De Christo mountains on the southwestern horizon, and the blood reddish mountains had a crown of fiery reds and oranges, fading to fuchsia and purple sky in the east. Both men were spellbound by the beauty. Stratton pulled off his floppy, gray, felt hat, that he characteristically always wore. "Bought me a new hat," he gestured the hat toward Steven. "From a hat store down in the Springs. First thing I did after Pearlman gave up the option."

"That so," Steven really didn't know how to respond. He took the hat and examined it. "Nice hat," he handed it back to Stratton. A wagon pulled out from buildings far below.

"There goes Frank Woods," Stratton observed of the figure of the wagon and horse toiling below, backed by the sunset. "He don't never quit working, night and day. Him and his brother Harry come in here on bicycles less than a year ago and started a wood and coal hauling business. They made good and their father staked'em. So, they bought a placer claim down there that had been hopefully platted into a town. Harry is a good salesman. 'Every Lot's A Gold Mine', is Harry's motto," Stratton chuckled. They're calling it Victor, after one of the original pioneers.

Steven watched the wagon creak along the road far below until it disappeared around the flank of Squaw Mountain below and to the southwest.

"Harry does the sellin' and Frank does the haulin'," Stratton stated matter of fact. "Them two is gonna' end up owning a large part of this here pie. Stratton slapped his hat on his leg once and fitted it back on his head. "Come on over to the shaft," he invited Steven. "Got something that I want to show you."

They walked the short way to the head frame and Stratton had the ore bucket exchanged for a platform. When it was ready, he and Steven stepped aboard. Stratton gave the order to be lowered to tunnel number four. They went down about eighty feet, Steven judged. There was a crosscut at that level.

Stratton lit a kerosene lantern that was at the entrance to the drift. He handed the lantern to Steven, reached and lit a second one for himself. He gestured for Steven to enter first. Steven stooped and made his way along the tunnel. He made his way over and passed several sacks of ore near the entrance. He duck walked

177

forward into the drift.

About thirty feet in, he began to see sylvanite. As he went farther, the seam got richer. The face of the vein was some thirty feet in length. It was three to nine feet in thickness, which would indicate that it extended down for at least a hundred feet. That volume and the assays that he had done of the material indicated millions and millions of dollars' worth of gold in sight. Steven's eyes widened in amazement at what he was seeing. Statton's dark eyes glistened in the lamp light.

"The joy of it's mostly in the finding of it," Stratton whispered low. He let Steven examine all he wished without further comment.

The vein was tending upward on the side they were not removing ore from yet. Steven understood immediately that the vein might extend to the surface somewhere north and west of The Independence ground. If the vein apexes on the surface of some other mine, that other mine would have a claim on the vein to wherever it extended. Even if it didn't, often court cases claimed that it did, and the expense of the fight often ended the dreams of small operators, even with good ore.

When he had seen it all, he went back to where Stratton was examining ore with a rock pick. Signs of single and double jacking showed in the tools around, and the holes drilled into the rock face where charges would be set as the miners followed the vein downward.

"Seen enough, "Stratton chuckled.

"Amazing," was all Steven could say.

"Pretty much," Stratton agreed. "How about some supper," he asked?

"I'm ready," Steven agreed. "It was a long day at the assay furnaces."

"Stratton led back to the platform and the man standing by at the top winched them up when he heard the call.

They made their way back to Stratton's small cabin. Stratton began to set out plates and utensils. He had a fire going on a Franklin style stove, and a pot sat on top. He took a wooden spoon and stirred what was in the pot. The smell of red pinto beans filled the room. He got down a jug and sat it in the middle of the crude wooden table in the center of the one room cabin. Steven sat in a rocking chair on the porch, overlooking much the same view they had enjoyed together earlier. Victor had a few lights and campfires showing. To his right due west, he could look down on the lights of Barry and Anaconda. He could hear Stratton shuffling inside preparing supper.

"What part of the country are you from, Mr. Stratton," he asked at last?

"Me, I hail from Ohio, just across the river from where Bob Womack was born in Kentucky."

"Mr. Womack has been really good to me, Mr. Stratton," Steven appreciated Bob.

"Call me Win, Steven," Stratton paused and came out to the porch. "Womack's a drunk," he told Steven. "You can't count on him, and you can't believe anything that he tells you. He's full of hot air like all these cowboys around here." He went back inside. Steven could smell smoked ham frying on the stove. The smell of strong coffee brewing wafted to his noise. He was really hungry when Wen called him to the table. He ate the beans, fried smoked ham, and sour dough bread voraciously.

"Don't get me wrong," he said at last. "Bobs got a heart of gold, but he's a drunkard." He paused and poured more coffee, but this time spiked it strong with the contents of the jug. "I like liquor as well as the next man, in fact, Bob brought me to Cripple Creek, and we's pards for a while." He stopped and seemed chagrined. "But, he's a drunkard."

"How did you come to be here at Cripple Creek," Steven ventured to ask?

"Oh, I worked my way west, when I couldn't take my father makin' a dog of me, or my six sisters infernal eternal chatter and fuss. I knew carpentry, as my father was a boat builder on the Ohio River. I came to the Springs in 'Seventy-Four', and opened up a carpentry shop there on Pikes Peak Avenue. Business was real good, and I made money, but it weren't enough adventure." He eased the stove door open and added a log. He offered Steven more coffee and added to his own cup with another generous pour from the jug. He offered to Steven, and he spiked his coffee also.

"I bought me a claim north of Fairplay. Had a nice name, The Yretaba Silver Load, southwest of here in the San Juan Mountains. That's all it had. I threw away twenty-eight hundred hard earned dollars, but I loved the adventure. I loved the high mountains, and the clean air. I liked being by myself way away from everything, and then," he said with a wink, "donkeys don't talk back."

He added another drop from the jug to his and Steven's cup. They talked on and on into the evening. Stratton told him of the old days, and the Leadville strike. He told about the opening of the territory. Steven told him about the link he had with the early survey by the Van Hayden Party. Win returned a story about the Mt. Pisgah hoax.

"This cabin," Win told him was a hunting cabin in the middle of nowhere owned by a rich silver king from Leadville named Major Demary. He loved to make Bob Womack out to be a fool, mocking him all over the Springs. There he was sitting on a fortune, and Bob trying to tell him, all the time. He abandoned the cabin in the mid-eighties, so I took up residence. Life's funny sometimes," Win poured another round for him and Steven. Now, there was very little coffee in the cups.

"What do you think of the mine," Stratton asked?

"There is millions of dollars in gold ore showing.

Win, you just might be one of the world's richest men."

"That's pretty much how I see it," the normally anxious Stratton was relaxed, and unimpressed with himself.

"There's just this one problem," Steven leveled with him. "The vein doesn't apex on the Independence ground."

"Yeah, I've been thinking about that. That's why I asked you up here, can you figure where it might apex?"

"Northwest of here," Steven told him. "The vein is tending that general direction, but now the specific spot where it will surface," Steven paused, "there's just too many variables."

"I can see that."

The men paused for a moment and a coyote howled in the distance. Win poured another round from the jug.

"I'm curious," Steven confessed. "You brought that assay in six weeks ago. What happened in the meantime?"

Stratton paused and sipped his cup and fingered his wispy, white mustache. "Well, you knew I'd optioned the Washington, but the buyer was just running a stock scam. He knew The Washington was showing some paying ore and bet on the flurry of activity that came with Count Portales purchase of the Buena Vista. He knew the ore probably would play out or remain low grade. I knew that I would probably get it back, and yesterday, I did." Stratton took a sip from the cup.

"You know, I figured I was finished up here, and told Guyot to rig me a sellers assay. Well, I went back to the Springs to find a carpentry job, but nothin' happening. Cleveland's demonetarization of silver has caught all those millionaires in Colorado Springs unawares. They were all overextended, and some are going under. Their incomes were cut in half, net values in half. Many with too much credit out are ruined, along with the banks that had loaned them money. Projects are sitting half finished, credit is frozen. Even successful builders like Joe Dozier hadn't a single project on the horizon. Laborers and their families along Shook's Run is eatin' prairie dogs. Joe advised me to come on back and see what I could get out of Cripple Creek. So, back I came." Stratton poked up the fire and added a stick.

"When I got back," he continued, "this man Pearlman was waiting for me, and he was hot to buy the note on the Washington, because it's a producing mine. It's all about the stock promotion you see, about bilking suckers."

Steven nodded that he understood. He sipped his cup along with Stratton.

"Anyway, I didn't like Pearlman. He's exactly the kind of speculator working for a syndicate that we don't need in here. He kept pessterin' so I offered him the Independence on a five thousand option, and a hundred and fifty thousand note," Steven's eyes got big.

"Not a bad deal for Pearlman, from what I've seen tonight."

"No, no," Stratton agreed, "but then it was just an unproved mine." Stratton paused a long time. Finally, he asked, "Ever had a dream come true?"

"You mean worked to achieve, or get lucky?"

"No, I mean, you ever dreamed of something, and then had it happen, exactly like you dreamed it?"

"Maybe," Steven confessed, "I've never been sure. It just seems like it sometimes."

"Well, I dreamed of that vein you saw before I ever saw it." Stratton paused to let that sink in. "Pearlman," he began again, "took an option at the end of May, and the next morning I went in and cleaned out all my tools, and got done with three of the drifts. There was an abandoned fourth drift, and I remembered I had an old drill in there, so I crawled in after it. When I got the drill, I was

182

worming my way backing out and just poked at a loose rock in the sidewall. That was when I remembered the dream, and that was when I found the vein, just like I dreamed it." Stratton paused a long time. He poured another round from the jug.

"Well, five nights ago, on July 27th, Pearlman and I had dinner at the Palace. He complained throughout dinner that the Independence was a bust, and that he would be lucky to get his option money back from the ore that had been mined. After dinner we settled in front of the big fireplace and had cognac and cigars. The option was running out the next day. My blood ran cold, when he mentioned that he was thinking of putting men in the abandoned number four tunnel the next morning. Then he complained again about wasting more money on a bust. I was in a dither," Stratton confessed.

"Suddenly, Pearlman pulled the option note from his coat pocket, and said, 'Look here, old man, how would you feel about taking this option back tonight?'. Well, I tried to reach for the paper, but my hand was shaking fearfully. I was afraid that I couldn't grasp it, or that Pearlman would guess what the matter was. Finally, I managed to croak out in a shaky voice, 'Why don't you just throw it in the fire', and he did." Stratton leaned back and stretched.

"That was lucky, "Steven shook his head in disbelief of the story.

"Not lucky, lad. Providence," Stratton said.

They regarded the light from a three-quarter moon was flooding the hillside. They sipped another drink and listened to the night noises. A shuffling scuffle of someone walking past could be heard. Stratton moved to the door and looked out. A dim figure could be seen in the moonlight, struggling under a huge pack on the person's back. The sound of a foot slipping on gravel came next, and then a surprised cry, and a whop of a heavy sack falling to earth. Silence followed for a few moments, followed by frantic scratching sounds. Finally, a score of epitaphs followed that would have blushed a sailor. Steven had joined Stratton on the porch, and now a scream of pure frustration came from the distressed man. Win went inside to get a lantern. "Darn you Elizabeth Yates," a voice with a high nasal pitch and decidedly Irish accent yelled out.

At this, Win took the lantern and headed toward the figure on the ground with Steven following him. "Whose out there," Win called out.

"Win it's Jimmy Burns," a contrite voice called out. They reached Jimmy in a few moments and the lantern showed him tangled in a pack and unable to get loose or get his footing and get up.

"Jimmy, what the hell is goin' on here?"

"Cut me loose, Win," Jimmy whined.

"So, you're talkin' to me again?"

"Ah, Win, I didn't mean nothin' by it. You were just so," he struggled for a word, "negative."

Win pulled out a pocketknife and cut a strap, which let Jimmy slip out of the pack. When he had Burns untangled, he invited him up the the cabin. "Looks like you could use a little drink." It was a sure invitation that Jimmy was loath to refuse.

"That's a real good idea," the little Irishman agreed. "Grab that pack strap," Jimmy told him with a gleam in his eye. "I got something that I want to show you." The two men grabbed the heavy pack and began to drag it along. Steven grabbed a strap, and helped pull it off the ground, and the three of them hefted it to the inside of the cabin.

"I heard you yell 'Elizabeth Yates'," Steven asked?

"I've seen you," Jimmy looked at him. "You work for Guyot, eaugh," he gave the Maine statement of self-agreement. "I was jus' frustrated," Jimmy explained. My sisters made the packs for us, but the buckle broke on this one the other day and Elizabeth works with our sisters sewing. I got her to put the buckle back on. Only, I didn't notice that she got it on backwards, and when I fell, I couldn't get the buckle to release, and I couldn't get loose from the pack."

"What's in the pack, "Stratton was curious. He had guessed that there might be something going on up at what the Irishmen from Maine called the Portland Mine."

"Win, you're not going to believe it. It's high-grade." He opened up the sack and they all looked at chunks of the ore. It was good high-grade sylvanite, exactly what Stratton was pulling out of the Independence.

"What do you think, Steven," Stratton deferred to him?

"It's from the same vein as the Independence vein. The Independence vein is a continuation of the Portland vein," Steven felt fairly sure of this. "Where is the Portland, from here," he asked?

"When the Lawrence placer was formed into a township, down where Victor is growing now, McKinnie thought he had some flat area that would suit better as platted lots, so he shifted stakes, south. Everyone along that side of Battle Mountain followed suit, and last January, it left a small sixty by sixty-foot area unclaimed. About ten days later, Jimmy come walkin' by and discovered it wasn't staked, so he staked it, and claimed it for him and Jimmy Dole, and they called it the Portland cause they both came from Portland Maine."

"Win," Jimmy whined, "I sure been missing you. We needed your advice something terrible."

"Well, you should've asked," he responded. "I sure been curious about all that buzzin' around you been doin' up there. Is that Fred Harnan I been seeing with you two up there?"

"Yeah, Harnan's been helping us."

"He quit me down here. He was separating ore for

me. He's a good man, experienced with his brother in Leadville."

"Well," Jimmy took a swig from the jug, "when you was tellin' me what a bust, to make you walk up and see, it just riled me bad. We got a shaft down about thirty-five feet, but, hell, me and Jimmy didn't know what gold ore even looked like. Harnan come along one day after sortin' ore for you, and we got to talkin'. We told him that we didn't even know what we were lookin' for, and he looked around on our pile of rocks, and right there on top, found a piece of sylvanite. He asked what we'd offer for him to find a vein, and so me and Dole offered him a third interest. Damned if he didn't go down the ladder, look around, had me move the ladder, and low and behold, he found it." Jimmy was really getting excited. He was relishing proving Stratton wrong about the Portland claim being a bust. "We've pulled seventy thousand dollars out in three months, just packin' it out by night on out backs."

"Is that a fact," Stratton was pleased. He was fond of both the Jimmys, and now a idea had coalesced in his mind. He took a pull at the jug and his countenance became shrewd.

"Why haul it out by night," Steven asked not quite seeing the whole situation.

"There's been previous claims," Jimmy explained. "They're bound to some of 'em file lawsuits on us. We're trying to get enough ahead to fight those claims in court and protect our claim."

"Seventy thousand's not going to be nearly enough," Win spoke up."

"It'll make a good start," Jimmy protested.

"They'll enjoin you from further recovery until a settlement of the suit, and they'll let it drag until you're strangled."

"Win, you're always so pessimistic."

"I'm being realistic, Jimmy." Stratton punched the

air to make his point. He paused for a moment, and looked at Steven. "I've got the same problem," he confessed.

"How so," Jimmy questioned?

"Sooner or later, it is going to be known where this vein's apex is," Stratton pointed out. "A very rich man will buy that mine, and through lawsuits, injunctions, whatever it takes, he will force all the other owners on that vein to sell to him. He will consolidate this whole area."

Jimmy rubbed his head, and his voice whistled through his nose. "What're we agoin' a do?"

"Stratton looked determined. "Jimmy, if you boys come in with me, between the Portland and the Independence, we'll lick every jawbone lawyer in Colorado. And we'll buy Battle Mountain."

"We can do it, Win," Jimmy stuck out his hand on it. They had a rollicking laugh and a round from the jug. Feelings were running high.

"Tell me Jimmy," Stratton asked, "what are you going to do with your millions?"

"Well," Jimmy snapped an answer in his raspy, high voice, "I'm going to make a million and get a beautiful wife and send my brats East to school and build a house as big as General Palmer's. And then I'm going to tell those damn millionaires in Colorado Springs to go to hell!"

Chapter 16. Legal Trouble

Steven went to work with Stratton and Burns surveying the Portland vein. Even after a great deal of work, the apex remained in doubt. The wealth of the find began to draw attention, even though they brought out wagon loads of ore at night. It was late October of 1893 when the secret could not be kept. By the next month, there were twenty-seven lawsuits in the court, amounting to over three million dollars in claims for damage by right of apex.

On a bone numbing cold day in early December, Steven crunched through the snow along Bennett Avenue. He noticed the warm smell, the aroma of pies and bread cooking as he passed Elizabeth's Place. He looked to catch a glimpse of her and saw some movement in the kitchen at the back. He trudged carefully on, as a thaw and refreeze had made treacherous footing on the ice along the walkway. He turned in at the Palace Hotel and stomped off the snow from his boots.

He made his way along the ornate passages to the third-floor suite, which had a grand stairway leading to a richly apportioned and lavishly decorated foyer. Steven rapped lightly on the door. Winfield Scott Stratton, very nicely dressed in coat and cravat, opened the door.

"Steven," he greeted him. "You've made it at last."

"Sorry, Win," he apologized, "the path was a bit slow to negotiate this morning."

"Quite alright," he motioned him inside. "I would like for you to meet Verner Z. Reed," he indicated a man seated behind him at an ornate writing desk of impressive proportions.

Steven stepped forward to shake hands. "This is

the young mining engineer, Steven Marks, who has been doing the survey work on the Portland Vein," Stratton continued his introduction. Stratton didn't mention that he was investigating veins other than the Portland.

Reed rose and met him halfway. Steven felt somewhat crudely dressed with both men in fine suits. Verner Z. Reed was in a finely tailored suit of Edwardian style. Ruffled and starched collars with lace edges. His handshake was firm and full of energy. His skin had a flawless complexion, and his mustache was waxed with a fine little point to its ends. He was the epitome of style for the spring of eighteen-ninety-four. He followed the fashion, and it suited his posture and manner.

"Can I offer you a cigar or cognac," he asked Steven?

"No thank you," Steven replied. "I don't smoke, but I'll take a rain check on the drink for another time."

Reed went back to his desk and pushing the tails of his coat back so that he didn't sit on them, seated himself. Steven and Stratton took seats on the opposite side of the desk. Reed arranged some papers and studied them for a few moments.

"What we need for you to do, Steven," Reed spoke smooth as silk, "is give a bill for survey work to the Burns-Doyle-Harnan Partnership, dated October 30th, eighteen-ninety-three. To your knowledge, Walter Crosby did not own the Portland claim at that time, but the Burns-Doyle-Harnan Partnership."

"That's easy enough," Steven agreed to the billing.

"We will want you to testify to that fact in court about six weeks from now."

"That is how the bill will be made out. That is the facts," Steven smiled. He understood that Reed was causing the twenty-seven suits that were filed to specify the wrong defendant party. The suits would have to be refiled, and Steven had no doubt that another billing for survey work would go to still some other name, so that the complaints would still be against the wrong name, frustrating the plaintiffs.

"How are the purchases of adjoining claims coming," Stratton questioned?

"I've secured an option of the One-Eyed-Jack," Reed pointed at a map and turned it for Steven and Stratton to see. They looked at where he was pointing.

"I already know the general tending of those nearby veins," Steven pointed at three places. "There are counter claims of apex that can be made against some of the nearby claims."

"I have already filed those suits," Reed's eyes fairly sparkled.

"Stratton clapped his hands, "Irving Howbert has given me unlimited credit at his bank," he informed Reed.

"Aha," Reed became more animated, "are you brave enough to borrow."

"The gold is showing. It's just good business."

"I want to declare a dividend on the Portland Stock," Reed proposed, "a big one."

"How big," Stratton questioned with admiration and understanding dawning on his face.

"One Hundred Thousand," Reed cocked an eyebrow.

"Do it," Stratton hit the table with his fist. "The stock will go through the ceiling," he laughed.

"I'll issue a million shares of common stock to hold the price down. We'll raise enough money to keep them stalled in court until they either give up and sell or exchange their holdings for Portland stock. It may take a few months, but there is no one on the scene that has the money to fight us long."

"We'll see an end to the suits, and a true consolidated mine."

"That's right," Verner sat back, and lit a cigar. He

190

poured he and Stratton a cognac and they toasted the gambit.

Steven added a congenial 'here, here' to the toast to join the men in spirit, even though he didn't want the liquor this early. He was amazed at the overall cleverness of this very smooth and elegant man. He was awed by the swiftness with which he was boxing in the other claimants.

"Give me a list of actions," Stratton told Reed, "And I'll have Jonah Finn do the filing."

"I've already made that list, Win," Verner produced a list with instructions already made out and handed it to him. Stratton was sure that he had picked the right man to lead this fight.

Talk turned to city improvement in lighting and water delivery, and then to trout fishing on warmer days. The meeting broke up. And Stratton suggested that they eat lunch as they left the suite and walked down the staircase.

"Join me at Elizabeth's Place for lunch," he suggested. "I'm meeting Finn there shortly."

"That sounds like a good idea," Steven agreed, and then as an afterthought, "I've seen some man with her from time to time?", his voice raised in pitch at the end to indicate a question.

Stratton threw an apprising gaze at him. "Most likely her simple minded brother, Harry," Stratton told him. "Never known Elizabeth to have a beau," he shook his head. "Strange," he mused, "she's an attractive woman. People figure something in her past," he shrugged and turned the corners of his mouth into a frown.

They walked two blocks east and entered the warm eatery. Good smells of savory meats and fruit pies accosted their senses. There were neat tables with simple dried wildflowers and spice plants. Homespun checked tablecloths covered tables that sat along the edges and in two aisles in the thirty feet by fifteen-foot front room. A window alcove formed a nice imitation Victorian entrance, so common in 'Little London' as they called Colorado Springs. Most of the tables were full, and a man in top hat and long waistcoat, with exaggerated long sideburns motioned to them.

"This is Maurice Finn," Stratton did the introduction, "Steven Marks, Maurice. He surveys for the Portland Company."

"Pleased to meet you, Mr. Marks," Finn stuck out his hand.

"Call me Steven, please."

"And call me Jonah, as most do," Finn corrected Stratton.

"Sounds like a bad luck charm, 'Jonah'," Stratton complained. "I've got too much seafarin' heritage. I call him Maurice. Here Maurice, some work from Reed," Stratton handed the instructions to Finn, whose eyebrows shot up more and more as he read the proposed legal filings.

"You're taking on the whole bunch, head on."

"Verner's got a plan," Stratton assured him. "Now what about the buyouts?"

"I've been able to get you close to a hundred acres in claims around the Washington and Independence claims."

Stratton just shook his head in the affirmative. "Good work Maurice. I'm hungry. Here's Elizabeth. My usual, Elizabeth."

"Lunch or breakfast usual, Mr. Stratton," she queried him? "You never know what time of the day it is for you," she kidded him. She made eye contact with Steven and gave him a smile of recognition.

"Lunch, I believe, Elizabeth."

"Are you sure, or do you just believe?"

"Lunch, positively."

"What's on that special," Finn asked, pointing at

192

the chalk board menu?

"Meatloaf comes with potatoes and turnips, with peach pie and coffee for six bits."

"Sounds good," Finn agreed.

"For me, also," Steven said, and then asked, "but could I have hot tea?"

"Sorry, just coffee made, and I've got too much," she indicated the other patrons impatient for service.

"Coffee, then is fine," he agreed.

She wrote the orders and moved on around the room. Disappeared into the kitchen. Harry appeared at the door of the kitchen and looked out at the crowd. She came back with a huge blue enamel coffee pot, and refilled cups around the room, ending with filling the set ups for the three.

Stratton and Finn discussed specific plots of land, some that Steven had already been surveying. The consolidation of Battle Mountain was becoming a reality, and Stratton was on the top. Elizabeth brought their meals, and the planning stopped as the men enjoyed.

"Elizabeth," Stratton said, "I swear you could cook for the angels."

"But I do, Mr. Stratton," she shot back. "I cook for you, and your friends."

"Good cook, and politic, too," Stratton gave her sarcastic praise.

"Oh, you know, you might not like my politics, Mr. Stratton," she was coy.

"You might be surprised at what I might like, Elizabeth."

They smiled at each other and left it there. She went to wait on others and went back to the kitchen. Finn and Stratton talked a little more, agreed on certain immediate action and Finn shook Steven's hand, and put on his gloves in preparation to go on his way.

"One word to the wise, to both of you, very

193

quietly," Stratton lowered his voice. "Get out and get every loose stock in the Independence. Quiet like, while the suits are still pending, before Reed makes his next move," Stratton pointed at the tabletop. Steven knew that he meant the dividend. He had saved a few dollars up, and this was going to be a good bet.

"Thanks for the advice, Win," Jonah Finn shook Stratton's hand, and went out the door, and walked past the front window going east on Bennett Ave.

Win went over the next few days on survey assignments. When the specifics were out of the way, a discussion arose about which they had been over in theory before.

"These veins are tending, as we thought they would," Steven unfolded a map he was working on. "This follows the theory that there is a single throat to the ancient volcano that made the several Brecia tube formations that we see these sylvanite veins formed in." Stratton turned the map and looked at where Steven was pointing.

"How deep," Stratton asked?

"It's hard to say, at this point," Steven shrugged. "Deep, over a thousand feet, certainly, maybe all the way to the floor of the mountain chain. Maybe as deep as the desert floor, that's seven thousand feet."

"A cave of pure gold?"

"It's been known, several times," Steven assured him. "Never in a caldera of this size, nowhere near."

"That means a giant cave of pure gold."

"This is the possibility."

"Well, Steven, my lad, you're my leprechaun, and I'm not turning you lose until you find me that cave of gold."

"Would that I could." They both laughed at the fantasy of it.

Customers got more scarce, as the lunch hour

faded, and Stratton, full of coffee, wanted some whiskey to top off an excellent day.

"Come on over to Johnnie Nolan's," Stratton pointed across and up the street, "where we can get some whiskey to take the edge off all this coffee. Elizabeth, you don't serve no Irish coffee," he complained.

"No apology, Mr. Stratton, there's no whiskey available at Elizabeth's Place."

"Bah," he said, "might as well be in Hayden's Placer, with those T-totalers of Ed De LaVergne's."

"I told you, you wouldn't like my politics," she said from the kitchen door. "Carry Nation is coming to town, you know."

"My God woman, now you've ruined my digestion." With that, Stratton stomped out in a real pique, without another word to either of them.

"I hope I didn't push him too far," Elizabeth had a worried look. Stratton was one of her best customers.

"He's moody," Steven assured her. "He'll get over it."

"He sure must hate Carry Nation," she observed.

"Well, he's a hard drinking man. He drinks a substantial amount of whiskey every day, ever since I've known him, and it seems to be increasing with increasing success."

Elizabeth made no comment but went back into the kitchen and began to clean up lunch and prepare the pies for the supper menu. Steven could hear someone splitting firewood in back of the kitchen and assumed it was her brother doing what he could to help.

Steven lingered, hoping to get some more conversation with Elizabeth. They had not exchanged two dozen words since the night of the fandango. He was again feeling nervous in a way unusual for him.

Two strangers, to him, came in the door. One was slick, with well-oiled hair tonic, waxed mustache, much like the style that Verner Z. Reed wore, much the fashion of the year. He had a derby hat on, a very handsome face, and smooth complexion. He looked like a faro dealer. His companion was ruddy complexioned with reddish, sandy hair, big boned and square toothed. Both men were shorter than Steven, but the man who looked to work outside outweighed him by thirty or more pounds. He looked like a rancher from the cut of his clothes and the western style Stetson hat that he wore square on his head. He had an enigmatic and vicious looking smile on his lips. They sat with their backs to the door facing the kitchen. They talked low, putting their heads close together to speak. They made Steven uneasy for some reason that he couldn't fathom.

When Elizabeth entered the dining area from the kitchen, she almost dropped the picture of water she was carrying. She sat it shakily on the table and turned to face the two men. She was pale, as all the color had drained from her cheeks. Her mouth moved, but she couldn't make any words come out. Inside, she was shouting 'go away'.

"I come for my wife, and the money she stole from me," Raff Janek barked at her, rough.

"I'm not your wife," Elizabeth set her lips in a firm tightness.

"You are my wife," Raff yelled at her, "and you run off with my money."

"And you've stolen valuables from me," Soapy Smith put in on her. Steven began to tense. He did not like the tone in which this was happening. She could not withstand this vicious aggression.

"I took my brother from slavery," she countered Soapy Smith's charge.

Harry heard the noise and came to the kitchen door. He saw Soapy Smith, and a grin spread on his face. He remembered Smith as a kind master. He had been beaten at both the marble quarry and the stable, but Soapy had only used the boy for sport, and everyone ridiculed Harry. He didn't mind. He started through the door.

"Harry," Elizabeth commanded, "stay in the kitchen."

"Now, I don't know what Raff wants with a skinny little bitch like you, but I figure this place is just about worth that indenture contract." He pulled a paper out of his pocket and spread it in front of her. "This is a Quit Claim Deed to this property. Sign it, or I'll take your brother with me, right now," he thrust the document toward her and held out a pen.

"We'll forget the money you stole," Janek piped up. "But you're coming home with me. You're my wife," he said with a triumphant thud of his fist. The two men obviously thought they had her boxed in a corner.

"You men go too far," Steven stood up.

Soapy Smith looked sideways at Steven and then checked him up and down for a weapon. A habit of many fights. "You don't want your nose in this, mister. It's none of your business."

"I won't sit by while Elizabeth is abused," Steven asserted.

Janek grabbed him with all the years of pent-up rage. He got hold of clothing and threw Steven backwards through the door, which busted out of the pine it was hinged on. He was on Steven in a second, but Steven managed to fend off a couple of roundhouses blows and connected with a stiff jab to Raff's chin when Soapy Smith got his arms from the back and pinned him. Janek began to pummel him into unconsciousness with blows to his face and ribs. Suddenly the blows stopped.

Elizabeth had stuck the gun barrel against Janek's head. The barrel of the gun she had taken from Smith's drawer on that day of liberation. "I'll blow your head off," she stated firmly, "if you hit him one more time."

She stepped back out of his reach and aimed the

bore of the big forty-five colt at Smith. Smith recognized the gun. "Let him go," she commanded. "You know that I will shoot you," she warned. Soapy let Steven's arms loose and he slid to the plank walk. Soapy reached and felt a prick on his neck where Elizabeth had stuck him two years earlier.

People were stopping on both sides of the street. Someone yelled, "You want Hy Wilson, Elizabeth?"

She shook her head. "They're leaving," she said firmly. Smith looked at Janek and motioned with his head.

"This ain't over," Smith threw over his shoulder. "I'll have that restaurant for what you owe me," he threatened again.

"A man's got a right to his wife," Janek asserted lamely. They slouched up the street and disappeared through the door of the Buckhorn.

Elizabeth slumped against the wall in despair, then pulled herself together and knelt to see about Steven. She sat the gun in reach and brushed the blood matted hair from his face. Two men coming along Bennett Avenue helped her move him inside and sat him at a near table. He could sit up, and she gave him a napkin to hold against a bleeding lip and went for water and cloth. Harry stood at the kitchen door right where Elizabeth told him to stay. The pistol lay on the table in front of Steven.

She returned in a few minutes with warm water, cloth, alcohol, and iodine. "I'm so sorry Mr. Marks," she said, carefully dabbing the wounds on his face with an alcohol-soaked cloth. "You seem to be attacked whenever you come near me."

"I had begun to notice a correlation," he winced from the sting of the alcohol on the cuts. Their eyes were very close. They made eye contact, for a long moment, they looked at one another.

"Who were those men," Steven asked, as if he had a right into her secrets? She withdrew a step.

"I'm not sure I can talk about that." She turned away.

Steven let it go. "Go with me for a surrey ride," he blurted. He had fantasized this for days, and now he was making a mess of it. "This afternoon," he coaxed.

"I couldn't this afternoon, I'm open until late." She paused and then said, "I close early tomorrow for Christmas day. We could go then."

"Then, I'll rent a surrey. That one with the bright red wheels from George Welty."

She laughed. She had a nice surrey of her own that she kept stabled. "I've always wanted to try that rig out," She laughed again. "I've seen Pearl De Vere in it several times. You know who Pearl is?"

"I believe," Steven said defensively, "that everyone knows who Pearl is. A very flamboyant woman."

Uh, huh," Elizabeth agreed with him with an appraising judgment. "I've got to get this place ready for the next meal."

"I'll see you tomorrow evening, then," Steven walked to the broken door, picked it up and sat it beside the torn door frame. He shrugged, she shook her head and started sweeping.

Steven wandered over to Johnnie Nolan's Saloon. Stratton was well on his way to a good drunk, in celebration of his new acquisitions.

"Well, Knocked Down Marks," he laughed. "What the hell happened to you?"

"I'm not sure, but I'll take that drink that you offered earlier." Steven washed the blood out of his mouth with swishing the whiskey around. "I need to know who a couple of gents with whom I've just become acquainted, are, and what their business is in Cripple Creek."

"Where are they?" Stratton was quick. Bob Womack was drinking in Nolan's at the time, and had moved close to hear Steven, seeing he was bruised and bleeding. Steven led the three out of Nolan's and east along Bennett Avenue to the Buckhorn. Steven described the two men along the way.

When they reached the Buckhorn, Stratton and Steven went all the way to the back, looking over the crowd. Bob went to Mother Duffy. "Just sold the Womack Placer," Bob bragged to her. He showed her a wad of one-dollar bills, that he had gotten off Johnnie Nolan for large bills that he had been paid for the claim. "I'm gonna give this money out fer Christmas to the kids in town," Bob told her.

"Bob, that's sweet," she gave him a friendly pat on the cheek. Bob blushed.

"Say, Stratton and Steven Marks is lookin' for a slicker in a derby with a thin mustache, waxed to a point, and a heavy-set man in a Stetson, on the prowl together."

"That's Soapy Smith and some rancher from up in the Gunnison. Word is, his wife ran off. They been asking a lot of questions about Elizabeth Yates, and how and when she bought and built the restaurant. Had their heads together with a shyster lawyer named Hadley, earlier this afternoon."

"Win, Steven," Bob called and motioned the two over. Mother Duffy told them the same, as much as she knew about Smith, which she knew from Creede and Denver. She warned them both that Smith could be very dangerous. Bob acquired another shot of whiskey and then left the Buckhorn.

By the time that Win and Steven had finished talking with Mother Duffy and exited the Buckhorn, Bob Womack had positioned himself in front of Johnnie Nolan's and was giving out one-dollar bills to kids getting in line all the way up Bennett. Steven and Win watched in amusement, and Stratton cautioned Steven about what they had learned from Mother Duffy. "It looks like Elizabeth has a secret past that is catching up," he warned.

Stratton bid him a goodbye and walked toward Myer's Avenue for continued revelry. Steven watched the line of present takers increase, with some miners joining in the line. Bob good natured, handed out dollars, and some of the men laughingly got in line a second time. Bob's inebriated brain caught what was going on, and he swung a fist at one big boned, and skinny, hungry miner. He knocked Bob flat with a right hook. The few dollars he had left blew into the snow, and children and miners scrambled for them.

Johnnie Nolan came out of his saloon and saw Bob in the street, face down in the snow. Steven helped roll him over and get him back on his feet. He helped Nolan get Bob inside the saloon. Bob sobbed his way through some coffee. He had caught a cold, and now he was all spent.

Steven walked a shaky Bob back to his cabin in Poverty Gulch. Steven was tired and beaten almost as bad as Bob, as he trudged back to the frame shack that he rented in Victor.

He checked on Bob the next day, which was Christmas morning. Bob was extremely ill, and some of the black crib girls along Poverty Gulch had been making him soup and coaxing him to eat it. Bob was in a bad way and Steven went into town and talked with deputy Peter Eales who went to the Western Union office, and wired his sister Lida, and informed her of Bob's condition. Lida came and took Bob back to recover in Colorado Springs, but Bob never really returned to Cripple Creek to live there again. When Bob arrived in Colorado Springs, the newspapers heralded "Winfield Scott Stratton, Cripple Creek's first millionaire." Bob was heard to say, "Poor W. S., all that money."

After Steven had informed deputy Eales about Bob Womack's condition, he wanted to walk down to the restaurant, but hesitated. He would certainly see her later

201

that day. He went to Welty's Stable and arranged for the surrey.

Elizabeth worked through the breakfast and lunch hour. She hoped she would see Steven, but shortly after lunch, she saw the lawyer Hadley come in, who presented her with a Letter of Demand. It read, "for restitution of services lost in lieu of a contract of indenture, a Quit Claim Deed, to be signed for the Bennett Avenue property, building, and business, as appertained."

She wouldn't sign. He threatened criminal complaints against both her and Harry. By the time he left, she was in a desperate frame of mine. She could think of nothing else, except worrying. What could she do? Take Harry and run again. All her money was tied up in the restaurant. She was finishing up late Christmas Eve in the afternoon, when Steven pulled up in front. She had completely forgotten.

She began to fix her hair, then thought how silly, with all the trouble facing her. He hitched the horse at a front rail and with a cursory exam of the door where she and Harry had reattached it, came inside.

"Ready," he asked?

"Harry," she called, "you close up and stay close."

"Aw, right," Harry came to the kitchen door, and then followed them outside. He watched then get in the surrey and waved to Elizabeth with obvious mixed emotions that he was trying to deal with inside himself.

As they passed the Palace Hotel going west on Bennett Avenue, a light snow began to condense out of the already dry air, indicating even colder air settling into the valley.

The horse snorted but kept a good trot, as they turned right a block, passing wooden houses with smoke curling from all the chimneys, and children throwing snowballs at each other, and threatening to throw them at the surrey. They turned left on Carr Street and headed up the eastern slope of Mt. Pisgah.

"I know a place toward Four Mile, where an old stage road toward Guffey goes across a ridge, and there is the grandest view of the Sangre De Christos," her breath condensed in the cold air in puffs.

"Show me the way," Steven popped the reins and the gelding sped up, but then he pulled to tightly on the reins, a beginner's mistake. He was alternately giving 'go faster' signals and then pulling back on the lines, giving mixed signals, until the frustrated horse lay his ears back.

"He's going to get the bit in his teeth," she warned Steven at the top of Mt. Pisgah hill as they started to descend.

"Whoa," Steven called, but it was too late. The gelding had the bit between his teeth and Steven could no longer hold him, as he ran away at full speed run down the sloping curve around the back of Mt. Pisgah.

Elizabeth took the reins. "Give him to me," she yelled. They were in a dangerous run. She stood on the front rail of the surrey and pulled back with all her weight. The geldings neck bowed, but he didn't give up and slacked very little in an outright run around the curve and down the hill. When she figured the neck muscles were tired, she gave him some slack, and sure enough, he stretched his neck up and out. That gave her a better angle on the bit in between his teeth, and she suddenly popped the reins with all her strength that she had left. It snapped the bit from between the horses' teeth and pulled his tongue painfully down. Now, she had him under control.

She brought him to a total stop. "I think maybe you better keep the reins," Steven said sheepishly. She drove on, turning on the old stage road leading southwesterly. She drove them slowly up the grade to a spot overlooking the Sangre De Christo range in the western distance. Light snow sprinkled down. Welty had placed a thick buffalo robe across the seat. Steven bagged the horse with a feed bag of oats, and they pulled the buffalo robe around them as the western sky turned from orange to purple.

Their faces were close. He smiled at her and the cold cracked his lip, where it was badly bruised. It bled a little, and suddenly, she kissed it, very tenderly. She tasted his blood. In a rush of emotion, she was overwhelmed with the thought that the same fist that beat her had beaten Steven. She started to kiss each bruise. He felt her tears wet his hair.

After a while, they just held each other in a contentment that neither had known for a long, long, time.

"Have those men bothered you again," Steven ventured.

"They sent a lawyer around to demand things."

"Who are they?" Steven already pretty much guessed the answer from what he had learned at the Buckhorn."

"One is a man I was forced to marry when I was fourteen," there it was out. "The other held a contract of indenture on my brother from when we were orphaned, and he was apprenticed to a man who sold him."

"Can that be legal in this nation," Steven asked?

"Where are you from," she was suddenly curious?

"I have applied for citizenship," he gave his quick answer.

"That is not what I asked."

"I'm," he hesitated, "Spanish," he confessed at last.

"I would never have guessed that. Steven Marks doesn't sound like a Spanish name."

"My given name is Stefano, and Marks was suggested at Ellis Island, since Marquez, my sir name, would bring a lot of unwanted attention, and perhaps worse."

"Stefano," she said to herself. "I would have never thought with your English accent," she was surprised.

"A good teacher from London."

"Oh," she knew he was educated. I'm a cedar chopper's daughter, from a poverty stricken, and dirt-poor small town. I've been married. That must rattle your Catholic sensibilities," she mused.

"I was raised Catholic," he agreed. "I'm not sure I hold to much of it, except maybe the Golden Rule."

"The gold rules here," she said cynically.

"I don't know United States or Colorado law, but Mr. Stratton is trusting a very clever and well-connected man from Colorado Springs. If I can get him to advise you, would you like to talk with him?"

"If Mr. Stratton trusts him for advice, I could hardly do better, could I?" She smiled at his concern. "What is his name?"

"Verner Z. Reed," Steven told her, and he's living in the front suite on the third floor of the Palace Hotel. I'll see if I can arrange a meeting."

The horse had finished with all the oats in the feed bag, and stomped impatiently, dumped in front of them, which made them laugh and pull the buffalo robe up over their heads. After a while, Steven removed the bag and took the reins. He kept the surrey in a slow walk all the way back to town in the growing twilight.

He had no trouble arranging a meeting with Verner Z. Reed, who was always ready to try to right any wrong in defense of womanhood.

Steven opened the door at the appointed hour in the afternoon of the next day, and after introductions, discretely left the room.

Elizabeth took a seat, and Verner moved to pour tea and sit at the edge in a more personal arrangement. She was nervous and could say nothing.

"You have a legal problem," Verner stated.

"Yes." She didn't know where to start.

"You have a husband that you have left, from a

youthful, forced marriage," he continued.

"Yes." She paused. "We were orphaned when Pappa was killed." Her voice began to break.

"You stole money when you left," Verner probed to get the story.

"I took my inheritance that came from my father's hard work."

"How much?"

"Three thousand dollars, which was less than what Raff got from Pappa's account," and then she lay the stock certificates for Yule Marble on Verner Z. Reed's desk. "And, these certificates, which are probably worthless."

Reed's eyebrows went up. He had just that very morning read in a New York paper, brought west on the train, and then brought by stage from Divide, that the monument to Abraham Lincoln was to be made of white marble, and money was to come to a vote in this session of congress.

"Worthless," he questioned? "Perhaps not. Do you know how you father came by this stock?"

"He was hauling coal to the steam saw at the marble mine. He was killed by a slab of marble that fell on him. The stock must be in payment for haulage."

"What about this other man, Smith," he questioned?

"My brother was indentured to the marble cutter in Yule, who sold his contract to another, and then it was sold again to a stable owner in Creede, who sold it to a saloon so that Soapy Smith ended up with it, having him work in a saloon in Creede."

"Contracts of indenture cannot be transferred," he told her. "Dismissal of the apprentice breaks the contract, as they are specific to a task." He let that sink in. "You will have no worries there." He paused again. "Tell me about this forced marriage."

She didn't respond. She didn't know how to tell

something she tried so hard to forget.

"I'm a writer, you might know," Verner tried to break the barrier. "Here is my first book _Lo-Ta-Ka_," he signed it 'To Elizabeth', and handed it to her. "Read page one-thirty-two, second paragraph," he said.

She thumbed to it and read. She visibly reddened, and a little gasp escaped her lips.

"Pretty racy, huh," he smiled. "Win Stratton burned it," he laughed.

She looked up at him.

"Now, I want you to tell me every detail of your forced and abusive marriage."

Elizabeth didn't know why, but she did, in a flood of anger and tears. When it was over, Verner offered her a silk handkerchief, placed an arm around her shoulder and led her to the door.

"You have absolutely nothing to worry about. This will be fixed by noon tomorrow, and you will not hear of these men, nor see them again," he promised.

Deputy Sheriff Peter Eales mounted the stairs to the adjoining second floor rooms at the Concord. Joe Wolf had no choice but to confirm the tenants in the two rooms were the men Eales was looking for on the day after Christmas.

Eales already had Wolf in his sights for several bunco scams and Soapy Smith staying in his hotel was not what Wolf wanted known.

Eales eased his gun out of its holster and used the butt to wrap on the side-by-side doors. Inquiring voices came from inside.

"Jefferson Smith," Eales called, "Raff Janek, come out here. I'm Deputy Sheriff Pete Eales."

The doors opened and both men, startled by the abruptness, open only a crack. Eales was backed by two more tough looking deputies.

"Both you men come out," Eales commanded.
Both did. "You men get your hats and coats on," he said.
The two deputies with a hand on their gun butts waited in
the rooms while the two men got warm clothes.

"What's the problem," Janek asked? He wasn't
used to being arrested, Smith was, and he kept silent.

"You two are wanted for questioning by Sheriff
Wilson," Eales told them on the way down the stairs.
They went toward Bennett Avenue from where the
Concord stood on Myers. When they reached the Palace
Hotel, instead of continuing on toward the station house
and sheriff's office, Eales directed them inside.

"This ain't the sheriff's office," Smith objected.

"That's right," Eales told him. "You're such a
smart feller." Smith knew better than to give Eales an
excuse to handle him, as Eales had a rough history with
offenders.

"We don't have an overabundance of good women
in this town. But we do jay hawkers," Eales chided them.

"If we're not going to the sheriff's office, where,"
Smith demanded?

"First, to the woodshed," Eales smiled. "All in
good time."

He marched them upstairs to the front third floor
suite. Lawyer Hadley sat in the foyer with Sheriff Hy
Wilson and Judge Colburn from Colorado Springs.
Hadley gave both men a shrug. He was likewise in the
dark.

Wilson opened the door and led them into the well-
appointed room. The deputies stayed outside, while
Sheriff Wilson motioned the two toward the elegantly
dressed man behind the desk. He made no pleasantries.
"Sheriff, if you would retire to the foyer with Judge
Colburn, I may need you shortly."

Wilson left the room and closed the door quietly

behind him.

"Hadley," Reed began, "you're known around for the fast one you pulled on Tim Houghton and defrauded him of him claim. A lot of people liked Tim, and you ruined him and drove him to drink, causing him to lose his mind. Now, you've teamed with these two and are attempting to defraud an orphan and her brother of their property. Get out," he said flatly, "and if I hear of anymore fraud on your part, I will see you disbarred." He pointed at the door, and Hadley, wanting no more part of this action, slunk out.

"Who are you," Soapy Smith snarled.

"A mediator in this case, and you have no need to know my name. I have filed a writ of Fraternus Amicus with El Paso County, which is allowed under recent Colorado Law, to act as a 'Loving Brother' in the case of orphans. This is in the interest of Elizabeth and Harry Yates."

Both men started objections, with Smith spouting, "that little thief," and Janek, "that's my wife." Verner Reed held up his hand to stop them.

"I have three possible courses of action against you, Mr. Janek. Foremost, you married the girl under suspicious circumstances of conflicted interest, at an age that is now illegal in Colorado. You will sign this annulment agreement, or there will be a divorce filing, and a criminal complaint. Under current Colorado law, she would receive half of your assets, including the sale of your ranch and cattle. In the criminal complaint, charges of white slavery, and conspiracy to defraud an orphan of her inheritance, will be made. If found guilty, and I'm sure that you will agree that you will be found guilty when this deposition is read to a jury," he handed Janek a paper listing the abuses that Elizabeth had endured under him. "If this goes to trial, you will serve time in Canon City, and such crimes are looked upon as pedophilia by many

209

men in jail. Men with such charges against them rarely live to the end of their sentences."

He left Raff to read the paper and started in on Smith. "Mr. Smith, your claim to a contract of indenture of Harry Yates is groundless and opens you to a charge of slavery. Colorado frowns on the abuse of the slow minded. You will sign this manumission paper discharging Harry Yates from any obligation, or you will spend time in Canon City, right beside Mr. Janek." He handed the paperwork to Smith.

Both men stood for some time studying the papers. "You will sign these papers, now, or Hy Wilson will take you into custody after Judge Colburn has signed these warrants for your arrest on the respective charges. If you sign, Wilson will take you to the county line and set you upon the road. This is your choices," he told them firmly. "Make it now."

Both men bent and signed the papers where indicated.

"Now get out," he dismissed them as garbage. At the door, he indicated to Sheriff Wilson and Judge Colburn that he had what he needed.

Verner Z. Reed, flamboyant righter of wrongs, and protector of orphans and women, watched the deputies escorting the two down the street to get their gear, and out of town.

He lit a cigar and chomped down on it in the side of his mouth. He had a glass of aged cognac in his right hand, in his left, he had the news of the vote on the Lincoln Memorial. He would take twenty-five percent of the Yule Marble Stock Certificates for his trouble. "God," he mused to himself, "how I love righting wrongs, and making a fortune being a hero."

Chapter 17. Labor Trouble

Smith and Janek had to walk the 18 miles to Divide after Hy Wilson turned them loose at the town boundary. Janek left on a train for Denver from Colorado Springs, with Soapy's sage advice, "You win some, and you lose some." He never could see why Raff had ever wanted Elizabeth Yates. He couldn't stand independent women, and this one had proven dangerous to him. Still, he wanted to know who he was against, and he sought out a knowledgeable man. On one of the fine streets overlooking The Springs, he had the taxi driver stop and wait. The driver, Sherman Crumley, knew Soapy well, but was surprised to find that he knew the rich banker, Irving Howbert.

After hearing the description, Howbert knew who was involved. "He's a very successful real estate investor named Verner Z. Reed," Howbert told Soapy Smith. "Stratton has taken a liking to him. I knew that he was in The District, and advising Stratton. He's a local white knight for charity causes and the like. Put Hy Wilson on you, did he? Well, they can be handled. Stratton's borrowing money from me." Howbert knew that the history of most hard rock mines was that they required more capital to work them than most mines could ultimately sustain, and ended up being conglomerated by rich owner bankers, like himself, who held the notes to the machinery.

"The depression is going to get worse, in spite of Cleveland's single metal policy. There's going to be pressure to cut wages at the mines in the district, and there is going to be labor trouble just like in Idaho. Forget this petty quarrel you have with this woman and go back to Denver. I want you to look around for the toughest men you can find, for strike busters. Put together at least a hundred men that have a taste for Irish blood." With those instructions, Soapy climbed back into Crumley's cab and caught a train for Denver.

The mine owners grew richer. Everywhere the talk was of the depression. Poor looking for work flooded into the district. As the mine owners grew even more rich and greedy, the labor organizers moved in. There was a meeting of the mine owners to try and fight the collective bargaining, and to drop wages to take advantage of the surplus of labor in the District. Some of the mines dropped wages to under three dollars a day and raised the hours per day to a nine hour day. Trouble began with the first announcement of this policy. Stratton made a compromise with the workers and recognized the Western Federation of Miners as a union, which prompted many of the other mine owners to say, "Statton's just not one of us." When Jimmy Burns said everyman had the right to collective bargaining, the Colorado Springs newspaper reported that several men in The El Paso Club billards parlor died of apoplexy on the tables.

Stratton signed a contract with the WFM, initiating the three dollars and twenty-five cents per day wage and the nine-hour work day. This move totally alienated Stratton from the other owners and even caused trouble in the Portland Company among some of the owners who grumbled but had to follow Jimmy and Win's lead.

Steven was kept busy during the winter and that spring with court dates, and important work for the Portland Company, with little time for social life, but he and Elizabeth did have a surrey ride into the country on several Sundays, when Elizabeth could get free of work. They had a favorite place to go, overlooking the Sangre De Christo mountains and the valley that stretched out toward West Four Mile.

There was still trouble brewing, and union men

were replaced by scabs, which brought a shutdown of the roads leading to some of the large mines. The militia was called in and some of the men intimidating the scabs were arrested and brought to a mock trial where Tarsney, the Adjutant General under Populist Governor Waite, acquitted them. This infuriated the mine owners. Finally, food and other essential services were denied to any member of the WFM. Guns and whiskey came out to the fore, and the talk got dangerous on both sides.

During a calm period, after the mock trial, the leader of the WFM, John Caulderwood left Jack Johnson in charge while he made an inspection trip to Leadville. Stratton was afraid that violence would break out with Caulderwood out of town, and placed guards around the Independence mine property. Soapy Smith brought the Denver Gang, a group of one hundred violent ex-police, who had just lost their jobs by order of Populist Governor Waite, which was a very unpopular move in the Republican stronghold of Denver. They came in to help El Paso Sheriff Bowers quell the striking miners. This move set in motion the chaos of a confrontation between the Bower's Denver ex -police, Governor Waite's state militia, and the striking miners on Bull Hill. The situation became a powder keg waiting for a match, and a group of newly released criminals from the Cannon City prison under the leadership of Jack Smith, who called himself General Jack Smith, provided the match. General Jack Smith has taken control of the enraged miners from Johnson, who Caulderwood left in charge. A train was on its way from Colorado Springs on the Midland Terminal with the Denver ex-police, and Johnson could not control the situation, but with the train on its way, gave Jack Smith orders to stop them.

Jack Smith and Shorty McLain edged over the little incline and observed the entrance to the Independence. Minutes earlier they had overpowered the guards at the

Strong Mine and had gained control of the mine except for an area where Superintendent McDonald and two other men had barricaded themselves behind a locked steel door in an old powder room on the second level, that had become an ore storage area for high grade ore.

Bob Mitchell, the headguard on duty for Stratton at the Independence saw a flash of light and movement from a copper brad in Jack Smith's hat. He stepped back into the entrance and called in the other twenty guards from the perimeter and informed them that they had company. They had heard some muffled explosions, and pops of shots coming from the direction of the Strong mine. Mitchell went down to the sixth level to where Steven Marks was working on mapping, measuring strike and dip of the various veins running through the walls.

"We've got some movement outside that don't look good," he told Steven. "You'd better come up topside. This would be a bad hole if someone blew the entrance, it could take days, or weeks to clear."

"Would they go that far," Steven questioned, but he stopped taking measurements and started moving toward the shaft leading to the lift platform.

"The spies that are out, say that the pot is about to boil over." It was at that moment that they heard the first explosions many levels above them. The walls of the mine shook with the explosive force, and dust spread thickly into the air. With concerned faces, they stepped onto the platform and signaled to be taken up. The platform began to move upward. More explosions were heard, and the platform stopped. A few minutes later it started again and they arrived at the top to the heavy smell of cordite. More pencil charges of dynamite were hurled into the entrance. The guards had fled the smoke and explosions, and taken positions outside, but had nothing to shoot at, as the explosive charges were flung at them from behind rises, and large outcroppings.

At that moment, a lull occurred, as Jack Smith scampered down the low rise and met a wagon on the trail coming up from the Strong mine. The wagon was loaded with cases of TNT, and dynamite. Smith grabbed off a case of dynamite and struggled with it back up the hill. Now he made larger and larger charges and hurled them into the entrance area around the Independence head frame.

Steven and Bob Mitchell were driven back into the Adit entrances by the increasing force of the explosions, as the guards became concerned that the entrance and head frame would collapse, they had moved to defend the edges of the entrance building. Jack Smith knew just how to do it, as it had been done at the Coeur d'Alene some months before, and he had been there to see it. As he had scared them away from the entrance Adit, and was now driving them with pencil charges to the downhill side, and flanking them to the uphill side. The guards had kept up a withering fire, but the pencil charges were thrown at them from behind cover, and their defensive fire was totally ineffectual. Slowly, Smith and McLain and a dozen others backed by twenty more men with rifles, had driven the Independence guards downhill from the mouth of the mine, until they were in an undefendable position. With dozens of charges being hurled downhill on them, they had no choice but to finally flee downhill, pell mell, scurrying away as rifle fire chased them along and shots whizzed overhead.

Jack and Shorty gained the entrance and sent men in to look for any guards still inside. They found the headguard and Steven just back of the platform area and brought them forward to Smith.

"Well, well, Knocked Down Marks," Jack Smith smirked, "make the acquaintance of Dynamite Shorty McLain, he said. Then by way of explanation to McLain, he said, "He's the one got knocked down dancing with

215

Elizabeth Yates at the Social Club last fall. He's Stratton's man, a mining engineer."

"Engineer," Shorty spit," I seen him around spyin' things out last week at the Portland."

"Where's Caulderwood," Steven asked? "Stratton has a contract with the WFM. Why have you attacked a man who's on your side?" Steven could smell that both men reeked of whiskey.

"Caulderwood's in Leadville on WFM business," Smith informed him. General Johnson is in charge at Altman, and I got orders to stop a train load of damned deputies from Denver that that damned Episcopalian Republican, Howbert got Soapy Smith to hire. He got every damned thug on the Denver police force, and they're coming up grade on a special train, right now. But we're gonna make a little surprise for them." The man was in a raving rage. Steven didn't try to reason with him again. This had been building for months, ever since the foreman at the Buena Vista tried to put men on a nine-hour day, while reducing the wage to two-seventy-five, the previous August, and had to take the order down or be beaten. A man approached them from the direction of the Strong mine.

"We've got the charges under the platform and the boiler, just like you said," he directed his words to McLain. "We've got the rest of the dynamite on a wagon headed here now. That gave Smith two full loads of dynamite. Goodly amounts of liquor had been brought along from the stores and mining offices, wherever a bottle could be found.

"Time to move," McLain directed to Jack Smith. Another man arrived from over the top toward Victor. "General Smith," he addressed Jack Smith in military terms. "The engine and two flat cars of deputies just pulled out of Victor headed this way."

Smith and McLain looked at each other and

216

nodded. McLain went downhill toward the Strong mine. "There's a new agenda, now," Smith spit at Steven. "To hell with the three-dollar, eight hour day. I'm gonna put a wrinkle in the plans of those dammed Clevelandites. This place is the venom in their fangs, and I'm going to stop the flow by blowing up every gold mine on this mountain. We'll see how that sets with W. C. Whitney and gang." He was taking a swig from a pint bottle every so often to keep up his courage. Steven could see his hand shaking. There was no doubt that the men coming at them on the train would attack front on and shoot to kill. "Stack that dynamite in here, away from a stray bullet," Smith ordered. They sat Steven and Bob Mitchell down against a wall and proceeded to unload the two wagons full of cases of dynamite and stacked them all along the wall opposite where the men sat. About fifteen minutes crawled by. There were excited voices at the entrance, and then a mighty explosion rocked the mountain. Steven found himself hurrying to the entrance. No one stopped him as the men around him watched as the Strong head frame sailed high into the air and pieces of steel and pulleys reached an apex and began to descend on the train pulling two flatcars of armed men. A second explosion rocked the valleys around, and the Strong boiler shot high into the air, so the men at the Independence entrance had to look up as it reached its highest point, and it too began a quickening decent on the trainload of men. With the little engine belching smoke, and spinning its wheels in reverse, steel, pulleys, and cabling rained down on the Denver deputies, who dropped their rifles and covered their heads with their hands in a futile attempt to protect themselves from the rain of debris, rocks, and steel falling all around them.

In about 30 minutes, Mclain arrived with men guarding three prisoners. Superintendent McDonald was bleeding from the ears. One of the other men cried and babbled in an uncontrollable hysteria. They were taken to

217

the mining town of Altman.

Johnson sent orders to Smith not to destroy the mines, at least not yet. It was an ace in the hole for now. There was plenty of dynamite in the other mines of Bull Hill. He ordered Smith to send that wagon load of giant powder on a train down the track and ram it into the deputy train south of Victor. Which they tried to do by stealing a train in Victor, but the train derailed on a curve and killed a cow and three goats grazing in an alpine meadow. About midnight, the two groups came together in a gun battle where two men got killed and five striking miners were taken captive.

Altman at over 10,600 feet was the "highest city in the world". It was on the saddle between Bull Hill and Bull Cliff. General Johnson had fortified Bull Cliff with logs, and had a fake cannon pointed at Victor. It was close to three of the Districts largest mines. The Buena Vista, the Victor, and the Pharmacist. It consisted of a school house, six groceries, as many saloons, four restaurants, boarding houses, two hundred unpainted shacks, twelve hundred men, women, and children, and one telephone.

Altman overlooked several square miles of Bull Hill and Battle Mountain. John Caulderwood had been mining on these slopes for years. He was born to mining in the coal mines of Scotland, at nine, and had mined the Pennsylvania coal in his teenage years. He was educated at the McReesport School of Mines. Things had gotten tough. He had seen it before. He had been a Mollie Maguire and had paid the professional price of being black-listed for it. Now just like then, all the good work was ruined by violence. Caulderwood returned to Altman from his tour of mines for the Western Federation of Miners on the morning of May twenty-sixth, eighteen-ninety-four, to find his strikers besieged in a state of war.

Steven could hear Caulderwood's voice from where he was being held and called out to him. Caulderwood heard his name called from the back of Smith and Peter's Saloon, where the men had been placed by the strikers.

"Steven," Caulderwood questioned when he saw who it was? "How did you get involved in this mess?"

"John, they've attacked Stratton's Independence, and I was there doing some mapping. They blew the Strong Mine all to pieces. Jack Smith is drunk and crazy. Last I saw of him, he was headed out with two wagon loads of TNT to blow every mine up that he could find."

"Johnson managed to stop him." Caulderwood seemed totally disheartened. "He sent Smith word to sober up and chase those damned deputies that Howbert brought in from Denver."

"How come Denver police are involved," Steven questioned?

"A few days ago, Governor Waite tried to fire some Denver firemen and policemen, that he saw as being too Republican for his Populist taste. They holed up in the Denver City Hall with guns out every window, and Waite ordered Adjutant General Tarsney to blast them out. Tarsney rolled cannon and gatling guns in and postured and threatened for the whole day with half of Denver having a picnic watching along Fourteenth Street. Finally, better sense overcame Tarsney, and he withdrew. Waite was humiliated. El Paso County Sheriff Bowers gave him a chance to save face by requesting the militia to keep order in Cripple Creek. Earlier, I had been able to negotiate with Tarsney to withdraw his men, and honored warrants that Bower's brought up from the Springs to arrest Western Federation men who had intimidated scabs and interfered with the operation of the nine hour mines. I thought I had things under control. Tarsney acquitted all the men charged, and I needed to go on an inspection tour of mines in Leadville. I left Johnson in charge, but his authority was usurped by Jack Smith and that bunch of convict anarchist from the Canon City prison. Apparently,

Howbert hired Soapy Smith to recruit some hundred or so of the ex-police fired from Denver by Waite, and they decided on a frontal attack on Bull Hill and the strikers. Johnson got word of it and ordered Jack Smith to blow up the Strong Mine, as it was next to the track that the deputy train was coming into the District on. Things just spun out of control from then on." Caulderwood looked beaten.

"I've ordered Johnson out of the area and have put Smith and some of the rowdier men in jail here in Altman, but it's too late," he shook his head in chagrin. "They stole a train in Victor and loaded it with TNT and sent it downgrade to try and ram the deputy's train. Fortunately, it derailed on a curve and only killed a cow and three goats, but they went and engaged the deputies in a fight last night about midnight, just south of Victor, and two men were killed and five miners taken prisoner."

Caulderwood shook his head again at the mess. "Now, there is no telling what will happen." Caulderwood paused for a minute and seemed lost in thought.

"Can I do anything to help," Steven offered?

Caulderwood looked shrewdly at him and nodded. "Follow me," he said. Steven followed him to the front of Smith and Peter's. Through the saloon doors he could look down on the whole panorama of Battle Mountain and Bull Hill. Men milled in knots, angry talk coming from every direction. Caulderwood moved behind the bar and got pen and paper. "Peters," he turned toward the proprietor, "please stop serving drinks." Peters immediately closed his bar. Caulderwood began to write a note and when he finished he brought the note to Steven.

"Steven," Caulderwood said, "please go to Father Volpe and ask him to tell the wives to bring their men home," he handed Steven the note. "This should be a pass to get you out of here safely."

Steven took the note and read it. "Ask Father Volpe," John continued to instruct, " to ask the saloon keepers to close their doors."

"I'll see what I can do," Steven opened the swinging doors and started to leave.

"One more thing," Caulderwood stopped him with a hand on his shoulder. "Get down to the Springs and see what's going on and then send me a note about what to expect. I don't mean spy," Caulderwood was apologetic, just help me restore order and a speck of sanity, if you can."

"I'll do what I can John," Steven shook his hand.

"I'm so tired of this," John continued. I'm caught between men rich as Midas, trying to squeeze out one more penny, and anarchist that want to stand it all on its head." He looked at Steven full in the face. "Steven," he said, "do you suppose when this is over that you might teach me to assay?"

"John," Steven told him, "I'd be glad to do that."

The men smiled at each other, shook their heads in dazed confusion, and Steven walked toward the road leading out of Altman down to Cripple Creek.

After talking with Father Volpe, Steven was able to walk part way and catch wagon rides into Divide and get a train into Colorado Springs early afternoon of the next day. He got off at North Park Station in old Colorado City, as a large crowd was gathering there. As he approached, he could see Stratton and Sam Strong on the podium with the current Mayor and Irving Howbert, Judge Colburn and other dignitaries. The usually pale Stratton was beet red and very animated to people talking all around him.

"You all know," the mayor began, "that I am a tolerant man, with nothing against a man's religion even if he does kneel to that Pope Leo XIII. But when men seize private property of men who have long struggled, and when murderous action is used to force their unholy cause, I say 'Enough'!" The crowd burst into cheers. They began to chant back and forth, "Enough", and also chants of "Impeach Waite", and "Hang Tarsney", broke out through the crowd. Steven worked his way toward the front, intent on getting a word with Stratton if possible.

Now, Judge Colburn rose to speak. "I call on every able-bodied man and boy to wrest Bull Hill from the insurrectionists before the insurrectionist despoil the Springs' fair womanhood and slit the throats of its little children." The crowd roared with anger. The ground seemed to shake under Steven's feet. A cry of, "Give Bloody Bridles Waite what he's asking for," rose in a chant from one section. Steven recognized that this chant came from a Waite speech where he had said that it was better that blood run "bridle rein deep" than civil liberties be usurped. It had curdled the blood of and cooled the ardor of many of his Populist supporters.

Now a lady in lacy full-length dress stepped forward. "I'm Susan Dunbar, president of the Colorado Springs Lady's Auxiliary, and we are fully prepared with bandages and dressings to take care of our wounded heroes," she announced proudly, and then added, "should that need, unfortunately, occur, we are prepared, and with water to fill canteens for the campaign. Oh, also, we are fully counseled in comforting the dying." She nodded in the affirmative, as if to say, 'that should about cover it'.

A cry began to go up for Sheriff Bowers to swear in deputies, and hands of men shot up in the crowd both volunteering and demanding to be sworn in, until an eager throng buzzed around Bowers until he mounted the podium and swore in, as deputies of El Paso County, some twelve hundred men in the crowd. It was decided what would be required for each man to bring, and they were ordered to form at Hayden's Divide the following noon.

As the crowd broke up, Steven was able to work his way forward and approach Stratton.

"Win," he called to him.

222

"Steven," he turned, "I was worried when I heard that you were taken in the mine with Mitchell when those worthless guards let themselves be run off from my Independence." He was still boiling mad.

"John Caulderwood came in this morning from Leadville. He sent Johnson away and locked Frank Smith and his drunken gang up in Altman. He sent me to Father Volpe to try and get the women to bring their men home and get the saloon owners to close. He's doing everything that he can to stop the bloodshed."

"I knew that John was out of town," Stratton said. "I was afraid when he left that things might get out of control. But, hell, I never imagined that they would attack the Independence. I done told Bowers and Hagerman to hire me a whole brigade of men to get my mine back." He was in as mad a rage as Jack Smith had been, and only a little less drunk. Whiskey was playing a big part in the trouble. Steven could see it being passed around.

The man that Stratton had been conversing with stepped forward. He couldn't help but overhear, and he was intrigued. "I'm William S. Slocum, President of Colorado College," he introduced himself and stuck out a handshake to Steven. "Did I understand you to say that you had recently come from Altman, and had been in conversation with John Caulderwood?"

"Yes, sir, that is where I have recently been."

"How did you come there?"

"I was taken prisoner by the Jack Smith gang when he attacked the Independence."

"And how did you manage to come here?"

"John Caulderwood wrote me a pass out of Altman with instructions to try and calm the area."

"I would very much like to try and calm this situation, also. Do you suppose that you could put me in touch with Caulderwood?"

"I believe that I can," Steven had already planned a

return trip for Caulderwood. Perhaps there was still a chance to avoid bloodshed.

Several days later at Hoosier Pass just north of Bull Hill, Steven arranged a meeting of the two men, who had come to represent opposing armies within the United States. A formal exchange of prisoners took place by the two illegal forces. Superintendent McDonald and the two other miners from the Strong mine were traded for the five miners taken in the midnight shootout south of Victor.

Steven introduced Slocum to John Caulderwood, and the formal exchange was made as had been agreed to by both sides on a treaty of sorts that had been drawn up and passed back and forth. At the end of the exchange Slocum was still trying for further reconciliation.

"Mr. Caulderwood," Slocum proposed, "Governor Waite and me would very much like to have you join at Palmer College with the mine owners, and everyone sit down and work these differences out to the benefit of all."

"I would be happy to join in just such an effort," Caulderwood assured him.

After the meeting broke up, Caulderwood sought Steven out to thank him. "Steven, I really appreciate your efforts in being a go between for the WFM and the county."

"I hope that we can help in some way," Steven knew the problems.

"The owners will accept the three-dollar, eight hour day," Caulderwood was sure, "but they're going to want someone's hide for the violence. Mine among others," he looked Steven in the eyes, honestly.

"Governor Waite will Pardon," Steven gave the inevitable conclusion.

"If they don't lynch him," Caulderwood pointed out the obvious problem of making way through a belligerent crowd. "I would like you to go with me," Caulderwood asked, "As a friend, as a bodyguard," he shrugged. "Those attitudes in the Springs scare me," he admitted.

"Sure, John," Steven assured him. "I'll go with you." Steven was curious to be in the middle of this struggle. It seemed that there might be a solution in conference as Slocum was saying. He was aware of the history being made.

Some six days later, they sat together in the hall at Palmer College. The mine owners had refused to shake Caulderwood's hand or even acknowledge his existence. John had grown pale and went into the hallway. The crowd outside was growing, and it was not friendly. Steven had staked out a seat along the hall, and he and Caulderwood sat opposite each other. They listened as the Populist Governor Waite, with long white beard and hair like an Old Testament prophet regaled the owners with tirade after tirade about their unholy quest for money at the expense of their souls. He "forsooth", and "shamed" them with stories of their own opulence right out of the local papers with the plight of the men who worked their mines. He held up right beside the opulent new hotels being constructed with obscene profits from the mines, the misery of the workers. He puffed and turned red, then purple. He pounded his flat palm upon the table screaming, "Gentlemen, for shame!". He turned his back on them and then walked about the room, appearing to pray for their redemption, and mercy upon their souls in their time of Judgment.

He came back to his seat, and this time pounded the table with his fist, and reminded them that he was in charge of the Militia. He asked Sheriff Bowers about the unauthorized force at Hayden's Divide, and to what was its intent? At this point Bowers rushed out to try and learn that very thing from Commissioner Boynton, who had decided that he could run things better than Bowers and had placed three reporters in jail at Divide and cut the telephone wires.

The mine owners smiled at this, knowing that they were slowly pressuring Boynton into doing something. They finally agreed with Waite to accept the eight-hour, three dollar day. Stratton had already agreed to a nine-hour three twenty-five compromise before the attack on the Independence. They would under no circumstances agree to pardon those guilty of criminal acts. Those men would have to be arrested and stand trial, and that especially meant even "John Caulderwood".

The meeting broke up and a large crowd surrounded the building calling for Waite and Caulderwood, with calls for a rope mixed in. While a dignitary called the crowd around for a speech in the front of the building, the Governor, John, with Steven leading the way, as a scout and advanced guard, went out a back basement door and hurriedly made their way to the train station.

When they got to the station, Sheriff Bowers was waiting for them. He handed Governor Waite a written request. "Boynton is going to try and lead those fools on a frontal assault of Bull Hill," he told Waite. "He has to be stopped for his own good. Those Bull Hill boys will make mincemeat of all these fine men and friends of mine. Sir," he begged Waite, "won't you bring the Militia in between these two parties determined to spill blood?"

"Thank you Sheriff for requesting Militia assistance for El Paso County. I'll order Adjutant General Tarsney in between the two belligerents immediately."

They shook hands with the Governor, who departed on a train for Denver, while Steven and Caulderwood headed back to Cripple Creek on the Midland Terminal as far as Divide and then walked back to Altman. They managed to move unrecognized through the enraged camp as Boynton marched the men to and fro and gave endless speeches to bring the hot heads to a fever pitch.

226

Word of Waite's visit and then word that Tarsney was moving the militia to El Paso County reached Divide at the same time as Steven and John made a stealthy departure.

"Steven," Caulderwood told him, "I'm in this to the end and there is no telling what the end will be, but it's going to be hard to avoid violence. These men are not going to just give up, on either side. Tell Father Volpe what is happening, so that he can be prepared, as much as he can be."

"I'm not going back to Cripple, John. I'm going to Altman with you."

"You're not a miner. This is not your fight."

"I may not be a miner, but I work for wages. I can understand the mine owners being angry at the mine takeovers, but I've seen them piss on the groceries, and then refuse to sell food to the strikers and their families that have been blacklisted. It's not right," he shook his head. "I'm going with you, if you've got room."

"You're buyin' into a mess of trouble, I guess you know that."

"I want to be there. I support the Western Miners. Greed is no substitute for good business."

They walked on along the wagon road leading toward Beaver Valley, crossed the open land and climbed the back of Raven Hill and walked south to Altman. As they approached through the woods, they could hear the shouting of angry men. Men with guns at the ready approached and crouched behind trees. Caulderwood called out to them, in fear that someone with a nervous finger might take a shot.

"It's Caulderwood," they heard the message go up the trail.

Men surrounded them with anxious eyes. Tired and worn and hungry looks came from not only the men, but women and children, who had come down to see what

227

the shouting was about.

When a large group had gathered, Caulderwood held up his hands to stop the questions that flooded after him.

"They accepted the three-dollar, eight hour day, but they won't give up prosecution of the men that they say committed criminal acts."

A disgruntled murmur stirred through the crowd of men.

"How many and which acts," a voice shouted?

"Well, the Strong Mine explosion for starters. Any destruction of property."

"What are we gonna do," the cry went up?

"The problem," Caulderwood told them, "is that Bowers has lost control of the deputies he swore in, and Commissioner Boynton has control of about one thousand deputies over at Divide. Now, Bowers has asked Governor Waite to order Adjutant General Tarsney to bring the militia back to the District, but Boynton is mounting an attack, probably before Tarsney can arrive."

"We're gonna fight," a voice rose. Joined by many others, "We'll fight."

"We won't give up," Caulderwood held up his hands for quiet. "We can hold them off until the militia arrives, maybe we can negotiate an end that we can all accept."

The talk went on most of the night and very little sleep came until near daylight, when guard posts and lookouts had been perched atop the highest points looking down in every direction. Steven slept on the porch of Peter's and Smith's store with twelve other men, and many more inside. The lookouts began to come in near noon to report movement up Beaver Valley.

Men quickly rallied to every tree and rock just short of the clearing of the alpine valley that ran northwest to southeast on either side of Beaver Creek. The troops, with gatling gun, which was broken, and one cannon, which no one knew how to fire, paused short of the opening of the valley in the woods on the north side . In fact, very few of the men of the El Paso deputies had ever fired a gun before recently in Divide. On the other hand, many of the miners were crack shots.

Caulderwood called the men chosen for their sharpshooter ability around him. These were the men who would take position in the forward tree line. "You all understand," he instructed again, "that you are to shoot to miss until we are hit. We will not be the first to draw blood, and anyone disobeying this order will answer to me."

Across the alpine valley, Winfield Scott Boynton stepped out in front of the troops and surveyed the hillside and top of the rise of Raven and Bull Hill. "Men," he yelled gesturing toward the ominous rise in front of them, "they've seen us coming and fled. Follow me," he gave a forward signal and started across the clearing and crossed Beaver Creek. Not waiting for the gatling gun or the bulk of the force, he marched his way bravely forward to within about seventy-five yards of the tree line on the south, when his hat flew off. Angry bullets whizzed past his ears, and puffs of dirt rose by the dozens all around the left and right of his feet.

The troops behind Boynton dropped to the ground as bullets cut the dirt in front of them. Boynton, too, fell face down on the ground. The firing continued for several more seconds before it suddenly ceased. Boynton and the troops made a wise retreat to the north tree line of Beaver Valley.

Action ceased, until close to midnight, when Steven awakened on Smith and Peter's porch, to the sound of sporadic gunfire from the woods all around the base of Raven Hill's north side. Boynton had ordered a night attack, but when the troops met warning fire from the guard posts and began to return fire, they became disoriented and blasted away at each other, not knowing friend from foe. The only good thing to come out of the night attack was the fact that no one was killed, and only two men slightly injured. The gunfire continued with less and less firing until past one o'clock the next morning, and signal sentries continued to fire in code until past daylight, when outposts arrived to confirm that Adjutant General Tarsney had led the militia into position between the El Paso County deputies and the Western Federation of Miners.

Tarsney sent word to Boynton through Sheriff Bowers to stand down, which Boynton refused to do. There was a great deal of pressure on him from all the bluster that had made its way back to Colorado Springs. He was in a pique and marched his men to and fro and sent out patrols in all directions, trying his best to look military. The standoff continued into the next day, when Boynton sent the Stratton Brigade up Bull Hill in a frontal assault. Tarsney ordered Bowers to again stand down, and the order was obeyed just short of rifle range.

The Stratton Brigade turned its gatling gun around as at a funeral, and sang to the tune of "The Grand Old Duke of York":

> Oh!
> The Sheriff of El Paso County
> With all the Sheriff's men,
> He marched then up the hill, and then
> He marched them down again.
>
> And when they were up they were up,
> And when they were down they were down.
> And when they were only halfway up,
> They were neither up nor down.
> Oh!

And again, they sang over and over all the way

down.

Steven and all the miners, watching from the log ramparts along the top of Bull Hill breathed a collective sigh of relief. Tarsney ordered the miners to surrender to him and lay down their guns. They complied and Tarsney's militia marched into Altman to the cheers of the desperate men.

The next day Boynton ordered the entire contingent of El Paso deputies through the center of Cripple Creek, with a band playing, and all flags flying. They were, in fact, a mob, and they broke out every store window along Bennett Avenue, including the front windows of Elizabeth's Place. He continued out the south road toward Victor. The miners watched from the top of Bull Hill. Steven looked on as the militia and the miners struggled to understand what was happening.

As Boyton's mob of deputies marched along the lower road, as they neared Anaconda, Tarsney called to Boyton from the higher road about a hundred yards above him. "Commissioner Boynton," Tarsney yelled. "What, sir, have you got in mind?"

Boynton halted the march and called back, "We are going into camp around the Independence mine to protect against further damage to the property, valuable to us all."

Tarsney could accept this plan but warned, "If you or your men take one step toward Bull Hill, I will be forced to blow you off the side of the mountain into Wilson Creek!"

The march proceeded to the Independence Mine, and the Battle of Bull Hill came to an end.

Several days later the twelve hundred deputies had a grand parade down Tejon Street, with the police, and firemen, five hundred home guard, the county jail guards, with Susan Dunbar's Ladies Auxiliary bringing up the rear. All Colorado Springs turned out for the gala.

They marched to the courthouse where "three

hearty groans were given for Governor Waite and his man Friday, Thomas J. Tarsney."

Susan Dunbar gave thanks "to all the women for their willing devotion in sending their dear ones to the defense of our home. The city feels the high honor due not only the courageous men at the front, but the quiet heroines at the fireside."

Steven and John Caulderwood sat at Smith and Peter's saloon after dark on June twenty-second. "There's a warrant being issued on me," he told Steven over a beer. "I'm going to Denver and let things quiet down. I'll have to surrender and stand trial, but I may be able to control where that is, and who the Judge turns out to be."

"Do you know what the charges will be?"

"They will try to implicate me in the order to blow up the Strong mine."

"You weren't even in the area," Steven dismissed it.

"They will try to make a case," Caulderwood shrugged. "I'll plead that a man has a right to defend himself against an unlawful force."

A slight man with a slouch hat came in and asked to use the phone. The bartender made it possible and collected the fee for a three-minute call to Colorado Springs.

"Alamo Hotel," the stranger said, and then "Adjutant General Tarsney." They heard the man say, "Urgent."

Steven and Caulderwood looked questioningly at each other. In three minutes the bar tender collected another two bits for the extended time. The man pulled the slouch hat down, and a smile brushed his lips. A muffled cry of 'Help' escaped the receiver as the stranger hung up. He strode quickly to the door and disappeared into the Altman night.

"What do you suppose," Steven left the question

hanging.

"I know my men," John said, "and I never saw that one before."

At the other end of the phone line, the night clerk brought Tarsney the message, and he had quickly gotten dressed and come downstairs. As soon as he clutched the phone, four men entered the Alamo hotel foyer and pistol whipped him on the head. They pulled a bag over his head and carried him to a waiting taxi carriage. Joe Wilson carried a bag full of feathers and a can of tar filched from a local building site. Sherman Crumley, an ex-Dalton gang outlaw, drove the hack away at a run.

Sam Agard was on duty and making his rounds, when he saw the kidnapping take place. He chased the hack up the middle of Tejon Street, blowing his whistle with everything he had, until Pikes Peak Avenue, where he met Police Captain J. W. Gathright. Agard reported a possible kidnapping to Gathright, who ordered him sharply to, "Stop making all the fuss, and go back to your beat."

The hack left town along the Austin Bluff Road, and turned in at the home of William A. Otis, a Cripple Creek mine owner. There behind his barn, they kindled a coal oil fire and warmed the tar.

"Take off your clothes," one of them ordered Tarsney. He sputtered but complied.

They smeared him with warm tar and then dumped on the feathers. They walked him out to the Santa Fe line at the east edge of town.

"Tarsney, you were warned to leave town. You've brought this on yourself. Now walk toward Denver and keep walking." Which is what Adjutant General Thomas J. Tarsney did until he reached a farmhouse later the next morning.

Elizabeth was worried about Steven. He was reported by Stratton's men as 'kidnapped' by the strikers in late May. He had not come to the restaurant until late June when the Battle for Bull Hill was over. She had to stop herself from running to him across the room.

"I've worried about you," she began.

"I got deeply involved in the strike," he told her. I didn't get a chance to get you word. But I hated to break our regular buggy rides," he referred to the bi-weekly and sometimes weekly outings they had taken since December.

"Is the trouble over," she asked? She remembered how real it had been when the troops and the gatling gun had marched past the restaurant, breaking out windows.

"For now, things are getting back to normal. The mines are producing, and the Florence and Cripple Creek narrow gage is coming in around from Victor by the Fourth of July," he noted. "Then it will be much easier for me to come over from the Independence or my shack in Victor to see you."

That made her smile. "The F.&C.C. coming into Cripple Creek is going to set off a party that is going to last days," she reflected from previous July 4th celebrations in Cripple Creek. The town had always gone all out for Independence Day. "Everyone will be there," she predicted. "There will be thousands of people."

"I'll come in on the first train," he proposed, "if you will come and meet me."

"That would be fun," she agreed. "After all this strife, I'm ready for a parade other than military." She remembered again the armed, marching men who had passed so recently in front of her eyes.

Steven came in on the F.&C.C. train arriving July, 2nd . The Fourth of July party started two days early and ran well past. Everyone was there to greet the first train. Photographers recorded the crowd and train from every angle. There were twenty-seven photographers present. The crowd was enormous.

Elizabeth spotted Steven first, and holding on to Harry, who would not be left behind on such an exciting day, stayed close, as they moved toward the part of the train's mid-section where Steven was exiting from the arriving cars.

Emma Carr was following along for company, as George had got into conversation with Sheriff Hy Wilson, as Peter Eales walked the crowd looking for any weapons that might be showing. Finding a firearm in Cripple's 'no carry' zone fattened the school fund and Peter was well into working on a brand-new brick wing all by himself.

Emma gave Steven a hug when he got down from the train. It was like being hugged by an angel. He was being welcomed into the family, the close central family of the early District. The crowd surged around them, and the train belched a sooty, black, and smelly, almost blinding cinders and smoke. They moved away from the train where the wind was not blowing ash on them.

They had to yell in each other's ears to be heard above the crowd noise. Steven saw W. S. Stratton talking to some men, with his typical floppy hat, with some of the men dressed in top hats, bowlers, Stetsons, and an assortment of rough and fine dress. Lola Livingston stood close by to Stratton, with a half dozen Meyers Street girls of her employ, looking on and watching the crowd around Stratton.

The train whistle blew. Speeches were being made by principals involved in the project. "That's the Socials," Emma pointed out. "Charlie Tutt, and Spencer Penrose, they call him Spec, along with Charlie McNeil, and that big blond hanging onto all three is Sally Halthusen." Steven had seen Sally riding her big white horse up Bennett Street. "They're the talk of the town," Emma concluded.

"I wouldn't care for any of them," Elizabeth said pointedly, "and Sally is just an amateur." Steven noted the glaring look that Sally was giving Lola Livingston at the moment.

"Who are they," Steven questioned?

"The tall one is Spec Penrose," Elizabeth pointed. "His partner Charlie Tutt is between Win Stratton and Sam Strong. I don't know that other man with them." They saw Emma pointing at them, and then Elizabeth, so one of them said something to Stratton, who looked up and motioned for Steven to come over. He tried to get Elizabeth to come along, but she and Emma excused themselves.

"Steven," Stratton said, when he reached the group, "this is Charlie McNeil, and he's going to process some ore for us. Charlie, this is my engineer in charge of assaying, among other matters, for the Portland Company, and my own shipments also." McNeil took Steven's hand in a firm and sure grip.

The train whistle sounded longs and shorts, and repeated, then chugged back for the siding turnaround to get ready for the return trip. Steven stayed with the group. They were talking about a bold new plan.

"Spec Penrose wants to mill low grade ore," Win told him. "Now the little producers could use a sampling works, and we would all benefit. Charlie McNeil has a new chlorination process showing good promise."

"I've heard of its discovery and use, with moderate results in the Transvaal," Steven told him. "That's about all that I know about it."

"Well, Charlie, here is getting good results on even

low-grade ores, and I want you to work with him. I'm going to help bankroll a milling company, with Spec and Tutt, and McNeil, so see what you can do to help them find the proper price to pay for the various ores."

The talk slowed, and Steven excused himself and went back to find Elizabeth and Emma. He found them talking with Father Volpe and the Barbee family, Mabs, and Joince, and Kitty. She and Elizabeth were in conversation about berries.

"The raspberries are showing red color. They'll be ripe, dead ripe and past in a few days," Elizabeth told her.

"We need to get the pots and tents ready," the other woman said.

"What's this about raspberries," Steven asked? "You know that I love that jam you serve.

"Well," she told him, "Here's your chance to find out where it comes from. We go camping for several days, and all the families that are interested in picking berries go along. We can store a winter's supply, and I buy any excess for the restaurant."

"I might arrange to go along on a picnic like that," Steven agreed.

"Oh, not a picnic," Elizabeth corrected him. "It will be hard and hot work over the fires, after the berries are picked."

They were distracted by an excited movement of the crowd, as a door to one of the train cars was pulled back and presents to Cripple Creek from the farmers of the Arkansas Valley were unloaded. Out came flats of flowers of every sort, followed by fruit from the area, and all over the world, even bananas, and fruit that was out of season. A pile of watermelons was placed along the side, and the children dug in voraciously, and were soon soaked from the juice that ran down their chins.

They watched the crowd and laughed and talked with everyone they knew as everyone was here for the grand event. Steven stayed with Elizabeth until after dark. Harry had gone off on his on to someplace unknown, and Elizabeth was concerned for him. Steven assured her that he was known around the town, and he would be all right. Roman candles and pinwheels of fireworks set the night alight with colors of fire. The echoes of the explosions coming back from the sides of bowl of Cripple Creek reverberated around, adding to the big base drums being played by the marching bands.

They said a reluctant "good night" and kissed, separating with plans to meet the following Sunday morning, for a Sunday and Monday picking and preserving outing. Elizabeth's Place was closed for the 4th, which was Monday, and that let many others go picking, as they would normally have had responsibilities on a weekday. Elizabeth promised to provide a tent, as he had none. She thought she could borrow one from the Poseys.

Sunday dawned clear with a balmy mid-summer glow on the horizon. The wagons of six families met and trained out the south road toward Victor. Steven drove Elizabeth's buckboard with Harry sitting on a tent on the back with glass jars packed all around him. The jars tinkled merrily against their glass caps as the buckboard bounced along. They made their way into eight mile canyon or Phantom Canyon as it was coming to be called, and followed the stream along to a camp site they knew from years before.

The place was shaded by huge Cottonwood trees, and water was plentiful from a spring that fed the creek. Good water could be gotten from this spring near the side of the stream.

Mama Posey took charge of setting up the big kettles of various sizes for the berries, and her big blue enamel coffee pot. Each had its own fire, and the men gathered and chopped firewood and placed it around.

Raspberries abounded in the stream flood plain and

up the sides of the stream and adjoining gulleys for miles, in patches all along the valley floor.

From time to time the stillness of the wilderness was interrupted by the Florence and Cripple Creek railroad as one train after another made its way up Phantom Canyon. Sometimes the engineers would see the group of berry pickers and wave and blow the train whistle. The people would all stop what they were doing and wave back. The rest was silence and bird calls, with the sound of tent stakes being driven and wood being chopped.

Soon the picking began in earnest. Harry, Steven, and Elizabeth took the eastern side of the stream. Sam Posey with Jake and Betsey Hoopolieth went on the western side. Soon, buckets of raspberries were flowing back to the camp and Mama Posey's simmering pot of berry syrup. Mama stayed busy keeping the fires just right, but not so hot that the syrup was scorched.

When she had a batch ready, she would call Elizabeth, or one of the other women that was experienced with the process, to come help. Then they would carefully ladle the jars full, and then set the glass caps in place, submerge the jars into scalding hot water in the final kettle. They would allow the jars to heat and then, taking the hot jar and holding it with a rag, tilting it slightly, pour bees wax around the edge. This would fill the adjoining crack between the jar and lid. When the jar cooled, a vacuum was pulled on the inside of the jar, and the wax kept it sealed. No bacteria could grow, and thus the sweet syrup was preserved.

Things proceeded well until late in the afternoon. The Winchester family was staying close to Steven. They were a family that lived near the Barbees on Golden Avenue. Mr. Winchester seemed to want to talk to Steven about mining and carried on a stream of conversation with questions about Steven's experience in Europe and in Cripple Creek.

Harry had gone off looking for a private spot to relieve himself. He just had his pants down when the F.&C.C. train came into the clearing behind him. It blew its shrill whistle. Another form rose out of the raspberry's bushes between Harry and the train. It was huge and brown in the shadows. It's growl mixed with the whistle, and grew to a roar. Harry glanced over his shoulder and took a pull at his pants and missed, so he just ran out of one of the legs.

Steven, Elizabeth, and the Winchesters heard him yelling as he came up the trail.

"B—Bb--Bear!" He stammered it out.

Ol' Mose was coming along behind Harry in his slow deliberate way. He was known to mosey and that had given him his name. The slow walk was the result of bullet put next to his spine by Warton Pigg years earlier. He growled and slobbered berry juice as he came, a totally terrifying charge of fang and claw.

Harry just kept running, right past the little group and on down the trail in the woods. Mrs. Winchester screamed at the top of her voice, which in a few seconds alerted Jake and Betsey Hoopolieth across the ravine. Steven stepped in front of Elizabeth as the bear did a full charge, breaking off at the last instant. It was a faux charge and a challenge. The next charge would end in contact. The bear roared at them while showing his whole eleven-foot reach, making himself as big as possible to the enemy.

The whine and whiz of bullets coming far too close, was followed by the reports of rifle shots coming from the Hoopolieth sister and brother.

Ol' Mose heeded the shots and the smell of cordite that they brought, dropped abruptly, and turned and disappeared, crashing through the dense brush. He shielded himself from the rifle fire, as he chose to flee, this time.

The four humans huddled for a moment in shock at what might have happened. When they could move, they went toward the main camp.

"What were those shots?" They heard Mama Posey call Jake and Betsey. "Sam?" She called him. "What were the shootin'?"

"Bear, big bear," Jake called back. He and Betsey were moving toward camp from the other side.

"Everyone all right," she asked? Elizabeth, Steven, and the Winchesters came into camp.

"Harry, Harry," Elizabeth began to call.

"Everyone is fine, I'm sure Mr. Winchester assured Mama.

"Sister," Harry called from the edge of the camp, from behind some bushes. "Sister."

"Come on, here," she called.

"I can't sister. I messed my pants."

That brought a laugh to what could have been a tragic confrontation.

Later, that evening, around the campfire, they recounted the day.

"I might have hit him," Betsey Hoopolieth claimed. "He ran off didn't he?"

"He don't like guns, that's why he's still alive. He don't hang around where there are men and guns," Sam Posey told them.

"Well," Betsey slapped her 30-30 rifle, "he can't stand up to no thirty caliber, hundred and thirty grain, high velocity load." Betsey was a crack shot and fancied herself another Annie Oakley. She had done some carnival shooting with her brother Jake doing rope and whip tricks.

"Warton Pigg put a thirty-caliber shot right in his spine from a cliff above him, when he caught Ol' Mose in a trap that was set under water on a lake shore where he came to drink. He took that shot and pulled off two toes to

241

get away. That's how I'm sure it's Ol' Mose cause those toes are missing on the tracks he left today."

"He must not have hit a vital spot," Betsey insisted.

"Maybe not," Sam shrugged. "It's one big, tough bear."

"I'm going to bed, sister," Harry said.

"Fine, Harry, you know our tent. Sam," Elizabeth asked, "Where is the tent for Steven?"

Sam and Mama gave each other a look.

"Why, I believe it must be still on the wagon," Mama moved from the fire to the area where the wagons had been unhitched. The horses were chomping hay, some with feed bags, in a staked rope line.

Elizabeth followed her and watched as she rummaged through the bags and tarps with a perplexed look, talking to herself. "Now I know it must be here somewheres."

Elizabeth smiled politely. "Did you put it in the wagon, Mama," she asked?

"No, dear. I believe Sam did. Sam," she called, "did you get the other tent loaded?"

"No, Mama," he called back. "I thought you did."

"Well, dear me," Mama flopped a tarp back in place.

"What am I going to do now," Elizabeth asked Mama Posey? She saw a twinkle in the old woman's eye. "You and Sam did this on purpose, didn't you?" She accused her.

"Now Elizabeth," Mama advised, as she moved back towards the camp, "you can't catch flies with vinegar."

"You and Sam have put me in a very embarrassing situation."

"We're helpin' all we can," the old woman winked. Then added, "you all are jus' learnin' to be a family. That's all."

"Mama, that wasn't the plan, "Elizabeth protested.

"Well don't that beat all," Mama sagely advised. "Sam," she called, "you didn't load the other tent, and now Elizabeth is upset," she blamed it on him. "She says that now there's no tent for Steven."

"Well, can't he sleep in her tent with her and Harry? It's plenty big."

"They ain't married, dummy," Mama derided his ignorance.

"Oh," he spoke with exaggerated slowness. "Well now, back in my courtin' days we solved a problem like this with a bundling board. Everyone stays on their side of the board."

"Sam," Mama gave mock praise. "You always have a solution to bell the cat with. We got no bundling board."

"Here," Sam threw his crooked old stick cane at her feet. "Here's a bundling board. And, if'n he don't mind it, Elizabeth you use the cane on his head," Sam smirked, and then in a low tone added, "jus' be careful which head you hit." Only Mama Posey was supposed to hear, but several laughs rose around the fire. Elizabeth was too embarrassed to speak, and totally lacking an acceptable solution, turned and walked stiffly to her tent.

Mama said good night, and Sam rose to join her. Winchester moved closer to Steven.

"I came on this berry picking outing to ask you something," Winchester said to Steven, after the crowd had thinned to its tents. Only Jake and Betsey and Steven sat with him.

"Did you?" Steven was curious.

"You might know that I have finally gotten the lease on the Doctor-Jack Pot."

"No, I had not heard that."

"Well, I have, but I've no money left for the development. It has over twelve levels that need exploring. I only have enough money for a few blastings and a few days of mucking. It's a big chance, I know, but if I can hit a vein right off, I might be able to put it back in operation at a profit."

"Yes," Steven agreed. He could see where this was leading.

"Your experience in the area makes you the best man to advise where to drift in. Would you consider looking it over and advising for a share in what we find," Winchester asked?

Steven didn't hesitate for a moment. This was the kind of thing that he had hoped for. Stratton paid him well, and in shares sometimes, but this was more. This was a chance to own a significant piece of a producing mine.

"I'd be glad to do just that Mr. Winchester, and from what I know of the area around the Doctor-Jack Pot, the chances are better deep, around the 10th and 12th levels."

"When can you look her over," Winchester was anxious. "The clock is running on the lease and option."

"I can find some time by mid-week, maybe on Wednesday," he promised.

"Very good," Winchester was really pleased. He had the promise that he had been after on this trip. The one that he needed from someone with expert knowledge of the area around the Doctor-Jack Pot Mine.

Winchester excused himself and left for his tent, leaving Jake and Betsey with Steven around the fire.

"I'm goin' after that bear in the morning," Betsey said with great determination.

"Betsey, that's crazy," Jake told her. "Why would you want to shoot that old bear?"

"Why Jake," she defended her enthusiasm, "that's Ol' Mose, the most famous Grizzly in the whole state. If'n I killed him, I'd be famous. Ned Buntline might write one of them dime novels about me. I'd be famous as Annie Oakley."

"You could end up bear shit, too," Jake warned.

"I ain't a'feared," she stuck out her chin.

"Then you ain't got good sense," he tossed a stick into the fire to end it and stalked off to his tent.

"Well," Betsey said to Steven after some time spent gazing into the fire," I guess if'n I'm goin' after that bear in the morning, I'd better turn in."

"Good night," Steven bid her. He wondered what the next day might hold for her. He watched the fire a little longer and then picked up Sam's cane and walked to Elizabeth's tent.

Harry was snoring when he stuck his head inside the flap. "Elizabeth," he questioned? She said nothing but moved slightly as if to make room. "I'm putting Sam's cane down between us." She turned face up, but didn't speak. He was as quiet as he could be, but Harry awoke and turned to look at him.

"Are you two going to have sex now," he asked? Elizabeth's body went rigid. No one spoke for some time.

"What do you know about sex," she asked him.

"Oh, I know all about it," Harry assured her in a confident voice.

"How's that," she continued to question him?

"One of the girls down the alley in back of our place gives me sex for the money you pay me, sometimes."

Elizabeth was shocked. Harry had become a grown man while she still thought of him as her little brother. "Which one," she asked him?

"Bessie. You don't know her. She likes me, and I take her left over food."

"You're taking food from the kitchen to her?"

"Only stuff people leave on their plate and don't eat. Don't seem like it should go to waste, and Bessie

245

shares it with some of her friends."

Elizabeth was silent for a long time. Steven could hear her steady breathing.

"Sometimes Bessie lets me stay when she has a customer. I just pull up a blanket and roll in a ball in a corner, and don't no one know I'm even there. I can roll up small," he offered.

Nothing was said for some time. Finally, Elizabeth told him, "It's all right Harry. You don't need to roll up."

Words stopped and the camp silence settled into the tent. The bundling board stick lay between the two, but fingers found fingers through a curved part in the stick.

There were promises in those fingers, tenderly touching. Elizabeth had never enjoyed this type of innocent love play before, and it made her feel light as a feather. She felt as if she were floating, and fell into a dreamless and peaceful sleep, fingers entwined.

Early the next morning, well before good light, the camp began to stir. Mama Posey had the blue enamel coffee pot full of strong coffee. She was already building up the cooking fires so that nice hot coals would be soon ready for heating more syrup. Betsey Hoopolieth was saddling her horse, tightening the cinch strap and examining the latigo for any twist. Jake stood next to her trying to dissuade her.

Mama Posey got wind of the idea Betsey had in her head and came over to where she was saddling up. "We didn't come on no bear hunt," she began. Betsey kept working her gear. "This is many fewer buckets of berries," she chided. "Jus' remember that when you're a digin' into the jam this winter." She could see it was doing no good. "Ah, what's the use? Tryin' to talk you out of somethin' when your head is set is like sayin' sic'em to a bulldog." She stood looking and worrying as only a mother can do.

"Betsey," Jake tried again, "don't go."

Betsey put her rifle in its boot and swung into the saddle.

"Jake, you got to go with her," Mama ordered. Jake's shoulders slumped, but he moved to saddle his own horse.

"I'm goin' to pick up his trail," Betsey pulled her horse around. She was all smiles, pert and pretty with yellow hair gleaming in braids in the morning sun.

"Jake rode after her as fast as he could saddle. She was looking at some tracks in the creek bed, and just as he got to her, she rode on down the trail.

Ol' Mose was not hard to follow in the soft earth of the valley floor. Sometimes he crossed hard ground, but rocks were moved and Betsey had no trouble finding the markings.

When old Mose crossed a stream, there were those three toed prints deep in the mud from a frame that started in the springtime at over one thousand pounds and this time of year, with him fattening up for winter, over eighteen hundred pounds of grizzly bear.

Jake could never quite catch up to Betsey as she trailed in front of him all morning. It was about noon when she found a spot she was pretty sure was the place the bear had bedded down for the night. It was between some rocks with a ledge above. She pulled her rifle and dismounted her horse and began to look around.

The F.&C.C. noon train came up Phantom Canyon and the noise of the train drowned out the whinnying of her horse as it shied away and ran.

The first indication she had was the smell of damp fur. She knew he was behind her. She had the rifle in hand in front of her and she laid it on her shoulder pointing backwards. She pulled the trigger. The explosion in her head was not the rifle going off. That was the last she remembered for some time.

She awoke once. The bear was sitting on his

haunches with his back turned part way to her, and he was watching her in a sideways manner from time to time. Their eyes met and locked. Betsey tried to be dead. Dead.

He came at her again in a fury. He grabbed her head in his jaws and she thought he would crush her skull. He shook her fast, as if he wanted her to understand, or die. She was still conscious when he marked her all over her face. She was his. She was his meat.

Jake saw Betsey's horse come running, terrified, back down the trail. He knew that something was wrong. He rode faster.

"Betsey," he called over and over. He found her smashed form where it lay.

"Betsey," he wailed. He bent down to her. She was unrecognizable. Her hair was a crimson oozing mass. Her face was chewed like pounded round. He listened for her heart and thought he heard a beat. "Betsey."

He got his rifle and looked around nervously. This had just happened. He spread a tent he carried out flat, made a traverse, and placed Betsey on it. He started back to camp as easy as he could go and still maintain enough speed to get back to camp by dark.

They heard three shots in the distance and asked each other if they had heard the shots. A few minutes later the shots were closer. Men rode out to see what the warning shots meant. They were soon back with the news. Betsey Hoopolieth was mauled by a bear, and they were bringing her, or what was left of her into camp. Mama collapsed and had to be put on a cot.

Betsey was alive it was determined, and plans were made to take her to a doctor in Cripple Creek. "The town of Victor is having a Fourth of July parade today," Steven said. "The same problem in Cripple Creek; who might have an office open?"

""There's a new woman doctor in town opening an office right down the street from me on Bennett,"

Elizabeth told Jake. "Her name is Doctor Anderson, and she's a surgeon. Jake, she is the best chance that you have of finding a Doctor on July 4th. She will probably be working in her office, across the street in the next block, just a few doors west of my restaurant."

Jake rode ahead to try and find a doctor. He found the office with "Doctor Anderson-Surgery" on the door and burst into the office.

"Are you Doctor Anderson," he asked to the petite, dark haired, young woman?" She looked up from the task of arranging her office.

"Yes," she told him.

"My sister's been mauled by a bear and she's tore up and bleeding bad. They're bringing her in from Eight Mile Canyon."

Susan grabbed her bag and quickly chose bottles from her stock. She tightened her hair bun against a trip in the wind, and asked Jake to go on to Alonzo Welty's stable, down the block, and around the corner to get a buckboard ready, and then bring it to her office. She was ready when he got back with the buckboard. Susan took the reins and Jake mounted up. They took off toward the Victor Road at as fast a pace as was safe.

They met Steven and Elizabeth with Betsey in the buckboard just north of Anaconda, and pulled under a tree in a glade. Susan tended her as best she could. When Betsey saw Jake she tried to talk.

"I saw him thinkin' Jake. He was thinking about killing me." Her eyes brimmed with tears. "He let me live, Jake. He let me live, but he marked me real good." Blood gurgled from between her teeth where her mouth was torn badly.

"Hush now," Doctor Anderson ordered. "I'm going to give you a little laudanum. It will make you sleepy. Try to swallow this." She gave her a potion from a vile.

"Who are you," Betsey asked?

"I'm Doc Susie," Doctor Anderson soothed her worry, "and you're going to be just fine."

They lifted her into the doctor's buckboard where some clean padding had been placed. They were turning to head to the office when Sam and Mama Posey caught up and joined them.

Doc Susie cleaned and sewed almost all the way through the night, until dawn. She took one-hundred sixty-seven tiny stitches, as small as she could make them. She sewed the flap of scalp back on the right side of the back of Betsey's head, where she had first been hit. Then she went to work on the face. It was a jigsaw puzzle but only a small piece was missing from the left corner of Betsey's mouth. Doc Susie managed to sew Betsey's face back together. Now if only no infection set in, which was always the worry.

She came out about daylight to face the crowd of worriers in her small office. Elizabeth rose to meet her, as the doctor pulled off a bloody smock.

"She's going to be fine," Doc Susie assured the haggard crowd, who had watched through the night.

"What about her face?" Elizabeth asked the question everyone was afraid to ask.

"Well," Doc Susie smiled. She knew when she had done a good job, and she was tired. "She may smile a little crooked, but we got most of the parts in the right place, I think."

Mama Posey burst into tears and Sam held her looking accusingly at Jake, like he should have been there to stop the bear. Jake just rubbed his face and blubbered like a baby. He had been so frightened that she was dead when he found her, or that they would lose her from blood loss.

"Thank the Lord," someone said.

Steven made his way along third street south, avoiding the crowd waiting for the interurban line's Arrow Electric cars that ran up the center of Bennett Avenue. He made his way south to Myer's Avenue and then turned into the pink brick structure of The Old Homestead. He waved at Spec Penrose sitting next door at the Topic Dance hall having a morning cup of coffee.

He entered the door into the well appointed and plush receiving room. He made his way along the stairs to the second floor viewing area, and down the hall to the room that he was familiar with from many visits. He rapped lightly on the door.

A lovely dark-haired, dark eyed beauty opened the door to him. Lola Livingston stood in bodice and garters. Winfield Scott Stratton lay on the four-poster bed behind her. He was propped up by thick pillows, with various papers spread in front of him.

"Come in, come in," he impatiently motioned and called Steven into the room.

They talked about the business of the day. He gave a report on how the chlorination process with Charlie McNeil was coming. Production rates and projections for the Portland and Independence groups were discussed in detail for the coming week.

Lola Livingston dressed and excused herself.

"By God," Stratton was beaming a smile this morning, "this is the way a man should live." He took a big swig of ten-year-old single malt whiskey from the glass in his hand. "I may not go back to the Springs for a month."

"It must be expensive," Steven reflected.

"Not so's I'd notice," Stratton assured him. "How are things at Wilson Creek," he asked?

"I'm doing fine. It's close to the work, and I've gotten drawing tables put along the wall with good light. I'm all fixed up, except running water, but the cistern is working right now."

"Well, I guess we could afford to modernize it a little."

"Not necessary," Steven could stand the inconvenience just like Stratton had for years. Stratton had given him use of the cabin near Wilson Creek when he had moved to the house in the Springs. When he was in Cripple Creek now, he took a swank room at the Palace, or stayed at The Old Homestead, as he was now.

They finished the business of the day, and Steven departed. He passed Lola Livingston in the hallway talking with a man seated in the upstairs viewing area. Three or four of the girls were posing for him behind the viewing glassed in area. Steven found he was not immune to the charms of the paramours. The sights and smells, and sounds coming from some of the rooms, and the pleasant, soft settings, fixed themselves in his mind. Everywhere he looked, suggestive eyes beckoned his.

He made his way outside. Spec Penrose was still drinking coffee at the Topic, and Steven joined him.

"Morning, Spec," he greeted.

"Morning," Penrose was somewhat sullen.

"You sound peeved," Steven ventured.

"I just put on a friend of mine from Denver at the real estate office to collect rents for me, and he went into The Old Homestead to see Lola, I knew she was with Stratton, over there. He went in forty minutes ago, and hasn't come out yet." He drank another sip and set his cup down hard in consternation.

Sally Halthusen made a fine figure on her big white

horse. She stiffened when she saw Spec sitting at the table in the Topic.

"Hi, Sally," Penrose called jovially to her. Sally didn't turn, she rode on, her solid rump twitching with the gait of the horse. "She won't talk to me," Spec laughed.

"I thought you two were an item," Steven quoted what he had heard.

"Awe, she wants to get married, right away. She wants this big ranch up north and west in the Platte River country. She wants all these fancy thoroughbred horses. I got tired of her yap." He shaded his eyes against the morning sun and watched her ride southeast. "She's got her eye on Tutt now," he chuckled. "He's got his hands full, that's for sure. She's ridin' up to Tutt's cabin."

"Tom Sharkey fights here tonight," Spec told him, changing the subject to more recognized sport. "Otto Floto arranged it against Jim Flynn. The "Sailor Boy" and Bob are going for a fast four rounder. The whole Upper Tens will be here," he referred to the ten biggest producing mines and their superintendents.

"That would be a fine sight," Steven agreed.

"If A. E. Carlton comes and Ethel Frizzel is there, we might see a hair pulling cat fight with the lady that Albert is with tonight, as prelude to the main event. Word is that Ethel filed a lawsuit on Albert for breach of promise."

At that moment a man emerged from the front door of The Old Homestead. "Charlie," Penrose yelled, "what in hell took you so long? Did you get the money?"

"Not exactly," the man stuck his hands in his pockets and started walking to join them.

"What does 'not exactly' mean?"

"Well, me and Miss Livingston had a long talk, and now Spec, don't get mad. Me and her decided that I should take the rent out in trade."

"Crap," Penrose swore, "she did it again. I can't

253

send anyone to collect from her, and I've never been able to withstand her either. That woman is good at it."

Spec began a conversation with the man, and there being nothing of interest to Steven, he rose and ambled on west along Myers Avenue. He was just turning to the north and headed uphill when Pearl De Vere came around the corner from the Welty stable. She was dressed in a stunning red velvet suit, with matching hat and feather, and sitting tall and erect on a spirited horse that she loved to ride side saddle, called "She Devil". She passed by him and the smell of her famous, and fine French perfume caressed his nose.

Everywhere that Steven looked he was confronted face on with sex. It was a springtime mountain phenomenon. He found himself in front of Elizabeth's Place, just looking in the front door at her. She saw him and smiled and continued with the work that she was doing. A strand of hair fell across the sweat on her face. She brushed it aside and noticed Steven still looking at her. She gave him a quizzical look. He made up his mind that he was going to have to talk to her. He felt like he might just bust wide open with his need for her.

Betsey Hoopolieth was helping in the restaurant, and Harry hustled and bussed dishes, while Betsey washed. The red and jagged scars, with stitches still showing, told of the terrible mauling that she had managed to survive. He sat and ordered breakfast and coffee. The two girls chatted about a planned shopping trip they were going to make that afternoon after the lunch crowd had cleared out. The recession that had struck the country had put most things on half price sales, and fine dresses and men's suits had been reduced from sixteen dollars on average to around eight.

"Steven," Elizabeth invited, "come along with us and shop for clothes."

"I have some paper work at the Mining Exchange,

but I can be finished by two-thirty or so, and I'll try to catch up with you two ladies in one of the shops along Bennett." Then as an afterthought, "Elizabeth, there is a fight at the Topic tonight, and everyone that is anyone is going to be there. Want to go with me?"

Bare knuckle fisticuffs was not Elizabeth's idea of fun, and she used her duties at the restaurant to beg off the invitation. "Why not come by after the fight, and I will be closing, we might still have a chance to visit," she offered when she saw the disappointment on his face.

He brightened at that, and they made plans to see each other that evening, as well as Steven promised to try and find the two that afternoon for some window shopping along Bennett.

What Steven hadn't told Elizabeth, could not tell, and it was an important confidence, was that he had a meeting at the Mining Exchange with Josiah Winchester. There was very good news to give and plans to discuss concerning the Doctor-Jack Pot Mine. Steven had followed up on the offer to partner with Winchester, and shortly after the excitement of the berry picking outing, had begun an investigation of the potential of the old abandoned mine.

He had begun by charting strike and dip of the various veins in mines that he had worked in the area. The Doctor-Jack Pot had been a grand producer in its early days, but the vein had pinched out, and the owners had gone broke looking to recover the lead. Eventually the mine was in receivership, and the abandoned shaft was overgrown. The shops had been removed, and the claim was considered by all to be worthless. Worthless in everyone's estimation except Josiah Winchester.

Winchester spent a lot of his time in Denver, buying and selling mining stock and promoting. He made little money at it but had managed to save the small amount that the First National Bank in Denver wanted for the lease. They would have taken any offer, considering Winchester a fool to try the claim. This had given him the name around the District as "Windy Joe", and almost everyone was laughing at him behind his back. Steven knew better.

After careful calculations, he was sure that the vein must be findable somewhere between the abandoned and deep tenth and twelfth levels. Winchester was tapped out with just acquiring the lease, and had borrowed money from Herbert Warne, a fat and lazy old man, who now resided in the Winchester home, sitting in the choice spot in front of the fire, while Mrs. Winchester swept around him, and he ate gumdrops one after the other, without ever offering the children a single candy.

Steven had invested mostly time but had also hired a small crew with his own money to clear the way to a promising section of the twelfth level, and had begun a crosscut. With Steven's careful calculations, they set the first charge, and when the dust cleared, and torches brought, sylvanite ore glittered with gold flakes, dazzled the miners.

Steven waited for Winchester in the foyer of the Mining Exchange. Josiah entered right on time, tall and erect, with a quiet dignity. Mabs Barbee's face appeared at the window for an instant. The girl was always running all over town peeking in windows, and Winchester, whom she called Uncle Si, was a favorite neighbor of hers.

"Bon Chance, Steven," he gave a Natchez greeting, and put out a hand, that was long with finely formed fingers, with immaculately manicured nails. He had a warm and trusting personality that effused confidence and charm, in an enchanting Mississippi drawl.

"Josiah," Steven returned the firm handshake, "let's go into the conference room over here," he indicated a nearby room with plush accommodations, "where we can spread out some papers and talk in private."

256

Steven led the way to the conference room, and they seated themselves at one end of a long table. Spreading out charts, and taking out notebooks and pencils, they began to make plans for serious work on the twelfth level of the Doctor-Jack Pot.

"The assay is great," Steven showed Josiah the reports from the assay office in Anaconda, near where the mine was located. "There is thousands in gold showing, and there's more. But we are going to need some capitol, more than I can come up with. Is Warne good for any more money?"

"Warne was good enough to make a loan, but I don't want any more money from him," Winchester disclosed. He's a bit of a nuisance to the Mrs., and I think I will go to Denver and form a company to raise the money. I have a lawyer there named Archibald M. Stevenson, who has served me very well in dealings with First National Bank of Denver, and with this assay, and a new holding company, I can issue enough stock to the bank to get the capital to begin."

"That sounds like a good course of action, and I think that I can squeeze out a few more dollars from my own money to keep development work going until you can put it together."

"I will issue a million common shares, and what blue chip that I can get the bank to recognize as capital assets. There is really none too little salvageable capital assets to speak of, so for the time being, Steven, you may have to take common stock to offset your investment in time and money. Is that going to be alright with you?" Winchester looked anxiously at Steven.

"That is the gamble that I am willing to take Josiah," Steven told him straight up. "You know that I have learned that you are a man of your word."

A warm feeling of friendship came over the two men, as they each found someone that they could trust.

They went over the exact equipment that they would need, cut the expenses to the bone, and figured the manpower that it would take to stope the section that was filled with gold, in sight. Figuring shipping and refining cost, they came up with a projected profit for the first three months of work. It was healthy, and they smiled at each other, and shook their heads in agreement.

The meeting broke up about two-thirty that afternoon, and Josiah left the Exchange building confident that his ship had at last come into port. Steven rolled up the paperwork and took it to an office that Stratton kept in the building, and placed the papers in the safe, and in jubilant spirits, walked along Bennett Avenue, looking for the two shopping ladies, and window shopping for a new suit, while the prices were good.

About two that afternoon, Betsey and Elizabeth were slowly walking along the north side of Bennett window shopping when they came to the Cabinet Saloon. In one window hung the sign, "Fortune Telling, Tarot Card Reading, Know Your Future." Smaller letters on the sign read "mines located, love life revealed, health and happiness foretold." Then in big bold letters at the bottom, "Madam Vida De Vere."

"Elizabeth," Betsey suggested, "let's get our fortunes told."

"I don't put much stock in such nonsense," Elizabeth frowned, but then looking at Betsey's disappointment, "but if you would like, I'll go with you."

Betsey beamed a smile that threatened to pull out stitches. The two women entered the parlor and were met and escorted to a waiting area by a young girl. The interior was dimly lit, but magical symbols and mystic tapestry hung on the walls heralding the value of the art of divination. They waited in a plush surrounding of well upholstered chairs and couches, opposite a curtain covered in Egyptian hieroglyphics.

After a wait of some ten minutes, the curtain suddenly parted and a dark haired, slender woman made a dramatic entrance. She said not a word, as she looked from first one woman to the other. Madame Vida De Vere was dressed in a long gypsy dress, full of color and embroidered with mystic designs from hem to bodice. She had an erect posture, and a face that was both smooth and lined in character. She had a classic Romanian nose, long and sharp pointed at the tip. She motioned for the women to follow her, and parting the curtain, led them into the reading room.

Symbols lined the room, and she seated herself behind a table that had a single object in the center covered by a red silk cloth with a golden fringe around the edge. She motioned for the two women to take their seats opposite her in chairs that were arranged on the opposite side of the table. "You have come to learn of your future," she told them in an Eastern European accent.

"Can you read our fortunes," Betsey blurted. "I would love to know what the future holds."

"The stars foretell, they do not compel. Are you here for a Tarot reading, or do you want me to gaze at your future in the Crystal Ball?"

"Oh, the Crystal Ball," Betsey effused in infectious enthusiasm.

Madame De Vere turned her gaze on Elizabeth. "And you," she asked.

"I don't believe in such things," Elizabeth told her flatly.

"I see," the gypsy nodded. She then held out her hand, palm up.

"How much," Betsey asked? "How much for a Crystal Ball reading?"

"Let your conscience be your guide," she demurred, and waved the hand slightly to make the point.

Betsey pulled out a five-dollar gold piece and

259

placed it in the hand. Elizabeth looked in her purse and found a one dollar Greenback. Madame De Vere accepted the gold piece with a sly smile, while she gave a sharp snort at the Greenback, but tucked that away as well. "Let us begin," she said, and with a flourish, pulled the silk cloth from the top of the object in front of her to reveal a stunningly polished Crystal Ball almost twelve inches in diameter. She looked at Betsey, "Please place the tips of your fingers on the base like this," she showed Betsey how to touch the supporting base with just her fingers.

When this was done, she let her head fall back onto the back of the chair that she was sitting in, and as her eyes rolled into the top of her head, let the eyelids droop, until they were almost closed. She remained in this position for close to a minute, and then her head came forward, and she stared intently into the center of the Crystal Ball. After a few moments she began to speak, in a voice that was her own, and yet different, slightly higher in pitch, with a hint of excitement. "I see two brown eyed children. They are a boy and a girl. They wear the feathers of the Red-Tailed Hawk in their hair. They are your grandchildren." Moments passed, as she stared deeper and deeper into the Crystal. Betsey stared with her, and she caught a hard sharp breath of anticipation. The gypsy woman began to speak again. "I see a clear, sparkling, blue lake, high in the mountains. I see living waters flowing from the lake to the people below. The children and the lake are one." There was a long pause, and then the enchantment was gone. "That is all," she said with finality.

"Grandchildren," Betsey had tears in her eyes. "Thank you, oh, thank you." She was so very pleased, that Elizabeth was glad that they had come.

"And now you, my little unbeliever," Madame De Vere turned to Elizabeth. "If you would place your fingers on the base." Elizabeth did as she was bidden, feeling somewhat foolish. The gypsy woman again let her head fall back, and then in a few moments gazed into the Crystal again. At first she had a confused look on her face, and then a look of trouble that soon took on the visage of terror. She moaned and then slumped in the chair, and did not move for many moments. Fear seized Elizabeth that the woman had been struck by a stroke.

"Madam," she finally asked her. "Are you alright?"

The gypsy stirred and then sat up. A stoic look came across her face. "Your fate is unknown," she told Elizabeth. "It is still to be formed. I can only tell you that in your hour of need, a man's strong hand will be the saving of you."

Elizabeth got a look of consternation on her face. "Indeed," she huffed. "A good Greenback for that?" The air hung thick between them. Madame De Vere said nothing more and seemed to be removed in trance to other matters, as the women rose and left the parlor.

Outside, Steven emerged from the Mining Exchange building into a bright and cool afternoon. The street was alive with hundreds of people walking up and down. An electric Arrow car moved down the center of the street on its steel track loaded with shoppers and tourists. There were over twenty thousand people living in town now, and many more thousands in the small cities that surrounded Cripple Creek on all sides. Prospectors led mules, phaeton carriages carried men and women in fine dress with high stepping matched, and blooded horses pulling them. The harnesses glistened black with polish and ostrich plumes adorned the heads of horses and ladies. Occasional motor cars, Stanley Steamers, threaded their way through the menagerie of people, horses, donkey's, dogs, carriages. News boys ran among the crowd hawking papers from the latest edition to arrive of the New York Times to The Cripple Creek Crusher, just off the press.

The train had just arrived from the Springs. A train arrived every few minutes now, as the Midland and the Florence lines competed in a life and death struggle for passengers and freight. Collbran and Gillett had completed the Midland Terminal into Cripple some months behind the F.&C.C., and men and women strolled down from the station that commanded a grand position at the east end of Bennett Avenue. They came in throngs of people, walking dogs or twirling their parasols, and walked west along Bennett in a slow procession. Steven recognized two of the strollers. Count Portales and his cousin-wife, Bertha, the Countess, came past. The Count sported his full dark beard, a three-piece suit, topped by a pork pie hat. He puffed his pipe in his right hand and carried a little dachshund in the crook of his left arm. The countess was being pulled along by two great Russian Wolf Hounds, who stopped to sniff each of the many telephone and electric poles they passed, as well as the brand-new fire plugs.

This brought back memories of his first day in town, and the first time he had seen Elizabeth that Sunday morning some three years earlier. He thought of those cozy days The Angelic Emma Carr had gone off to join her husband in Oklahoma. George Carr had left to get in on the Cherokee Strip land rush with Joe Wolf, when the editor of the Cripple Creek Crusher had waged a campaign against Joe's crooked wheel at the Clarendon, and run Joe out of town. George Carr had liked Oklahoma, and Emma had joined him there, never to return. They were missed, and those halcyon days were gone.

Steven stepped aside to let the Count and Countess, with their dogs, pass by. The Silesian Lord and master of Glumbowitz was rumored to be selling the Broadmore Property just west of the Springs to Tutt and Penrose, when it failed as a gambling establishment. Tutt and Penrose were making a fortune along with Charlie

MacNeil and Stratton, milling low grade ores from the small producers using the new chlorination process. Several new mills, and one huge one was in phases of production and construction.

The cozy community had been replaced by a bustling and thriving modern city. Very few modern buildings existed. The original greenwood, false fronted stores, stood weathered, dried and cracked, and many were unpainted.

Horses and riders, mixed with mules, donkeys, and old prospectors, treaded among the carriages, buckboard, phaetons, electric cars, and foot traffic. Except for shabby clapboard, wooden store fronts, this could have been mistaken for St. Louis, or even New York City.

Steven caught a glimpse of Elizabeth and Betsey just coming out from the Cabinet Saloon that contained the fortune telling of Madame Vida De Vere. He hurried to catch up to them. Rinky-Tink piano music flowed from the saloons he past, and he recognized the frenetic banging out of "Do You Like Tootie Fruitie" as he passed The Buckhorn. The windows along the way were filled with goods on sale. He caught up with the two ladies as they stopped gazing at the work in the window of the photography studio just passed Johnnie Nolan's at the corner of Third Street.

"Oh, Steven," Betsey greeted. "We had our fortunes told, and I'm going to be a grandmother."

"I don't doubt it," Steven laughed at her obvious joy. "And what was your fortune?" He asked Elizabeth.

"I don't believe in such nonsense," she told him, and turned back to the pictures in the window.

"She's got an unknown future," Betsey revealed.

"So do we all," Elizabeth chastened her, and then brightening, and hooking an arm through Steven's said, "let's get our pictures taken."

They all agreed to this novelty and went in to have

the flash powder blind them several times, as the photographer poised them on his couch. They strolled and shopped until the evening dinner hour approached and the two ladies went back to work at Elizabeth's Place.

Steven had tea and scones with raspberry jelly and lingered there until around six in the evening, when he headed for The Topic where the crowd was beginning to gather for the fight.

The Topic was about sixty feet wide and over a hundred fifty feet long with a high ceiling on the first floor. A ring, twenty by twenty was built up in the center for the Friday night fights, which Otto Floto promoted each week. Tiers of seats rose on all sides with only a narrow aisle between the seats and the ring.

Steven found a seat on the west side near the center. The crowd was growing, and bets were being made. High grade ore of sylvanite and calaverite, with gold crystals as big as a thumb nail were coming out of every pocket and being matched to other crystals side by side. Cripple Creek miners would bet high-grade on which way the wind would be blowing at the drop of a hat. Gold coins matched gold coins, and Greenback matched Greenback dollars, but high-grade was the preferred bet, and everyone had some.

Frank Peck was one of the first of the millionaires to arrive, passing out cigars to anyone that wanted one, until the air was purple with cigar smoke. Boys moved in the stands selling bottles of ice-cold beer. Spec Penrose arrived with Grace Carlyle, his new sweetie from the Mikado. Tutt came in with Sally Haltusian. The two groups ignored each other, although the men came together for a moment to place a bet with each other.

Stratton came in with Lola Livingston in a pearl and lace gown with matching white lace hat. They went to a reserved section almost directly across from Steven. Sam Strong came in with his girl from The Homestead. A.

264

E. Carlton came in with Ethel Frizzel on his arm and took a box seat on the north. Evidently Ethel and Albert had settled their quarrel.

Otto Flotto was making the rounds of the ring on all sides and making secret sign language as to numbers to his boss, H. B. Levie, who owned the Butte Opera House, which Otto managed for him, down the street to the west. Levie was the king of the tenderloin, owning many of the cribs east of The Homestead, where foreign girls worked, and toward Poverty Gulch, where the black prostitutes were found. Levie chomped on a big cigar and wrote in a book the information that Otto was relaying to him in hand signals. More and more of the rich mine owners and their superintendents gathered into the reserved box seats.

A warmup fight was started. They were two unknowns that Otto had found, brawlers from the local bars, who were eager to make a name, and maybe escape the muck bucket and climb to stardom in the ring. They went at each other in a savage one round all out fight. The betting and noise swelled. The drinking became more profuse, and the smoke thicker.

The first bout came to a sudden end with a terrific right hook and a knockout. The ring was cleaned up and the bets settled, and a new round of betting commenced. Jim Flynn came to the ring first and took his corner. The "Sailor Boy" made his appearance and entered the ring. He flexed and postured for the crowd, amid cheers and catcalls.

Jimmy Burns had come in alone and took a box seat near Stratton. Jimmy Doyle came in and looked around and saw Burns, came the other way to near Steven and took a regular seat on one end. Steven saw Stratton notice and frown. The word was that the two were on outs with each other over a dispute about managers, and hot accusations had been flung back and forth with each man thinking that he had been cheated out of his fair share of some of the Portland bonanza. Stratton had tried to talk some sense into them, but their stubborn Irish nature had caused the quarrel to continue. The two men glared at each other across the ring.

The Woods brothers came in from Victor and took box seats near Stratton. The Bernard brothers came in with Joncie Barbee. They were slapping him on the back and offering to buy him beer. The word was that they wanted to buy his Ajax mine for ten thousand dollars, and that Barbee had accepted their offer, but papers had not been signed.

The referee called the two pugilists to the center of the ring and they touched gloves. The bell rang for the first round, and the men met in the center. They sparred and tested each other's reach and circled for an opening.

Flynn let loose a mighty round house hook and Sharkey blocked it and knocked Jim's head back with a stiff straight jab with his left hand to the left cheek of the fireman, which snapped his head back. The crowd exploded with cheers. The "Sailor Boy" moved in with more jabs but couldn't connect a solid punch as Flynn gave ground and circled the ring backward. The crowd booed and hissed, trying to make him stand and fight. The bell rang for the end of the first round, and the men went to their corners.

It went round after round with Sharkey connecting jabs and Flynn throwing murderous hooks, just when he seemed all in. In the eighth round the exhausted men clinched in the middle of the ring and the referee moved in to separate them. Flynn threw a hook in the separation and the referee gave him a warning.

More high-grade ore came out of pockets. The betting grew heavy. The crowd had blood in its eyes. They hooted and jeered. They booed when the tired men clinched and cheered when a blow connected. Some of the women approached one fighter or the other with promises of sexual favors. Others yelled obscenities at their manhood if they clinched. Round after round it went, and after fourteen rounds, they were still on their feet and still swinging.

Steven had seen enough, and he had some very important talk to have with Elizabeth. She would just be finishing up at the restaurant and he waited for the end of the round and then made his way through the crowd and outside. He walked along Myers and turned north at third street and went to the restaurant.

Elizabeth was just finishing, and she looked up and smiled at him when he entered. "Who won," she asked?

"It's still going on," he told her.

"You didn't stay until the end?"

"No, I knew that you would be finished with work, and I wanted to talk with you," he took a seat at a nearby table and motioned her to join him. She propped her broom in a corner and sat across the table from him, with a perplexed look crossing her face. From his tone and actions, she could tell this was important.

"What's going on," she asked, placing her hands palms up on the table.

He took hold of both her hands. "Elizabeth," he had a pleading in his voice, "I have always been fond of you from the very start, the first time I ever saw you that Sunday morning."

"She raised an eyebrow. "I'm very fond of you also," she squeezed his hand. He squeezed back. A fluttering feeling crossed his stomach.

"I love you Elizabeth, and I want you to marry me."

She withdrew her hands, then saw the hurt look that came into his eyes. She reached and grabbed his left hand. "I love you too, Steven, but I've been married, and I'll never marry again."

He looked away and stared at the floor for several

267

moments. He was choked with emotion, and he didn't know how to counter this. "I know that it was bad for you," he finally said, "but this will be different, I swear it."

"It's not that, I know that you're a good man." She paused to collect her thoughts. "There are legal implications to marriage for a woman. I like my freedom, and I like my independence, and the business that I own. It all changes for a woman when she marries. And then, there's Harry," she shrugged.

"Harry is no problem, and he is far more independent than you recognize," he argued. He knew he had taken a wrong turn when he saw the steel come into her eyes. "We can manage with Harry," he tried to soften it. Neither spoke for some moments, but the soft hand play that they had begun in the tent that night came back into their fingers. The shadows of the evening grew long with the last rays of the sun fading into night.

"The hugging and kissing are wonderful," he began again. "But they've set me on fire. The girls at The Old Homestead are touching me and enticing me." He shook his head and a pleading entered his voice. "I'm human. I need more, Elizabeth, I need you."

She began to understand. Although she was damaged in her desire, the long and tender courtship that she had experienced with Steven had awakened some strong emotion. "This is not so much about marriage as it is about sex," she told him. "I've seen you going in and out of the houses on Myers, The Homestead, and Lola Livingston's house next door." There was an implied accusation. "I assumed," she let it hang, "like all the men."

"Not all," it was his turn to be offended and hurt. "Elizabeth, I want marriage and a family," he protested. "I would never be with any of those women. Statton practically lives there these days. He has me meet him and give mining reports there at Lola's, or since The

Homestead is nicer, he rents a room and has Lola join him there." He tried to explain. "When I'm there, there are continuous flirtations and an atmosphere of enticement. I don't know how much more I can take, and I don't want that." He searched deep in her eyes. "Elizabeth, I want you, and only you," he confessed his deep desire.

She paused and thought for a long moment. "I don't want to be married," she stated flatly again, "and I don't know about children, I never got pregnant with Raff, and I don't want the syphilis."

"I have never been with any of those women," he swore again. It's not safe, but I'm crazy with your kisses. Please don't stop loving me. I need you more than anything."

"I can give you what you need," she looked him full in the face, "but I will say when."

He felt a rush into his loins and felt his face flush. He squeezed her hands in agreement. "I can't kiss you anymore," he said, because I can't stop." He rose to leave. "Make it soon, Elizabeth," he said somewhat sternly. "Make it soon." He left quickly and strode toward the train station with exhilaration in his heart, which was pounding in excitement.

He came over from Wilson Creek on the F.&C.C. every day for the next week to eat at the restaurant in the late afternoon, when customers had slowed. He sat quietly and said little. Elizabeth thought he had eyes like a sad little puppy.

Shortly after the full moon, she came close to his table and leaned down and whispered in his ear, "Two nights from now, on Tuesday night. I'll come into Victor on the seven o'clock F.&C.C., if you'll meet me at the station.

It sent an electric shock through him. "I'll be there with bells on," he promised. She laughed and stroked the back of his hair with a tender touch.

Tuesday seemed to take forever coming. Steven had enough work to keep him busy. There was always work for the Portland Company, and now he was working in his off hours on Winchester's Doctor-Jack Pot. Stope mining had begun with the money borrowed through Stevenson from the First National Bank of Denver, and shipments would soon be made. The results were still secret, as Winchester was using some of the money to buy back small amounts of stock that he had sold in the past. Steven rolled up the sheets on his desk that he had constructed by a window in the front room, which he used as his office. It would not be right to let even Elizabeth know of this good fortune until Winchester was ready to make it public.

Rain clouds began to threaten a summer storm in the early afternoon, and he worried that a violent storm might delay or change their date but threaten was all that happened. He continued to clean and sweep his bachelor quarters, and cook a stew of chicken and rice, with carrots and onions. It was basic fair, and it would not be possible to impress her with his cooking, as she was the expert there.

It was time to go meet her at the train. He left in haste, then he came back to get an umbrella, just in case, and taking a last look around hurried to the train.

She was in a light-yellow summer dress with a matching parasol, and carried a small bag with her trousseau, and a picnic basket, that she handed off, as he kissed her on the cheek when she stepped off the train onto the platform.

"I was afraid the rain might come and keep you away," he told her. She smiled shyly and hooked an arm through him. At that moment it began to drizzle, and the wind picked up so that the umbrella did little good. It was not far uphill from the station to the Wilson creek house, just below the imposing structure of The Independence mining operation.

The house was surrounded by a split rail fence, and the yard was large. The privy was behind and on the east side, uphill from the house on the right when standing in the front yard facing the house. There was a large L shaped porch, with several straw chairs, and a hand pump at the east end that drew water from the cistern below. The main entrance door was just to the left of this pump. He held the door open and she entered.

The room seemed cozy in the late afternoon sunlight that slanted through the west window by Steven's desk. There was a Franklin stove near the center, and a table and chairs by a window looking south and down on Victor.

"I've made a chicken stew for us," he went to the stove and stirred the pot. He added wood to the fire and noticed that he would need to bring in wood soon, as even summer nights were chilly, and they were both a little damp from the rain. "But I've neglected to bake any bread," he confessed.

She had taken the basket from him and set it on the table. With a merry twinkle, she pulled out a loaf of French bread and showed it to him.

"Perfect," he laughed.

"And" she said pulling a bottle from the basket, "a bottle of my own homemade Raspberry wine. But I'm afraid that I haven't brought a corkscrew."

He searched through the drawers and failing to find one, got an ice pick and pushed the cork into the bottle. He then got two glasses, and with her holding the glass, he poured, using one hand to hold the bottle and the other to push the cork out of the way with the pick. They clinked glasses and took a sip, each looking at the other over the rim of their glasses.

He got down some bowls and began to set the table. Her feet were wet from the walk and she unlaced her high-top shoes and took them off, pulling off her stockings. Steven watched her as he stirred the stew to heat it some. This was a very suggestive move on her part.

There was a huge bear skin rug between the Franklin stove and the south wall, and she went to it and rubbed her bare feet in its fur. "This is a fine thick pelt," she observed.

"There's a story there," Steven told her. Stratton bought the rug from Warton Pigg. He shot it way back in the 70's. You know that he is obsessed with hunting Ol' Mose. He's been after that bear for over thirty years. One spring he surprised this one coming out of its den. It was a female, and after he shot and killed and skinned it, he got spooked, and high tailed it out of the canyon country and back to his ranch. He is sure that she was Ol' Mose's original mate, and the pelt made him nervous that Ol' Mose was going to slip up on him someday for revenge, so when Stratton saw it and liked it, Wart made him a great price. He practically gave to Win."

"Ol' Mose's mate." She shook her head in wonder and knelt down and rubbed her hand through the thick and silky fur.

He had the table set and the stew served, and he slid a chair out for her to join him. Such grand attention brought a smile, but when she tried to compliment his efforts, he rebuffed it with assurances that it was only plain fare, and nothing beside her cooking, or even the light and crunchy French bread. They ate mostly in an awkward silence as to their coming union, and when they finished, he suggested that they sit on the porch and watch the last rays of sunlight. The sky was clear to the west over the Sangre De Christos, and that set the sky on fire from underneath, matching the blood red of the mountains that turned into fuchsia, and then a pinkish gray until the final rays were almost gone. They had consumed the better part of the tart and tasty Raspberry wine, and were both feeling its mellow effects. He saw her shiver in the coming night air.

"You're cold," he said.

"A little, my feet are bare," she wiggled her toes. Several passersby had looked at the couple and Jimmy Burns had even "hallowed" them from a distance and then stood shading his eyes and squinting into the setting sun, unable to make out clearly or believe that it was Elizabeth on the porch with Steven.

"Let's go in," he suggested, and they went back inside. The fire was low, and he went to get more wood. He made a trip to the privy while he was out.

When he came back through the door, he almost dropped the wood and caught his breath in a gasp. She was standing next to the stove warming her hands, and she had changed into a white silk negligee. It was sheer, and transparent, and reached almost the floor. She had pulled covers and pillows from the bed in the back room and had them laid on the bear skin rug behind her. He dropped the wood with a thud and went to her and they kissed and sank down onto the nest she had made for them.

They kissed for some long time, and he pulled a cover over her shoulders, and went to build up the fire. He got down a goat's milk cream with aloe, that was so good for the dry skin at this altitude, and warmed it in his hands before rubbing it on her feet. This was a luxury that she had never known. He worked up her legs and onto her back and rubbed the muscles between her shoulders. She sighed in contentment.

Finally, she began to undress him, intending to rub the cream on him in return, but she didn't get the chance, as once they were naked and started to kiss, a passion engulfed them. When they slept, the fire would die down, and he would try to build it up quietly, but she awakened each time, and they made love again, and again.

Susan Dunbar rose from her chairman's seat to thank all present for the successful campaign. "We owe a special thanks to Elizabeth Yates, of Cripple Creek for bringing us early warning of this despicable form of so-called entertainment, this throwback to the dark ages of civilization. Joe Wolf and his matadors will not be marching with our organization in its Third Annual Flower Carnival." With the bang of her big gavel, the meeting broke up. She sought Elizabeth out for a word.

"Elizabeth," she caught her, "the organization will reimburse you for the cost of the ad."

"That is not necessary," Elizabeth told her. "I want to use my own money as my part of stopping this atrocity." She unfolded a piece of paper and handed Susan Dunbar one of the two sheets. "It reads like this: It can be nothing else than a blot upon the reputation of Our State and of El Paso County if this monstrous troupe is allowed to disport itself in public. We of Colorado Spring pride ourselves upon our interest in education, culture and all advancement. Then let us protest against the retrograde movement toward the dark ages. May we redeem ourselves by keeping bull fights from our borders and may we keep our Flower Carnival within the bounds of Refinement and Beauty. This," she continued, "will go into the Gazette here in Colorado Springs and also into The Cripple Creek Crusher."

Steven arrived at Elizabeth's Place early afternoon of August 23rd, eighteen=ninety-five, with no notion of the part that Elizabeth had played in opposition to the advertised Bull Fight.

Sally Halthusen's big white horse with Joe Wolf in

274

complete Senior Jose' costume, with the extra large sombrero, could be seen at the head of the column gathering at the eastern end of Bennett Avenue, in preparation for the parade.

"Joe Wolf is dressed in Spanish costume and riding Sally Halthusen's big white prancer back and forth at the end of Bennett," he called to Elizabeth to come look. "That big seven-foot cowboy Charlie Meadows is doing rope tricks on one side of the street and Jake Hoopolieth is jumping through hoops on the other."

"Well," Elizabeth came over and looked out the door, "there is no harm in Jake, but I can't say that for the rest." She barely glanced at the parade, and he couldn't get her out of the kitchen to see the man and woman matadors dressed in red silk and trimmed in gold. It was such a taste of Spain to him and brought back memories of his youth. He noticed Elizabeth's preoccupation with her other tasks and regretted not being able to share.

When he excitedly told her that he had tickets for the two of them for the next day in the Gillette Arena, built in the Beaver Creek clearing, Elizabeth was less than thrilled. She did want to be there, but she wanted to be there with some type of law enforcement that would shut the bullfight down and lock up the promoters. She didn't know how to tell Steven of her opposition.

Betsey Hoopolieth had been watching her brother do rope tricks as the parade of matadors, picadors, and promoters walked the length of Bennett Avenue. She turned in at Elizabeth's Place to say 'hello'.

"Hi, Steven," she gave him a hug. "Aren't they just grand," she sighed. All the red silk with golden embroidery that the matador wore had captured her imagination.

"They are grand," Steven agreed. "Jake was twirling a good loop."

"Howdy, Elizabeth," Betsey smiled. "I just saw

Doc Susie and she took out the last of my stitches. Betsey beamed a smile and showed both sides of her face.

Elizabeth came over to examine Betsey's scars. They were still red and raw, but it was all healing. "Yes," Elizabeth stated firmly. "That's going to heal up just fine," she reassured Betsey.

"Oh, I wouldn't go so far as to say that. Fine is not for me. But them silk outfits sure looked good, didn't they. I like Senior Jose's green velvet git up too." She went to the kitchen and gave Harry a hug.

"Hi, Betsey," Harry stopped to look at her face. "You're getin' all put back together," he concluded.

Betsey bounced back to the door. "See you all in Gillette," she waved and took off toward the disappearing parade. It seemed to be stopped in the street. When Betsey caught up with Jake, she could see that something had happened. The men all had worried looks on their faces. Joe Wolf dismounted the big white horse that he had ridden on during the parade down Bennett Avenue.

"This time it's got Secretary of Agriculture Morton's signature on it. There will be no getting around it this time," she heard a man tell Joe Wolf.

Wolf never lost his composure, or even his fake Spanish accent, that he had acquired in Mexico recently, while looking for a matador and fighting bulls. He neatly squared the giant sombrero he was wearing. "We'll just have to find fighting bulls from some ranch near," Joe calmly instructed.

At this, Matador Marrero stepped closer. "But will these bulls know how to fight," he said with a thick accent. "Fighting Bulls are chosen and bred for generations to react properly to the matador." Mrs Marrero came closer to support her husband, although she understood little of what was being said. Her head bobbed vigorously up and down.

"I'll find you the best bulls you've ever fought,"

Senior Jose' assured the two matadors.

"Jake, what's happenin'?" Betsey tried to understand.

"They stopped the bulls at the border," he told her.

"Jake," Joe Wolf called out to him, "where can we get some good bulls?"

"The Welty's is selling bulls down in the Four Mile country, so is Captain Gross, and Wharton Pigg. They all raise bulls for sale to the neighbors. I know Wharton Pigg's got a good one he would sell."

"We need some men to drive them to a central location so that we can haul z'em up to zee arena in Gillette," Senior Jose' continued in his fake Mexican accent.

"I'm sure that Alonzo would let me use some men from the livery to go down to Four Mile and bring them in to Wharton Pigg's place. He has the best pen and loading chute."

"Jake," Joe Wolf directed him. "Take, Arizona Charlie Meadows, and Kid Meadows with you and go on over to Alonzo's Livery and see if you can get that started. We'll be along there in a few minutes, as soon as I can get rooms for the entourage at zee Place."

Jake headed off down the street toward the livery when Betsey gripped his shoulder. "Jake," she admonished him, "you ain't fixin' to sell him Waterbucket, are you?"

"Betsey, we won't never get a better price for him than sellin' him to Joe Wolf."

"Jake, that's Pied's great grandson. I bottle fed that calf just like I did his grandma. I saved her from the wolves and like to caught my death of cold. You said it was the start of our herd. Now you want to sell the best bull we've ever had?"

"If Joe Wolf will take him, it's the best money we'll ever get, and with that money, I can make the entry fee for the Cheyenne Rodeo. I might win that championship silver buckle." With that said, he pulled away and strode on down toward the livery stable around the corner.

Betsey was crushed by her brother's unfair behavior toward what was hers as well as his. She remembered the day that the little calf had hung a water bucket around his neck and had gotten his name. Now, he was a fine animal, jet black, and all bull, just coming into his full size at three years old. Betsey turned back toward Elizabeth's Place to try and get some solace for the wounds in her heart that were worse than the wounds on her face.

She burst in the door. Elizabeth and Steven looked up from a table where they had sat down to cheese and apples, which had turned early in the cool mountain air. "Jake's gonna sell Waterbucket to Joe Wolf," she bawled. Elizabeth stood and went to her and Betsey sobbed on her shoulder.

"What's going on Betsey?" Elizabeth held her. "What's happened?"

"They stopped Joe Wolf's fightin' bulls at the border and they're agonna get some from the local ranchers. Jake is taken' um down to Four Mile to Wharton Pigg's ranch where we lease pasture. He's gonna sell Waterbucket to be in the arena, and slaughtered in the ring."

"Waterbucket is a bull that Jake owns?"

"He's mine too," Betsey cried.

Elizabeth held her and looked accusingly at Steven. He looked back with a 'what did I do' expression on his face. She was already boiling mad about this whole affair, and Steven's enjoyment was adding insult to injury.

"Where is Jake now," Elizabeth asked sternly.

"They are meeting at Alonzo Welty's stable and then going to Four Mile to gather the bulls." She sat and put her elbows on the table. "He said, with the money, he could enter the Cheyenne rodeo and maybe win the silver

278

buckle. That's my bull as well as his and he's got no right to sell the best bull we ever had."

Now Steven could see that the reason for all the tears was Betsey felt Jake was betraying her. Both women were giving Steven looks that were making him uncomfortable.

"I think I'll go down to the Welty Livery and see what's going on." Neither woman acknowledged his intent, and in an awkward moment, he eased out the door and walked down the block and around the corner to the livery.

He arrived in time to hear Jake tell Alonzo, "The Joe Wolf Grand National Bull Fight Company would be good for any expenses."

"We need some men," Alonzo said out loud and looked around him. Steven was the first man he saw. "Can you ride to push cattle," he asked?

"I can ride," Steven shrugged.

"Nothin' to it," Alonzo assured. He quickly gathered eight men, including himself, Jake, and the Meadows brothers. He had mounts and spare horses brought out from the pens. The horses were saddled, and Steven mounted up with them and headed west to West Four Mile. They rode to Wharton Pigg's ranch and had outriders go to the Grose, Witherspoon, and Welty Ranches. These were the men raising bulls in the area, and it was decided that each rancher would round up and bring two bulls to the Pigg Ranch.

Jake, Steven, Arizona Charlie Meadows, and Kid Meadows rode out into Whart Pigg's pasture to a bull that Jake pointed out. An Angus of some quality, but not to compare with the brawny monster that Wharton Pigg selected.

The five men chased the big black bull the length of the field twice, before he selected the gate that led to the pen and the loading chute. Steven's part was easy, just to stand his horse and block the way and slowly herd the bulls into the holding pen. The other ranchers brought their bulls to the loading area, until the men were working by lantern light.

They loaded them into carts one at a time, and by midnight Steven went with the last cart and followed along on horseback to Gillette, where the arena had been constructed by a swarm of carpenters bought with Joe Wolf's credit with various local banks.

The night was getting very late when he turned his horse over to Piala, a Ute stable hand that had come along to wrangle. He walked back to the Wilson Creek Cabin that Stratton let him use. He heard one discordant note as he was leaving. A quarrel had broken out over the feed promised the bulls.

"It ain't right, Mr. Carleton, to let these animals go hungry on no technicality," he heard Jake say to A. E. Carlton.

"My contract," Carlton shot back "is for feed for bulls arriving from Mexico, Mr. Hoopolieth, from Mexico. Mexican fighting bulls, arriving from Mexico, not some local stock brought in to be slaughtered in a farce. The whole scheme is falling apart. No sir, I'll not advance credit to feed these animals. These are not the animals that I am contracted to feed, but these may be the animals that I own for the contract that wasn't fulfilled, for the money I should have made, feeding bulls that were stopped at the border, through no fault of mine."

Carlton stalked away from the penned up animals. Steven hated to see the bulls go hungry but there was nothing that he could do about it. Jake and Steven locked eyes, and Jake shrugged his shoulders in perplexity, and chagrin at the man's attitude.

Steven made his way back to the Independence property and climbed into bed. He was up at daylight and splashed water on himself. He decided he needed more and heated water on the wood burning stove and made a shallow bath in the big claw footed tub. He was able to catch the 7:30 train out of Victor into Cripple Creek a little before eight. The streets were already blooming with traffic heading on the roads leading from Cripple Creek to West Beaver Park in Gillette.

Steven arrived to find Elizabeth still unprepared to make the day's outing. "Where did you disappear to yesterday," she asked idly? "Did you go down to the livery?"

"Alonzo and Jake were getting ready to go down to the ranches around the Four Mile area and round up some bulls," he told her. "They asked me to come along with them and help," he proudly told her. He felt included in the group.

She didn't see it that way. "You helped them round up bulls after the Mexican Bulls were stopped at the border," she asked accusingly?

"We got two bulls from Bob Witherspoon, and two more Captain Gross brought in to Wharton Pigg's. John Witcher brought in three, and me and Jake and Arizona Charlie Meadow, cut out two bulls at Whart Pigg's, and pinned the whole bunch. By midnight, we had them carted up to the holding pen in Gillette." Steven was proud of his night's work. Elizabeth fell silent, but she was very sharp with Harry and would not hear of him going to the event.

Steven was a little perplexed and excited to get moving. Finally, she signaled she was ready to depart. She had said that she would prefer to walk over to Gillette, some four miles, mostly uphill. The day of August 24, eighteen-ninety-five was cool and clear and about seventy degrees Fahrenheit. A very nice summers day for a walk in the mountains, and they joined a column of people moving along. They emerged from the road through the woods to a glade overlooking West Beaver Park and the Gillette town site, very near where the labor war took

281

place. Spec Penrose and Charlie Tutt had developed some real estate in the area and had built a racetrack. Joe Wolf and Charlie Meadows had led fifty carpenters there a few days earlier and built many more seats, thrown up in tiers of twenty rows. They had driven a log rampart seven to eight feet high around an arena area two hundred and fifty feet square.

All around the arena seats were five layers of various carnival games; saloons, flim-flam barkers hawking prizes, and tents where maybe worse took place. As Elizabeth looked down from the ridge overlooking Beaver Park, she was repulsed. Steven was eager to move ahead with the crowd. "Come on," he encouraged, "we need to get to the gate so we can enter early and get a good seat." He tried to hurry her along.

They moved several hundred yards closer. That was when Elizabeth locked eyes with Soapy Smith. She stopped walking.

"Come along, Elizabeth," Steven called from ahead, then walked back to where she was stopped. Smith went back to the business at hand, and Elizabeth moved hesitantly forward.

She saw Spec Penrose standing with his arms folded, watching the crowd with a serious look on his face. She recognized Francis Hill shaking papers in Joe Wolf's face. Joe pointed at the mayor of Gillette and turned his back on Hill who continued to scream, "the Humane Society will see to it that all of you are locked up!"

The crowd poured money into the coffers of the carnival games. Smith's soap game, with money wrapped in some of the bars, and a shill in the crowd to yell 'eureka' whenever one of them pulled out a big bill to entice the crowd, made up one in ten of the booths. Many more stands promoted the shell and pea game. The good tricksters had large crowds fascinated with their speed and skill and were fooling the betting miners out of their hard earned wages.

As they walked through the menagerie of booths and tents, Elizabeth caught glimpses of even more sordid human behavior. Behind one tent, a man was using a syringe to inject morphine or cocaine into his blood stream. Both drugs were serious addictions to many of the working men in the district. Working girls were milling in the crowd looking for customers, and an occasional tent flap was thrown back as a finished customer emerged or a new one entered. They made way through five layers of con games, saloons, and cribs. To Elizabeth, it was like walking through a cesspool.

Still, there were many women curious enough to be among the crowd. It was a late start for the gate, and many of the miners had turned their pockets inside out to indicate that they were out of money, long before the ticket window opened. Even so, some three thousand people bought two, three, and five dollar seats. Steven made sure that he was near the first gate that opened, as he had advance tickets. He had bought five-dollar seats and they entered the gate that would allow them access to those 'best' seats.

They had just sat down, when Betsey Hoopolieth joined them. "Jake sold Joe Wolf Waterbucket," she told Elizabeth with a stern expression.

"I know," she nodded at Steven. "He went with Jake and Alonzo to get the bulls. They brought them into Gillette about midnight.

Betsey gave Steven a frown. The crowd continued to pour in, but many seats were still not filled when it slowed to a trickle of people and then stopped. The crowd began to anticipate the show and some rhythmic stomping of the seats started and stopped in sporadic pockets here and there throughout the stands.

Arizona Charlie Meadows entered on the big white horse that Sally was letting him use. Kid Meadows entered just behind him, followed by the two banderilleros, holding their ribboned barbs in a ceremonial way to display the flowing color. They lined up against the far side of the arena opposite a grand master of ceremonies platform built over the gate that the bulls would soon enter through.

Joe Wolf mounted the podium in a giant black sombrero and a green velvet suit with silver buttons down the front and silver conchos along the outer seam of his pants. He had on patent leather boots, ankle high, spit shinned to a mirror finish by Amos, the boot black. "The Grand National Bullfight will come to order," he boomed. "Today, for your entertainment, we have two of Mexico's finest matadors. Matador Marrero, of world renown reputation, and his lovely wife, the only female matador in the world," he made it grand as he could. With a few more gracious accolades, he introduced the "incomparable, the only, Arizona Charlie Meadows, and his brother Kid Meadows as picadors," he barked. Each man stepped forward or moved his horse forward as they were introduced. Charlie struck a note of awe with the crowd, and they gave a collective cheer for the giant cowboy. He was quite the figure with his seven-foot frame, long flowing blond hair, over his shoulders, like a scout from the previous decades, looking very much like Buffalo Bill Cody in his fringed leather pioneer garb.

After the introductions, Senior Jose' had wanted trumpets or bugles to sound, but all he could get was a flute. He turned the stage above the gate over to the flautist, who played a stirring rendition of a part of the opera "Carmen". At the conclusion of the flute music, Senior Jose', with a flourish, threw an iron peg to the toreros, a symbolic key that was the command to open the gate. Jake Hoopolieth swung the gate open and the first bull trotted into the arena, looking bewildered and feeling hungry, as he hadn't a bite for almost twenty-four hours.

The bull was the big black that Wharton Pigg had brought in. Betsey peaked through her finger and was relieved that it was not Waterbucket.

The animal ran the length of the ramparts twice searching for an escape and then came to a stop near the far end from the entrance gate. The crowd noise rose at first and then died away as the beast turned first one way and then the other. The banderilleros moved in on him, and as he turned his attention to them, they split to either side. While one drew the attention of the confused animal, the other attempted a run at him from the opposite side.

Neither of the two were very sure of this bull's experience in the ring, and Garcia, the first Banderillero, did a poor job at barbing. The ribboned barb missed its mark and in moments shook loose and fell to the ground. Banderillero Sandrea did no better on his first pass. The performance lost energy, as the two fell to arguing loudly in Spanish over strategy to dart this ranch animal. After five more attempts at placing the ribbons, only one barb stayed. Intended to guide the blade of the matador, it was far out of place. Few in the crowd knew its purpose, but Steven understood that it was poorly done. Elizabeth noticed the frown on his face, which went with her mood perfectly, as she had seen more than she wanted already.

Now the two picadors moved in on the animal. They brought the bull to the center of the ring and used the seventeen-foot pikes to good effect. They soon had the animal bellowing in pain and pawing the ground in an absolute fury. As soon as the bull began to paw the ground and shake his horns at the men on horseback, Arizona Charlie Meadows signaled to his brother, and they pulled back to the far edge. The matador came out into the center of the arena, dressed in black satin trimmed in gold embroidery. A roar went up from the crowd and the bull stood stock still near one end.

Matador Marrero held the cape out, spread in front

of him. "Ah hah, Toro," he called softly, then stood motionless. For Steven, this brought back a flood of memories from his childhood. For Elizabeth, the show was becoming an unspeakable horror. She saw the pain in the animal as it stood bellowing from the torment at one end of the entrapment.

The crowd had fallen totally silent, caught in the moment. After several minutes, the animal saw the matador and turned to face him squarely. Finally, he charged. Marrero didn't move, but held the cape out, and passed the bull around him. The animal turned and came back. Marrero expertly passed him back and forth in the classic dance done by the bull and matador. He ended it with the move called "The Veronica". A movement where the matador stands in front of the cape and passes the bull in a circle around his body, leaving the bull bewildered looking for his target, standing still, while the matador strides three steps away, pulling the cape off over the horns and turning his back to the bull in triumph, while the exhausted animal is stopped in dejected defeat. He let the bull recover and then challenged him again. This time, when the charge came, he sent home his barbs. The bull flinched away.

Elizabeth heard Steven say "Bravo". Matador Marrero signaled. Jose' Wolfe blew a silver whistle. Kid Meadows bought the rapier. Marrero poised, back arched, almost on tip toes. "Ah Toro," he challenged. The animal, very weak, charged him again. The matador thrust his rapier from the top into the heart, and the first bull fell dead.

Steven was on his feet in a moment. "Bravo," he called over and over. It was a great bullfight, fought on the slope of Pikes Peak. Such memories of Spain flooded his mind. Elizabeth was appalled. She and Betsey stayed seated. The next bull would soon come out, and Betsey was scared it would be Waterbucket. The two women held hands.

El Presidente, Senior Jose' Wolfe felt a tap on the shoulder. Sheriff Bowers was looking him square in the eye. "Joe, you and this whole shebang is under arrest by complaint of Francis Hill and the Humane Society."

"You can't arrest me, I'm already in the custody of Gillette Constable Lambert."

"That so?"

"I'll take you to him."

"Lead on, Joe."

"Charlie," Joe yelled, "keep the show going." Charlie Meadows nodded that he heard.

Joe led Bowers to the Torero's dressing room where Constable Lou Lambert, a director of The Joe Wolfe Grand National Bullfight Company waited, as planned.

"I've had Joe, and all the others in custody since morning," Lambert told Bowers.

"I'll accept that," the El Paso County sheriff agreed cordially. He was glad to be able to step out of it. "I had to arrest on the complaint," he explained. "Hill has influence and friends. You're going to have to arraign him now. That's the only way that I can let you keep custody."

They called down Gillette Justice of the Peace Keith, who quickly not only arraigned, but tried and acquitted Joe on the spot. The judge was also a director of the event. "I could of seen the rest of the show," Keith complained, when he levied a fine of five dollars each for court costs on the four Mexicans, including the lady bullfighter, the Meadows brothers, and Jake Hoopolieth. "I been cheated out of part of my ticket cost," he pointed his gavel at Joe, "so stop trying to bargain me down to twenty-seven-fifty. The fine stays like I said." He banged his gavel, but the show was over by the time he could get back to his box seat in the stands.

Elizabeth was saddened and sullen. Steven hardly

noticed in the exhilaration of the day. Betsey Hoopolieth had a plan. She said her goodbye to Steven and Elizabeth, as they moved through the departing crowd.

Betsey explored the holding pen area and climbed the rail fence to see where her bull was. She noted the various gates that led to an exit. No one seemed to be watching the enclosure.

It was near midnight when a slight figure in a gray serape and straw hat slipped over the railing and climbed into the pens with the remaining bulls.

"Waterbucket," she called softly. The bull stirred and came after the sweat feed that he knew always came with Betsey. She scratched behind his ears, and hugged him like a big dog, then slipped a rope through the nose ring and led the docile animal to the first gate. She opened the sliding wooden latch as quite as possible, making only a scraping sound. Two more gates and they were free, but at the last gate leading to the outside, a form stepped in front of her.

Piala had been sent by Alonzo to watch the animals, which Wolfe had only promised to pay for. There were now several interested parties that realized the bulls, alive or dead, might be the total assets of the company by the time this all shook out. Now, he and Betsey locked eyes in the dim moonlight. Neither said a word. Betsey knew who he was. She had seen him around for years. He had been at Judge Castello's store when she was five and first remembered going there. For his part, Piala had been in love with Betsey Hoopolieth since the first time that he had ever lain eyes on her. They had never spoken. A long moment passed.

"He's mine," she stated flatly.

"Piala turned to the latch and opened the outside gate. He watched as she led Waterbucket away into the darkness.

Steven went alone to the Sunday show. Elizabeth

would not consider going. She pleaded that she couldn't
be away from the restaurant again. It was just as well.
The crowd was less than three hundred people. The first
three bulls were Herefords, and they refused to fight. The
Meadows brothers chased them back and forth as the
terrified animals ran for their lives. Two bulls, from the
remaining stock, were goaded into a charge, and Matador
Marrero dispatched them as if bored.

The Monday show was canceled and Maurice Finn,
working for A. E. Carlton, swooped on the remaining live
animals, and the meat from the two kills.

"Say Wolfe," Finn badgered Joe, "there's one bull
unaccounted for." Carlton was the first of many creditors.
Even with only a breach of contract complaint, being first
in line with a bulldog lawyer like Finn, he stood a good
chance of getting possession of these few assets. With
Alonzo's men yet to be paid, not to mention the owners of
the bulls, the court would consider that they all had
extended credit to Joe Wolfe's company, and were
therefore just a few more creditors in line right behind A.
E. Carlton.

By Wednesday, Francis Hill had managed to get
the company locked up on a warrant by District Attorney
Blackmer. Arizona Charlie's Meadow sat in a hot jail cell
in the Springs with clothes pins pinning his hair up on top
of his head. A crowd of giggling young ladies had
gathered outside the cell windows to see the stars,
including the matador. Members of the Cheyenne
Mountain Club bailed out Wolfe and the Meadows
brothers. They hated Francis Hill for stopping their pigeon
shoots. They staged a wild west show that weekend and
performed bulldogging, and calf roping, both on the
Human Society hit list. With this money they bailed out
the matadors, but the other lesser figures of banderilleros,
and Jake Hoopolieth were forgotten and remained in the
clink.

Steven had brought paperwork down to the Mining Exchange building and then walked up Bennett to Johnnie Nolan's passing by the new water hydrants that were being installed for fire protection. He talked for a moment with Joe Moore, a leader in the volunteer fire department and then entered Nolan's. N. B. Guyot, who was holding forth in an obviously funny speech, as everyone was laughing and hooting, turned his way. Steven moved into the group to listen.

At about the same time, Betsey Hoopolieth arrived at the back door of Elizabeth's Place. "Hello Harry," she hugged him as she came through the kitchen. Elizabeth was seated at a table going over receipts. She saw Betsey's serious face and set her pencil down.

"Hello Betsey," she greeted. "What's the matter?"

"Elizabeth," Betsey's voice quivered. "I need help."

"How can I help?"

"You know Jake's in jail down at the Springs?"

"I had heard, but thought they had all been bailed out."

"Not Jake, they just forgot him."

"What did Jake do, but open the gate," Elizabeth wondered aloud.

"The judge said that started it all." Betsey shook her head. "Now everyone is chasing Joe Wolfe for their money, from Spec Penrose right on down to Alonzo Welty."

Elizabeth smiled at the whole bunch getting what they deserved from such a spectacle. "You need money to get Jake out," she jumped ahead to a conclusion.

"I can't leave my brother in that hell hole," Betsey told her.

"How much?"

His fine is fifty-four dollars," Betsey shook her head.

"I can do that," Elizabeth reassured her.

"Thanks, Elizabeth, but I won't take charity, plus, it's more complicated."

"What then?"

"A. E. Carlton has a claim on the bulls left, and he knows that one is missing?"

"One's missing?"

"I took Waterbucket Saturday night," Betsey confessed.

"Oh, Betsey."

"Now, Sheriff Bowers is looking for him as rustled. They can still hang a rustler."

"What can we do," Elizabeth was puzzled.

Betsey had thought it out. "if you can get him slaughtered, he should be worth the bail. You know where to sell the meat, and there will be nothing for Bowers to find."

"That makes me a receiver of stolen goods," Elizabeth frowned. Neither woman said anything for a long moment.

"I just knew that you have animals dressed all the time and butchered. I got nowhere else," Betsey begged.

Elizabeth decided. "Betsey, you bring him down to Alonzo's, and I'll make the arrangements. She got fifty-five dollars out of her till and gave it to Betsey, who thanked her and went out to bring Waterbucket to his fate.

Elizabeth called Harry in from where he was sitting out back. "Harry, go down to the Welty stable and tell Alonzo or George that I'm sending another beef down to butcher. Tell them that Betsey Hoopolieth will bring him in this evening, and butcher him right away and bring me the meat."

N. B. Guyot was just winding up a long satirical account of Francis Hill's fight with the Cheyenne Mountain Club over horse tail docking, and pigeon shoots. He had recounted the lunacy of the last week in a hilarious rendition of all the gossip going around. Arguments raged pro and con, as to whether Joe Wolfe was hero or scoundrel. Steven had arrived in time to hear most of it, and after a couple of beers was in a great mood.

"Yes sir," Guyot concluded, "was it cruel to slay those animals in that fashion? Hell yes," he answered his own question, "but a far greater cruelty was perpetrated, gentlemen, by A. E. Carlton, who refused to feed the poor, doomed beast a last meal."

The crowd of tipsy men roared in good humor to the perceptive speech. Steven chatted a little more with Winchester, who was in the crowd. Things were looking very good for the Dr. Jack Pot on the newly reopened twelfth level. About dusk dark he left Nolan's and walked past Joe Moore's crew of firemen that were putting their tools away for the day and went on toward Elizabeth's Place.

He entered in a jovial frame of mind, totally oblivious to the storm that was about to break. "Guyot just told the funniest account of this whole bullfight fiasco," he laughed.

"I see nothing funny about any of it," Elizabeth sharply told him. She had never spoken to Steven in this tone before. Harry, who had heard Elizabeth in moods like this, and knew about her displeasure with the bullfight, had arrived back from taking the message to the livery. He went out the back door to avoid the storm. Steven's head snapped around to look at her.

"It's funny like a skunk in the house," he kidded her.

"Stefano Marquez," she spit his name at him, "I don't think I know you. You are brutal and insensitive. You cheered at torture. I don't understand you."

"Elizabeth," he tried to reason with her, "you butcher beef almost every day. This is a beautiful ceremony that celebrates the dependency that the animals have on us, and on us the animals. It is like a dance."

"It's a horror show, and I just don't think I even know who you are."

Steven caught fire. "Elizabeth, I don't think I like this kind of talk from you."

"I don't think I can stand anymore," she tried to continue, but words failed. They locked eyes fiercely.

He rose and turned to go. Any more talk was going to make it worse. "You know where I am," he said at the door, "when you come to your senses." Then he was gone.

Elizabeth was numb. The shadows grew darker. There was a knock on the back door. She struggled up and found Piala with a wagon in the back.

"I've brought the quartered-out beef, Miss Elizabeth," he told her. He could see immediately that something was wrong.

"Please bring one forequarter in to the butcher block here and take the rest to the cook at The Place Hotel," she instructed in a weak voice.

"And what do you want done with the offal and the skin," Piala asked?

"Oh, Oh," Elizabeth tried to answer and then broke. She ran from the back into the dining area and fell into a chair at a table in a dark corner. The tears began to flow, and then her body shook in great sobs.

Piala followed her to the dining doorway, and as she heaved with the crying, moved closer and stood quietly beside her, without touching her. Finally, when she got a little control, he asked. "Can I help?"

She shook her head and wiped her eyes with a tablecloth, "No, Piala, thanks, but there's nothing for it," she said through the tears.

Steven was hurt and angry. He had shared a dream with Elizabeth. He was alone and in a foreign land; he depended on her for understanding, and now that was shattered. It was worse for the way she had seemed to reject his heritage from Spain. From the beginning of this farce, it had been an emotional roller coaster ride. All his memories of bright gaiety from his youth seemed smashed in a ditch.

For Elizabeth, the whole affair was fraught with images that brought back all the fears and anxiety of a world of cruelty, with the images of that day at the fair grounds in Gillett searing her soul. The horror of seeing Soapy Smith running the gaming tables, the seamy greed and corruption that loomed that day along with the terror she felt in empathy for the tortured animals had been too much of a shock. It was going to take time to sort it out, and both of them turned away from the grief and heartache that their love had thrust upon them to work, something that they could cope with.

Both buried themselves in the jobs at hand, and left the fear and rejection to smolder in the depths of their minds. Time passed, and they hurt. The hurt turned to anger and the anger brought a resolute stubbornness. Without communication, they drifted farther apart, and so a month went by, and then two.

Christmas was approaching. The town grew gay around the two lonely lovers. Steven stayed away from Cripple Creek and worked at the Wilson Creek house or in the mines. If he had to go to the mining exchange, he would find himself longing to go to the restaurant, hungry for a look at her, and gazing down the street hoping for a glimpse. Once or twice, he thought he saw her. It would cause more pain, and he would turn away. Elizabeth would find herself gazing toward the Mining Exchange and determinedly turn away and back inside.

There had been a huge strike in Poverty Gulch, of all places. It had been near where Bob Womack had found the original piece of float that had assayed and started it all. There were some diggings through the years, claims and abandoned holes, but nobody had hit the vein. So it always was in Cripple Creek District. Where one man gave up, another at a later date, dug a few more inches and struck a bonanza.

There were several claims in the area that were considered worthless, when a dashing young banker, with budding political aspirations, from Denver named James Sheahan had gotten the bug, and with money that he had from his Denver investments, bought and consolidated the lot. He put men to blasting into the mountain side, and almost immediately, they struck it. It was big, and soon Stratton was milling good ore for him.

Sheahan came down from Denver many times to oversee the new mine, and he and Win became friends. They were making each other loads of money, and when a man did that, Stratton liked to entertain. He introduced the young dashing bachelor to the pleasures of Myers Avenue, and through Lola Livingston, he became acquainted with the madame of the Old Homestead, Pearl De Vere. As Lola was exclusive to Win for some long time, Pearl become the exclusive paramour to the handsome young Midas of Poverty Gulch.

Pearl had always had an aloofness from the men she serviced, but as she realized that she was getting older, this time she was struck hard. In spite of her firm rule of her heart, this time it got away. She was secretly in love with her lover, for a madame, a dangerous turn of mind. This frame of mind was enhanced by the gifts that the dashing Sheahan showered on Pearl.

The big news, as Christmas approached, at the end

of eighteen ninety-five, was the party being planned by
Pearl De Vere at the Old Homestead. Stratton and
Sheahan had framed it up, and Sheahan insisted on footing
the bill. The rumor was that it would be the grandest party
that had ever taken place in the District, the most lavish
affair that had ever been in Cripple Creek. A tropical
garden was imported with orchids, gardenias, and palm
trees. Denver orchestras were coming down to play
dances. Wild turkeys were iced and brought from
Alabama. Caviar was ordered from Russia, with cases of
French champagne to wash it down. And to top it off, a
beautiful French gown of pink chiffon, laced with seed
pearls, and costing the enormous price of eight hundred
dollars was ordered by the young Midas, for Pearl De Vere
to wear. Her imagination ran wild. He must love her like
she had fallen for him. It was a fairy tale romance, and
Pearl was now deeply in love, and in anticipation of a
proposal.

Steven witnessed some of these developments. He
brought mining reports to Stratton at Lola Livingston's or
next door to the Old Homestead and had come to be
casually acquainted with Pearl. The night of the party, he
was totally enchanted by the hostess, who waltzed with her
Midas in the stunning Parisian Gown. Stratton drank too
much. He almost always did these days. The young midas
did also, and as women want what other women have, one
of the younger girls, a new one, enticed Sheahan into one
of the rooms.

The party was gaily going on and the madame was
the hostess, so her attention was elsewhere, but eventually
she came looking and found Stratton nursing eighteen-
year-old single malt Scotch whiskey. Steven and Win sat
in a side parlor, and Steven had noticed the enticement,
which had somehow brought a black mood on Win, who
had a dark side from his youth that Steven little
understood.

Pearl entered the room with all smiles and grace, and looked questioningly around with a puzzled expression. "Where has James gone off to," she asked Stratton?

A sinister expression crossed Win's face. A devilish smile curled his lips. Steven could see this but knew little of the abuse as a child that Stratton had suffered, smothered by a flock of older sisters. Those experiences and the episode with Zerula Stewart had left him with a masochistic bent that he had never overcome. That and the fact that he had never been able to buy Pearl, and the whiskey brought it to the surface.

"You're in love with him, aren't you?" He hit her in the face with her secret. She made no answer to her secret being revealed but simply widened her eyes and inclined her head and smiled demurely, as if to ask again where James had gone.

Stratton's eyes narrowed and got mean. "He's went off with that new girl of yours Lola Bell, the young pretty one."

Pearl's face looked as if she had been shot through the heart. She gasped, and a hand involuntarily fluttered near her mouth.

Stratton continued the cruel barrage. "When he gets married, he'll marry a young Denver socialite." He paused to let it sink in. His eyes got blacker. "You're just an old whore," he snarled.

Her eyes brimmed with tears, and she choked, turned and left the room as in a daze. Stratton took another sip of whiskey, looked over at Steven with a satisfied grin. He looked the very visage of Satan himself.

"I think I'll call it a night," Steven said excusing himself.

"What's your hurry," Stratton slurred, "the party's just getting started."

Sometimes people's behavior could be completely

inexplicable. Steven made his way outside. It was cold, bitter cold. A throb of loneliness struck his core, and he pulled his coat tighter and walked northward and east the short way to the midland Terminal. He had to wait nearly an hour for a train to Victor. It was a cold, lonely ride home on Christmas Eve.

He spent Christmas alone at Wilson Creek. It was two days before he came back to Cripple Creek to consult drawings at the Mining Exchange. Newsboys were running with papers everywhere.

"Pearl De Vere dies from morphine overdose," he heard a boy yell. He stopped the kid and bought a paper and read the story on the front page of the *Times*.

"Pearl De Vere, madam at the Old Homestead, died early today from an overdose of morphine. According to a denizen in the house, a gay party was in full swing when Pearl excused herself, saying that she felt indisposed. She refused to let anyone go with her to her room. She was in high spirits all evening, a woman said, and never seemed happier or more carefree. No one could offer any reason why the Madam should want to end her life. The body was discovered by the wealthy patron of the lavish affair. It was lying across the bed fully clothed in the ball dress that came only last week from a salon in Paris. The name of the patron could not be learned. It was understood that he left suddenly on business in Denver. Funeral arrangements will be announced later pending words from the deceased's relatives in the East.

Steven sat on a bench in the station and read it again. A man as generous a Winfield Scott Stratton, who gave coal in winter to the poor, had the birds fed on frozen days, built churches, reimbursed cheated partners, and dozens of other acts of charity, could let whiskey demean his soul such that cruel words had cut this delicate flower down. The prestigious men at the party would scatter from the scandal like a covey of quail flushed from a bush. He

298

shook his head in the realization that the sense of community would collapse. Many things would change. The ugliness of death would despoil everything it touched, as tongues would wag about everyone that had attended.

The day of the funeral was cold and blustery. Steven felt that he should be there. He took a position behind the Elks Club, who were in full regalia with maroon fezzes with brightly polished golden crossed swords on the hats. Joe Moore led the band, and they came first. He played the Death March all the way down Bennett Avenue from Lampman's funeral home to Mt Pisgah cemetery, the big base drum beat a slow and solemn cadence.

Pearl's coffin came next in a black hearse with glass windows pulled by two black horses, with the coffin almost entirely covered by red and white roses sent by miners and admirers. Inside the coffin, she remained dressed in the Parisian ball gown. Her Eastern relatives had left her to a paupers grave when they discovered that she was not the dressmaker to the rich that she had pretended to them, and Johnnie Nolan had started a movement to have the dress sold in order to bury her, but at that moment an anonymous letter had arrived from Denver with ten one hundred dollar bills inside instructing Farley and Lampman's to give her a fine funeral.

The hearse was followed by the red wheeled phaeton that she liked to drive, with a huge spray of pink carnations in the seat, and the spirited blacks that always pulled her around town being controlled by a man walking beside. Next came the Elks club members in the costumes followed by the few adults that wished to mourn. People's faces could be seen in the second story windows along Bennett, curious enough to watch but not wanting to be seen as participants. Only a group of rag tag children followed along behind the carriages of veiled women friends from the tenderloin.

As they passed Elizabeth's Place, Steven saw her turn away and go back inside, with body language stiff with judgment. They proceeded slowly onward through a biting wind to Mt Pisgah where huge bon fires burned to thaw the ground enough for the grave diggers.

Father Volpe could not be persuaded to read at what was ruled a suicide, and the scripture reading was left to an Elks Club official to read a short passage of "Judge not, least ye be judged." Then Joe Moore raised his coronet and played sweetly, "Goodbye Little Girl, Goodbye." The coffin was lowered and the chilled crowd began a fast retreat in reverse order with the veiled ladies, now with their veils lifted, making a clattering carriage run back down Bennett, laughing and talking.

Steven dropped dirt on the coffin, thinking of the waste of a young life. None of the prestigious men who had been at the party were there. They had all fled to their mansions in Colorado Springs and Denver and had no comment and were not to be seen. They would play in much more circumspect indulgences from this point on, with the girls coming to them in private rooms, by secret arrangements. The gay abandon and wild parties were over for many and on temporary hold for all.

Joe Moore's band was the last to leave, with members cross fanning their arms to keep warm from the wind. Where Mt Pisgah road met Bennett Avenue, he struck up "It'll Be a Hot Time In the Old Town Tonight", and the band kept it up all the way back into town. Steven saw Mabs Barbee sitting on a rock at the far Western end of Bennett with her head buried in the crook of her arm. Her shoulders shook with the tears that flowed.

He followed the procession then hurried back to town, shivering with the cold wind. Elizabeth was on the porch at the restaurant, and they stared straight at each other as he passed close. She was frowning and he clearly read her lips as she silently mouthed, "like all the men," to him, then turned and disappeared back inside.

He made his way back to the train station and stared blankly and sadly out the window at the piles of gray talus stacked everywhere, and the leafless aspen trees, dark and dormant in the bitter cold of an alpine winter.

Chapter 22. The Fires

Things weren't the same in Cripple Creek after the funeral. Win Stratton stayed away at his home in Colorado Springs. The gay and sometimes wild times of The Socials, as they had come to be known, were gone, at least for the moment. The snow came long and deep that January, and the District was wrapped in a thick white blanket that seemed to last and last. Men struggled to keep the tracks clear. An eerie quiet set in that winter, broken only by the chugging of the steam engines as they labored to pull the grade into Victor, and the shrieking of the brakes as they came down grade into the station at the Midland Terminal in Cripple. The snow lay deep and drifted all around and seemed to dampen the sounds of the muffled explosions that now happened in the mines at a deeper and deeper level. The only break was at noon each day as the whistle they called the Mockingbird blasted out.

Steven worked his duties at the Portland and then went to Anaconda and directed work at the Doctor-Jack Pot. It was painful to come to Cripple Creek. He missed Elizabeth fiercely and nothing could fill that ache of loneliness. But he realized that she would have to come to him, and he continued to hope that their love for each other would eventually win out over the pride and strife necked obstinateness. He just didn't know how to heal the breach, so he buried himself in work and stayed away.

Elizabeth, too, tried to hide in work and there were always plenty of hungry men to feed. She and Harry and Betsey were kept busy. A new interest took much of Betsey's time. The Ute Indian, Piala, came often now to Elizabeth's Place, and it was obvious that an affection was growing between he and Betsey. The laughter they shared, the holding hands, the private talk in the afternoons when

302

business got slow before dinner hour was like a knife that cut into Elizabeth's consciousness, making her painfully aware of what she had thrown away in shunning Steven. She too felt the pain of loneliness, and even Harry was often off with his girlfriend from the tenderloin. And although she disapproved, she realized that it made Harry happy, as he whistled when he worked cleaning up the tables and dishes these days. The two mainstays of her emotional life were otherwise occupied, leaving Elizabeth alone to ponder the course that she had chosen. Many times, she found herself out on the porch and looking toward the Mining Exchange building. She never saw Steven there as she sometimes did in the past. The longing built in her like a hunger, and she vowed to go to Wilson Creek, then a stiff resolve would darken her with pride and stubbornness, and she would think that it was all just too complicated, and better left alone. Many men tried to flirt with her, but she rebuffed them all. She had none of it. It was all too painful, so a stubbornness that had always served her well in the past, kept her locked in place, and darkened her heart.

It was the night of April 1st , eighteen-ninety-six that she had the dream. She woke at exactly midnight as the pendulum clock in her bedroom above the restaurant was striking. When she came awake, and she counted the strikes. There were twelve. The dream was still vivid in her mind, and she wondered at such a strange dream.

It began with the smell of smoke. That impression lasted, and she had never had a dream with a smell in it before. But even awake the thick scent of smoke seemed to linger in her nostrils. She had the horrifying impression of fire. She seemed to be being carried and fire was everywhere. Fire was on all sides. Embers blew along the path, and even the sky was filled with shooting flames. A vague feeling that this was Bennett Avenue came over her that she could not shake. The scene changed. A little girl's voice called to her from far away. "Mommy," it said. "Mommy," it called insistently. "Wake up, Mommy, wake up." In the dream, she had opened her eyes to see herself, yet not herself, but a small child in pig tails that looked exactly as she had looked as a child.

"And who are you?" She had asked the child in mocking delight.

"I'm your little girl," the child retorted with firm petulance.

"And where did you come from?" Elizabeth continued the game in a mock sing-song voice that seemed to be a routine that she shared with the child.

"I've come from heaven," the little girl answered, "to be with you. Wake up, Mommy. I'm hungry."

Elizabeth had awakened at that moment. She listened to the clock strike and counted the strikes. She heard all twelve. It was a very unusual dream, and she didn't return to sleep for many hours, as she lay restlessly in bed and mulled through the events of her life.

Winter dug in and held on until late in April, and a huge snowstorm descended on the town the night of April 12th. The next morning snow was piled everywhere, and Mrs. James D. Yambert trudged through the snow that morning down to the corner of 3rd and Bennett and into Johnnie Nolan's to report that the roof had fallen in on the house that she rented from him at her house on Carr Avenue. Nolan scratched the back of his head and told her that there was nothing to be done about it until the snow had melted some so that workmen could be hired to clear away the collapsed boards and a new roof put in place. Several days went by and most of the snow had melted, and still workmen did not appear, so she walked back down a second time and extracted a promise from him to get it fixed. More time went by, and still no repair, so back she came a third time, in a pique over the ruin at the house, and his lack of concern. Again, he promised her that he would put men right to work on it. Time went by, and still nothing happened.

Steven had come into Cripple Creek to talk with Winchester, as they had a meeting at the Mining Exchange building. He purchased a Times at the Midland Terminal, and took a few minutes to read the front page, as he was early. The date said Saturday, April 25th eighteen-ninety-six. The sky was clear, and crisp as a light dusting of snow had filled the cracks here and there, with winter tenaciously hanging on. A soft, warm and light wind was blowing from the southwest. An article halfway down the front page caught his eye and he read.

Dr. Whiting expounded on the healthy virtues of mountain air, and another article, a little farther down the page, was an interview with Mayor George Pierce, who was quoted as saying, "Our splendid system of waterworks and well-disciplined firemen makes it possible to control and extinguish the most serious conflagrations; henceforth, out citizens can be free of this terror."

He admired the new brick Midland Terminal which was having the finishing touches put on it by workmen, and then strolled down the north side of Bennett, admiring the framing of the new National Hotel which had been completed to its four-story height.

After the meeting, about one o'clock that afternoon, he left the Mining Exchange building. He had turned resolutely away from looking toward the restaurant and was walking back east along Bennett Avenue when he noticed Otto Flotto, crossing Myers and walking very fast along the west side of 5th street, coming from the direction of the The Central Dance Hall. He continued east for a short while and heard Flotto's hobbling steps running behind him getting closer. Otto had just passed him in one hell of a hurry when pistol shots rang out. Steven stopped and listened and the shots continued in a series of six, and then six more. Otto Flotto seemed to speed up, crossed

Fifth Street, almost being run over by one of the Woods Brothers' transfer wagons full of coal, and disappeared into the Midland Terminal building at the east end of Bennett. The repeated pistol shots in a series of six was the signal for a fire and for the volunteers of the fire brigade to come running.

Men began to listen, and some of them who were volunteering began to run toward the station located in the center of the block at the new City Hall, and the new six-hundred-pound fire bell located there began to clang, others ran straight for the pistol shots. Steven changed his direction and went west and followed along down Third. He was beginning to smell smoke, and as he came close to the corner of Myers and Third Street, he saw smoke bellowing from the center of the block on the south side. A few more steps and he was able to see The Central Dance Hall was in flames. They were mostly on the second floor, and coming out the windows and lapping at the cornice work headed for the roof. The new Gardiner non-interfering alarm box at the corner had not been pulled, and so Steven reached it and pulled box twenty-one.

There were women running from the rooms with their arm's full of possessions, and he saw Harry at the bottom of the west side near a stairwell with some of the women throwing things down to him that he caught and piled at the edge of the street. Firemen arrived with a hose, and soon had it connected to the new fire plug at the corner, and they lay it to the center of the block and played a stream of water on the flames, and the flames began to abate some. They wet the surrounding porch, and one of them came up the stairs and broke out windows facing the street so that water could be streamed into adjoining rooms on either side of the room that was on fire. It was at that moment that the hose a few feet from where Steven was standing began to swell, and then the fibers gave way and the hose burst. Yelling back and forth began between the volunteers, and one of them ran toward the nearby station to get a coupling to fix the break. The fire began to gain ground.

The rooms to the west caught first, and women frantically climbed onto the porch. The stairs on the west side caught from falling window frames filled with fire, and the women on the porch were trapped. One of the firemen threw them a rope, and they attached it to a post and one at a time climbed over the railing and slid down the rope with Harry catching them as they got near the ground.

The Mockingbird, the steam whistle located on Xenia Street at the El Paso and Fremont Electric Light Company and Power Station, began to whistle its shrill call, in a series of six short bursts, and then just began a continuous loud burst. The man arrived back with the coupling and two of them cut the hose with a knife and fitted the device in place and tightened the hose clamp, but by this time the whole building was in flames, and the flames were spreading to adjoining structures to the east and west of The Central Dance Hall. The Union Dance Hall caught on the east, and Casey's Secondhand Store to the west was already in flames.

The flames shot high into the air, and the heat was becoming intense. Telephone poles in front were catching on fire and the insulation was burning on the wires strung along the south side of Myers. There were both the J. A. Whiting company located in City Hall, and the R. P. Davie Hose Company from the southwest corner of 1st and Bennett station volunteers fighting the fire at this point, but they lacked a chief to co-ordinate. It was doubtful that a chief could have done any good, as men had to move back from the south side and let it go, as the building fronts crashed into the center of Myers.

They began to play water on the buildings on the

north side of Myers, spraying water on The Topic, and The Old Homestead in an effort to keep the flames from spreading to the north side. The wind was from the south, and it began to blow harder, as the fire was making its own wind now. Steven watched in horror as embers floated across the sixty feet of Myers Avenue and landed on the roof of The Topic. The roof caught fire. It spread to the roof of The Old Homestead. Then it spread to the roof of Lottie and Kittie's Place and on east to The Library. Women gave up trying to save possessions and fled for their lives. Those two structures were gone, and the fire spread west among the buildings that fronted Myers on the north side. Crapper Jacks caught, then the Red Onion. Next, ex-fire chief Jordan's My Friend Saloon caught at the end of the block and Steven had to move up the alley on 3rd, as the fire jumped the street and caught the Morning Times building on the west side of 3rd Street. All Myers was ablaze on both sides from 5th street and all along the south side to Third. Soon the whole street on both sides was an inferno.

Now a frantic effort to save the business district on Bennett Avenue's south side began. The crib houses in the alley along between the two streets were first dragged away, but this could not happen fast enough, and men were giving out from the effort, so giant powder was brought in, and the crib houses were blown up. This created rubble that went up fast, and the fire spread to the base of the new Post Office on the south side of Bennett. Next it spread to Fairly Brothers Furniture Store next to the Post Office.

Steven moved farther up the hill as the fire grew west along Myers, and began to try to help pull hoses into position for a stand along the high wall that divided north and south Bennett. A woman in a black dress and white shirt smudged with soot came by him carrying a parrot. He saw Mabs Barbee looking on in horror just up the hill from the corner. The woman with the parrot ran by her going up Third Street with the parrot screaming, "Good Luck Suckers," over and over again as it tried to maintain its balance by flapping its wings, holding on the to the arm of the running woman.

Steven realized that the fire was going to catch the Mining Exchange Building, and ran for Stratton's office, and put important papers into the safe there, and when it was full, gathered what he could and ran downstairs where a larger safe was being rapidly filled by other men.

With no fire chief to direct them, men hooked up eighteen hoses to various water mains and tried to lay lines to the Bennett Avenue business district. The water pressure gave out, as they had hooked up too many hoses to the main that fed the lines. A lack of an experienced fire chief that knew main sizes and locations was sorely felt. Bennett Business district was catching from 3rd street east. The Gold Mining Exchange Building was becoming totally involved from the roof down. The First National Bank next door was starting to catch on the roof and in front, as embers blew across from the south side, which was now ablaze in a solid front of fire.

The City Hall was next to catch, and Chief of police Jim Marshall and jailer Tom Ryan opened the doors of the jail and released twenty prisoners, who ran west along Bennett until they came to several barrels of whiskey stacked in front of Kline's Saloon. Kline had some men working on rolling them away, and some of the released prisoners cheerfully joined in rolling barrel down west on Bennett past Elizabeth's Place, where she stood anxiously watching, and then south on second into the Midland Terminal Office back lot, where they broke open the head of one of the casks and proceeded to dip up whiskey and get roaring drunk.

A valiant stand was made, and the fire is contained east of 3rd street, but when Johnnie Nolan's Saloon at the corner caught fire, it was too hot, and hoses had to be abandoned where they lay. What hoses still worked were concentrated on the west side of 3rd Street, and Weinberg's Clothing Store got soaked and torn up by water pressure, but the fire was kept east of this corner by valiant effort.

Steven had gone out the back of the Mining Exchange Building as the front became a mass of flames, and embers and flaming boards from the roof fell into the alley behind. Looking west, he could see the roof of Johnnie Nolan's Saloon starting to catch, and he turned east and went to the Midland Terminal Building at the east end of Bennett. He climbed to the roof and help relay buckets of water that were used by several men to douse embers that were catching the roof of the new structure. He could see Elizabeth's Place two blocks east and could see that she was all right for the moment and watching from her porch. Houses on the south side of Carr were starting to catch. The fire was moving north with alarming speed, so when a train pulled in from Victor with a chemical fire engine and the Victor volunteers, a great cheer went up from all around.

The train also carried several cases of dynamite, and these got handed down and placed in a protected area. Some of the drunk prisoners from the jail, very tipsy on Kline's whiskey, found their way into the Midland Terminal at the east end of Bennett. One noticed the dynamite, and laughingly handed the sticks out to his drunk buddies, who began to run all over the north side of town tossing sticks of dynamite around into houses like they were firecrackers. Peter Eales and some of the other deputies saw this going on, and shot several of the men, leaving them where they lay.

The burned out homeless gathered at the reservoir and helplessly watched as the fire threatened to climb to them. For some strange reason, The Family Liquor Store at the northeast corner of Myers and 3rd , and the

Methodist Church at the corner of Carr and 4th Street were spared, although the Baptist, Episcopal, and Congregational Churches on corners across from the Methodist church all burned. Houses along the north side from Eaton and Golden north were too widely separated for the fire to continue, and it began to slow and extinguish. The wind died down as dusk began to fall, and the fire burned itself out. Water was still being played on hot embers at midnight.

Sheriff Marshall swore in one hundred deputies, of which Steven was one. Badges were cut from tin cans, as all the badges had burned up in City Hall. At 11:00 PM, J. P. Lindsay, cashier at the First National Bank, sat on the warped safe amid smoldering ruins. Fifty-three arrests were made that night, and the prisoners were held in the basement of the Midland Terminal.

Many businesses were back in business by night fall, and the next day. The First National Bank had wired for instructions as to how to open the safe, but it opened the next morning on the combination, and everything inside was intact. The bank moved to the Bi-Metallic Bank and moved in with the Mining Exchange Bank on the south side of Bennett in that block, near the businesses that were between there and next to Elizabeth's Place. Weinberg's Clothing Store held a fire sale and sold water damaged goods to try and offset the loss from the streaming fire hoses. George Holland rented a building next door to Elizabeth's Place and built a stage, while the fire was still burning to the north and west, and gave a performance that evening with some of the Taxi Dancers that Harry had brought to the restaurant that afternoon. The first new structure was built. A temporary stay from the brick-only order was given, and many new buildings started out of wood, just like before. Then they were argued about in legal terms, as the town council realized that they might not be able to get them torn down without

311

a lawsuit for each one. The stay was quickly rescinded, and brick and mortar replaced lumber along the front of Bennett, and men vied to see who could complete the first new structure. By Monday morning The Morning Times put out a paper from its temporary quarters on Golden Avenue. People of the town, with homes left, took in the ones burned out, and soon everyone had a place to stay.

Rumors flew thick from person to person that the fire was intentional in order to plunder the vault of The First National Bank, which had one hundred thousand in cash on hand that day, but police discounted this as talk. Still, when pistol shots were heard on southwest Myers Avenue on Monday afternoon, a crowd gathered around yelling "hang him" until it turned out that it was only a man practicing with his pistol at a target. Insurance sold briskly, even though the price was ten percent of value of the property for one year.

Steven was exhausted, and without sleep for over twenty-four hours, and he went back to Wilson Creek on the train to Victor after some of the deputies were told that they could stand down. There he fell into bed too tired to bathe and slept through Sunday and into Monday. He cleaned up Monday and was sore and tired all day. Feeling better by Tuesday, he attended duties at the Independence and then went late Tuesday afternoon to Anaconda to check on work at the Doctor-Jack Pot.

He awoke Wednesday and cooked beans through the morning and did paperwork and worked on drawings until about noon, when he fixed beans and bacon for lunch. It was while he was eating that he heard the first of the explosions coming from Cripple Creek.

Shortly after noon, The Portland Hotel on Myers between 3rd and 2nd Streets, caught fire. Waitress Bessie Kelly went into the kitchen for an order, where she found the back kitchen wall, behind the stove, aflame. She ran into the office crying "Fire." Bartender, C. H. Kelly, suddenly saw flames shooting through a stovepipe hole over the bathroom, possibly coming through from the kitchen. Grabbing the money in the till, that was all he was able to save, as The Portland Hotel went up fast.

There was a light well above the kitchen and flames spread to the roof and involved the entire structure within minutes. Next door at Green's Cafe, waitresses ran to their rooms to get personal effects, but the stairwell was catching fire, and they had to run back through the flames, leaving everything.

Six shots were heard with fear throughout the town. The volunteer fire department responded. The Davie Hose company was first on the scene, but a hose was loaded wrong end first when rolled up by exhausted men the Sunday morning three days earlier.

By the time hoses were hooked up and streams of water were played on the conflagration, the entire building was on fire from sidewalk to cornice. The water had no effect. Embers landed in the El Paso Lumber Yard across the street on the north side of Myers and there were more fires starting than men could get water to. The lumber yard began to catch fire.

Harry was finished with the noon crowd clean up and Elizabeth had gone to the loft bedrooms and was writing events from the previous Saturday in her diary. She had just written, "Thank God it's over," when pistol shots pierced the air. She counted in terror, as they were coming from close by and west behind Elizabeth's Place. She looked out a back window and could see smoke coming toward her on a stiff wind blowing out of the southwest, and smoke was pouring across the top of the El Paso Lumber Yard. She could see workmen carrying furniture out the 2nd Street door of The Booth Furniture Store and Mr. Booth was wetting blankets and placing them on the furniture in an effort to stop embers, which were already spreading on the wind, from burning the fine furniture, as the items were loaded onto wagons that were pulling up in the street and the alley behind, on the north side of his building. She was numb with shock. It was all happening again. The Mockingbird was screaming, and men were shouting, running everywhere. She went down to the kitchen and looked out the back door. Embers and tar paper floated on the wind acting like incendiaries wherever they landed. She could see the roof of The El Paso Lumber Yard catching fire less than four-hundred feet from where she stood, and thick choking smoke filled her nostrils.

She went to the front and pandemonium reigned on Bennett, as men tried to load possessions into anything with wheels. She could see Dr. Susan Anderson's office that Dr. Anderson shared with Dr. Verbay three blocks west on A Street and Bennett at the northwest corner. She was loading arm loads of medicine and bandages onto a buckboard with the white eyed terror showing on the face of the hobbled animal hooked to the surrey. Wagons hurried by going east along Bennett to the burned-out section, where men frantically kicked goods off and headed back across 3rd Street to try and get another load.

A terrific explosion went off behind her and just to the west, as men used cases of giant powder to try and stop the lumber yard fire. Cripple Creek miners always used two cases, and scorned using a few sticks, as two cases were always better than one, to their way of thinking. It simply spread the fire faster as embers went high into the air and floated all the way to Mt. Pisgah.

Men pulled fire engines and equipment to the corner of Bennett and Second Street, and she could see them as she looked west, playing water on the third floor of the Masonic building, which had escaped Saturday's conflagration, because it was a solid brick structure. Ammunition stored at The Wright Hardware store began to explode in staccato bursts, as if a war had started. North and south from 1st to 2nd, Myers was totally engulfed.

She heard explosions of cases of giant powder set in The Booth Furniture Store and saw furniture sail high into the air. Debris rained down on firemen and bystanders, wagons and horses, injuring many, as pieces of furniture rained down onto Bennett Avenue in front of her. She seemed rooted in the doorway to the porch. Finally, she forced herself to go west to Second Street and looked south, standing in front of the Bi-Metallic Bank for shelter from flying objects.

Firemen moved in with more hoses and attached them at the corner of Bennett and Second Street. Men yelled at them to get back, and Elizabeth shielded herself against the brick walk of the bank. Charges had been placed in Harder's Grocery Store, and the crowd moved back, trying to warn the firemen, but they were too absorbed in getting hoses hooked and didn't hear, or chose to ignore the danger, when the dynamite went off. The men were pelted with flying bricks and as the smoke cleared, the street was littered with injured men.

More men rushed in to help the injured as a second charge went off, injuring most of the good Samaritans. Fireman George Griffith lay in the street missing his head. The crowd moved back farther, fearing a third explosion. She saw a familiar shuffling walk. Harry came into the smoke and helped carry wounded away. Others joined him. Elizabeth was stunned and called out to warn Harry, but she could not even hear herself, as she seemed to have lost her voice.

She could look from the corner along 2nd Street and saw Mr. Howell standing on top of Murry's Saloon, holding hose and playing water across onto the Masonic Building when the building was blown out from under him. He did a graceful full flip in the air and landed on his feet in the center of 2nd Street and walked away through the debris and disappeared into the smoke walking south, in a daze, but otherwise unhurt.

Steven had heard something of the explosions that first were set to stop the fire and had gone out to look over the mountains between. Smoke curled high into the air, and although he couldn't believe what he was seeing, a panic and sure resolve seized him.

It was seven miles to Cripple Creek, and as he approached the Midland Terminal Station in Victor, no train was in sight. He paused only a moment to look around, and then began a brisk walk along the tracks, as using the trestle along the way would be the fastest. It took him a little over an hour and fifteen minutes to walk to Cripple creek, and as he got closer there were more explosions and the smoke climbed higher and thicker. He seemed to hear a voice in his head telling him to hurry.

He arrived at the trestle crossing Poverty Gulch at about 2:30 to a bedlam of frantic activity that lay in front of him as wagons vied for position to unload goods in the middle of the burned-out section from Saturday, among the cement mixers and brick stacked along Bennett Avenue readying the new structures going up.

He saw the Palace Hotel at 2nd and Bennett on the northwest side explode, and he thought that he caught a glimpse of Elizabeth coming back up Bennett in a hurry headed toward the restaurant. He had trouble getting through the debris and piles of goods and ran north up hill to Carr Avenue and crossed to 2nd and came down. As he passed the corner of 2nd and Bennett, a dejected Sam Altman was viewing the ruins of the old and new parts of his Palace Hotel. The fire had crossed Bennett in the middle of the block between 1st and 2nd and was advancing east along the north side. The Bi-Metallic Bank had been blown up and the fire was catching in the rubble.

Elizabeth had abandoned her position at the corner of 2nd and Bennett, where she had been watching the brave fight that firemen put up along 2nd Street, between Myer's and Bennett. This is where she had seen Harry's heroic acts.

As she hurried back toward the center of the block, The Bi-Metallic bank was destroyed by dynamite when it caught, in a futile attempt to save the rest of the block. The clerks in The Mining Exchange Bank locked valuables and cash into safes, and so did the clerks of The First National Bank, who had moved in with them, for the second time. They abandoned the structure and they flooded out the front door just as Elizabeth came hurrying by.

She began to hurry faster as she now saw a man on horseback with a rope around her restaurant trying to pull it down and away into the center of Bennett. "Hey you stupid cowboy," she yelled at him, as he tugged on the building with his horse backing like it had a calf roped and the structure bent under the strain. She ran over and ducked under his rope and went inside and got the first stick she saw, which was her broom, came back and began to beat on the man as high as she could reach, and then beat the horse on the head.

Steven came around the northeast corner past the Pulin Block at this moment and seeing what was happening began to run toward her. He was about halfway there and running as fast as he could.

As she was bashing the cowboy and his horse, a man came running west along Bennett. As he passed her, he yelled, "Lady you better run for your life, 'cause I just put thirteen cases of dynamite under Weinberg's Clothing Store."

The cowboy, hearing this, threw the rope in the air and wheeled his horse west, and kicked him into a full run. Elizabeth looked around dazed and then took several steps toward the porch of Elizabeth's Place and set her broom down leaning against a post. Steven was now close, and he yelled, "Elizabeth," with all his might.

She turned and looked at him with a blank expression, and seeing who it was, reached up to pat her hair in place, and then took several steps toward him. The concussion from the blast knocked everyone within a block to the ground. The windows along Bennett just disappeared. Elizabeth was picked up by the force of the blast and thrown several feet forward and knocked face down into the dirt. Steven was knocked on his back.

He didn't know how long he was unconscious, but when he awoke it was a scene out of Dante's Hell. There was fire everywhere around him. He struggled forward to find her stricken form. Her hair was bloody, and the back of her dress was in shreds. He scooped her into his arms and looked frantically for a way to go. The whole block was aflame on both sides.

Pearce Pharmacy was in the middle of the block on the north side, and he made for that doorway, as it was the only building not yet totally in flames. She was hard to carry as she was limp and he was stunned, but he staggered into the pharmacy as fire closed in behind them.

He made his way out the back into the alley, but could not see which way to go. He finally decided to go towards 2nd Street, and as he emerged from the alley, the ruins of the Palace Hotel blazed in front of him. He passed firemen on his way uphill as he struggled to carry her out of the fire. The firemen were now fighting to keep the fire from spreading north, and they were laying hoses along 2nd from Carr Avenue hydrants to try and contain the fire to Bennett Street. The boilers in the basement of the destroyed Palace Hotel were reaching critical temperature, and with the pipes bent and contorted closed, the boiler exploded injuring more firemen.

Hot metal flew past Steven with a whining sound as he staggered north along 2nd past Carr. He turned east on Eaton and soon the smoke lessened a little, as he joined a throng of people fleeing houses along Carr and Eaton, just north of the burning business district.

The city was now completely overwhelmed, and a stream of people crowded Eaton and Golden, as the houses along Carr were mostly in flames. The wind pushed the fire in a solid front north into the residential section. The fugitives pushed wheelbarrows, pulled wagons, and even pushed baby carriages loaded with what worldly goods they might save.

They all fled up hill, toward the reservoir, and Steven trudged on with Elizabeth unconscious in his arms. The throng hustled along with one mind, to escape to the water of the reservoir. Somehow, he found himself there among the people. He recognized Mabs Barbee and her mother Kitty, and he lay Elizabeth down and fell on the ground himself, with his heart pounding as if it would thump out of his chest.

He recovered, somewhat, in a few minutes as they watched what was left of the fire brigade use dynamite to blow a fire break north of Golden Avenue as the fire consumed everything north of Myers and east of B Street to the west. That was practically the entire town.

Furniture, table legs, dishes, cooking utensils, boards of houses, sailed high into the air, and the crowd had to watch and dodge objects that came hurtling their way. More and more people crowded around the reservoir, with the moaning of people separated from everything that they owned, and the crying of babies, for want of food and comfort.

Johnnie Nolan came through and seeing Mrs. Yambert among the homeless, a smile broke out on his big Irish face, and he yelled at her, "See how smart we were not to fix that roof!" But his jovial expression changed when he saw Steven with Elizabeth lain out on the cold earth unconscious. He knew Elizabeth well, and he liked her, and he liked Steven. He promised that he would do something as soon as he could, and he went off to look for a blanket, but there was none to be found.

Below the reservoir a short way stood The Sister of Mercy Hospital. They could clearly see a brave stand of firemen protecting the hospital where many of the injured were stacked in the hallways. Doctors there were taking care of people as best they could and the badly injured and those in need of amputation were transferred to Pikes Peak Hospital where Dr. Liggett and Dr. Crane performed operation after operation, some minor, and many amputations. The firemen blew a fire break around the structure and used the last of their water and strength to protect the hospital and the injured inside. Steven saw Harry moving among these men, pulling hoses and sometimes helping hold a nozzle when other men's strength had played out.

Elizabeth was breathing and had stopped bleeding. He used the bottom of her dress to wrap the oozing wounds on the back of her head and wadded up the rest of the bottom half of her dress to cushion her head. That was all he could do for now.

At about three PM, as Steven was laboring to carry Elizabeth up Eaton Street, Jimmie Burns was using the telephone that was located in Maurice Finn's house on Golden Avenue. From here, high above the city spread out below, he could see the devastation and the advance of the holocaust as the fire marched northward. On the other end of the phone line, in Colorado Springs was Win Stratton. The citizens of the Springs could see a yellow haze towering above Pike's Peak and knew that something incredible was happening, west, on the other side of the mountain.

Mayor J. C. Plumb had gone to Stratton's house thinking that he might know something. The phone had rung and it was Jimmy Burns on the line, and Stratton repeated what he was told, as it was happening, to a gathering group of men. Verner Z. Reed came in with an anxious look. Spec Penrose came in with an even more worried look, as he had owned The Topic, which went up on the Saturday before. Now he listened as Win described the fight to save The Penrose building just south of Edinburgh. The explosion damaged the building, and the smoke kept Burns from seeing what was happening south of Bennett. Irving Howbert came in and stood listening as Stratton reported the minute-by-minute story.

"The Davie Hose House has caught, and the fire and embers are spreading west now," Stratton repeated what he was hearing. "A solid line of fire is spreading north from B Street on the west to 3rd, at the edge of Saturday's ruins. Most houses on Carr and Eaton are in flames and embers are spreading as far as Mt. Pisgah cometary. Just below the reservoir a last stand is being formed to try and save the injured at The Sisters of Mercy Hospital. They're blowing homes all around the hospital in an attempt to keep fire from the building. A huge crowd of people, at least five thousand, has gathered at the reservoir, and more are walking there every minute. A solid line of fire is marching north from the western edge of the city to the devastation of Saturday's fire, and they are beginning to blow up houses along Golden to try and stop its advance. Embers are catching structures on fire as far north as Pikes Peak Avenue.

"Jimmy," Stratton said into the phone, "I'm going to bring a train of relief supplies. Reed and Howbert are here with me with Spec and Mayor Plumb. We're coming, so I'm going to hang up now." He put the phone down and turned to the other men. "We've got to move and move fast," he said to them. "We need a special train, and all the supplies we can find. Charge everything to me, and we'll divvy it up later."

He picked the phone back up and called the agent in charge at the Midland Terminal office and ordered a special train. Then he called the bakeries in town an bought every loaf of bread there was, over one thousand loaves and had then sent them to the Midland Terminal. He then called the largest grocery in town and ordered cases and cases of canned meat, condensed milk, and diapers.

"Let's move men," he urged. The men volunteered assignment and within thirty minutes everyone had a duty. Stratton drove to the Midland Terminal to see about the trains. Irving Howbert sent twelve freight wagons to Sheilds-Morley wholesale grocery, and the goods were loaded and sent to the depot. Stratton called Giddings Department store, N. O. Johnson's dry goods, and Perkins and Holbrook's wholesale, buying every blanket in each store.

E. R. Stark and H. C. McCreery collected one hundred and sixty-five eight-person tents at Barnes and Sons, and McCreery, who was an Alderman, got word to Colorado City to have the big tabernacle tent ready to load on the special train when it came through.

By 5:00 PM, a train load of supplies had been gathered and the relief train left out with Sheriff Winfield Scott Boynton in charge. They stopped at Colorado City to load the tabernacle tent. Spec Penrose served as brakeman and Harry Johnson helped fire the coal box. By 6:15 they were making fifteen miles per hour as they chugged up Ute Pass. They had to slow at the big trestle as they had to use on of the heavier engines and caution was necessary crossing the bridge. Then they poured on the coal all the way to Divide, where the special was switched to the last eighteen miles of Midland Terminal tracks for the pull through Gillette and Victor and on into Cripple Creek.

Word spread at the reservoir that help was coming and cheering and whoops went up as they could see the lights of the train shortly after dark, as it came into Gillett, and again at Hoosier Pass. The refugees shivered in the

322

cold and tried to stay warm around camp fires. Around 9:00 PM the lights of the engine could be seen coming around Gold Hill to the south and cheers broke out as fire flew from the brake shoes as the relief train high balled down the hill and screeched to a stop at the Midland Terminal.

Men met the train carrying oil torches made of rags wrapped around sticks and soaked in coal oil. Woods Brother's transfer wagons were waiting, along with other wagons that were available and goods were loaded on to them and brought to the hoard of people waiting at the reservoir.

Jimmy Burns had come over to the reservoir about dusk dark and Steven had seen him and told him of Elizabeth's injuries. Now Burns showed up with a wagon with tents, and he and Johnnie Nolan pitched a tent while Steven wrapped Elizabeth in two blankets. When the tent was ready and two cots were brought in, they lay her on one of the cots and Steven, at last, had her sheltered and wrapped against the night chill.

Harry came looking along the edge from where he had been putting out embers below. He was totally covered in soot and smoke. Steven called to him, and he made his way up to the tent, and Steven hugged him and brought him inside. "Sister," he cried when he saw Elizabeth's stricken form. Steven put his arm around Harry's shoulder. Tears were running down both their cheeks, putting streaks in the soot on their faces.

"She's going to be all right, Harry," he assured her brother, but he was far from certain of that.

Chapter 23. The Awakening

It was after midnight before Steven lay down on the cot next to Elizabeth. Harry had curled at the end of her cot and fallen asleep from exhaustion shortly before. When Steven awakened it was good daylight. Elizabeth was still unconscious and Steven was afraid to touch her. She was warm to the touch, and he was relieved.

Harry was not in the tent, and he was nowhere to be seen on the outside. Steven walked away from the crowd to relieve himself, but there was little to relieve and he was becoming dehydrated. Coming back to the tent, he saw the gypsy woman, Vida De Vere, sitting outside a tent nearby, smoking a pipe. He passed her and she said nothing, but her eyes followed him. He had not been back long and was sitting on a cot holding Elizabeth's hands when Harry came in with a bucket of water.

"Water," he said to Steven.

Steven dipped some from the bucket and drank and then splashed some on his face. "How is Sister Sarah," Harry asked?

"She is still asleep," Steven told him. "The sleep is good for her to get well," he added a positive thought to try and ease Harry's worry. "The water was a good idea, Harry," Steven told him. He wet his finger and placed drops of water on Elizabeth's lips. He removed the bloody bandages from her head and tore off the ruined spot, then wet the rest by pouring a little water over it with cupped hands until he had it soaked. He took the sopping wet rag and lay it gently on the forehead.

"They're giving out canned meat and crackers," Harry told him.

"That's good, Harry, see if you can get us something to eat."

Harry went off to get them some food and Steven continued to watch her. He held her hand and squeezed it gently. "Don't leave me Elizabeth," he begged her.

Harry was back soon, and Betsey Hoopolieth and Piala were with him. "Hello, Steven," Betsey hugged him. "How is she?"

"I don't know," Steven confessed. "She's breathing, but she hasn't made a move or even a sound."

Betsey felt of her hands, spoke to her, calling her name and felt her head and face. Piala stood quietly. "She's not running fever," Betsey observed.

"I need to get her to the hospital," Steven said.

"The hospitals are full and overflowing, and there is already some sickness. I saw Dr. Anderson on the road when we came in. It's just awful, unbelievable. We weren't in the city," Betsey explained, and then looked at Piala. She sat silent for a few moments on the cot beside Elizabeth. "I think I know where Doctor Anderson is working, and I'm going to go ask her to come here."

"Thanks Betsey," Steven was grateful for the help. He wasn't thinking all that clearly yet.

She and Piala left with promises to be back soon, and Harry and he opened the canned meat and crackers and ate it, washing it down with water from the bucket, drank with cupped hands. So many amenities were missing, but he was so grateful for the efforts of Win Stratton and the others on the relief train.

It was in the early afternoon that Steven and Harry heard horses outside, and looking out found Betsey and Piala back. Doctor Anderson was coming up in a buckboard, and after greetings all around she went inside the tent to examine Elizabeth, asking the others to wait outside. She emerged in a short while and came to talk to the group. "Help me turn her over so that I can dress her wounds." She got solutions of medicine in bottles from her buckboard, and Steven helped her turn Elizabeth and watched as she dressed the bloody injuries.

"She's in a coma from a bad concussion," she told the group. "Dehydration is the worse problem, now. Given time she will awaken, but with no way for her to take in water," she shrugged, "she may never wake up."

Steven almost crumpled, and Harry became agitated. Betsey frowned and reached for Piala's hand. Doctor Susie looked at each one of them. "I won't lie to you," she told them. "Only time will tell. I'd take her to the hospital, but with all the injured, there isn't a bed, and with the exposure to the nighttime air, we already have many sick, and it will get worse. She can absorb some water through her skin, so bathe her with water as best you can. Moisten her lips and keep her mouth wet. That's really all that can be done." Having said that, she climbed back in her buckboard and left, promising to come back when she could. "you can find me at Pikes Peak Hospital," she told Betsey, "so keep me informed, if you move her."

The afternoon dragged on, and Harry and Piala went off to survey the damage to the downtown area, and see if there was anything to recover from the restaurant. Betsey worked to keep Elizabeth wet, and Steven went for more water.

Shortly after Steven left, Betsey noticed a shadow of someone standing outside the tent, and looking out, found Madame Vida De Vere there. The two looked at each other. "How is she," the gypsy asked?

"We don't know," Betsey told her. "She won't wake up." The gypsy woman opened the tent flap and went in with Betsey following her.

She didn't touch Elizabeth but sat beside her thinking. Betsey began to wet her again. This was the image that the gypsy had seen when these two had come for a reading. Much of what she did was sham, but sometimes strange things happened to her, and this was one. Through these women, the gypsy had foreseen the disaster and felt somewhat her own fate. It had stunned her at the time. It had been a true waking vision, but she had not been able to see the outcome for Elizabeth or for herself.

She had seen Elizabeth, unconscious, and had felt the fire in her mind's eye, and it had stunned her that day. She had recognized Steven this morning as the man in the vision who had saved Elizabeth from the fire. It had been a powerful and unusual event, truly physics, among many sham tricks. She pondered this as she looked at Elizabeth's stricken form. "Leave us," she told Betsey.

Betsey hesitated for a moment, and then did as she was bidden without asking any question. She stepped outside the tent and left Vida alone with Elizabeth. The gypsy removed a necklace from her own neck. She looked at the pendant in her hand. It was a cross with an inverted tear drop for the top. It was an ancient Egyptian symbol of eternal life called an Anka. She had always worn it since she was a little girl. Now, she placed it around Elizabeth's neck. "Not a bad bargain for a paper Greenback," she said to the unconscious form. She exited the tent.

Steven and Vida came face to face. Steven looked questioningly at Betsey and then back at the gypsy woman.

"I have placed a talisman around her neck," Vida told him. "Leave it on her until she awakens, then return it to me."

"What nonsense is this," he questioned setting the bucket down and holding the tent flap aside. He looked in to see. Elizabeth was as he had left her, and he checked to see, saw the pendant and came back out of the tent. They locked eyes and Vida looked deep into him.

"And what is it that you do believe in young man?" She asked him directly.

Steven looked away, flinching, at her gaze. "Not much," he admitted.

327

"When is the last time that you have been to church," she asked?

Steven looked back at her questioningly. He didn't regress on his first day in Cripple Creek but went farther back to the day of his mother's funeral. A cloud passed across his continence.

"It's you who needs to awaken," she pointed a finger at the heart in his chest, then turned and strode back toward her tent and campsite.

About an hour later, Piala and Harry came back from the ruins. Harry carried a lump of metal, silvery with ash mixed through it. He was still covered in soot, and although Steven had used water and cloth to wash up, he knew he didn't look much better.

"Gone," was all Harry could choke out. "Gone." He held out the lump of metal. "Silver," he said, "and the stove."

"Good work," Steven told him and hefted the lump of melted coins.

"The city is already starting to rebuild," Piala spoke up. "Her cast iron stove can be cleaned. There's a sign on the lot. It say, "Lots must be cleaned by the 4th of May, or the city will clean them. Cleaning bills to be paid by May 10th or the lot will be considered abandoned and sold at auction to pay any charges: By Order of The City Council."

Steven hefted the silver. "Maybe sixty ounces," he guessed. "With the price of silver down to seventy cents an ounce, after refinery charges, maybe thirty Greenbacks." He turned to Harry. "Does she have a bank account," he asked?

Harry shook his head 'no'. "Sister didn't like banks," he said.

"Piala," Steven asked a favor, "can you hire a wagon and driver to take trash away, if I pay for it?"

"Wagon prices are high," he told Steven.

"I have the money, but it will take days to clean the lot, and I want to stay with Elizabeth and keep her wet."

"Harry and I can clean the lot," Piala assured him.

"I'll help you with Elizabeth," Betsey assured him.

After a little more planning, Piala and Harry went to start on the lot. Betsey found friends nearby to help get Steven a hot meal. Steven sat holding Elizabeth's hand, and bathing her with a soaked rag. He thought about what the gypsy had said to him and rolled the pendant in his hand. It was so much like a Christian cross, except for the inverted teardrop at the top. After he had eaten a hot sandwich of bread and cooked meat, and drank water, he was feeling stronger, and he washed his hands and face the best he could. His clothes were a mess, but it didn't matter. He asked Betsey to watch Elizabeth, and he walked down to St. Peter's Catholic Church.

St. Peter's was undamaged by the fires, and he knew Father Volpe from several meetings during the labor trouble. He lingered outside for a few minutes and then resolutely walked inside. The pews had been removed from the sanctuary, and people were camped all over the floor. Cots and bedding were spread wall to wall, mostly filled with women and babies. Babies squalled and cried. Steven saw Father Volpe at the front of the sanctuary and approached him. The Father saw him coming and broke off talking to a woman and came to meet him.

"Father Volpe," Steven began after they had shaken hands. "I need to talk to you." Father Volpe could see the concern on his face and motioned for him to follow and led him to the vestry in the back to one side. He sat, and motioned Steven into a seat.

"Father," he began, "I'm troubled and need to talk to you."

"As a priest?" Father Volpe asked, seeing that this was serious.

"Yes," Steven admitted.

Father Volpe placed vestments around his neck and motioned Steven to follow him to the confessional, taking his position on one side and guiding Steven to the other.

"How long since your last confession," Father Volpe began when they had assumed their seats.

Steven didn't answer for some time. "Long," he said, "many years. I haven't confessed since my childhood, and my mother's death."

"I see," said the priest. Neither spoke for a long time. "You have something on your mind," the priest stated to him.

"You know Elizabeth Yates," Steven began.

"Yes," Father Volpe confirmed.

"She's been injured," Steven told him. "She's in a coma and won't wake up. I'm bathing her with wet rags to get her some moisture as the doctor has instructed, but I'm afraid. I'm afraid that she will never wake up."

"She is special to you," Father Volpe asked?

"Very special, and I want to pray for her, but I don't know how."

"I see," the Father paused. "You are intimate with her," he asked?

"Yes, we were, but we argued."

"Are you married," the priest asked?

"No, but I have asked her, and she wouldn't."

"But you have sex with her."

"Yes."

"Was that the trouble between you?"

"No, we argued over the bullfight. I am from Spain in my youth and she hated the bullfight."

"So you offended her?"

"I guess that I did. We argued. She said that I was brutal. She was married before to a brutal man."

"She is divorced?"

"The marriage was annulled by court order as she was too young too consent. She won't consider marriage

330

again. He stopped. This was the type of nonsense about the church that he hated. It inferred legal questions of ownership and property as pertained to women. The priest could sense his antipathy. "I need you to pray for her Father. I need her in my life." He was at a loss for words.

"I will," Father Volpe assured him. "I want you to go to the alter and light a candle for her."

Steven left the confessional and did as he was told. It was nonsense he felt, but he did it and then left the church feeling hopeless and worn worse than when he had come inside.

He returned to the tent and bathed her repeatedly. He watched her far into the night, and talked to her, telling her how much he loved and needed her and begging her to wake up. He couldn't sleep, and sometime after midnight, he went randomly walking about the ruined town. He found himself in front of St. Peter's again and he slipped quietly inside.

People were sleeping everywhere, and he moved along the edge being careful not to step on anyone. He moved close to the altar and just sat looking around. The loss of his mother's life swept over him and he felt the anger and resentment of losing both his mother and his father. That anger and grief had turned him away from faith in anything.

He began to try and pray, pray to something that he really did not believe in. he knew that he needed it to be there. He went deeper into his need. He felt his soul empty and his heart ache. It ached for his mother, and his father, and Elizabeth. It ached for every injustice that he had ever experienced. The senseless death of Pearl De Vere even crossed his mind. He tried to put the feeling of existential loneliness into words. Words failed. He went deeper, and tears ran down his cheeks. He cried for the whole world, for a lost humanity, until finally he was empty, needing, mumbling, "Abba, Abba," to himself and

331

calling for help.

At that moment, he felt a light touch on his shoulder. He looked up to see Father Volpe standing there. "Steven," he said, and sat down beside him and put an arm around his shoulders. "I couldn't sleep," the priest told him.

"I need her," Steven looked through tear blurred eyes. "I don't know how to do this."

"You're doing fine," Father Volpe patted his shoulder. "We don't any of us know, but we have to ask, and then have faith," he said.

"I don't know how to have faith," Steven told him.

"We have to expect a miracle," the priest looked toward the crucifix above them. "Sometimes it happens, and sometimes not, but we must expect it to receive it."

They sat in silence for several minutes. "I have been praying for Elizabeth," Father Volpe told him. "I have an idea," he confided. "I want you to bring her here to the church. It's the best place for her, and we will put her in my room. I will find other quarters. I have a bathtub and running water, and you can place her in the tub and soak her for an hour, take her out and tend her in my bed. You can soak her over and over. It may help."

And so, the following morning Steven, Harry, Betsey and Piala moved Elizabeth to St. Peters and Betsey and Steven began to soak her every few hours. They then used the water for themselves to clean up. Betsey found other clothes to dress Elizabeth in and Piala found clothes for Steven and Harry. They took shifts tending her and doc Susie came by and approved completely.

It was near morning, going into the fourth day that the first moan came from Elizabeth. Betsey was watching and she awakened Steven from the pallet in the corner where he was sleeping. "She moaned," Betsey told him.

He jumped up and went to her. He patted her hand and called her name. He asked Betsey to find some lotion.

Betsey came back in a few minutes with mineral oil used for babies. Steven began to rub it on her feet.

Elizabeth was dreaming. She was underwater and she held a baby in her arms. She knew the name of the baby very well. The baby needed to get to the surface. She went up and up, and when she broke the surface there was fire everywhere. She couldn't remember the baby's name. She had to submerge to get away from the fire.

She knew the baby's name very well when she was beneath the surface. It needed to get to the surface. She tried again. Again, she forgot the baby's name. Over and over, she sought to reach the surface. Over and over, she had to go back under, as she either dropped the baby, or she forgot its name. She had to reach that surface and somehow stay there.

He was rubbing her feet with oil. She moaned again, and her eyelids fluttered. "My baby," she cried out, and she heard it clearly, but Steven only heard her moan.

"Where is my baby," Elizabeth said. She opened her eyes and looked into Steven's eyes.

"What baby," he asked her?

She was puzzled. She shook her head back and forth, 'no'. "I don't remember its name," she said. "Funny, I know it well, but now can't recall."

He put a wet rag on her forehead. "Steven," she said thickly through parched lips.

"Yes," he confirmed.

She looked right at him and he knew that she recognized him. "Ice," she whispered, "ice," and then went back to sleep.

He left Betsey watching her and ran to where Father Volpe was in morning prayer. "Father, she woke up. She asked for ice," he told him excitedly.

"We can maybe find some of that," he said. "They brought some up on the second relief train to keep perishables." The Father was gone a few minutes and

Steven went back to where Elizabeth lay. The priest brought ice and Steven broke it into tiny pieces in a bowl and placed some into her mouth.

He did this with several pieces and after a little while, she began to chew it with her mouth. Her eyes opened and looked around her. "Thank you," she whispered softly.

It was a joyous day. Harry was so excited to have Sister Sarah back. Her recovery was rapid and soon she could eat. In a few days, they moved her to the Wilson Creek house, as soon as she was strong enough to ride the train. When Win Stratton found out about it, he insisted that Elizabeth come to Colorado Springs to his house there, as it had indoor plumbing. They moved her there the next day, and Betsey went with her to nurse her back to health.

Harry, Steven and Piala got the lot cleaned off and recovered what they could, which was one big cast iron cooking stove. Brick buildings were going up all around and several times men, both known and unknown to Steven came by inquiring about the lot and if it might be for sale. They made Harry mad, and he told them it was 'Sister Sarah's, and not for sale'. Steven thought about it, and he had an idea.

He went to the First National Bank in Cripple Creek and asked for an appointment with Bert Carlton. He got on a schedule, and two days later at three in the afternoon, he got in to see Carlton.

The office door said A. E. Carlton. The new bank had been completed in record time. Workmen still moved about putting finishing touches on the new building, but the main part was finished in a little over a month since the fire, so it was the first week in June when he sat down to talk with Carlton.

Bert Carlton was cool at first. "What type of salary do you make," he said off-handed. "Stratton pays you what, five dollars a day. That's fifteen hundred a year less expenses, and you don't own the lot. Elizabeth Yates owns that lot." Carlton was well aware of the situation. "She should sell out," he told Steven. "The City will never let her rebuild a little clap-board business like she had before."

Steven was chagrined. "I have some savings," he ventured.

"How much," Carlton countered?

"Three hundred dollars," Steven told him.

Carlton sneered. "That's hardly collateral for the building you have in mind, now is it. The building will be close to twenty thousand to build and furnish a two-story brick like you're talking about. Why, fire insurance alone will be close to two thousand a year, taxes another three hundred. No, it just won't do."

Josiah Winchester is giving me several thousand shares of the Doctor-Jack Pot mine," Steven offered.

Carlton's interest picked up. "I hear they're shipping good ore. What's the value of that stock?"

"Probably around ten thousand," Steven asserted.

"What's the liquidation value?" Carlton scratched on a pad. "Maybe six thousand," he figured. "You would be willing to sign that over for a building on a lot you don't own?"

"Yes," Steven didn't hesitate.

"We would have to have a first lien on the lot as well," Carlton told him.

"I can form a joint venture with Elizabeth Yates, and we can give you a deed of trust to both the stock and the lot."

"Hmmm," Carlton twirled a pencil. "I want to see the ore in sight at the Doctor-Jack Pot."

"I can arrange that with Josiah Winchester," Steven assured him.

A few days later Josiah Winchester showed A. E.

Carlton around his mine and gave assurances that Steven would be good for the loan. Winchester was a trusting man, and an optimist. Carlton asked some simple questions about the mines' liabilities and Winchester assured him that the note for the beginning work would be payed off soon, and the mine would be unencumbered. He told him that the note was held by The First National Bank of Denver, and gave him the name of his attorney there, Mr. A. E. Stevenson. Carlton seemed satisfied, and the paperwork was prepared and after Steven signed it, it was taken to Elizabeth to sign, and Winfield Scott Stratton signed as witness to Elizabeth's signature.

And so work began on the new two-story building that was to house the new Pardner's Restaurant," as Elizabeth insisted it would be called. On September 15th, 1896, it had its Grand Opening, and they cooked on new stainless-steel equipment, as well as made bread in the old cast iron oven, the only thing that came through the fire. The town was growing again and busting with growth from another five thousand people that had come in to service the city or build the new buildings. More ore was being shipped every day.

At the Grand Opening of "Pardner's Restaurant," there was a big presentation for Harry and he was was presented with a special recognition for his heroic acts during the fire. Also, as a surprise, they asked him to take a job as janitor in the new fire station, that was to have a full-time staff of firemen and equipment. The town now wanted more than a volunteer fire department, and money had been set aside.

Steven, Elizabeth, Piala, and Betsey, who was now showing pregnant with her first child, watched proudly as Harry had a badge pinned on him. Piala and Betsey had been married in a Ute Indian ceremony, as she couldn't legally marry him under Colorado law. It was a joyous day.

336

Life quickly assumed a routine for the restaurant and the group did well together. Steven and Elizabeth stayed together at Wilson Creek, or mostly in their room on the second floor of the new brick building. Steven never talked of marriage. He was waiting for Elizabeth to mention it. She wondered but held her tongue. Old habits die hard.

The following Sunday, they packed a picnic lunch, closed the restaurant, and Steven, Elizabeth, and Harry went for a buckboard ride out toward Four Mile, to their favorite spot overlooking the Sangre De Christo Mountains to the west, with Harry sitting on the back swinging his legs.

A small lake was nestled down in the valley below. "Look said Harry, "a bear."

A bear was in the waters of the lake furiously splashing water up and over his head.

"I think it's Ol' Mose, splashing in the water," Elizabeth squinted into the distance and shaded her eyes to see. "What is he doing?"

"I can hear him growl," Steven said, as he cupped a hand to his ear to better hear.

Harry moved closer to the edge and watched the bear intensely for several moments and then turned with a smile on his face. "I think," he said slowly, "he's growling at the rainbow."

Bibliography

Sprague, Marshall, *Money Mountain,* Lincoln, Nebraska: University of Nebraska Press, 1979.

Kaelin, Celinda Reynolds, *Pikes Peak Backcountry,* Caldwell, Idaho: Caxton Press, 1999.

Cornell, Virginia, *Doc Susie,* Tuscon, Arizona: Manifest Publications, 1991.

West, Elliott, *The Saloon on the Rocky Mountain Mining Frontier,* Lincoln and London, Nebraska: University of Nebraska Press, 1979.

Carson, Kit, *Kit Carson's Autobiography,* edited by Milo Milton Quaife, Lincoln/London, Nebraska: University of Nebraska Press.

Smith, Toby, *Kid Blackie, Jack Dempsey's Colorado Days,* Ridgeway, Colorado: Wayfinder Press.

Lee, Mabel Barbee, *Cripple Creek Days, Forward by Lowell Thomas,* Lincoln/London, Nebraska: University of Nebraska Press.

Williams, Lester L., M.D., *Cripple Creek Conflagrations, The Great Fires of 1896 that burned Cripple Creek, Colorado,* Palmer Lake, Colorado: Filter Press.

West, Beverly, *More Than Petticoats, Remarkable New Mexico Women,* Guilford, Connecticut: TwoDot, An imprint of The Globe Pequot Press.

Adams, Ramon F., *Cowboy Lingo, A Dictionary Of The Slack-Jaw Words And Whangdoodle Ways Of The American West,* Boston/New York: The Houghton Mifflin Company.

Thompson, Atlanta Georgia, *Daughter Of A Pioneer, A True Story of Life In Early Colorado,* Portland Oregon: Binford & Mort Publishing.

Mackell, Jan, *Cripple Creek District, Last Of Colorado's Gold Booms,* Charleston SC, Chicago, Portsmouth NH, San Francisco: Arcadia Publishing an imprint of Tempus Publishing Inc.

Garraty, John A., *The American Nation, A History of the United States Since 1865,* Harper Collins Publishers.

Feitz, Leland, *Victor, A Quick History, Colorado's City of Mines,* Colorado Springs: Little London Press.

Feitz, Leland, *Victor, Ghost Towns, A Quick History, Ghost Towns of the Cripple Creek District,* Colorado Springs: Little London Press.

Feitz, Leland, Cripple Creek!, *A Quick History, The World's Greatest Gold Camp,* Colorado Springs: Little London Press.

Feitz, Leland, Myers Avenue, *A Quick History, Cripple Creeks Red Light District,* Colorado Springs: Little London Press.

Wommack, Linda, *Colorado Gambling, A History Of The Early Days, 1991*

Brown, Robert L., *Cripple Creek Then and Now,* Denver, Colorado: Sundance Publications, Limited.

Mac Iver, Kathi, *Maggie,* Cripple Creek, CO.: Columbine Press.

Courtesy of Nancy Fromm, Cripple Creek Library, use of the microfich archives of early Cripple Creek News Papers.

Many, many articles from the internet written by historians of the area. Maps and tourist information by the Cripple Creek Chamber of Commerce.